PLAYING BY HEART

JB SALSBURY

PROLOGUE

TWO MONTHS AGO...

BETHANY

W ill the heartbreak ever stop hurting?
I figured after a few days, the pain in my chest
would go away. Even now, as I rub the sore spot on
my sternum, the emptiness only intensifies. From the backseat of
my car, I stare through blurry eyes at the neon DQ sign across the
parking lot and bring the bottle of Malibu rum to my lips. Tilting it
back, I gulp, then I gag at the pungent coconut flavor. I accept the
burn and twisting in my gut as my punishment. I deserve this after
how badly I messed things up.

I was too needy.

Too in love and somehow blind to my own faults.

My head is heavy as I look at the gray upholstery to my left, then
to my right. I can still smell him here. Tears fall in sloppy splashes
from my chin to disappear into the fabric. Poetic, really. The last
place I remember feeling happy is right where those tears belong.

I sniff back my emotion and take another gulp of rum.

My phone lights up in the front seat—another text from my

roommate asking where I am. I snort as I imagine her reaction if I told her what I'm doing. She'd be pissed, accuse me of wallowing.

I take another sip.

Maybe she'd be right.

If only there was a way to erase some of the past. A way to start over. Try again. Maybe he'd give me another chance.

A small voice in my head whispers I might not be thinking clearly from being three-quarters of the way down a bottle of booze, but I close my eyes and push away the nagging voice of reason.

I just want to be rid of the memories.

I set the bottle down next to me and thumb the book of matches I had kept in my purse. The gilded resort emblem catches the distant streetlights. We were happy there. At least, I think we were. Memories bring a fresh onslaught of tears. I close my eyes, and the darkness makes me sway. I throw down a hand to keep from toppling over. The scent of coconut rum permeates my nose.

Moving slowly, I snag the bottle, but I'm too late. Its contents soak the cushions of my backseat.

"Great..." My voice sounds foreign, lazy, my tongue thick and heavy.

I fumble with the door handle and kick the thing open before crawling out and spilling onto the asphalt. Deranged laughter falls from my lips and mixes with my gentle sobbing.

"I'm a mess." I flip over onto my back, then sit up and stare through the open back door of my car.

My mind's eye flashes with images of naked skin pressed against naked skin. Hands gripping, lips sucking, the sound of our love-making wrapping us in a blanket of ecstasy.

Whispered words between heated moans...

I love you.

I close my eyes as more tears spill.

You're the kind of woman a man marries.

Anger stirs in my gut, chasing away the heartbreak. I open my eyes and glare into the backseat.

Before I'm even aware of what I'm doing, a lighted match flies, then another, and another, each one burning out in the air. I look down and rip at them furiously, lighting the entire book before tossing it away.

"Burn," I growl through a cascade of sadness.

Flames crawl up the fabric.

I feel my lips pull into a deranged grin as I watch what was left of us burn, and with the flames, the pressure in my chest lightens. With stiff, robotic movements, I stand and grab my phone and purse from the front seat.

I give the fire one last glance and nod. "Good."

Now I can start over. Become a better person, the kind of woman he'd never leave.

Drunk, I stumble away without a single regret.

1

PRESENT DAY...

JESSE

I know what's happening the second the freezing water hits my face. I've felt it before. The bite of the cold combines with the bruising force of ice cubes, and I'm aware of the degree of trouble I'm in by the force with which they're thrown. On a scale of one to ten, these cubes bitch-slapped me at an eight.

I put my hands up to protect my face—admittedly too late, but my reflexes are for shit. My skin stings like a motherfucker. A low growl of irritation reverberates in my foggy head as I cling to the cold and try to peel my eyes open.

I'm more fucked up than I thought.

"Wake up, Jesse." The disappointment in my manager's voice is as familiar as the ice-bucket wake-up call.

My mouth tastes like a garbage dump in a one-hundred-year-old wasteland. I rub my eyes, push away a few small chunks of ice, and roll toward the voice. Peeling back my eyelids takes effort. I'm tempted to use my fingers to pry them open, but I don't because I've got a reputation for bouncing back after a party. At the ripe age of twenty-eight, nearly the Golden Years for a rock star, I refuse to admit I'm getting too old for this shit.

"What time is it?" My voice sounds as if it's being raked over broken glass, which is about right considering my throat feels as though it's coated in thorns.

After a long sigh and frustrated puff of breath, the man speaks. "I think the question you mean to ask is what *day* is it."

With every blink, more blood flows back to my eyes and his blurry form comes into focus. He offers me a tall to-go cup and my mouth waters. I clear my throat and sit up slowly. The walls spin until I swing my legs over the side of the bed and plant them firmly on the carpeted floor. The world stills. Works every time.

I smile, feeling victorious as I grab the coffee. The first few sips do wonders for my throat, and when I speak again, my voice sounds a little more like me—still rough as usual, but less *Walking Dead*. I run a hand through my hair and feel it sticking out at all ends—again, my usual. "Are the guys warmed up? I have a good feeling about today. We laid down some pretty sick tracks yesterday."

Dave's eyebrows shoot to his hairline. For as young as the guy is —only a few years older than me—he looks double his age with bags and premature wrinkles around his eyes. He's every bit the high-powered LA talent manager and works the parental scowl better than my parents ever did. "Is that right? You laid down sick tracks yesterday, did you? Good feelings?"

My smile falls a little. He's doing that *question* thing he does when I'm in really big trouble. "Um..." There's never a right answer when he gets like this. He's not looking for answers anyway—or rather, he is, but there's only one answer he wants to hear. "Sorry, did I fuck up again?"

"Did you fuck up. Again."

Oh shit, it's the non-question repeat of my question.

I must've fucked up again.

I toss aside the comforter and stand up, because action is always the best response to Dave's anger. *Just get up and start moving.* There's a cold breeze between my legs. The naked puzzle piece works to make a full picture that points to why my manager of ten years is looking at me as if he caught me fucking his sister.

My toes flex on the luxury shag carpet. I swing my gaze to the floor-to-ceiling windows overlooking downtown Los Angeles. My stomach sinks.

"I'm not at the house," I mumble.

"What gave it away? The crystal fucking chandeliers? The fact that not a single one of your band members is here with you? Speaking of, where the fuck is Trey?"

Oh shit, we've graduated to *rapid-fire* questions. Not good.

My head throbs when I turn around to take in the room. The filigree wallpaper, white-gloss molding, tables covered in empty bottles of Dom and Macallan, and the remnants of white powder my nose must've missed.

I spot the door on the far end of the room and I nod. "He's probably in there."

Dave leans back in some ornate, French-style foo-foo chair, crossing his arms as if he's waiting for the fireworks show—a.k.a. my memory to fall back into place.

"Look, I'll grab my shit and meet you back at—" I step on something. I peer down to see a ripped condom wrapper. And it's not alone. At least a dozen are scattered all around the bed.

From the look on Dave's face, he saw them before I did, and he shakes his head as more disappointment tightens his expression.

Right, I need to find my clothes. I twist around, and every muscle in my body screams in pain. My gaze snags on a head of bleached-blond hair on the pillow next to mine. All right, so I picked up a groupie and brought her back to a hotel room for a night of absolute debauchery. Dave can't blame me for that.

There's also a lump at the foot of the bed. A big one.

I rip the comforter back to reveal two bare-ass-naked women.

"Huh..." I would've thought I'd remember them, but my mind is a black hole.

"Huh? *Huh?!*" He's yelling now.

I cover the girls back up and spot my jeans on the floor. I slip them on as quickly as possible without falling face first into the bedside table. "Look, I know you're pissed."

"Pissed? You think this is pissed? No, I'm fucking beyond pissed."

His voice follows me as I make my way around the room, searching for my shit. My wallet, where's my phone—oh my shirt!

"This is a PR nightmare! I ask you for one thing, one fucking thing, and you can't even do that! I rented you a mansion with a top-of-the-line recording studio for the band and even that's not enough. Your album was supposed to release in six weeks, Jesse! Six weeks!"

The door at the far end of the room opens and my bodyguard, Trey, comes stumbling out, wearing nothing but black boxers. "What the fuck is going—oh, shit." He sounds like a kid who got caught with his dad's *Playboys*. "Dave."

My manager's head whips around and glares at the six-foot-five wall of pure muscle as Trey cowers a little. "You're fucking fired."

"Hold on." I spot my phone on the coffee table and snag it. "Don't overreact. This isn't Trey's fault."

He stabs a finger toward the spot Trey is no longer standing in. My guess is he's on a mad dash to grab his shit too. "It's his job to keep you safe."

"I'm a grown-ass man." I pull my T-shirt over my head.

"Really? A grown-ass man, huh?" He gets right in my face. At just over six-feet tall, I've got a few inches on him, but you'd never know it by the way he's glaring at me. "Then tell me, what day is it?"

I have no idea, so I chuckle. "What does that have to do with anything?"

"I want you to tell me—"

A symphony of female whispers erupts from the door Trey came from as he ushers two girls in tight mini-skirts out of the bedroom.

They lock eyes with me, and I smile. The brunette with big hair runs up to me and throws her arms around my neck. I stumble backward —thanks to my hangover—and hold her around the waist to keep from taking us both down.

"You're so hot." She smells like stale perfume and last night's binge. "I love you."

"Thank you, sweetheart. I love you too." I loosen her arms from my neck as Trey hooks her around the waist from behind and pries her off me.

I notice he's holding the other one back too, her big eyes rimmed with black makeup as she blinks at me. After eight years of mega success, I fall easily into meet-and-greet mode and flash her a lazy grin that has her reaching for me.

"Party's over, ladies." Trey escorts the two women out, then he goes to fish the girls from the bed I slept in.

I lock myself in the bathroom, take a piss, splash cold water on my face, and check my phone so I can finally answer Dave's question about what day it is. The piece of shit is dead.

I brace my weight on my arms and hang my head. The last thing I remember is working on music at the mansion. Nathan and I got into it over a drum solo he wrote, and I left to grab a drink and cool down. Trey took me to a little dive bar where he knows the owner, and we were drinking Jameson, I remember that. Connecting the dots, we must've gone somewhere else, picked up some chicks, and grabbed the penthouse for the night.

Maybe it wasn't the smartest thing to do with the deadline for the album looming, but one night off seems reasonable.

I grab the little bottle of free mouthwash and try to gargle the taste of rotten ass from my throat. I'm sure Trey had the girls sign NDAs before we made it to the hotel. No matter how drunk or high we've gotten, he's never let me down when it comes to making sure my private life stays private.

When I open the bathroom door, I'm grateful to see the bed empty. The door to the hotel room closes, and Trey comes into the living room, looking apologetic. Dave is on the couch with one of the women from my bed. Her back is toward me as she speaks quietly to my manager.

"Please, you can't do this. Think of the band," Dave whispers.

The blonde is sniffling, and Trey hands her a tissue before looking at me. I grin and he refuses to meet my eyes. What the fuck?

"I'm sorry, I can't go back." More sniffles.

What the hell is going on?

She pushes back her long hair, and her profile catches me off guard. "We're in love, Dave. I know it's not the answer you want, but it's—"

"Kayla, please—"

The name is a punch to the ribs. "Kayla?"

She whirls around to face me and—oh fuck!

I rip my hands through my hair and close my eyes. "I didn't. No, I didn't, I didn't, I—"

Warm, feminine hands come around my waist, and she presses herself to my front. My eyes pop wide open to stare at the ceiling, but my hands stay firmly tangled in my hair.

"Jesse, it'll be okay. We'll tell Nathan—"

"Shit." I step back out of her arms and look at her as if seeing her for the first time—her tight red mini-dress, long thick hair, big lips, and even bigger eyes as she stares at me in shock. "Listen, Kayla, this was fun and all"—I think. Flashes of us kissing hungrily and falling into bed assault me. Yeah, it was definitely fun.—"but I have to think of the band."

"What?" She blinks slowly. "What are you saying? You told me we were forever. You said..." She clears her throat as her eyes fill with tears. "You told me you love me."

Dave groans and throws his hands in the air before falling back on the couch and rubbing the shit out of his face.

"I do love you." Love the way your lips feel against my skin, love the way you worship me in bed, love the way you apparently let me bring another woman into bed with us, but... "You're engaged to my drummer—"

"Ex-drummer," Dave groans.

I whip my gaze to him so quickly I get dizzy. "What do you mean ex-drummer?"

Dave stands and stares at me with cold-hearted detachment. "Nathan quit. Three days ago."

"That's impossible! We were recording yesterday—"

"Five days ago."

"No, I was—"

"Nathan called me and told me you walked out, throwing a hissy fit, five days ago." He pinches the bridge of his nose. "Kayla broke up with him the next day to run off with you, and he quit."

"Jesse"—she tugs on my shoulder—"come on, baby. We don't need this."

"Wait, I need a second." My head pounds and my gut churns.

"Sure, yeah." She rubs against my side, tucking in close. "Whatever you need."

Her presence is annoying and confusing. I step out of her hold. "Trey, please make sure Kayla gets home."

My bodyguard gently ushers a crying Kayla toward the door.

"You told me you love me!" The door closes behind her, and I hear her yelling all the way down the hallway to the elevator.

"Jesse—"

"It's all right. I'll talk to Nathan, tell him whatever he needs to hear to get us back into the studio."

"Jesse—"

"Let's get the fuck out of here." I move toward the door. "I need to use your charger. Phone's dead." My hand is on the doorknob.

"*Jesse.*"

My hand freezes as well as my feet. I've never heard him say my name like that, half dying man and half drill sergeant.

I turn around, and Dave nods at the couch. "Sit down."

I glare at the piece of furniture, imagining all that was done on it that I'm grateful I forgot. God, I slept with Nathan's fiancée.

What can I say? I love women. They make me feel fucking awesome and they do whatever I want. Once I asked a woman to get naked and squat-waddle around the room while flapping her arms like a chicken and she did. I laughed my ass off at the time, but after the fun, whenever I remember it, something that feels an awful lot like guilt digs in. No matter how much I drink and drug up, that unwelcome shit manages to worm its way in. Every. Single. Time.

Like now.

Fucking Kayla. But come on, clearly she and Nate already had problems if she'd sleep with me. If anything, I did the guy a favor. He was going to devote the rest of his life to a woman who dropped him like a bad habit just because I told her I love her. If I could explain that to Nathan, he'd understand and we could go back to making music.

"We'll talk on the way back to the mansion." I jerk my head to the door.

"We're not going back to the mansion." He shakes his head and frowns. I have to give the guy credit—he doesn't lose eye contact with me, not even to blink. "You're killin' your career, man."

I suck in a shaky breath. "I'll pull it together. I promise. I know I dropped the ball—"

"Dropped the ball? This is the first album you were set to put out that wouldn't have had a single Jesse Lee original song on it. You used to be the best songwriter in the business and now we can't get you to write *one*."

I run both hands through my hair, and although my head throbs and my stomach is sick, I think I may still be a little fucked up from last night because his words should shake me up a lot more than they do.

Something's wrong. I'm numb.

And getting more numb every day.

I've worked so hard to get where I am. Two Grammys, platinum albums, sold-out worldwide tours, and the monster in my soul is still hungry. No matter how much I feed it, it always demands more. So I pour into it. I snort happiness, fuck euphoria, and as soon as I think he's satisfied, I blink and he's hungry again.

"I get it. I've been fucking up. I know, and..." God, am I about to beg? "I can do this. I wrote 'Massive Attack' in less than an hour and won a Grammy for that. I can do this, I promise."

He steps close. "You're out of time."

That's okay. I can fix it. "I'll call our label, tell them I had a stomach bug or—"

"You used that excuse three weeks ago."

I jerk my head toward him. "Okay, well maybe I got strep, or fuck, I don't know, help me out here. This is bullshit." The monster in my chest yawns and stretches its reptilian arms, awake and gearing up to roar. "Have they forgotten how much money I've made them?" Oh God, the rumble of the monster's putrid growl swirls in my throat and there's no way to hold it back. I tower over him. "I need more time, and you're gonna make it happen because you work for me. You hear me? You all work for me. Arenfield Records is *my* bitch, not the other way around. Call them and tell them they'll get their fucking song when I'm ready to give it to them. In the meantime? Tell them to go spend the millions I've made them on some chill."

He stares at me with dead eyes, as though he's heard this tired-ass Top 40 song before and wants to change the station.

He's not the only one.

"What?" I'm practically panting now. I need a shot of whiskey and a white line.

"They dropped you."

"Excuse me?"

He shrugs.

"They dropped me?"

"Yes."

"Bullshit." I laugh, but the stern, no-nonsense look on Dave's face sobers me. Maybe half-sober is more accurate. "They can't fucking do that! My contract, they—"

"They can, they have. It's over."

My career, the band—oh shit, the guys are going to kill me. Chris has a wife and baby to support, Ethan would die if it weren't for playing music, and Nathan's already going to kill me. It's over? I grip my stomach and stumble to a half-filled ice bucket. A cough turns violent as I dry heave and I feel my ribs protruding beneath my shirt.

When I made it big, I was two hundred pounds of muscle and stamina. Now I look like one of those skinny runway models in Milan. I embody the strung-out rock star and everyone who knows me wouldn't tell me shit at the risk of evoking the monster. Everyone except Dave.

After coughing up air and mint-flavored spit strings, I wipe my mouth with my forearm and stare at my hands braced on the table. I'm covered in tattoos, but the little of my natural skin that shows through is the color of cocaine—pure fucking white. When was the last time I saw the sun for more than a mad dash from the back of a car to the front door of a bar? Years?

"What can I do?" My words drip with desperation and defeat.

"Nothing." His voice is resolute. "It's over. I'm sorry—"

"*Please.*" I cock my head to look at him but can't meet his eyes. "I'll do anything."

Silence expands between us for what seems like forever.

"There might be one thing," Dave says, and I hold my breath. "It's non-negotiable. I think we can get the label to reconsider if you go."

I pinch my eyes closed. "Go."

I don't need to ask where. I've been through it before. They're sending me back to rehab.

I blow out a long breath and try to calm my racing heart. *Breathe, Jesse.* I've done rehab a few times. I can do it again. If that's what it takes, I can do it. There's always a nurse who can sneak me booze and pills. Twenty-eight days of wooing an orderly for travel-sized bottles of liquor is easy.

"All right." I straighten up and roll my head around on my neck. "I'll go."

"Now."

"What do you mean now?"

"From here. Right now. No negotiating."

"Fuck. Like *right* now? What about my stuff? I need to get some things from my place—"

"Already done."

Guess that's the benefit of being a millionaire—I don't even need to pack my own shit. Still would've liked to have one more night to get drunk, pass out, and pretend my life is awesome and not a complete shit-storm.

"Fine." I shrug as I force the monster to accept this is what needs to happen to stay on top. "Twenty-eight days."

"Ninety."

My eyes burn as they practically fall from my skull. "Three *months?!*'

"That's the deal."

I lock my hands behind my neck and stare at the ornate wall-paper on the ceiling. Who the hell wallpapers a ceiling and how come I didn't notice that before? Whatever. Ninety days. I can do ninety days. I'm sure I'll be able to worm my way out after twenty-eight, good behavior and all.

"Fine." I groan. "I want the private double at La Mar Recovery, top floor, and none of that group shit they tried to get me to do last time. I'll agree only to one-on-one." I make my way to the door, and this time, Dave doesn't stop me.

He hands me a Dodgers ball cap and a pair of black Ray-Bans. I pop them on as we emerge into the hotel's hallway and move toward the elevators.

"Dr. Hanson. Tell him I'm only working with him and make sure I have that blood orange Pellegrino on hand. Last time they only had lemon. I hate that shit, it tastes like I'm drinking Mr. Clean." I smack the down arrow button. "I want my guitar too. Notebooks. Lots of them."

Inside the elevator, I lean on the back panel as the doors slide shut and Dave silently hits the lobby button.

"And none of that California cuisine crap they tried to feed me last time. I want Anton cooking all my meals." My private chef is the shit. He's originally from Louisiana and can infuse chronic into almost anything. "I want the same bedding I have at home. Same brand, thread count. Shouldn't you be writing this down?"

The elevator pings and we walk out into the lobby. Gasps and squeals erupt. I lift a hand and wave, smiling like the fucking rock star I am, and push through a crowd that forms before I duck into the back of a waiting limo. Dave crawls in behind me and closes and locks the door.

"Oh, one more thing—if I'm going to be locked up for ninety days, I want my fucking phone." I snag a fresh pack of Marlboro reds that are always stocked in every car I'm in, rip open the cellophane, and pop one between my lips.

Dave flips open a gold Zippo like a good little manager, and the flame dances in front of my face. The guy doesn't smoke, but he's always got a couple forms of fire on him for when I need it. He snaps the thing closed and tosses it on the bench seat across from him. "There's only one little problem with all that, Jes."

I suck in a lungful of smoke and exhale until the back of the limo is lost in a carcinogen cloud. "Yeah?" I pull off the ball cap to rub my head, and I chuckle. This should be fucking hilarious. "And what's that?"

"You're not going to rehab."

After weaving through the congested streets of downtown Los Angeles, the limo hops onto I-10 headed east. There's only one thing east of LA. Desert. Lots and lots of flat, boring, brown desert.

I want to ask Dave where the fuck we're going, but I won't give him the satisfaction of knowing I care. My concern is pointless anyway. My hope is we're headed to some quaint little personal reflection center in Palm Springs. If my label wants me to pull ninety days in the desert—which, btw, is more than twice as long as Jesus Christ did—I'll do it. I have to. For me, for my music, for the fans, for my band. Which reminds me, I need to call them.

"You got a charger?" I straighten my leg to fish my phone from my jeans pocket.

Dave holds out his hand, and I drop the device in his palm. I lay my head back and close my eyes while he takes care of getting it some juice. I hear the window roll down, and dry, hot air whips across my face. I open my eyes just as my iPhone gets tossed out the motherfucking window, and I whirl around in time to see it get sucked under a semi and blasted into a million pieces on the highway.

"What the fuck did you do that for?"

"No phones."

The ugly beast inside me cracks an eyelid.

"I have to call Nathan! You want me to make shit right with him, but you won't let me do it! My band needs to know I'm—"

"They know." He won't even look at me and speaks so calmly, as if he doesn't give a shit that he's ruining my life.

I practically belch as fury rises in my chest. I want to hurt him. I breathe through my nostrils and stare at my hands. My fingers clench into fists as I fantasize about wrapping them around his neck and squeezing hard. Unwanted images of my fingers on the frets of my guitar tease me and soothe a bit of the anger. I can't kill my manager. I have to rein in it, so I move through the chords of "Hurricane," the first song I ever wrote.

Six hours. Roughly.

It's hard to tell since I don't have a phone, but when Dave pulled out his, I made sure to take a peek. I've been stuck in the car for six hours. We passed through the Inland Empire, flew past Palm Springs, through Blythe and Quartzite, where Dave grabbed sandwiches I couldn't even look at without wanting to vomit. How long has it been since I actually craved food? Years? I ate because I knew I had to, but when did I last enjoy it?

I push those shit thoughts away without regret. I'll have three months to look back and question all the bad decisions I've made, and slowly starving myself won't even make the highlight reel.

We stopped at a deserted rest area so I could take a piss without getting hassled by fans. When we reached the outskirts of Phoenix, Arizona, the shakes kicked in and I desperately searched outside my window for the closest bar. My mind conjured ways to get away from Dave long enough to grab a quick few shots of anything. Another half hour and I was thinking I should've taken the mouthwash from the hotel this morning. It contained a little alcohol. Not enough, but something was better than nothing, right?

I am so fucked.

I have to close my eyes, hoping I'll fall asleep and wake up at the mansion with my band. I don't want these cravings. I want to write music. As those words move through my head, the monster laughs low, smoke coming out of his nostrils as he calls me on my shit. *You'd sell your fucking soul for a bottle of Jameson and a line.*

He's right.

I must've dozed off, because when I closed my eyes the sun was up and now the limo is stopped and it's dark outside. I rub my eyes and peek out the window. If it weren't for the rocks and cacti in the front yards of these shitty houses, I'd think we were in a rundown Los Angeles neighborhood.

When I look to ask Dave where the fuck we are, he's not there. I'm alone. My mouth waters at the chance for a drink. I dive toward the mini fridge, knowing it's a long shot. Surely Dave cleaned it all out before I got inside. My stomach sinks with a mix of craving and disappointment when I find nothing but Voss water.

"Shit." I search frantically out the windows. There's got to be a little neighborhood bar around here. Or hell, I could knock on any of these doors, and once they realize Jesse Lee is at the door, they'd offer up all the booze in their liquor cabinet.

It's worth a try.

Yes, this is the kind of shit that got me into this position in the first place, but what Dave doesn't know won't hurt him.

Convinced, I pop the door and hop out. Hot air slaps me right in the face and makes my skin wet. Either that or I'm suffering from withdrawal sweats. Either way, nothing a cold drink won't fix.

"Mr. Lee."

Son of a bitch. The limo driver is leaning against the hood with a smoke between his fingers. His eyes narrow on me as if he can read my intentions. Not that it would take supernatural skills—even I can feel the frantic crazy in my eyes.

So I drop the tension in my shoulders as best I can and scratch the few-days' beard growth on my jaw. "Yeah, man."

"You okay?"

"Great." I shove my shaking hands into the pockets of my jeans. "Where are we? Where's Dave?" *Translation: How much time do I have to get my hands on a drink?*

He jerks his head toward a small house with a crooked roof and a string of Christmas lights around the door. "You want a smoke?"

He holds out a pack and I take one then take his offered light.

Seriously, what are we doing here? Wherever here is. There's an old, beat-up minivan in the driveway and the lights are on inside the house, but all the cheap plastic mini blinds are closed. If I didn't know better, I'd think Dave was picking up some traveling weed from a poor white trash dealer in the middle of the desert, which would be fucking awesome.

I smoke the cigarette down to the filter in four drags then bum another one off the driver. I know him, he's driven me around plenty of times, but I can't for the life of me remember his name. "Thanks for the smokes."

He grunts and nods.

"Hey, um... are you a fan of my music?"

He chuckles and takes a long drag off his smoke. "Who isn't?" he says through a stream of smoke coming out of his nose.

"Cool, cool." I take another drag. "I'll get you tickets to our LA show for this next tour if you let me use your phone."

He raises one thick black brow, apparently thinking it over, then shrugs. "Sure."

He hands me his phone and I scramble to call my assistant/dealer before Dave shows his face. I stare at the number pad, quickly realizing that I don't know his phone number. In fact, I don't know anyone's phone number.

How can I not know any phone numbers? Not one?

9-1-1. That's all I got.

Dammit to fuck!

I hand it back to him, and he chuckles.

"Real funny." I take the last drag and flick the butt into someone's yard. I wonder if that was the smartest idea, seeing as we're in the middle of the very dry, very flammable desert. Or is it genius? A little scorched earth is a sure way to get me the hell out of here.

The door of the shitty little house opens with the sound of rusty metal rubbing on rusty metal. Limo Driver and I perk up as two men walk out.

The single string of Christmas lights casts the men in a weird orange silhouette, but I could spot Dave's shape and walk anywhere —average size, walks as if he's got a huge stick shoved straight up his type-A asshole. The guy with him is taller, my size. Something about him is familiar, but I don't dwell on that too much as I'm side-tracked by searching his hands for a big fucking bag of hydroponic. My mouth practically waters.

"You're awake." Dave's voice comes from the dark.

"Yeah." *Where's the weed?*

"Good." His face comes into view, and when he steps aside, I check out his friend's hands. Empty.

I groan and stare at my manager. "What the fuck are we doing here?" My pulse is kicking harder than usual and making me antsy. I need another cigarette, and if I can't get my hands on something to make them stop shaking—

"It's been a long time, Jesiah."

My breath freezes in my lungs.

You've got to be fucking kidding me.

Game. Over.

The monster jumps behind my ribs, electrocuted to life by the voice of my older brother using a name I haven't heard since I was seventeen years old.

I don't look at him. I can't look at him. Instead I glare at Dave as claws rip at my chest, pushing me to beat the fuck out of the presumptuous, meddling asshole. "Is this some kind of *joke?*"

"This is the deal." Dave's voice holds no hint of the fear he should be feeling. "Take it or leave it."

My jonesing brain struggles to understand what he's telling me. The deal. Not rehab. I still can't look at my brother. *"He's the deal?"*

Dave's face remains stoic, but the flash of pity in his eyes only manages to piss me off.

"After everything I've done for you." I shove his chest harder than I'd think I was capable of in my condition. He stumbles back but quickly recovers, only to come nose-to-nose with me. "You'd be blowing street performers for a chance to represent them if it weren't for me." I shove Dave again. "You hear me, motherfucker? You'd be nothing! *Nothing!*"

"Jesiah—"

I whirl on my brother, looking him in the eye for the first time and daring him to say my name one more fucking time. I haven't seen him in years, and except for the sensible haircut and button-up shirt, he looks the same. Dark hair, tan skin that he got from our mom's Italian side, and the strong features we both got from our dad.

Always the pacifist, he holds his hands up in surrender.

"You have a choice." Dave's voice calls me back to him. He looks a little pale. "You can leave here, come back to Los Angeles with me, and say goodbye to your career. Or..."

He doesn't need to finish that thought.

"Jesus."

My brother cringes.

I run my tongue along my teeth, my mouth dry, my skin itchy, my blood vibrating. "This is bullshit."

I throw open the door to the limo and crawl inside.

Dave mumbles, "Fuck."

I want to call him an asshole for not knowing me as well as he should.

I snag the three packs of smokes from the limo and Dave's Zippo he left in the cup holder, then I crawl back out. Dave looks relieved, and my brother nods solemnly.

I stare at the man who encouraged me to pursue music when everyone else told me to go into something more acceptable. The man who told me I could change the world with one song. The man who never, not once, gave up on me. Until he did.

I nod toward his house. "All right then, let's fucking do this, *Benjamin*."

2

BETHANY

There's just something about Sunday morning, am I right? The first day of the week. The day I can wash away the mistakes of the week prior and start fresh. Which is what I find myself doing every Sunday. I know I can't expect perfection—I am only human after all—but really, how hard can it be to go one week, seven measly days, without being a complete moral failure? *How hard?*

I straighten my lanyard and make sure my nametag is facing outward before plastering on a smile. (That's rule number one from church greeter prep class.) A big, fat smile. If I pretend I'm centered, secure, good, then that's the first step to being centered and secure and good. Fake it 'til you make it!

"Good morning, Mr. Gentry. Mrs. Gentry." The second rule is it's important to maintain eye contact as I hand them each a bulletin. "Welcome to church."

Mrs. Gentry squints through her bifocals at my nametag. "Thank you, Bethany."

"You're welcome."

Mrs. Diego flaps her hand-held fan so hard it blows her gray, curled bangs from her forehead. "Good morning."

"Welcome to church, Mrs. Diego." Using people's names makes them feel important and seen. Rule number three.

I continue working rule one through three until my cheeks hurt. "Good morning, welcome to church, Mr. and Mrs. Thompson." More smiling. "Good morning. Welcome to church, Mrs. Cash."

Sadly, she's not related to Johnny Cash. I asked. Apparently she gets asked often. Mr. Cash was a car salesman and died last year from emphysema.

"Good morning, uh... Mister... um..." Okay, he didn't seem to care that I don't know his name, so moving on. "Good morning." I go on and on until I'm sick of hearing my own fake-cheery voice. "Welcome to church—"

"Do I smell like vodka?" The hot breath accompanying my best friend Ashleigh's voice practically melts my earring.

More people pass through the doors. I hand them each a bulletin. "Good morning, welcome to church." I glare over my shoulder and hiss, "No. You smell like tequila."

She scrunches up her nose then leans toward my ear again. "Tequila... so like, bad morning-after tequila or good margarita tequila?"

My eyes bug out as I push my fake smile to its limit and continue to hand out bulletins. "Does it matter?"

"I think it does." She huffs into her palm to smell her breath.

"You're fine, just... we'll sit in the back row."

"It's *that* bad?" When I don't answer, she huffs more booze-breath in my face.

"Fine." She rolls her eyes. "I'll save you a seat."

She saunters away in her leopard-print skirt and red heels that she's paired with a sensible white button-up shirt. I don't know how she does it, but Ashleigh always manages to combine club clothes and church clothes in a way that looks semi-tasteful.

I stare down at my long, floral sundress complete with buttons from the bottom hem to the collar at my neck. I'm a bonnet away from looking like an Amish grandmother. Insecurity crawls over my skin, making me flush from my flat-sandaled feet to the tips of my ears.

"Welcome to church, Mrs. George."

I blow breaths upward to try to cool my face until the ushers relieve me by letting me know church is about to start. I find Ash in the last couple rows of the sanctuary, but the church is small, so we're really only twenty-three rows from the main platform.

The worship band plays as Ash leans into me. "So?"

When I look at her, she has one perfectly sculpted eyebrow arched over her chocolate-brown eye. "So what?"

Stupid question. I know what. She knows I know what.

I'm thankful for the music because she can't hear the dying animal sound that crawls up my throat. Appropriate, I think, as it's the sound of my broken heart.

"Well?"

I slip out my phone and open Instagram, making sure to keep the device low, on my lap, as I go to Wyatt's page. "He's not here. Weird though. His most recent post is from here in town, so I assumed he was back."

"Huh." She nods and says nothing that somehow says everything.

I'm pathetic. I need to move on. LOSER.

"I know, okay?" I close Instagram and flip the phone face down on my lap. "I just..." I can't let him go.

"I get it." She pops a Tic-Tac in her mouth and leans in to talk over the music as they gear up to drop the beat on "Great is Thy Faithfulness." "Remember when I cancelled Netflix and it practically killed me? I only lasted three days before I went back."

"Um... okay, but Wyatt isn't Netflix, and he broke up with me, I didn't break up with him."

"Still, it's almost the same thing."

"No, it's not even close to the same thing."

"Close enough." She winks. "Why don't you just call him and tell him you miss him, rather than stalking him and his new girl-friend at church? That's what I don't understand. You're practically salivating for a chance just to see him walk in"—she does a little flicking motion with her fingers toward the aisle—"and walk out."

"I'm trying to be the bigger person."

"By stalking him."

"It's my church too. Besides—"

"Shhh-shh-shh! This is my favorite part." She leans to the side to see around a big puff of teased and coiffed white hair. "Oh wow, he's wearing a green shirt. Good God, he's so hot in green..."

"Ashleigh, please remember you are not in a nightclub."

She snaps her fingers in my face. "Easy there, judgy. You have your reasons for coming to church. I have mine." Her eyes flare as they fix on the subject of her lust.

"Pretty sure there's a special place in hell for girls who have dirty fantasies about their pastors."

"I don't care." She licks her lips. "I just want one bite."

I look at Pastor Langley, and I totally get it. He's tall, dark, has perfectly balanced features and a seductive smile that has no busi-ness being on a man in his position. He always dresses appropri-ately, but his muscles fill out his oxfords in a way no woman could miss. He has no idea the temptation he flaunts to the women of his congregation. Pastor Langley is hot, I'll give Ash that, but he doesn't compare to my Wyatt.

My Wyatt. It's been two months since he broke up with me, and I still can't stop thinking of him as mine.

My heart thuds dully. I was really hoping I'd see him today. Maybe him and Suzette—*yeah, Suzette, what a stupid name.* They showed up at church together shortly after we broke up. What kind of a slut goes after a man who just broke up with the woman he loves—loved?

I squeeze my eyes closed and say a quick prayer that God would forgive my bitchiness—oh, and please forgive my profanity. Wow, great start to the week, Bethany. The sins are already lining up.

Is it too soon to call for a re-do?

If only I could go back in time to the weekend I took him to Sedona at that quaint little resort. That was when he first told me he loved me. A weekend for a lot of firsts—we made love that night. I really thought we'd end up together. There's still a chance that we will. We can be there again, back in that bed. Maybe we could honeymoon there.

I add fantasizing about another woman's boyfriend to my growing list of sins for the day.

Then quickly justify it because he used to be mine.

"This is my favorite part," Ashleigh squeals and claps as if we're at a male strip club. Not that I've ever been to one, but Ashleigh made me watch *Magic Mike*.

Pastor Langley takes his place at the pulpit.

"No one fills out a pair of tan slacks like that man." She groans and earns a scowl from the older couple in front of us. "What? You know it's true."

The woman shushes Ash then turns back around in a huff.

"She knows it's true," Ashleigh murmurs in my ear.

I grin and shake my head even though she's absolutely right.

Pastor Langley preaches on patience, on relying on God's timing rather than our own, but I struggle to pay attention as my gaze continues to scan the room. Maybe Wyatt came in late. Snuck in through a different door?

"What time do you have to be at work tomorrow?" Ashleigh asks while keeping her hungry eyes up front.

"Stop it, you're not coming to work with me."

"Oh come on! I have a bet with myself that he looks amazing in sweatpants. What does he sleep in? I'll drop you off and walk you in—"

"Ash. I can't risk losing my job just so you can get up close and personal with my boss. If you want to do that, you'll have to do it on your own."

"You're the worst friend ever."

I snort-laugh, earning another glare from the woman in front of us. "Sorry."

"Promise me you'll snap a pic if you see him in sweatpants. And I want the front angle." She winks and stares forward, tilting her head a little as Pastor Langley walks the platform, speaking animatedly about God. "Just one taste. One. Little. Lick."

"Oh my goodness, would you please be quiet!" The woman in front of us shakes her finger at Ash.

She and I sink into our pew, giggling until our stomachs hurt.

We manage to keep ourselves together for the rest of the service, and I jump up to open the doors as the final "amen" rings through the chapel. I say my goodbyes while searching for Wyatt's full head of wavy blond hair. After the door closes with the last of the congregation, I accept that Wyatt isn't here.

I wonder if he's sick. Maybe I should call him and check? I could bring him some noodle soup and—

"What are we grabbing for lunch?" Ashleigh hands me my purse. "I'm still hungover. I could use a burger."

"Whatever."

"Whoa." She gives me the side-eye as I pull off my lanyard and we walk to the parking lot. "Do I owe ex-fuckface for this splendid mood you're in?"

"We're at church. Easy with the f-bombs."

"We're in the lot. Besides, Jesus doesn't care."

Now I side-eye her. "I'm pretty sure he does."

She shrugs. "Agree to disagree."

"What?" My phone pings in my purse. I almost break the sound barrier getting the device into my palm. "Oh. It's Pastor Langley."

"Don't sound so disappointed. What does he want?"

I click open the text.

Little change of plans for tomorrow.

I text back.

Is everything okay?

The text bubbles appear then disappear, then my phone rings in my hand.

I jump, and Ash squeals when she sees his name pop up on my screen. "Ask him if he wants to meet us for lunch! Ask him if—"

I silence her with a hand in her face and hit Talk. "Hey, Pastor Langley, what's up?"

"Bethany, I'm driving so I couldn't text."

The sun is beating down on my head and my dress is clinging to my legs, so I motion for us to keep walking to Ashleigh's car. "Okay."

"About tomorrow."

"Yeah, is Elliot sick?"

"No, she's fine. This weekend was crazy or I would've reached out to you sooner, but, uh… there's something I need to discuss with you. Can you come over a little early tomorrow?"

"What time do you need me there?"

"Sometime around seven or eight? If that's okay?"

"Sure."

"Great. I'll see you then. Thanks."

The line clicks off, and Ashleigh stares at me through wide eyes. "He wants you there early! He likes you. You slut!"

I open the passenger side door and climb inside. "He's a pastor! He made vows or signed a contract or… I don't know how that works, but I'm his daughter's nanny and he's not some horny frat boy."

"He's a single man and I know single men. They all want sex."

"You should start paying more attention in church."

"Whatever. So if he's not having you come early to proposition you for sex, then why?"

"I know this might come as surprise to you, but a large majority of the population have entire lives outside of sex. And it's nice to know you listen to all my phone calls. Snoop."

She blows that off and turns the engine. "Oh! Maybe he's banging some chick in the church and he wants to talk to you about how he's going to handle it with the congregation or whatever."

"Have you not been listening to a single word I've said?"

She slams her palms on the steering wheel. "Whoever she is, she is so lucky!"

"Easy there, Miss Assumption."

"He's banging Anne-Louise. I'd bet my savings account."

"You have less than fifty bucks in your savings account."

She lifts a brow in my direction. "Now who's the snoop?"

3

JESSEJESSE

There have been a couple times in my life when I've wanted to die.

Once when I had the flu and was about to go on stage in front of a sold-out arena in Sydney. I had a temperature of 103. Dave kept saying we should cancel, but there was no way I would let down my fans because of a stupid microscopic virus. I planned to die on stage. Instead, I made that virus my bitch and had one of the best shows of my life. I collapsed before the last song and was rushed to the hospital, but fuck, it was so rock-n-roll.

There was another time when I wished I were dead, but I refuse to think of things that happened back before I was Jesse Lee, so fuck that.

I will say, even after those times, this here, lying on some crappy spring mattress covered in cheap, itchy sheets in a tiny cluttered room that's plastered in framed photos of the same smiling face... yeah, I'm ready to meet my maker. My body won't stop shaking, my skin is constantly wet, and I'm thirsty, but every time I try to drink water, my stomach rejects the fluid. That must be the reason for the handy-dandy bag hanging beside me and attached to the IV in my arm.

Curled into a ball on my side, I moan as a fist grips my guts and squeezes hard. Everything hurts—from my head to the tips of my fingers. Even my toenails feel as if they've been crushed with a hammer.

I need a bottle or a bag of coke or a fucking casket.

I push out a breath and groan. Hold my breath and hope to pass out and die. Flip onto my back—nope, that's worse. Roll to my other side, shove my face in a pillow, and want to scream, but I'm afraid the act of opening my mouth with any kind of force will send me into a fit of dry-heaving muscle spasms.

A deep murmuring comes from my side, and my eyeballs feel as though they've been peeled when I open my lids to find the source of the sound.

Ah, I should've known.

My brother sits in a chair close to the door, his Bible open on his lap. His gaze slides along the words as his lips barely move. Praying. Why am I not surprised?

"Do something... worthwhile... and get me a drink," I say between convulsive shivers.

His chin tilts up. I hate that he looks concerned. The two of us haven't been able to be in the same room without fighting since the night I grabbed my guitar and took a bus to LA.

"You're awake." He closes his Bible and sets it on the table next to him. "I wondered what kind of drugs they were giving you to keep you asleep for so long."

"Benzos." I shake so hard my teeth chatter. "Tell the nurse to stop being so stingy with the pills."

"You want me to grab Pete?"

My left leg cramps up hard. "Who the fuck is Pete?"

The dark, judgmental stare pinches his expression, and the beast inside me whips his scaly tail with the challenge.

"Love what you've done with your room here, *Benjamin*." I motion as best I can with one arm at all the photos.

His expression grows even tighter, and I catch a flicker of warning in his eyes.

"It's like a goddamn Maggie shrine in here."

My words hit their target, and he pushes up from his chair to take two steps toward me. I chuckle, partly because it's nice to see the good pastor still has some fire in him, and also because I might very well get him to smother me with a pillow and bring me the sweet fucking relief of death if I keep this shit up.

"She'd be proud to see you doing so well without her. I bet..." I brace to fight off a wave of nausea and clear my throat. "I bet you still have all her clothes. Maybe your next wife will wear them and you can pretend she's—"

"That's enough."

"No, it's not." I chuckle. "I'm not even warmed up yet."

"That's the drugs talking, you're not yourself—"

I burst out laughing because he has no fucking idea who I am or what myself sounds like. "Stop being a little bitch and get over your dead wife already."

He spins toward the door and grips the handle, but he mumbles, "I'll be praying for you, Jesiah." Then he walks out.

I smile. That was easy enough. I should have him killing me or kicking me out in no time. My eyes lift to a photo of Maggie on the bedside table. There's nothing special about her. She looks like an average girl on an average day. I never knew Maggie. I met her briefly when I went to my brother's wedding but ended up leaving early because the paparazzi got wind and crashed the party.

Fine by me. The booze was cheap and the bridesmaids were all Bible-bangers. Maggie seemed like an okay chick though. Perfectly blah and normal, just like my brother.

Three years later, Dave pulled me out of a recording session to let me know Maggie had died of some weird shit that happened giving birth to my brother's kid. I should've probably reached out, but I knew I was the last person he'd want to hear from and there was nothing I could say to make him feel better.

Yep. I don't need him and he never needed me.

I flip the photo down so I don't have to stare at Maggie's disapproving face. "Family. So fucking overrated. You should know that by now, Maggie."

My eyes focus across the room. I blink to clear the haze of fever-sweats. The chair. A blanket has been thrown over the back of it, but I'd recognize the carved pattern anywhere. How many times were my palms marked by that fucking pattern?

Why does my brother have it?

A violent heave wracks my body, and I cough and spit over the side of the bed, praying for death to come.

BETHANY

The bus stops a block from Pastor Langley's house on Palo Verde Road. Mid-March and its almost ninety degrees at seven o'clock in the morning, and my shoulder under my purse strap is wet with sweat. I'm grateful for the tiny breeze cooling my skin. Every year summer in the desert is as hot as I imagine hell to be, and I've made no move to relocate.

Because of Wyatt.

No, not because of Wyatt!

I have my friends here—okay, my one friend. My church... ninety percent of the congregation is twenty to thirty years older than me. My parents live only an hour away. And come on, what's not to love about Surprise, Arizona? Even the name is fun.

I'm scrolling through Wyatt's IG page, tapping on old photos to see if there are any new comments, but find nothing. Maybe he's still—I spot a navy pickup truck in the driveway, next to the pastor's minivan that's parked over the huge chalk rainbow drawn on the concrete. I shove my phone in my pocket and knock twice on the door before the lock clicks open.

A man with dirty-blond hair, who I've never seen before, answers. "Hey, you must be the nanny."

"Bethany." I respond to his kind smile with one of my own.

"Come in." He swings open the door, his free hand firmly wrapped around one of the pastor's coffee mugs that has THE SERMONATOR written on it. "Coffee's fresh."

He walks past me to the kitchen as if he's lived here all his life, which is really weird. I've been Elliot's nanny for two years and never seen another soul in this house.

"I'm sorry, but who..."

"Oh." He holds out a hand to shake mine. "I'm Pete, RN."

"RN?" I realize now that Pete RN is wearing blue scrub pants with a matching shirt. My gaze darts to the hallway that leads to the bedrooms. "Is Pastor Langley all right?"

"He's fine." He turns toward the cupboards and grabs a mug. "Coffee?"

"Uh... sure."

"Cream and sugar?"

"Yeah, that's great, thanks."

Elliot must still be sleeping. I've never been here this early. Usually when I come at nine o'clock, she's already at the table, eating cereal.

"Nice shirt." He eyes the logo on my left boob and lingers a little too long before grinning at me. "You work there?"

No, dumb dumb, I just like wearing a Pies and Pancakes uniform shirt. "I do."

"You have my favorite pie." He hands me my coffee with a smirk that makes my skin feel hot. "French silk."

"Oh, yeah." I accept the coffee. "It's one of our most popular flavors."

I move to the living room to avoid whatever it is he's doing that feels an awful lot like flirting. I set my purse on the couch and notice a pillow and folded blanket placed at the end. Is Pete RN sleeping over at Pastor Langley's house? *None of your business, Nosey Nancy.*

A door slams and I startle, spilling hot coffee on my hand. I lick it off before it drips to the floor just as Pastor Langley comes down the hallway. His hands are in his hair, his elbows high so that his T-shirt sleeves slide down to showcase his larger-than-pastor-sized biceps. He makes eye contact with Pete and frowns. Whatever non-spoken conversation they have doesn't seem like good news.

I turn my back to give them privacy, but then I hear someone coughing violently. I spin around as the RN springs into action and races down the hall. What the hell was that?

"Bethany, hey," Pastor Langley says on an exhale, heavy with relief.

Oh wow, he *is* wearing sweatpants. Ashleigh's going to kill me because there's no way I'm pulling out my phone to snap a pic.

He drops his hands from his head and motions to the dining table. "Have a seat?"

"Oh, sure." I scurry over and can't help but let my eyes travel down the hallway.

He grabs himself a cup of coffee and takes the seat across from me. His cropped brown hair is a mess and his eyes droop a little bit, as though he's in desperate need of a good night's sleep. "Thank you for coming early." He runs a hand over his head. "There have been some changes around here, and they may affect your willingness to continue work as Elliot's nanny."

I wonder if it has anything to do with the sick man in the pastor's room. I sip my coffee, trying to remain calm, even though it sounds as though I'm about to get fired. I can't get fired. I need this job. "Oh?"

"Are you familiar with…" He sets his intense green eyes on me, and it's hard to hold his gaze. "My background?"

"Um… not really. I only know about Elliot's mom…" I allow my words to trail off because neither of us need to hear me say "dying."

"Right." He frowns, and I hate the look on him. "Very few people know that I have a brother and he's… well, he's a huge pain in the ass."

I chuckle at the pastor saying *ass*. Seriously, how cool is he?

"We were estranged until a few days ago when his manager called, telling me my little brother needed my help. There was no way I could say no, even though, between us, it was really tempting."

I nod, afraid to say the wrong thing, but did he say manager? I'm guessing he's not talking about the blue-Walmart-vest-with-a-gold-nametag kind of manager. I know his brother can't be Pete RN—they look nothing alike—which means—

"So, uh… my brother has been staying with me. He's staying in my room because he's pretty sick."

Ah-ha! How sick? Cancer?

"But…" His face scrunches up as he looks at me. "He's getting better. Stronger every day, and I guess what I'm saying is, he's going to be here for a while. Three months, to be exact."

"Forgive me, but what does this have to do with me?"

He reaches over to the bookshelf to his left and I *do not* notice the straining muscles in his arms. Nope. No, I do not.

He slides a piece of paper in front of me. "I hate to ask you to do this. I hope you know I trust you implicitly, but the big boys in LA have their own rules and if you don't sign this, then you'll no longer be able to nanny for Elliot and that will really suck."

I blink at the sheet of paper. The header is the name of a law firm printed in a fancy font on pretentious cream-colored paper. The subject of the document: *Non-Disclosure Agreement*. I allow my eyes to follow along, line for line, the strings of ten-dollar lawyer words I don't understand.

Then I get to a name.

One name I've seen plastered on every gossip magazine headline, every entertainment news show, and every awards show in the history of Hollywood—or at least in the last five years.

"Jesse Lee?" I swallow back my reflex to choke. Nervousness has always made me nauseated. I set my eyes on Pastor Langley. "Your little brother is *Jesse Lee*?"

He nods solemnly.

My gaze slides down the hallway to the bedroom. "Jesse Lee is in this house?"

"He is." Pastor Langley slides a pen across the table. "And if you want to stay employed by me, and I pray you do because I'd be lost without your help, I'll need you to sign." He dips his chin toward the document. "I'm sorry, I know this isn't cool, but everything happened so fast and—"

"It's okay." Is it? Is it okay? There's a world-renowned recording artist a stone's throw from where I'm sitting. Jesse Lee, the rock-n-roll bad boy, the Coast-to-Coast Casanova, the guy who recorded a song with the sound of him pleasuring himself in the background until he... he... *until completion!*

"If you're at all uncomfortable with this, I understand. If you're a fan of my brother's music, I think it's best if you don't sign it."

"I'm not a fan." No way. Gross. I mean, his music is all right if you can get over the fact that he's a worldly, self-indulgent heathen. "Not at all."

"I figured as much." He grins. It's small, but it's enough to stick in my craw.

Why would he figure I'm not a Jesse Lee fan? I like music. I like all kinds of music.

Pete RN comes out of the bedroom, closing the door softly as if trying not to wake the person inside. The front of his shirt is wet and he has a small towel in his left hand. He makes eye contact with Pastor Langley but doesn't speak. Both men's eyes come back to me.

Right. I go back to reading the document. If I sign this, I'm not allowed to speak about what I see inside this house to anyone.

I'm not allowed to speak to the press. *Well, duh! Who would do that?*

No photos. No videos. No autographs.

All infringements upon this contract will constitute legal action.

This is ridiculous.

I scribble my name on the dotted line and slide the paper back across the table. The pastor exhales long and hard, and I sense the relief pouring off of him.

"It'll be fine, Pastor."

"Please, I've told you before, you can call me Ben."

"Right... okay."

He scoots back in his chair and takes a photo of the document before hitting some buttons on his phone. I assume he's sending it to the powers that be.

"Welcome aboard, nanny." Pete squeezes my shoulder then tugs my ponytail playfully.

"Uh... thanks?"

I don't really see how things will be all that different with the infamous Jesse Lee in the house. I'll still show up every day and sit with Elliot until we hop on the bus to go to preschool at noon. Then I'll scurry off to work at the diner like I do every day of the week. Surely adding a multi-millionaire, triple-platinum-selling, Grammy-award-winning man-slut to mine and Elliot's mornings won't be too disruptive. Hopefully he and Pete RN will stay in that back bedroom.

Pastor... er... Ben sets down his phone and looks at me in a way that feels like the sincerest of apologies.

"I'm going to be fine, Ben." Wow, it feels weird calling him by his name. "I'm here for Elliot. I'd never turn my back on her, you know that."

"I appreciate that, I do. But, uh, there's one more thing that's not in the contract, but I'm asking as a friend, as your pastor."

"What is it?"

"Please don't tell anyone Jesse's my brother."

"Oh, okay. Sure." I make a zipping motion on my lips and toss away the key.

He smiles with a full mouth of straight, white teeth and I can see it now. Add a sexy smirk, a head full of X-rated thoughts, a few dozen tattoos, and a little more height but less muscle... yeah, I can see how Pastor Langley and Jesse Lee could be brothers.

I wonder why all the secrecy.

4

BETHANY

The rest of the week is completely uneventful. I show up at the Langleys' at nine o'clock sharp as Ben gathers his things to head to the church. Pete RN stays in the bedroom with the superstar—I assume watching him sleep or whatever else nurses do with sick famous people. A flash of Pete RN giving Jesse Lee a sponge bath flickers through my mind, but I push it out of my head.

Elliot and I eat cereal and watch cartoons before I bathe her and dress her for school. I make her lunch while she practices her colors at the dining room table, and we're out the door to catch the bus. The week runs like clockwork.

So when I show up at Pastor Langley's on Friday, I expect much of the same.

The door swings open before I'm even across the yard, and Ben comes spilling out with one arm full of books and the other hand holding a huge travel mug. "I'm late for a meeting with the elder board. Go on in, Elliot's watching TV."

He gets to his minivan without dropping anything, which is

impressive considering he looks as though he hasn't slept in a month.

"Okay. Have a great day!" I wave as I jog up the couple steps to the front door.

"Thank you!" His car fires to life, and I watch him pull out cautiously.

When I get inside, Elliot's in her rainbow PJs, holding her stuffed tomato and watching *Veggie Tales*.

"Good morning!"

She turns around, her dark eyes settling on mine for a second before she smiles. "I'm watching *Silly Songs with Larry!*" She points at the television and turns back as the animated cucumber sings in a slightly annoying voice.

I drop my purse on the couch and squat next to her, kissing her head before pushing her dark curls away from her face. "Did you eat?"

Her mouth is open and she smells like Honey Nut Cheerios.

"I'm going to take that as a yes." I cross to the kitchen, where I can keep an eye on her as I clean up the breakfast dishes, and freeze when I see a sink full of plates. "Looks like someone's feeling well enough to eat again."

I haven't asked what's wrong with the celebrity locked in the back room, but I'm practically a PhD after Googling every symptom I've heard whispered around the house. Chills, vomiting, hallucinations, no appetite... my guess is flu or stomach bug. I can't imagine Ben allowing anyone in the house who might be contagious, but that might be why Mr. MTV is quarantined in the bedroom.

I keep that in mind while I rinse the dishes and put them in the dishwasher. I run the machine immediately and make sure to wash my hands and sanitize the sink when I'm through. When I hear footsteps in the hallway, I look up to see Pete RN making his way toward me.

"Mornin', Beth-nanny." He tosses a newspaper in the garbage and sets two coffee mugs in the sink.

One of those probably had Jesse Lee's lips all over it. I wonder how much something like that would sell for on eBay? I heard a waitress put Justin Bieber's dirty milk glass on eBay for $75,000! Of course, this mug could be carrying a highly contagious disease so...

"Hey, Pete. You're hilarious." I rinse the coffee mugs, kissing a potential seventy-five Gs goodbye. "Charlie Sheen."

"Nope."

Over the last few days, I've learned a little more about the playful nurse, like the fact that he lives in Phoenix and works in private care catering to the rich and famous. The problem is he refuses to disclose who he's worked for, but swears if I guess right, he'll let me know. So far, all my guesses have been wrong.

I wipe my hands and hang up the towel, waiting for him to speak. His posture indicates he has something to say.

"I need to run out for a bit."

"Um, *what?*" I try to remain calm by closing my eyes and attempting to lock down my suddenly racing heart. "You're leaving?"

"Don't sound so scared." He winks which, despite his handsomeness, makes him a little skeevy if I'm being honest. "I'll be back."

Is it okay for him to leave?

He laughs. "You're cute when you're confused."

I'll ignore that. "Are you sure you should leave? I mean, what if he falls or, like, needs something?"

"First off, he won't fall. Second, I won't even be gone for an hour."

My eyes dart over his shoulder to the hallway. "So he's feeling better then?"

He seems to mull something over for a second, as if he's trying to choose his words wisely. "There's no concern for any immediate health risks."

I wring my hands and lean over the breakfast bar to make sure

Elliot is still happily involved in her show. "He's not contagious, is he?"

His eyebrows pinch together. "No." A slow smile pulls his lips. "He's not contagious."

"Phew... great. I feel better."

He blinks a few times then shrugs. "Right, so I'm going to take off."

"Maybe I should call Ben and let him know." I pat my pockets for my phone before remembering it's in my purse.

"No need." Pete snags his keys from the bookshelf. "He already knows." He holds up his cell. "I texted him."

"Oh, so... okay. Cool." Ugh, why does my stomach hurt?

He checks his phone then heads out the door, leaving me alone. All alone with a four-year-old and a mega-millionaire rock star.

Rather than dwell and give myself an ulcer, I go about the day as though it's any other day. "Hey, Elliot? When this is over, how about we do some coloring?"

She doesn't peel her eyes from the screen.

"Okay, glad you're on board."

Until her episode is over, I'll tidy up the living room and pick out Elliot's clothes for the day. I throw together her lunch—cheese sandwich, sliced apples, a cookie, and milk. Maybe I'll get her bathed and dressed before we color, in case we lose track of time.

I head to the bathroom at the end of the hallway and freeze when I hear a moan from the other side of the master bedroom door. The sound stops and I wonder if I imagined it. I ignore my overactive brain and plug and fill the bath. When the water level is high enough, I shut it off and go to grab Elliot. My feet freeze again when I hear another pained groan coming from the bedroom.

I close my eyes and tell myself he isn't my problem. Jesse Lee is Pete RN's problem. But what if he's hurt? I chew the inside of my mouth, staring down the hallway, then back at the bath, then settle on the door.

A long groan of agony sounds again.

Oh no, he's really suffering.

My hand shakes as I grip the doorknob and I crack open the door. The first thing I notice is the smell of disinfectant, which—even though Pete assured me he's not contagious—brings me comfort when I stick my head inside the sick room.

I've never seen Pastor Langley's bedroom before. The door has always been closed when I'm here and I'd never snoop. Jesus is always watching.

Even now, I don't linger on the room but force my gaze to the source of the sound.

There, under nothing but a white sheet, is a tattooed, naked torso. Attached to that torso is a head topped with a full mess of brownish-red hair. *Oh em freakin' gee.*

There in the bed is Jesse Lee.

He's on his back, his head propped up on pillows, his chin pointing toward the ceiling and showcasing the most perfect male jawline I've ever seen—square, strong, and hard. I would say almost too hard-looking if it weren't for his pouty lips and long eyelashes. He licks his lips, and his white teeth emerge to sink into his thick lower lip.

At the sign of his pain, I'm jerked from my inspection and jump into action—only to stop abruptly when I notice his right arm shoved beneath the sheet. And it's moving in quick, jerking strokes.

I gasp and throw my hand over my mouth.

He moans and lifts one knee. The sheet slides off and down his lean thigh that's decorated in more ink. I stumble backward and whirl around only to slam into the doorframe. I fumble out the door and hurl it closed.

My breath comes in quick bursts, and my face is so hot it burns. A deep, gravelly chuckle followed by a soft sigh sends me pinwheeling down the hallway to Elliot.

Omg, omg, omg! He wasn't in pain! He wasn't in *any* pain. He was... he was... I can't believe I witnessed Jesse Lee pleasuring himself!

"Okay, it's okay." I try to calm myself as I scoop Elliot off the floor without bothering to turn off the TV. "Bath time!"

I race past the bedroom door and lock us in the bathroom. We'll be safe here until Pete gets back.

JESSE

That was fantastic.

If I had the strength to get up, I'd go kiss that woman on the mouth for the gift she just gave me.

I had been getting a bit nervous about my ability to get myself off. Didn't help that Benji's wife was smiling at me from all six hundred photos.

Then there's that motherfucking chair. I'd had the nurse cover it completely with a blanket, but that shit haunts me from behind the crocheted throw.

I didn't think I'd even get close to coming, but then the mystery woman poked her head in. I knew it wasn't the good ol' man nurse because he would've kept his cool and left me to my shit. My brother would've launched into a lecture on why jacking off is a sin.

She didn't do either.

I heard her sharp intake of breath. I knew for a few short seconds she was watching me, and I imagined she enjoyed what she saw.

None of the images pulled up from my memories of debauchery and triple-x-rated sex-a-thons did a thing for me, but that innocent little gasp sent me reeling. I saw stars, lost all feeling in my arms and legs, my throat went dry, and if I weren't already lying down, I'd have fallen on my ass.

I didn't even see her face, just a flash of a simple brown ponytail as she raced out the door. For all I know, she could be a beauty queen or a troll. Doesn't matter to me—I'd kiss the crap out of her for what she'd done.

I clean up with the cheap top sheet and toss it onto the floor.

"Junk still work? Check." I lie naked under the ceiling fan and soak in the first solid period of time that I actually feel… good.

Now that all the drugs and booze are exorcised from my system, I can work on my plan to get out of here.

I roll to my side then push up slowly to sit at the edge of the bed. Without any blood in my head, I brace myself on my knees to stay upright. My skull throbs with the new vertical position, and my body feels as if I went two rounds with Tyson. I lie back down and must doze off because when I wake up, I find the man-nurse in the chair, reading a magazine.

"So?" My voice sounds raw from not being used. "What's the word?"

He closes the magazine and stands. "Nothing, yet." He gathers the stack of gossip magazines and pack of cigarettes I sent him to buy and places them on the bedside table. "But there're four pages of celebrity photos before and after they got boob jobs."

I groan and push up to sit.

"Looks like you're still flying under the radar." He peeks at the top sheet still balled up on the floor. "New sheets?"

I grab the magazines and skim the headlines for my name, but it seems the nurse is right. "How long have I been here?"

He's gathering the sheet off the floor and stuffing it into a hamper. "One week today."

"Huh." And not a single fucking news outlet noticed I'm missing.

"You've been weaned off the meds—would you mind sitting over there so I can strip the bed?"

He offers me a hand, but I ignore it and slowly push myself out of bed. He's crazy if he thinks I'm going anywhere near that chair. I may be weak as fuck, but I'll risk falling and cracking my head rather than sit on the throne of nightmares. I stumble to the far side of the room. He tosses me a pair of sweatpants, and I appreciate that he doesn't stare at my naked ass and make things weird.

"Dave should be calling any minute to let us know what the next step in your recovery is." He goes about gathering all the dirty bedding. "Are you hungry?"

"Who's the girl?"

With his arms full, he looks at me. "What girl?"

I nod toward the door.

"Did she come in here?"

A slow smile spreads my lips at the memory of her innocent gasp and what it did to my body. "Yeah."

"Oh." He frowns, most likely putting together my nudity, the dirty sheets, and the girl, and coming to the most obvious conclusion. Wrong, but I won't correct him. "Uh…" He crosses to the door, stares at it for a second, then turns back to me. "She didn't mention it."

"That's not what I asked." Fuck, does this guy need me to write it down?

"She's no one. Just the nanny."

I've only been out of detox hell for hours at the most and already my body is jonesing hard for a thrill. Drugs and booze are out of the question if I want to keep my band together so… "She still here?"

"Nah, man. She's gone—oh, hold on." He fishes his cell phone from his pocket. "It's Dave." He hands it to me then leaves the room with the hamper.

"Eighty-three days to go," I say when I answer the phone.

"Nice to see you're in no hurry."

"Dave. I'm sober. Don't be a bitch."

"Pete says you're off the detox drugs."

"I am. And now I get to sit on my ass, bored out of my mind, for eighty-three days when I could be recording and making you millions."

"Here's what happens next. You'll have private counseling every day for the next thirty days—"

"You've got to be fucking kidding me."

"Down to twice a week for the following thirty days, then once a week for the last thirty."

"This is bullshit!"

"You'll also be meeting with an AA-slash-NA group daily."

"You seriously expect me to be able to stroll into some AA group without security? Are you fucking insane?"

"I'm making arrangements so it'll be safe, and everyone will sign NDAs."

"Why are you doing this? I'm sober! That's what you wanted, so why don't we cut the crap and get back to work?"

He's silent for a few beats too long.

"Dave!"

"Look, Jesse..." He sighs long and hard. "How much is your career worth to you? This is your *only* chance to hold on to everything you've worked so hard for."

The monster inside burps, and it bubbles up my throat. "I'm a fucking rock god. I don't need you or the band. I could walk out of this shithole house right now and be back on the Top 10 in one week!"

"That's where you're wrong. You're unemployed. You have no band, no label, and if you fight this, every label from Los Angeles to New York will blackball you."

"Not if they want to make money off me they won't!"

"Do you have any idea how much money Arenfield Records lost because of you in the last year? Cancelled shows because you had to be shipped off to rehab, all the studio hours they booked and paid for but you never fucking showed up? Not to mention the last album tanked!"

The hand gripping the phone shakes, and I resist the urge to throw the device into the closest wall.

"This is your only option. Take it or leave it, but know that if you leave, it's over. Done."

I rub my eyes and groan. How the hell did I lose control over my life?

BETHANY

"Pancakes and a side of bacon." I set down the plates on the table of three men who look as though they're pre-gaming before hitting a bar. "Can I get you anything else?"

When they assure me they're good, I check on my other tables. Friday nights at Pies and Pancakes is a lot busier than one would think. We don't serve alcohol, but we serve the one thing everyone who's been out drinking seems to crave.

Loads of carbohydrates.

"Excuse me?" A man in jeans and a T-shirt is dipping his napkin in his water glass. "Can I get more syrup? I spilled on myself." He brings the wet napkin to his groin area and rubs vigorously.

The quick visual takes me right back to this morning, walking in on Jesse. I spin away with an animated, "Sure thing!" and scurry off to the kitchen.

With the sound of sizzling breakfast meat on the griddle and the scent of sweet dough in the air, I try to forget what I saw Jesse Lee doing in his brother's bed. Funny, but trying to forget the visual only has me thinking about it more. Why is it we can't unsee the things we want to unsee? Why don't we have some kind of delete button to completely strike the image from our memory? I have a list of things I'd like to erase from my memory bank.

I fill up another small pitcher of syrup, then I deliver it to the guy who—thank goodness—has stopped cleaning himself.

But the damage is done as I replay Jesse's tattooed arm tucked beneath the bed sheet, his straining muscles, his chin tipped back, over and over on a loop—"No!"

The man looks at me, clearly confused.

"No, uh... no problem."

I need to get this off my chest. If I could tell Ashleigh about what I saw, she'd make me feel better—no one can normalize sexual stuff like she can—but that damn NDA means I have to process and get over this on my own. Alone.

Moving on. Think of something else. Stay busy and eventually I'll forget that I saw Jesse Lee having sex with himself. Sure. Totally something a female would forget.

I grab the box of sugar packets from storage and fill sugar ramekins in an attempt to forget, or at the very least ignore, my memories.

"Bethany, you have a new table," Mindy the hostess calls to me as she runs toward the employee bathroom. "Keep an eye on the front for me? I have to pee."

I put down the box of sugars and grab my pad and pen to take the order of the couple sitting in my section. My feet refuse to move when I see who the couple is.

Wyatt and Suzette.

Okay, be calm. Breathe.

I put on my most comfortable body language and force myself to their table. "Good evening, welcome to—oh wow, Wyatt? Is that you?"

I mentally cringe. Is that you? We dated for almost a year, as if I'd forget what he looks like? *Smart, Bethany.*

"Uh… yeah." He seems surprised to see me. "Hey, Beth."

I never liked being called Beth, but somehow Wyatt makes the name sound like royalty. "You're back from Hawaii."

He frowns. "How did you know I was in Hawaii?"

My mouth drops open a little as I try to come up with a non-stalkery-sounding excuse. I shrug casually. "You posted on IG, it passed by in my feed." No biggie. Not stalking.

"Oh, right." Uncomfortable silence stretches between us. "I didn't know you'd be working tonight."

"I work every other Friday and Saturday, rotating, that way I get one weekend night off a week." I pinch my lips closed to keep from rambling on about things he probably doesn't care about.

"Yeah, I, uh… I didn't see your car outside."

"Ah, yeah, well, my car? It's uh… Oh! Our pie of the week is pecan caramel, your favorite." I rush out my words, hoping to take the focus off my car and what happened to it. Without my permission, my face and neck grow hot with embarrassment.

"No pie tonight." His arm is thrown over Suzette's shoulder. My gaze sticks on his thumb softly caressing the bare skin at her bicep.

"You remember Suzette," he says.

"Yes, hi." She's beautiful—long black hair, exotic almond-shaped eyes, puffy lips in a constant pout, and I know from stalking her social media she has the body of a swimsuit model. Maybe she is a swimsuit model, although I think she would've included that in her bio. "It's good to see you again."

She grins. It's short and strained and super uncomfortable. But come on, we're all adults here. This doesn't need to be awkward.

"Can I get you something to drink to start?"

"Sure, we'll have two waters and we'll share a vanilla shake." Wyatt smiles at Suzette, which makes her cheeks turn pink.

I scribble on my notepad. Vanilla. Weird, Wyatt always liked chocolate shakes. "Great. I'll get that right out."

I'm grateful when I'm out of sight and can wipe the stupid grin off my face. Why does fake smiling hurt my cheeks and real smiling doesn't? Whatever.

I whip up the shake fast enough, adding an extra scoop of ice cream because I know Wyatt loves his sweets. Two straws, two spoons, I slide the tray onto my palm and move their way but stumble in my sensible black Reeboks when I see their faces smashed together.

The blood runs out of my head. My palms sweat. The tray wobbles, but I grip it in time to save the drinks. My heart sinks into my stomach as Wyatt's hand cups Suzette's jaw, his own jaw tilting to deepen the kiss. With a softball-sized lump in my throat, I push forward and clear my throat once I'm at their booth.

"Your vanilla shake." I set it down, regretting that extra scoop and the extra cherries on top. I place the waters on the table, hoping they don't see how badly I'm shaking. "Is there anything else I can get you?" I stand there, stiff and uneasy.

PLAYING BY HEART | 53

Suzette's chocolate-brown eyes flash to mine. "Nope."

"We're good. Thanks, Beth." The way he says my name sounds like an apology, which is sweet but he doesn't owe me that. Unless... he still has feelings for me.

The thought stirs hope in my chest and helps me to smile, genuinely smile, before turning around and leaving them to their dessert.

The night Wyatt broke up with me, he said I was the kind of woman a man settles down with. Suzette with her mini-skirts and big boobs, Wyatt used to refer to her type as arm candy. There's no way what they have is serious. He'll tire of her eventually, and I'll make sure I'm still in his life and available for when he does.

"Why do you like him?" Ashleigh is sitting cross-legged on my bed with a canister of Pringles in her lap and her hand elbow-deep inside it. "He has to know you seeing him with Suzette is going to hurt, so why would he do it unless he's a heartless cock-sucking bastard?"

I pick at my pink nail polish and wonder if Suzette ever wears pink. My guess is she's more of a black, blue, and red nail-color-wearer. "He said he didn't know I'd be there."

Her expression is pure pity. "Bethany. There are a million different places he could've gone. Hell, when he realized you were working, he could've left—"

"That would've been weird. I can handle seeing him with someone else." I don't feel the conviction behind my words, but eventually I will. Right?

She holds up her hands and shrugs. "Whatever you say."

I grab a short stack of Pringles while I try to convince myself that I meant what I said. I may not have the whole sexy exotic thing going on like Suzette does, but I have qualities. I work hard, live in a decent two-bedroom apartment, and manage to pay half of everything with my income. I volunteer at the church and I'm a nanny, for crying out loud. I may not be a bikini model, but I can rock a tank-ini. Oh my gosh... I'm a sixty-year-old woman trapped in a twenty-four-year-old's body.

I groan and drop back on the bed, handing Ashleigh my stack of chips. "Can we please talk about something else?"

"Yes! You've been tight-lipped about Pastor Langley all week. Why was he so eager to have you over there early on Monday, and please tell me you got a pic of him in sweatpants. Or pajama pants of any kind. Flannels?"

I hate lying to my best friend, but I can't give her the info she wants, except... "Yes, he does wear sweatpants. No, I didn't get a picture because that's creepy and totally inappropriate."

"Oh, come on! Not even one photo?"

"No, sicko! He's a man of God, not a nude entertainer!"

"Nude entertainer?" She bursts out laughing. "You're funny. You mean stripper? Porn star? Male escort?"

"Yes, all of those things. He's not them." I kick my legs over the bed and grab my phone from its charger. I open Instagram for the millionth time tonight and check Wyatt's page, but there are no new updates.

I don't know what's worse: watching them together and knowing their every romantic move, or not having any information as to what they're up to next?

"Moving on!" She caps the Pringles and rolls to her side, all her blond hair draped over my pillows. "Why did he want you to his house early?"

"Huh?" I pretend to scroll on my phone, sidetracked, until I can think of an excuse. I don't lie! I'm horrible at it. And some part of me is angry that Pastor Langley has put me in a position that I have to.

"Oh my God, did he hit on you?"

I jerk my gaze up from my phone. "No! Ew. No way!"

"Ew?" Her eyebrows pop high. "Ben Langley and the word 'ew' don't even fit in the same universe, let alone the same sentence."

"No, I know, I just..." I shrug. "It was just some changes to Elliot's schedule, that's all he wanted to talk about." I give her my back to keep her from seeing through me and knowing I'm a big fat liar who is going to burn in hell.

"Huh." She's silent for a few seconds.

"Well, I should get to bed. I'm exhausted."

We say good night, and she goes to her room.

I crawl under my comforter with my phone in my palm and pull open Wyatt's social media, then I go back to look at all our old photos he posted when we were together.

I fall asleep imagining we're together again.

5

BETHANY

The weekend went by quickly. Wyatt and Suzette were at church with his family on Sunday, but they must've come in through the door on the north side, so I didn't get a chance to greet them.

The sermon was about... um... okay, well, I wasn't really paying attention, but I do remember him saying something about going through trials and how God is with us or something like that. Sue me! I couldn't take my eyes off of Wyatt, the way he'd whisper things into Suzette's ear or hold her hand.

Ashleigh managed to drag me to our favorite froyo place before I burst into tears. I started my period that night, so I'm sure that's all that was.

My eyes still feel a little puffy as I ride the bus to Elliot's house. After my Wyatt-and-Suzette-filled weekend, I'm looking forward to seeing Pete RN for a good laugh—or at the very least, the ego boost his flirting gives me.

I step off the bus, and rather than check Wyatt's social media, I hit Play on my music and pop in my ear buds. Linkin Park is on rotation, and with the mood I'm in, I turn it up and growl the lyrics all the way to Pastors house.

"Good morning," I say when I let myself inside.

"Bethany!" Elliot comes racing down the hallway and throws her arms around my waist.

"Whoa! Someone woke up with some energy this morning."

She pulls back and looks up at me through a tangle of dark curls. "I have an uncle!"

I look down the hallway toward the bedrooms then back at Elliot. "Yeah, you do."

Is she just now learning she's related to a rock god? She races back down the hallway to her bedroom. I drop my purse on the couch, next to the pillows and blankets folded neatly on the end.

"Hey." Pastor Langley comes from the hallway dressed and ready for the day, his coffee mug in hand.

"Good morning."

He rinses his cup and puts it in the dishwasher then turns toward me. "My brother is up and moving around, so you may see him today. He's asleep still, but he has an appointment today. A man by the name of..." He reaches into his breast pocket and pulls out a business card. "Dr. Harry Ulrich." He stuffs the card back into his pocket. "He'll be here sometime this morning, if you could let him in?"

"Of course."

He smiles, but it's sad. "Just show the doctor to my room and he'll take care of the rest."

I look around the pastor. "What about Pete?"

"Pete's last day was yesterday."

"What?"

"Yeah." He frowns.

"That's good, right? That means your brother is better?"

He nods solemnly and grabs his keys off the countertop. "Yeah, he is."

He passes by me with a squeeze to my shoulder then disappears out the door.

Rather than sit and stare between the bedroom door and the front door, I go about my business. I pack Elliot's lunch then wonder if she even ate breakfast. I pop my head into her room to find her happily engrossed in Barbies.

"Did you eat breakfast?"

"No. I want eggs."

"What's the magic word?"

Elliot looks up from her toys. "Please."

I head back to the kitchen, making sure to keep my eyes pinned to the floor to avoid peeking at Jesse Lee's door, and whip up scrambled eggs, proud I've avoided so much temptation today.

I drop butter in the hot pan as a door slams down the hallway. "Perfect timing." I scramble the gooey eggs and turn toward the sound. "Your eggs will be ready in a..." I'm not met with the three-foot-something child, but rather a six-foot-something man staring right at me. I gulp. "Second."

His glare tightens.

I try not to be obvious while taking him in. I only want to assure myself he's not naked like he was the first time I saw him. Nope. Not naked. He's wearing a gray T-shirt and a pair of worn-out jeans that are frayed around his bare feet. Convinced he's fully clothed, my gaze bounces back to meet his. His eyes are similar to Ben's, but more hazel than green. His hair is wet as if he's fresh from a shower.

I clear my throat. "You, uh—" My voice shakes, so I clear it and wipe my hands on my shirt before stepping toward him and holding out my right hand. "You must be Jesse."

His dark brows drop lower and he takes me in the same way I did him, but my guess is he's not trying to convince himself I'm wearing clothes. Rather, I get the impression he's trying to imagine what I'd look like out of them. From his curled upper lip, I'd say he's not all that impressed.

My Pies and Pancakes polo and polyester black pants tend to do that to a man.

At the smell of my butter burning, I drop my hand and turn back to the stove. Clearly Mr. Poops Gold Records doesn't feel the need to be polite to the peasants, so I'll pretend he's not here. Which is really hard to do when he steps into the small kitchen, invading my space. I drop the eggs into the pan and watch them bubble, ignoring his presence as I assume he gets himself a cup of coffee. I'm grateful when I feel him step away and hear the sliding glass door to the backyard open and close.

I exhale and scoop Elliot's eggs onto a plastic Elsa plate, sprinkle on some cheese, and fill a matching Elsa cup with milk. "Elliot! Breakfast is ready!"

The thump of tiny feet sounds in the hallway, and she skids to a halt at the table before climbing into her booster seat.

I take the seat next to her and cut up the eggs a bit so they'll cool faster. "Give them a minute so you don't burn your mouth."

Her gaze is cast forward, so I follow to see she's staring at her uncle leaning against a wooden support beneath the patio overhang. He's not looking at us, so I check out the colorful tattoos that cover even the backs of his arms before disappearing under his T-shirt. His hair is short in the back and longer and messy on top and it's the strangest color. Not brown or red but something in between—whoa! I duck my chin when he turns around abruptly.

"Eat up," I say to Elliot, who doesn't seem nearly as flustered at being caught staring.

The sliding glass door opens then closes, and I hold my breath until the seat across from me slides out and Jesse sits in it with a loud puff of air.

"Uncle Jesiah, want some eggs?" Elliot forks a bite and shoves it toward him.

I grin at her forwardness while simultaneously wondering about his name. Is Jesiah his real name or a nickname?

"No. I only eat organic."

I pause at his tone—one I would expect between adults, but not from a grown man to a child.

Elliot's face falls and she frowns at her eggs as if they've grown legs. "What's organic?"

"It's all right, just eat." I shoot a quick glance at Jesse, only to see his eyes firmly planted in my direction. I do my best to ignore him when he's making it nearly impossible to do so. "Drink your milk."

I hope whatever fascination Jesse has with the side of my face ends soon, because my cheeks feel as if they're going to burst into flames. He sips his coffee, not once taking his eyes off me, and Elliot finishes her eggs, leaves her milk, and asks to be excused to her room. Desperate for a reason to get away from the table, I let her go, snag the dishes, and hop up as quickly as I can—only to trip on the chair leg. My face ignites in a red-hot blush.

I scurry to the sink and rinse off the dishes, hoping that when I turn back, he'll be gone. No such luck. He's still slouched at the table, his legs wide beneath it, his hazel eyes latched firmly on me.

I open my mouth to say, "What!" but he beats me to it.

"What's your name?" He's not smiling. His expression is as casual as someone who asked for the time.

"Bethany?"

He tilts his head as if questioning my answer then leans forward with his forearms on the table. He nods at the seat across from him, and my body automatically jumps at his silent command, my brain only questioning it once I've sat down across from him. His eyes bore into mine and I'm forced, after a few seconds, to look away.

One thing about Jesse Lee? It's impossible to absorb his attention head-on for too long. Small doses only.

"You wanna fuck?"

My gaze snaps to his. Did he just say...? As his words register, I push back from the table as if the piece of furniture has become a bedrock for immoral sex acts.

For the first time this morning, the man shows a hint of a smile.

A smirk, really. "Not here. The bedroom. And make sure the kid doesn't bother us." He stands, leaving his empty coffee mug on the table. "Hurry before I change my mind."

He doesn't even look at me as he walks away and disappears into his bedroom.

With my jaw in my hand and my other hand on my racing heart, I'm left sitting at the table, wondering what the hell just happened.

JESSE

The more time that passes, the more I'm convinced sex is exactly what I need.

I knew Dave would surround me with men—Pete, Dr. Harry, a men's recovery group. My manager doesn't have to say it to send the message loud and clear. NO PUSSY!

How he let the homely little nanny slip under his radar is beyond me. Maybe he figured she wasn't my type. He was right. She's so ordinary, she practically blends in with the eggshell-colored walls. But I remember the sound of her sweet gasp, and I imagine all the other sounds I could get her to make while she's wrapped around my hips.

Blood rushes like rockets through my veins to between my legs. Getting hard when I'm sober is such a different experience. The numbness from the booze and coke is gone and my brain is dry. Sex is going to feel phenomenal. I pop the button of my jeans and slip my hand beneath my boxers with a groan.

The little nanny better hurry up or I might finish myself off before she gets here.

I imagine her eyes were as wide when she caught me jacking off as they were this morning when she saw me in the kitchen. Big, innocent, I knew immediately she recognized me despite my brother's insistence that he wasn't telling anyone who I am. Fine by me.

I pull up the image of nanny whatsherface—fuck, what was her name? No matter. Her skinny legs, flat chest, and makeup-free face shouldn't do it for me, but what can I say? I'm desperate. She's female. And in that ridiculous outfit that does nothing for her already non-existent curves? Fuck, how is this shit keeping me hard?

My head lolls to the side and I check the clock. Twenty minutes have passed since I propositioned her and she's still not here? Maybe she's putting on a movie for the kid? I'll give her a few more minutes.

With my eyes closed, I keep myself on the edge, building and building only to pull back right at the cusp of a mind-blowing orgasm. I groan. Damn, I ache.

There's a soft knock at the door, and the sound alone almost sends me spiraling. I picture her walking in in some everyday cotton panties and piece of crap sports bra and I'll be damned, I'm still anxious to get at her. "Come in."

The door clicks open, and I expect to feel the heat of her thighs as she straddle my hips.

Instead, I hear the clearing of a throat.

A masculine throat.

I blink open my eyes and stare at the ceiling.

"Mr. Langley, am I interrupting something?"

I roll my head to the side to find a gray-haired man in a suit with a leather folder in his hand. "Yes."

He lifts a bushy white brow. "We have an appointment. You'll have to finish that up later." He steps inside and closes the door.

I slip my hand from my jeans and curse the nanny. I have the worst case of blue balls in the history of the male species, and it's all her fault.

6

BETHANY

My stomach is in knots.

With each mile, the pain in my gut increases until the driver slows at my stop. I turn my phone over in my hand, my eyes glued to the brown roof of Pastor Langley's house, and I can't get my feet to move me off the bus.

"Bethany?" Darrell, the bus driver, calls. "You okay?"

I shake my head and gather my things. "Fine, thank you." I sling my purse over my shoulder and smile at him before heading down the three steps, stopping short on the last.

Since my encounter with Jesse yesterday, I've been on edge. After he told me to meet him in his room, I got Elliot ready and we went to the park before school. The psychiatrist showed up as we were walking out the door, so I was able to let him in before jogging away. I couldn't sleep all night as I replayed Jesse's cold stare, his emotionless proposition, and his answering smirk.

One word throbs in my head at the thought of Jesse Lee —predator.

He reminds me of those sharks that chase down the rubber seals behind boats then sneak up from underneath them. That makes me the rubber seal.

"Are you sure you're okay?" Darrell says from behind me.

I stare at my feet and force them off the bus. "Yes. Thanks."

The air brakes announce my fate as the bus leaves me a few houses away from Pastor Ben's. During my obsessing last night, I wondered if I should talk to Ben about what happened. I even considered quitting as an option, but I need the money if I'm ever going to put my mistakes behind me once and for all.

"One depressing thought at a time there," I whisper and square my shoulders.

Jesse Lee is just a man, and at twenty-four-years-old, I need to be comfortable standing up for myself. With a shove of courage, I walk toward the house, and as I approach, I notice a sleek black car in the driveway. The rims are chrome, and I can see my reflection in them. The windows are tinted so dark, I can't tell if anyone is sitting inside.

I head to the house and knock twice before walking in, pausing in the doorway with my hand on the doorknob. The fight-or-flight instinct roars through my veins when a pair of bored and indifferent hazel eyes meet mine. They quickly morph to thin, angry slits, forcing my gaze away and into safer waters. It's not too late to turn around and run.

"Hi," I say to Pastor Ben, who smiles warmly.

"Bethany, come on in."

I step inside, feeling Jesse's eyes on me the whole time as I drop my purse on the couch. He's sitting at the kitchen table, next to a man I've never seen. I search for Elliot, but she's not in the living room, so I head back to her bedroom, needing the distance from Jesse before I pass out from lack of oxygen.

"Oh, hang on," Ben says. "Can we talk to you for a second?"

I wonder if maybe Ben found out about what happened yesterday and is going to fire me or lecture me on—*God, Bethany! Stop it! You're the victim here. You didn't do anything wrong.*

"Sure." I move toward the seat farthest from Jesse only to see Ben take it. The only other seat that's not less than a foot away from Jesse has Elliot's booster strapped into it. I lower myself to the seat right next to Jesse, but I keep my butt cheek on the edge farthest from him. "What's up?"

I risk a peek at Jesse, who has intensified his glare by tilting his head. Thankfully Ben speaks up and I give Jesse my back, or as much as I'm able while balancing on my left butt cheek.

"First off, I wanted you to meet my brother," Ben says, motioning to the man behind me. When I don't turn around, Ben frowns.

"We met."

Ben's eyes dart to the new guy, who then glares at Jesse.

"What?" Jesse barks.

Ben seems to shake off something. "Right, okay, good, so Jesiah, you've met Elliot's nanny, Bethany Parks." He doesn't allow too much silence after his statement. "This is Dave Mann, Jesiah's manager."

That explains the fancy car. The guy looks to be in his late thirties, dirty-blond hair, super blue eyes, but the set of his jaw tells me his boy-next-door look is a façade and he doesn't take crap from anyone—not even a spoiled rotten and rude rock star. "Bethany, it's nice to meet you."

Jesse taps his fingers on the table impatiently. Rhythmically, as if he's playing a song. I wonder if it's a nervous habit. Does this meeting somehow make him uneasy?

Ben says, "Dave had an idea, and I think you might like it."

I look at the guy, chuckling inwardly as I imagine him in a blue Walmart vest with a gold nametag.

"Jesse needs to get around, but I'm not comfortable with him driving himself just yet," Dave says. "Ben tells me you don't own a car. Do you have a valid driver's license?"

My cheeks get warm. "Yes, I do."

"Great." Dave slides me a black key fob. "The car outside is yours to use until Jesse is ready to drive."

"*What?*" I look at Ben, whose eyes are alight with excitement.

Dave continues. "I'd like to hire you to take Jesse to his AA meetings every day and bring him back here."

"AA meetings?" So that's what was making him sick. My stomach rolls over and I swallow back a surge of nerves. He's a drunk. I suppose it makes sense—sex, booze, rock-n-roll. "I, uh... I have to get Elliot to school by noon, so we catch the eleven o'clock bus and—"

"Jesse's meetings are at eleven thirty," Dave says. "You drop him off at the church, get Elliot to school by twelve, pick Jesse up and bring him back here, and you take the car with you when you leave."

I blink once. Twice. He's not joking.

"I have to be to work by two." As if that's an excuse? Why can't I think of a better excuse!

Dave's eyes narrow. "Do you have a substance abuse issue, Ms. Parks?"

"Me? No!"

His gaze narrows farther.

"I don't drink. Not even a little." Not since... I clear my throat. "And I've never touched drugs."

"You're missin' out," Jesse grumbles, earning a sharp glare from his manager.

Ben nods. "I vouch for Bethany on that. She doesn't mess around with drugs or alcohol."

Dave nods and grunts.

"The car is yours to use, Bethany," Pastor Ben whispers.

"That's right," Dave says. "Until Jesse is ready to drive himself."

The celebrity in the room makes a frustrated huff.

Dave ignores him. "I'll tell you what. When Jesse goes back to LA, I'll transfer it over into your name."

"You're kidding," I whisper. "This has to be a joke."

"Jesus, nanny, take the fucking deal already." Jesse's frustrated voice rumbles at my back, and I resist the urge to whirl around and give him a lecture about blasphemy.

"But…" I swallow. "That's a Lexus."

"It's just a car," Dave says.

"Just a car?" A burst of laughter jumps from my lips.

"It's a very nice car." Dave checks his watch as if I'm holding him up. "Do we have a deal?"

"So, you're saying it's his car and I'll be driving it until he's given the all-clear, then it's his car and when he leaves it's mine?"

Jesse drops his head back and groans. "For fucks sake, someone draw the genius here an illustration."

"Jes," Ben warns and then his eyes come to me. "This is a great opportunity."

It is. If my own pastor says I should do it, then… "Okay. I'll do it."

Dave slaps his hands on the table then stands. "Great. My ride is waiting outside."

"Dave," Jesse says in a demanding tone, boss to subordinate, "think about what we talked about."

Dave shakes his head. "I already told you it's too late for amendments."

"Fuck," Jesse mumbles, earning a glare from Ben.

"I'll walk you out." Ben jumps up.

"Bethany, thank you for your help," Dave says before walking out the door while murmuring to Ben.

As soon as they're outside, I stare at the key fob. A slow smile spreads across my face.

"You want to explain why you left me with my nuts in my stomach yesterday?"

I startle at the hostility in Jesse's voice. He's mad at *me*? Feeling a surge of anger, I whirl around and glare at him. "If that's your idea of an apology, you suck at them."

He leans forward, his colorful tattooed forearms braced on his knees. "You think I owe you an apology? For what? Offering you my dick?"

I cringe from his crass words and curse the heat creeping into my cheeks. "Well, yeah! You assume because you're *you* that any woman would want to sleep with you?"

He tilts his head while I absorb my own words.

"You're wrong." I grab the key fob and stand, desperate to find Elliot and get the hell away from this guy. "I have zero desire to have sex with you, *Jesse Lee.*" I hold up my hand and make a zero with my fingers. "Zilch."

He grins, a slow lift of the corner of his mouth that I could see women falling all over him for. Not me though. "Most women appreciate a man who offers himself up to be used for sex."

"I'm not most women. And you should know that a huge majority of women only have sex with men they're in love with."

He rolls his eyes, still grinning.

"You're infuriating." I shove the car key into my pocket.

"You're a child," he says through a deep chuckle as Ben comes back inside.

"Pastor Ben, would it be all right if I took Elliot to the park?"

He looks a little surprised before his gaze slides from me to his brother, where they narrow. "Everything okay?"

Jesse shrugs as if our conversation about sex was nothing more than a tiny annoyance, a fly buzzing by his face, easily swatted at and forgotten. "Just dandy, *Pastor Ben.*" The superstar assjerk stands and exits the room as though the world is watching, rather than just me and his brother.

As soon as he's out of sight, Ben looks at me. "I'm really sorry. He's..." He blows out a long breath. "Difficult to deal with at times. Well, most of the time."

I grin and shrug and rinse dishes to keep my hands busy. "Not at all. He's fine. I'm fine."

"Are you sure? Because if you change your mind or..."

I turn to look at him. "What?"

He steps into the kitchen. "My brother is a slave to his baser instincts, and I wouldn't put it past him to try to... to attempt to... uh..." He rubs the back of his neck.

"Seduce me?"

His expression turns sour and apologetic. "I'm sorry, but yes. His moral compass points in a different direction than the people you're probably used to being around."

I wipe my hands on a towel. "If you think that's true, you haven't spent enough time with my roommate, Ashleigh." Oh, how she would love that. "Thankfully, my moral compass is solid, so you have nothing to worry about."

I would never have sex with Jesse Lee. I imagine doing so leaves most girls feeling like a used Kleenex. No, thank you.

"I know you won't. Which is why you were the perfect option for his chauffer. Which reminds me, Dave didn't mention it, but he's doubling what I pay you on top of leaving you the car."

"Double?" I'm shocked, elated—holy crap, I'll be making over twenty dollars an hour, plus my Pies and Pancakes money, and a car... I'll be able to start a savings account! Not bad for a twenty-four-year-old.

I frown. I am *not* a child.

JESSE

"I don't know, doc, maybe it's nothing. Or maybe it's everything." I'm lying on my brother's bed, fully dressed in jeans and a T-shirt, my ankles crossed and my hands clasped over my stomach. "His dead, lifeless body swirled 'round and 'round until he finally disappeared in the deep, dark afterlife in the sewer. I don't think I ever recovered."

When I don't hear Dr. Ulrich's immediate response, I turn to see him glaring at me from over his tiny doctor glasses. This is day five of my daily therapy, an hour a day where I talk about my childhood in order to pinpoint why I drink... drank.

Newsflash—because I love the taste. Because I love how creative I feel when I'm smashed. Because getting hammered helps me sleep, tune out the world of chaos that is swirling around me. There doesn't need to be a deep dark reason why people do the things they do. Maybe they do it *because they like it.*

Type that in your fucking medical journals.

With a long, exasperated sigh, he removes his glasses and rubs his eyes. "If you plan on getting better, you'll need to start taking our sessions more seriously."

"I am taking them seriously." *No, I'm not.* This entire ninety-day stint is a big fucking waste of time. I'm just doing what I'm told so I can get back to living my life.

"Your dead beta fish when you were seven is not what I would consider a life-changing event."

I actually lied about being seven. I also lied about it being my fish. It was Ben's and he was seven. He cried when he had to flush his best friend Fins. He's always been a wuss. "That's awfully judgmental, doc. Just because you don't see it as life-changing doesn't mean it wasn't for me."

"If you want to continue to waste my time, then that's fine with me. I get paid either way." He slips his glasses back on and jots something on his yellow pad.

"Right, so then there was the time I was given meatloaf and my mom didn't tell me until after I ate that it was turkey meatloaf. Well, I don't eat birds. She knew that! She made me believe it was beef when she knew she was feeding me avian flesh."

"I'm sorry, time's up." He grips his leather pad and stands. "You'll have to save the rest of that story for tomorrow."

He can't seem to get out of here fast enough, which makes me smile. I check the clock. He left ten minutes early. If I can keep shaving away at the time frames, by next week, we should be only meeting for thirty to forty-five minutes a day. Progress.

I allow my eyes to close before I have to go out and hunt down my driver. When it's time to go, I find her in the living room, coloring with that little brat with the booger nose.

I was already annoyed when we got in the car. I had no idea how much more frustrating the ride would get.

First off, Bethany doesn't know how to drive. I've seen eighty-five-year-old grandmas drive more aggressively. Second, she puts on music for the kid on the way there, so I have to listen to pre-pubescent voices sing songs about washing their hands and doing math and shit. And third, she ignores me. Completely. So I'm stuck staring out the front window while a tiny brown-headed midget in the backseat talks my ear off about *nothing*.

Questions at rapid fire. "Why can't we breathe under water?" and "Where do cows grow?" Bethany does her best to answer. Most have been utter bullshit, but eventually she shuts up the little person.

We pull into the lot of Ben's church. The structure is nothing fancy, just a typical church that could easily moonlight as a small school, if you took away the huge cross out front.

She puts the car in a spot and hits Unlock. "You want me to walk you in?"

I glare at her. "Did I miss the part about sobriety disabling my arms and legs?"

I don't give her a chance to answer. I head into the lobby and look left then right and follow the scent of donuts and cheap coffee. Anger swirls, irritating the beast inside me. Why the fuck do I have to do this? I can stay sober on my own for the time it takes to write an album.

The AA room is filled with cheap, mismatched furniture arranged in a circle on shitty mustard-yellow carpet. Eight other guys are all shoving donuts down their throats and sipping from tiny Styrofoam cups.

One of the guys spots me and smiles. "Mr. Lee, you made it."

I pull my baseball hat a little lower over my eyes. He weaves through the Kumbaya furniture ring then shoves his hand forward. I shake his hand that's sticky with donut glaze. Slob.

"I'm Paul. Come on in, grab a coffee. We've got donuts—"

"I'm good." I wipe my hand on my jeans and cross to one of the three chairs in the circle. I don't want to get stuck on a loveseat with one of these drunks—ex-drunks.

Paul announces it's time to get started and the seats fill quickly. A few gazes dart toward me and widen, but when I glare at them, they snap their eyes away.

"I'm sure you've all noticed we have a new member," Paul says proudly. "Would you like to introduce yourself?"

I shrug. "I'm Jesse and I really don't want to be here, so if we could cut the formalities and just get this shitshow over with, that'd be great."

A few dudes blink. Others scowl. Fuck if I care.

Paul frowns. "Okay. Let's go around the circle and introduce ourselves to Jesse."

One by one, the sad fucks say their names and their drink, and most often drug, of choice. They speak about the stuff as if it's a family member that's died. I guess I can relate. I'd give anything for a bottle. How these guys can sit here and listen to each other whine without at least having a buzz is impressive.

I nod off twice during the meeting. I may have even slept for a bit because the last thirty minutes felt like only a few seconds.

I don't say goodbye, just hightail it out of there. I wonder how I'm supposed to call the blue-ball-giving nanny to let her know I'm finished, but that question is answered when I step outside and see the Lexus. Thank God.

When I pull open the door, she screams and jumps, her phone flying into the passenger seat.

I snag it and sit. "Calm the fuck down. It's just me."

"You scared me!"

"I'm so sorry, I wasn't aware I should knock." I look at her phone. "She's hot. Who is she?" I hand her back the phone, and she fumbles to close out the Instagram page she was stalking.

"No one."

"Her tits in that tiny bikini say otherwise. She's definitely someone."

Nanny's jaw clenches and she puts the car into drive. "She's... a friend. Well, she's not my friend. She's a friend of a friend."

"Oh yeah? Invite her over." I pull off the baseball hat and run a hand through my hair. "I could use a little physical therapy."

She whips her head around and I wink, which makes fire flicker behind her eyes. "Trust me when I say Suzette is not your type."

"*Suzette.*" I roll the name around on my tongue, not loving the way it feels. That doesn't mean I wouldn't love the feel of her on my tongue.

"Yep. Suzette." She spits the woman's name with venom.

Interesting. "Not a fan?"

Her chin tucks in as if I've offended her. "Of course I'm a fan. Well... I mean, I don't know her well enough to—"

"So that must be why you were stalking her social media page, checking out her bikini pics, yeah? You were"—I hold up my fingers for air quotes—"'getting to know her.'"

"Why do you care?"

"Because she's hot. Because I need to get laid. Because every single thing I used to do to make myself feel good I can't fucking do anymore, that's why."

"What about music?"

I open my mouth to say something shitty, but the words freeze in my throat.

Back in the day, there was no better feeling in the world than writing new songs. I'd get down the melody, jot some lyrics, and that alone would give me butterflies. Once a song was finished, it felt as if I'd created life. Making a tangible, animated something from nothing made me feel like a god. When did creating music stop giving me that feeling?

7

BETHANY

"Where is he?"

My eyes pop wide and I shoot up in bed. "What?"

I blink into the dim light of my bedroom as Ashleigh rips open my closet.

"Wyatt!" She disappears into my closet, pushes around my clothes, then stomps out. "Where is that fucksack?"

"Why would Wyatt be here?" I rub my eyes and check the time. Barely five in the morning.

She drops to her knees and checks under the bed. "He thinks he can hide from me?"

"Ash—"

"He thinks he can just swoop back into your life and use you for sex whenever he wants!" She rips open the drapes as though a man who's almost six feet tall could hide himself behind a curtain.

"Ashleigh, stop!"

She whirls around, still wearing her corset top and leather pants from her shift last night. She's a bartender at a club and her shifts tend to stretch into after hours, either for work or personal reasons.

"Wyatt isn't here." According to his IG post, he was at a comedy club last night with Suzette. My shoulders sag. "No one is here. Just me."

"Then who's fucking car is in our spot?" She points an accusing finger out the window.

Oh darnit. How to explain the car to Ashleigh without breaking the NDA? Hm.

"I'm going to management! Some asshole parked in our spot." She moves to storm out of the room.

"Wait! Ash, just..." I rub my face, trying to wake up. I ended up working until midnight last night and figured Ashleigh would be out all night, so rather than parking in guest parking and walking across the complex, I snagged our assigned spot. "The car's mine."

Her black-lined eyes pop open wide.

"I mean, I'm borrowing it... I guess." I can't lie, but telling the truth is also a no-no.

"From who?"

"From... Ben."

"Ben."

"Pastor Langley."

I wouldn't think it possible, but her eyes grow even bigger. "Oh my God," she whispers.

"No, don't. It's not what you think."

"I can't believe you didn't tell me."

"You know me better than that! Come on!"

"The text followed by a phone call, the early morning." Her eyes dart around the room as she ticks off each of her fingers. "You calling him Ben, the feeling that you're hiding something."

"You could not be more wrong."

She scampers to the edge of my bed. "Tell me everything. Is he a good kisser? Does he have a big—"

"Ashleigh!"

"Oh! Does he have huge balls?"

"Ew, what?"

She gets a dreamy look in her eyes. "I've always pictured him with a great big heavy sac."

"Okay, you know what?" I rip off my comforter and head to the bathroom, trying like hell to erase the last sixty seconds of my life. "I'm not doing this. You're insane."

"Wait!" She chases me and walks into the bathroom right behind me. "You're not kidding."

I hit on the water and push tangled hair out of my face. "Of course I'm not kidding! Pastor Langley is like a brother to me. You know that."

She chews on her lip. "Hm... then why is he loaning you that sickass ride?"

Giving her my back, I pretend to tweak the water temperature to avoid looking her in the eye. "There was someone creepy on the bus and Elliot got freaked out, so he got a car for me to drive until I get my own."

Sounds believable.

"Dang, how much does he make to afford a Lexus?"

"I don't know, I don't care. I'm sure someone in the congregation hooked him up with a deal. Can you just be satisfied with my answers and leave me alone to shower?"

"Yeah," she says absently as if she's still trying to piece things together. If she spent half the amount of think-time on her own love life rather than fabricating mine, she'd probably have a lot fewer one-night stands. "I have to get some sleep anyway."

She closes the door behind herself and I exhale a big breath.

In the shower, I squeeze a generous amount of shampoo into my palm and suds up my hair. There's nothing worse than smelling like breakfast meat, and that scent really clings to hair for some reason. I feel good about how I talked my way around the luxury car. If I only felt as good about my interactions with Jesse Lee.

Yesterday on the way home from his meeting, I asked about his music and his entire demeanor changed. He didn't speak another word and opened the door to get out before the car had even come to a complete stop. I felt sick to my stomach that I'd unknowingly offended him and equally sick that he was attracted to Suzette.

My hands freeze on my head.

I wonder if Wyatt loves her.

If he does, I should be happy for him, right?

I pull up to Elliot's house shortly before nine and sit with the car running in the driveway while my mom goes on about the nutritional value of beets and how gluten is poison.

"Have you tried that new keto diet everyone is talking about?" Her voice is conspiratory, and I consider telling her she needs a hobby outside of food-related fads. "Debra Espinosa lost twenty pounds on that diet."

There's movement behind Ben's open blinds. I imagine it's Elliot wondering which Disney princess will pour from the door of the luxury car.

"I'm pretty sure the keto diet is just the Atkins diet you tried back when I was in elementary school." I push the button—yeah, a button!—to turn off the car.

"I don't think so. This is new and—"

"I'm sorry to cut you off, Mom, but I have to get going."

"No problem, honey. Have a good day. Oh, and let me know if you hear from Wyatt." She says his name in a sing-song voice.

I frown because I think my parents might love Wyatt more than I did—do! More than I do.

Leaving my purse in the super-safe car, I trudge up the driveway, yawning thanks to Ashleigh's early wake-up call. Extra coffee today. Hopefully Ben has a fresh pot brewed.

I knock twice and push inside to find Elliot at the table and Ben dressed and ready in the kitchen, pouring milk into a bowl. "Good morning."

"Good morning," Ben says then brings Elliot her cereal.

"Bethany, Daddy got me Playdough!"

"So we'll be sculpting today." I kiss her head that's covered in soft fluffy curls. "Lucky Charms? Yum." There's a fresh pot of coffee in the maker. I head to it, and Ben hands me a mug. "Thanks."

He props a hip on the counter, and I notice he's dressed more casually today—jeans, plaid shirt untucked. "How did things go with my brother?"

I sip my coffee and already feel a little more alive. "Good."

He scrunches up one eye. "Really?"

"Yes, really." Ben doesn't need to know the gory details.

He frowns, then smiles. "Great." He checks the time on the microwave. "I better go."

"Have a good day," I call as he nuzzles Elliot's cheek, making her giggle, before he says goodbye.

"You too."

He leaves us alone, and I drop into the seat next to Elliot. "What did you watch this morning?"

"*Frozen*," she answers through a cheekful of colorful marshmallows. "Some of the ladies at church said it's satanic, but Dad says they need a theo-lowlogy lesson."

"Disney is not satanic. That's just silly talk."

"I know." She shrugs and continues to shovel food into her mouth.

"Do you want to do a puzzle today?"

She nods with milk dripping from her lips.

I drum my fingers until I can't stand it another second and pull out my phone to check Wyatt's IG page. No new posts since last night. I check Suzette's. Nothing. Groaning, I set my phone down and sip my coffee.

Ben's bedroom door clicks open, and my shoulders bunch with tension. I say a silent prayer that Jesse is in a good mood. His bare feet slap on the hardwood floor. When he passes me, I nearly choke at the sight of all his bare skin as he saunters around in nothing but a pair of shorts that I'm pretty sure are meant for sleeping only.

They're soft gray cotton and baggy everywhere but around his slender hips, where they hang low enough to see the top of his butt crack.

I'm glad he's facing away from me when he pours himself coffee. I study the parts of him covered in ink—his arms up to his shoulders, even his hands. His back doesn't have any ink, but raised discolorations slash across his shoulders, making me wonder if he'd been in an accident. He turns around. His stomach is also tattoo-free. I remember his thighs having ink. Even his calves have different pictures and words—oh no, he's coming this way. I swallow my nerves as he struts up to the table, his hips at eye level. I can't help but notice the massive bulge that moves with his body.

I squeeze my eyes closed as he takes the seat across from Elliot. If he noticed my staring at him, he's nice enough not to mention it. Maybe he's in a better mood today and we'll get through our short time together with minimal jabs—

"That shit you're eating will kill you," he says to Elliot.

My jaw falls open. Who says that to a child?

"What?" she says in her sweet voice as she stares at her cereal as if it's turned into earthworms.

"Don't listen to him."

She pushes away her bowl with a sad frown. "I'm finished."

"Okay, why don't you go watch TV?" I help her out of her seat, and she glares at Jesse, who shrugs and sips his coffee. "Go on." I give her a little push toward the living room, and the moment she's out of earshot, I whirl on the jerk. "How could you say that to her?"

He stares at me as if I'm dumb. "It's true."

"Says the guy who has filled an entire coffee can in the backyard with cigarette butts?"

"Doesn't make it less true."

"Lucky Charms won't kill anyone. It's lucky!" I bite down to keep from saying anything else because everything that comes out of my mouth around this guy makes me sound stupid. I head to the kitchen and rinse Elliot's bowl and my mug, placing them in the dishwasher and feeling eyes on me the entire time. "What?"

"What?"

"Stop staring at me."

He tilts his head, his hair an absolute mess of perfection. How the hell does he wake up looking as if he's about to do a photo shoot? "Turnabout is fair play, nanny." His gaze rakes along my body from my feet to the top of my head, and my cheeks must be bright red from knowing he did see me studying him earlier.

I stomp over and take a seat on the opposite end of the table. "What is your deal?"

He looks at me with boredom in his eyes. "Morning sex is my favorite."

I close my eyes, momentarily at a loss for words, then I find them. "Please, stop talking about sex around me. It's inappropriate."

A slow curve of his lips takes me aback. "I make you uncomfortable when I talk about sex."

"Uh, yeah! I think that's kind of obvious."

He leans forward, angling his body toward me, and I'm grateful for the few feet of table separating us. "You feel squirmy when I talk about sex. Like, suddenly your shorts are too tight."

"No, I do not."

"You get butterflies, not just in your stomach but in other places too." His voice is so deep. I don't think I ever noticed that in any of his songs. "Your boobs get heavy and ache to be touched."

I force a big, huge grin and even push out a laugh. "That's pathetic. Tell me, does this vulgar talk work on the women you bed?"

He frowns, and I grin even wider at my temporary victory.

"Because I gotta say, Jesse Lee, you should really consider a different tactic." I push away from the table. "Heavy boobs." I snort-laugh. "That's a good one."

I leave him speechless, and I'm grateful to be out of the room so I can release some of the tension in my muscles. He couldn't have been more wrong about how his mentioning sex makes me feel. Wrong, wrong, wrong.

Sure, I feel a little squirmy, as if I'm covered in cooties, but that's because he's a walking advertisement for an STD clinic. And yeah, I guess the weird flip-flop feeling in my stomach could be considered by some to be butterfly-like, but that's only because the thought of having sex with him makes me nauseated.

I know, I know, I'm crazy for not wanting to have sex with the Coast-to-Coast Casanova, right?

Wrong!

Being one of a million women isn't the same as being someone's one-in-a-million, no matter how amazing the sex would be.

JESSE

Day Fourteen

Seventy-six days to go.

Fuck, that sounds like a lifetime.

"Have you been journaling? Getting your thoughts down on paper like we talked about during our last session?" Dr. Ulrich twiddles his fancy gold pen while waiting for me to have some kind of emotional breakthrough. This therapy shit is all the same. Dig deep, crack open the coffins of the past, and air out the stank of putrid rotting flesh.

No thanks.

"I don't journal, doc."

"Why not?"

"Because I'm not a twelve-year-old girl."

He clears his throat, and I wonder how much Dave is paying this guy to keep him here and put up with my shit. I bet it's enough to buy him a warehouse full of those fancy fucking pens.

"How about music?" He flicks that damn pen toward the guitar in the corner of the room. "Have you been writing any new songs?"

"That's not my guitar. It's Ben's."

"I'm sure he wouldn't mind if you used it."

I'm already shaking my head. "Using another man's guitar is like finger-fucking his wife."

The good doc cringes but recovers quickly. "Would you like me to see if we can get your guitar here? I'm sure Dave would have it shipped."

I stare forward blindly. Playing a guitar in my brother's house makes me uneasy to say the least. Would he hear me and remember the days we'd play together, back when life was simple and my older brother was my hero? "I don't think so."

"You mentioned the only reason you're here is because you're supposed to write some music. Are you sure you're not ready to at least try?"

I shift in my seat and scratch the back of my neck. I could work when Ben's gone. He only comes in his room when he needs to grab clothes every few days.

A weird twinge pinches in my chest. I rub at my sternum. What the fuck is that? I hate to say it, but it feels an awful lot like guilt.

My brother takes on my drunk ass. I treat him like shit. Treat his kid like shit. Get off on making his nanny as uncomfortable as I possibly can. And he doesn't say anything about it. He feeds me, leaves me alone, and every night, he squeezes onto that piece-of-shit couch while I'm sprawled out on his bed, in his room—the one he shared with his dead wife.

"Are you feeling okay?" Doc pulls off his reading glasses and his brows drop low in concern.

"Never better, doc." I rub my chest again. "Never better. But, uh, I think I'll have Dave send my guitar over."

His face lights up and I roll my eyes. *Don't get your hopes up.* I haven't felt the creative pull since I've been sober. It's possible that without the chemical assistance, I've lost my ability to write music. No. Fuck that. I can still write.

He jots a few notes then asks me questions about my parents, what their marriage was like, and how it all made me feel. I ignore most of his questions or give one-word answers because, again, fuck this shit.

"That'll be it for today." He closes his leather folder and assures me he'll be in contact with Dave about my guitar.

It's almost time for my meeting. I take a piss and head out to let my ride know we need to go. She's on the couch with her arm wrapped around Ben's kid and a book open in her lap. She wore her hair down today, so it looks longer as it falls over her shoulder in a thick, dark panel, covering the logo on her stupid fucking uniform shirt. Her lips move, and I lean in to hear what she's saying. She's reading a story and changing her voice with each character, making Ben's kid giggle. For a moment, I get lost in the sound, the cadence of her voice and the soft laughter of the kid combined is almost hypnotic.

"Oh, hey." The intonation in her voice is replaced with a hint of panic. "Are you ready?"

"Nope, I just enjoy killing time here with my thumb up my ass."

She looks horrified before she mumbles something to the kid. They both get up, grab a couple bags, and head out the door. I slip on my baseball hat and hop into the passenger seat while they do the shit with the kid seat in the back.

We don't talk as we head toward the church, no different from the last few days. After she shut me down for sex for the third time, I gave up. My hand gets me the same result and this girl is bad for my ego.

The car is too quiet, so I flip on the radio. Two preset stations later, my own voice comes from the speakers. I grin and turn to the nanny, who gives me an uneasy smile.

"You like this one?" I ask.

She nods. "It's all right." Her pinkie finger taps the steering wheel to the beat. She's lying.

I lean back and listen to the lyrics, remembering the exact moment I came up with the chorus. "I wrote this song on my first tour. We were opening for 311 on their reunion tour."

"Oh, I thought this was a newer song of yours."

"It is. I wrote it, like, six years ago but kind of forgot about it until we needed songs for an album and I went looking through some of my old stuff."

"How do you come up with the lyrics?"

My reaction is to shut down, to say something shitty that'll get her to leave me alone, but that takes energy I don't have. "Different things. This one was inspired by the high I was on, ya know? I was so fresh, staring down the bright lights of superstardom."

"That's the name of the song."

"Yeah, genius." I chuckle.

She does a double-take and grins, probably shocked to hear me laugh. I have to admit, I'm surprised too. I frown and stare out the window.

Too quickly, my song ends and I change the station a couple times, searching for something—

"Leave it here! I love this song."

"Really? You're an AC/DC fan?"

"Don't be so surprised. I like all kinds of music." She drums her fingers on the steering wheel to "Dirty Deeds Done Dirt Cheap."

We fall into a comfortable silence for a few seconds until I hear a sound coming from her lips. I peek over to see she's singing the words.

Singing is an overly generous description for the sound coming from her mouth though. Holy shit... her voice is *awful*.

She not only butchers the song, singing notes that should only be used by parrots and dolphins, but she's fucking up the lyrics too. *"Thirty thieves, thunder chief. Thirty thieves and the thunder chief..."* She sings with the kind of enthusiasm reserved for opera singers and those on Broadway.

I rub my upper lip to hide my silent laughter, but she must catch my shoulders shaking, and the sound of dying animals stops coming from her mouth. "What is so funny?"

"I—" A burst of laughter flys from my lips. "I'm sorry."

"Why are you laughing?"

"That…" I clear my throat and tell myself to stop fucking laughing, but doing so sends another wave of laughter. "What was that?"

Her chin jerks back in offense. "Um, I'm sorry, I wasn't aware that you were uncomfortable with my singing in front of you."

"That wasn't singing."

Her jaw drops open then slams shut and she glares. "You are such a jerk!"

"Daddy says we shouldn't call people names," the kid pipes up from the back.

The nanny's face turns red, which isn't nearly as much fun as watching her lose her shit. "Your dad is right, Elliot." She shimmies her body as if she's a bird ruffling her feathers to look bigger and more intimidating. "I'm sorry."

"You should be apologizing to Brian Johnson for butchering his song."

Her eyes widen. "Oh my gosh, message received, okay? My voice isn't amazing."

"Oh, it wasn't just that. You fucked up the words too."

"Daddy has to put money in the curse jar when he says bad words."

Man, who made this kid the behavior police?

"How 'bout I give you a hundred bucks and you let me off the hook?"

"Okay!"

I turn back to my chauffer. "Tell me what lyrics you were singing."

She chews her lip self-consciously. "Isn't it… I mean, he's saying *thirty thieves and the thunder chief*, right?"

"No. Not even close."

"You're lying."

"Where's your phone?" I see it sitting in the space holder between us and snag it. "What's your password?"

"I'm not telling you my password!"

"What do you think I'm gonna do? Read your text messages and emails? This may come as a surprise, but I'm not interested. Not even a little."

She recoils as if my words hurt. I want to tell her she should really try to have thicker skin, but I don't care enough to exert the energy. "All fives."

I hit the fives. "Clearly you don't care if people break into your phone with that amateur pass—whoa... who's the douchebag with little Miss Hot Tits?"

She grabs for her phone, but I hold it out of reach. "No one."

"Another *no one?*"

She's forced to put both hands on the wheel to drive, and I take a closer look at the IG post. "'A night out with bae.' So these two are a couple. No one says bae anymore. Someone should send Tits here the memo. Why are you so obsessed with—" It all clicks into place. "You're into this guy?"

It seems as if she wants to deny it, but it's too late, I can tell I've caught her.

"He's my ex-boyfriend."

"Ahhh. And you want him back."

"I don't, I mean... I don't know, yeah, I guess so."

I study the photo. His current girlfriend is sex in heels while the little nanny here is... well, a nanny in ugly fucking sneakers. "Good luck with that. This chick is hot."

"Yes, well." Her jaw clenches. "Thank you for reminding me." We pull into the parking lot, and she throws the car in park and whirls on me. "Has it ever occurred to you that some people might actually find a person's personality attractive? That maybe it's not about how they look on the outside?"

I stare at her, bored, because I have an answer to that, but I don't think she's gonna like it.

She shoves her hand toward me. "Give me my phone back."

I hit a few buttons before handing her the device. "'Dirty Deeds

Done Dirt Cheap.'" I swing open the door. "The lyrics are literally the title of the song, genius."

She glares at me and I grin before slamming the door and walking away.

Funny... walking away and into the meeting room?

I'm still smiling.

8

BETHANY

When was the last time Pastor Ben cleaned out his freezer?

The question pours through my mind as I stare at the fresh packages of frozen vegetables stacked on top of bricks of really old frozen vegetables covered in ice-fuzz.

I peek at Elliot, who is happily finger painting at the kitchen table. She was occupied while I cleaned out the cupboards under the sink, and judging by her intense stare at the page, I'd say I have another fifteen minutes until she's ready to move on.

I pull everything out of the freezer and toss things that are inedible. Pretty sure frozen peas aren't supposed to be a solid cube of ice. Toss. Maybe after this, I'll see if Elliot wants to bust out the plastic pool. I usually wouldn't suggest that because it's a lot of work dragging it out of the storage shed, cleaning it, then filling it with water, but today I have energy to spare.

Yesterday at church, Wyatt showed up alone.

Alone!

As if that wasn't enough, he actually stopped and asked how I was doing. Some might say he was being polite and it's not out of the ordinary to make conversation with the greeter. But this wasn't that.

He smiled. He made eye contact as if he were really listening. I was about to ask him where Suzette was but decided against popping our temporary bubble by bringing her up.

I felt great about our interaction, ready to start the new week on a positive note.

I don't know why people hate Mondays. They're just as good as Sundays, a chance for new beginnings. And Lord knows I need a new beginning. After an entire week of Jesse Lee, I have a lot of repenting to do. That man is infuriating. He's selfish and thoughtless to how his words might affect other people. He's callous and arrogant, and... okay, he's kind of funny. I mean, when he's not making fun of me, which is hardly ever.

I've made a new vow!

I will no longer allow Jesse Lee to hurt me.

"What is *that?*"

Speak of the devil.

I sigh and turn toward the towering pillar of tattooed torso standing over Elliot's painting.

"I'm painting a ballerina." Elliot continues to swirl her hand covered in blue washable paint onto the page.

"Ballerinas aren't blue. They're pink." He heads over to the coffee pot and grabs a mug.

"Don't listen to him, Elliot. Art is interpretive, which means ballerinas can be whatever color you want." I slam the freezer door a little harder than necessary and scold myself. *Remember your vow.*

Jesse glares at me, and rather than jump with fear, I grin. Big.

"I bid you good morning, Jesse Lee. I trust you slept well." I walk past him with my head held high.

"I did, until I realized I'd woken up in a 1940s TV show."

I clear my voice and shake off his little jab. "It's no surprise you've managed to sweep women off their feet with your *charming* personality." I roll my eyes hard and make sure he's looking at me when I do it.

He leans back with his ass to the counter and sips his coffee, grinning a little behind his mug. "My getting a woman off her feet has nothing to do with my personality. It's got everything to do with my co—"

"*Do not* finish that sentence!"

He squints one eye in a way most women might find adorable, but not me. "Confidence. What did you think I was going to say?"

My face flames and I busy myself by tidying up around Elliot. The low rumble of his chuckle has me balling my fists and looking for something to throw at him.

The vow. Facing away, I close my eyes, exhale, and release the tension in my muscles.

"Hey, nanny. Any chance you've seen my package?"

My eyes dart open and I whirl around. "There you go again!"

I stomp toward him and hate the way his eyes dance with humor and a little confusion as he follows my movement. I stop directly in front of him in such a huff that his eyebrows pop above his ridiculously inhuman-colored eyes. Seriously, are those contacts?

"You just can't help yourself, can you?" I hiss-whisper. "I've asked you to never speak about s-e-x with me and you refuse to respect my wishes. Listen to me loud and clear, Jesse Lee."

He looks way too relaxed, even entertained, as he slouches against the cabinets.

"If we lived in a dystopian society and sleeping with you meant I'd get sunshine and oxygen and all the food I could eat as well as preserving the human race for future generations, I still wouldn't touch you." I step closer and his eyes flare, which pisses me off more. "I would rather die of scurvy and kill all hope for the survival of mankind than have s-e-x with you."

With my rant over, I'm suddenly aware of how close we're standing. I take a big step back and slam my back against the stove.

Jesse watches me, and the heat in his eyes would make me think

I've pushed him too far if it weren't for his grin. "So... let me get this straight. That's a no? You haven't seen my package?"

I'm about to scream when Elliot looks up and points toward the door. "Daddy put it over there."

What? I whirl around, and to my utter shock and disappointment, leaning against the wall by the TV is a tall, brown-paper-wrapped package.

Jesse smirks. "'Preciate that, kid." He crosses to it, and I gape, searching for the right words as he picks it up and carries it back toward his room. He stops to whisper, "It says a lot about you that you feel the need to spell *sex* like it's a dirty word." He winks.

When he slams his door, I finally shut my mouth, staring helplessly down the hallway.

I am an idiot.

I'm sick to my stomach. Again.

What I said to Jesse about not having sex with him after he was simply looking for a delivery... well, it was unacceptable and unfriendly. I don't know what it is about this guy that brings out the absolute worst in me, but I hate it. I attacked him when, for once, he didn't deserve it.

He didn't speak to me the entire ride to his meeting. He's done that before, and usually I don't take it personally, but after the way I treated him, I know his silence this time was personal.

I dropped Elliot off at preschool and had to race halfway across town to grab an apology gift. Thank goodness the Lexus is fast. I made it back to the church to pick up Jesse with five minutes to spare. My stomach is in knots. I picked up the peace offering so that I couldn't chicken out, but now, as Jesse could walk out those doors at any minute, I contemplate racing it to the nearest garbage can.

Do I really need to apologize? Surely misunderstanding what I perceived to be a highly inappropriate comment, in front of a child no less, would be forgivable with just a verbal apology. Oh crap, what am I doing? Once he sees what I got for him, he'll use it to belittle me and play upon my kindness.

I spot the nearest garbage can. Right by the double doors. If I run, I can trash it in time.

I pop open the door and check to make sure no one's watching, then I scurry to the can. I'm roughly four feet away when the door to the church swings open. My shoes squeak against the concrete entryway as I come to halt.

Jesse freezes when he sees me. "What are you doing?"

I shove my gift-bearing hand behind me. "Nothing."

He glares from beneath his ball cap, the shadow of the bill making his face look even more sinister than it does naturally. "What's behind your back?"

I exhale and accept my defeat by shoving the gift toward him. "For you."

He studies it. "Is that...?"

"Kale, spinach, parsley, green apple, lemon, and some weird word that starts with an A. Akey or..." I shake my head and shove the drink at him. "I don't remember."

He slowly takes the drink. "How did you know my juicing recipe?"

Oh wow, I knew this would be embarrassing. "You know, we should probably get in the car before someone recognizes you." I whirl around and scurry to the car, praying to God that my face will return to its normal color.

Sadly, God doesn't seem to be answering my petty prayers today.

Jesse climbs inside and my cheeks still feel as if they're being blasted with a blowtorch. I would hope that he'd notice and turn away, giving me some privacy to calm a little, but he has zero social graces. He angles his body toward me and stares, waiting for an answer.

Knowing it's unsafe to drive while my hands are shaking, I ball them in my lap. "I'm sorry, okay? That's all. I just... I felt terrible about our misunderstanding—"

"Your misunderstanding."

"Right. I felt terrible about what I said to you and so I brought you a peace offering."

He looks at the drink, takes a sip, and goes back to staring at me. "This is spot-on. How'd you know?"

"I Googled it. You'd be surprised the stuff you can find on the internet."

"You internet-stalked me."

"No!" My stomach twists a little, but I push back my nerves because I refuse to top off this humiliation party with a barf piñata. "You did an interview with some men's fitness magazine and you offered up the information."

He sips on his drink. "What else did you learn about me?"

"Nothing. I didn't dig that far." I know his favorite fish is sea bass, he hates filberts—which I believe are some kind of nut—and he only eats beef called Wagu, whatever that is. I punch the engine button and pull away from the church.

"Liar." He finally sits forward.

With his eyes off me, I relax a little. Silence stretches between us, and although it's uncomfortable silence, I'm still grateful for it.

When we hit the driveway, he speaks up. "Apology accepted." He pops open the door and climbs out before leaning down with one tattooed arm propped on the car's roof. "Oh, and I may've instigated your misunderstanding."

"What? Why?"

He shrugs and steps back from the car, a grin on his face. "You're entertaining when you're mad." He slams the door, punctuating his words.

Dick!

I back out of the driveway and speed off with a squeal of my tires, still hearing his chuckle through the open window.

JESSE

Day Twenty-One

One week until my twenty-eight-day mark.

I have to say, it's been a piece of cake so far. All I have to do is ignore everything I don't like, sleep as much as I'm able, and kill time in every possible way.

With my elbows on my knees, I stare at my guitar leaning on the wall by the closet. The best musicians in the world were at the top of their game while drunk and high. Kurt Cobain, Jimmy Hendrix, David Bowie. Sober those guys up and they'd never be able to create the magic they did when they were wasted. I should just pick it up, but what if I no longer have what it takes to create musical magic?

Discouraged, I drop my head into my hands and groan.

Hanging over the elastic waistband of my sweats is a roll of flesh that wasn't there weeks ago. What the fuck is that?

I jump off the bed and head out into the living room, where Ben is sprawled out on the couch with his kid curled up at his side, watching some cartoon. "Hey—"

"Shhh..." the kid says but doesn't take her eyes off the screen. "This is the best part."

I roll my eyes and watch some singing blonde make an icehouse out of magic that squirts from her hands. When it seems like the song isn't going to be over for a while, I drop down in the chair and wait. Whoa... blond chick just pulled her hair down and got sexy as fuck. Wait, no, I am not lusting after a damn cartoon. I drop my head back and wait until the singing ends.

"Ben, hey."

He turns his head away from the television only to have his kid grip his chin and turn it back.

"Keep watching, Daddy."

"Okay, princess. What is it, Jesiah?"

I grip the armrest of the chair. Why does he insist on calling me that? "I need to call Dave."

"All right. I'm not stopping you."

"I don't know his number."

"You don't know your *manager's* number?"

"I'm not doing this with you." I stand up, prepared to wait for Dave to call me.

"What do you need?"

"A gym." I slap my gut. "I need to move around, burn off all this processed food you've been feeding me."

He kisses his kid's head and slips off the couch. I follow him to the kitchen, where he pours himself a glass of water.

"Well?"

He looks at me thoughtfully, which makes me feel as if I want to curl in on myself, so I stick out my chest to prove a point. *You don't intimidate me anymore, big brother.*

"You can work out at my gym." He shrugs.

"No, I can't. If I go to a public gym and get recognized—"

"It's not public. It's at the church. You can use it whenever you want. They do yoga classes and weight training a few days a week, but you can work out around that."

"Wait, you have a gym at your church?"

"Physical fitness goes hand in hand with spiritual well-being."

That explains the extra bulk he's put on since I last saw him.

"When can I start?"

"I guess you'll have to talk to Bethany and see when she's available to take you."

I run my hands through my hair. Shit. How the hell is this going to work? I'm not used to having to ask for favors. I mention my needs and they're met.

This is uncharted territory.

I fucking hate it.

9

JESSE

"Thanks for sending the clothes," I say to Dave while sorting through the box of workout wear he overnighted me. I cross to the bathroom, and the 70s-era telephone comes off the dresser and thumps to the floor. "Any chance I can get a cell phone here soon?"

Fuck, it's frustrating to think I've made this guy millions and I'm begging him to get me my own phone. The monster has been silent inside me, but now I feel a scaly stir.

"You write me a song yet?"

I pick up the plastic phone cradle and slam it on the dresser. "That's how this works, huh? Necessities being divvied out as rewards?"

"More like you make an effort and prove you want your career back, then I'll start treating you more like a client and less like a child."

"I've been sober for almost a month!"

"You've been seeing Doctor Ulrich for a month and he says you're still refusing to participate in therapy."

"What the fuck? Isn't there some client confidentiality shit where he's not allowed to discuss what we talk about? I'll have his license revoked!"

"For what? Telling me you're not taking the sessions seriously? Good luck with that. You're down to seeing him twice a week now and running out of opportunities to get the help you need."

There's a rumble behind my ribs where the monster lives, but rather than rage, he rolls over and continues his hibernation. Pussy.

"What's going on with the band?"

"I told you, there is no band."

"Are you trying to get me to drink again? Come on, give me something to hope for here. If this is all a lost cause anyway, then why the fuck am I here?"

He's quiet for a few beats then clears his throat. "The guys are waiting to see what you write before they decide if they're going to stick around or not."

"That's good, right? I'll crank out a few number-one songs and we're back in business."

"The label isn't sold on you making a comeback. Whatever you come up with, it'll have to be good enough to win them over as well."

My gaze darts to my guitar that is starting to collect a sheen of dust. "I can do that. And what about Nathan?"

He sighs. "Nathan's out for good."

I run a hand through my hair. "That can't be right. He loves the music—"

"He loved Kayla."

Fuck, I have nothing to say to that, so I don't. What kind of man gives up his entire career for a chick? He clearly isn't the type of man who would die for his music, so we're better off without him.

"There's a drummer I've been keeping an eye on out in Las Vegas. If, and I mean if, you come up with a single that's reminiscent of the early Jesse Lee stuff, I'll see if I can get him to replace Nathan."

"If? Where's your faith in me?"

"Honestly? It died during your second rehab stay."

"I've been to rehab three times."

"I know. I gotta run. Get me those songs."

The line goes dead.

I stare at the leather-bound notebook and black Bic on the bedside table, then my gaze slides to a photo of Maggie, her hands on her swollen belly and her eyes dancing with joy while looking at me.

"How am I gonna do this in here? There is zero inspiration." I decide I need some fresh air and a cigarette, so I snag my Marlboros and a lighter and head to the kitchen to grab a coffee.

At nine thirty in the morning, I expect to find the nanny and the kid somewhere, taking up space and making too much noise, but the house is empty. Good. Maybe with them gone I can think —what the...?

I squint through the sliding glass door and into the backyard. There's one of those plastic kiddie pools, and the midget and the nanny are sitting inside it.

"She looks ridiculous." I slide open the door, and both sets of eyes come to me. "Don't you think you're a little too big for that?"

"Good morning to you too," she says as she bobs a plastic fish in and out of the water.

I don't know why the visual frustrates me so much. Maybe it's my conversation with Dave. Maybe it's the sheer idiocy of a grown woman in a baby pool. Maybe it's the fact that in a swimsuit, she's wearing less clothes than I've ever seen her in and I'm fucking horny and grumpy as shit, but she continues to reject me for sex.

"I need you to take me to the church gym."

"Oh, awesome! Are you taking Holy Yoga? Or Weights-n-Soul? I think they're starting a Zumba to Zion class. I bet you'd be good at that." She laughs and a little snort comes out, which is so fucking annoying.

"After my meeting, I'll go to the gym, so just pick me up an hour later."

"I can't. I have to be to work at two, except for every other Friday and—"

"That's not gonna work. Change it."

She glares at me. "If you don't like it, then drive yourself. My only job is to get you to your meetings."

God, this woman is impossibly stubborn. I drop into a chair a few feet away from the pool and light up my smoke.

"You can't smoke that here." Her big brown eyes dart toward the kid, who seems completely oblivious to my smoking.

"It's outdoors, it's not hurting anyone."

"You're setting a bad example."

"Says the woman in the baby pool." I squint at her breasts. "Is that a unicorn on your suit?"

"It's a Pegasus."

I take a long drag from my smoke and blow it in her direction.

With a growl, she stands up from the water, and I'm momentarily knocked off guard by her body. Her suit is far from sexy—it's a full piece that covers all her modest curves—but something about it makes me desperate to peel it off and discover what's underneath. She's not tall, but what height she does have is in long, toned legs and her hips are soft and round, something she hid well under her clothes.

She plucks the cigarette from my hand and water from her body drops onto my lap. "I'll take that."

She turns, and I watch her hips sway back to the pool, where she dunks my smoke in the water then tosses it into a bush. Apparently satisfied, she slaps her hands together and plops back into the water.

"You shouldn't smoke anyway. Amazing with all the smoking-related deaths every year that people still smoke. It's like the tobacco companies are saying, here's a gun with a bullet in it. Give me money and I'll let you put it to your head."

"Oh, but it's okay to say that in front of the kid?"

She frowns then looks at the little girl, who seems to be completely ignoring us anyway. "Elliot, never smoke. It's bad for you."

"I know," she says then kicks around, splashing me with more water. "I'm a mermaid!"

Flying horses, fish girls—I pretended I was a fire-breathing dragon when I was a kid. The world is filled with normal people who dream of lives of myth and legend. Simple on the outside and fire-breathing on the inside. Rock-n-roll superstardom is no different. I became what they wanted to see.

No argument. No fight. No resistance from me...

My pulse pounds in my throat. "Oh fuck..."

"Jesse!" the nanny scolds. "What is your problem?"

I blink at her. "I gotta go."

I think I just wrote a song.

BETHANY

Jesse jumps up from the lounge chair and bolts inside, clearly forgetting to close the door.

I sigh and get out of the pool to go shut the door. While I'm up, I keep an eye on Elliot, even though she can swim and it's only a couple feet of water, and grab two sugar-free popsicles from the freezer. My gaze darts down the hallway. Jesse's door is closed. I wonder if he's okay. I check the clock and see we have another couple hours before we have to leave, so I head back out to Elliot.

We hang out in the pool until our shoulders are pink and our hands are wrinkled. I dump the pool water and put her in a bath, then I get her dressed and leave her with her Barbies while I take a quick shower.

Finished and dressed, I realize we have ten minutes until we have to get Jesse to his meeting. I get our things together, hoping

Jesse didn't fall asleep or something, and finally go knock on his door. "We gotta go!"

He swings open the door, and he's still in his sleeping shorts. "I can't. I'm writing."

"What? No. You have to go. You can't miss a meeting."

He seems a little dazed, as if he just woke from the best dream ever and wants to get back to sleep to pick up where he left off. "No, call them, tell them I'm sick."

"You can't do that. Dave said—"

"I need to write a song and I'm on to something amazing, so just call them and tell them I'm sick." He turns around, and I follow his gaze to find a notebook on the floor, words and musical notes scribbled all over the open page. "Please, Bethany." He's never called me by my name before. "I need you."

I don't know why I'm nodding, but I am. "I…"

"Thanks so much. I owe you."

He closes the door in my face, and I stand there for a few seconds, wondering how I'm going to get Jesse out of his AA meeting without getting either of us in trouble.

* * *

"You told them I had diarrhea!" Jesse's eyes are wide as he stares at me from the mouth of the hallway.

I don't know why he looks so upset. I did what he asked and got him out of his AA meeting. I hide my secret smile. "You told me to tell them you were sick."

"Yeah, like a fever or pink eye, not the runs!"

"Elliot, hurry up!" We had been making our way out the door for school when she realized she forgot to grab something for show-and-tell. That was when Mr. Rock God thought to ask me what illness I'd given him. I zip up Elliot's My Little Pony backpack and glare at the furious superstar. "A little gratitude would go a long way."

His glare is all the thank you I get. Ungrateful, spoiled celebrity! "Diarrhea was the best I could do. Besides, no one ever questions diarrhea."

He rakes his hands through his hair, and although he finally has a shirt on, when he lifts his arms like that, it exposes that awesome part of his stomach that tapers and disappears beneath his—"Are you staring at my dick, nanny?"

My eyes snap to his that dance with humor.

"No, you disgusting pervert. I was not." I lean around him. "Elliot! Come on!"

"I'm still looking for my beagle puppy!"

I swerve around Jesse and down the hallway to help search for the stuffed animal. "Did you check under your bed?"

"You've got to be kidding me," Jesse rumbles from the doorway.

I spin around to find him glaring at a poster on Elliot's wall. "You have something against Justin Timberlake?"

He looks at me, eyes wide, jaw slack. "Do you ever watch entertainment news? He beat me for an MTV music award last year."

I stare adoringly at the image of J.Tim in a black leather jacket and a pair of jeans that fit him beautifully. "He's amazing. Just to be nominated alongside JT is an honor."

"Nope. Not even close to accurate."

Elliot pops her head up from behind the bed. "He's a good dancer. Can you dance?"

"I don't dance, kid."

She shrugs. "That's probaly why you lost." She ducks down to search for her stuffed animal.

Jesse's jaw drops open, and he glares at me. "She's been brainwashed. I can't believe my brother's kid doesn't have a single poster of me on her wall." He shoves a finger toward the poster. "I'm her freakin' uncle!"

Silence fills the room, and he looks stunned as he apparently processes what he said. His eyebrows drop low and he shakes his head, backing out of the room.

"I found it!" Elliot's arm pops up with the stuffed animal in hand.

"Let's go, we're going to be late." I usher her out and past a confused-looking Jesse. "You're right." I squeeze his shoulder, pulling him from his temporary daze. "You are her freakin' uncle." *Now act like it.* "Good luck with your song and there's some Pepto in the medicine cabinet."

I can't help but giggle at his answering growl.

Does it make me a horrible person that I got an insane amount of satisfaction from telling Jesse's AA leader, Paul, that he had a horrible case of diarrhea? I can't help it that I want the guy to be human for, like, one second. It's not natural to be good-looking and flawless all the time.

Maybe it was mean to give him fictional diarrhea.

But the look on his face when I told him... I grin. Why does being bad feel so good?

10

JESSE

"Jesiah, you got a minute?"

I peer up from my position on the floor, my back to the bed, guitar in hand and a pencil between my teeth.

"If this is a bad time…"

I pop the pencil out of my mouth. "Come in."

Ben opens the door with a plate of food in hand. He doesn't see me sitting on the floor right away, but when he does, he seems surprised. "Hey."

"Hey."

He crosses to a small end table by that fucking chair that I shoved into the corner and puts down the food. "I wasn't sure if you wanted to take a break to eat." He clicks on the floor lamp.

I blink blurry eyes at the time. It's almost eight o'clock. The room managed to get darker without me even noticing.

Ben stands across the room from me, his hands shoved into the pockets of his jeans. "I heard a little of what you were playing. Sounds good."

Feeling vulnerable and uneasy, I close my notebook and lean my guitar on the bed. "It's rough, but I'll get there."

Tension-filled silence stretches between us, and I wonder how much of this he'll put us through before he puts us both out of our misery and leaves. He rocks back on his feet and looks around the room. His gaze settles on a photo of Maggie with longing and sadness in his eyes. I wonder if he misses staring at her pictures at night now that I'm taking up his room.

I spot the food he brought me. Steak, potatoes, some kind of green vegetable. My chest twinges. "You can have your room back. I'll take the couch."

His gaze slides to mine. "No. I think you should have your own space, and I get up early anyway. Elliot too. This way we won't wake you." He goes back to the photo. "I can get these pictures out of here—"

"You don't have to do that."

"They make you uncomfortable, I get it—"

"No."

He seems confused.

I stand. "It's cool. I don't mind them. But if you insist on staying on the couch, you should take a few out there."

He smiles sadly and grabs the closest photo of his dead wife. He doesn't press the frame to his chest or kiss it like his expression led me to believe he would. Instead, he holds it at his side. I get the sense he doesn't want me to know how much it means to him. "Right, well... I'm going to shower and get to bed."

"Ben."

He stops at the doorway and turns around.

"Do you miss it? Playing." I lift a chin toward his dusty guitar. "Writing."

"A little, yeah."

"You ever think of going back to it?"

He shrugs, and I don't miss the way he holds the photo frame tighter to his side. "Not really."

"Too bad." I snag my food off the table and sit back on the floor to eat. "You were good at it."

He drops his chin for a few breaths then looks at me. "You comfortable on the floor?"

I eye the antique chair for the maximum amount of time I'm able to—which is all of two seconds. "You can't expect me to sit on *that* fucking thing."

The moment my words register, Ben's face drains of color.

"G'night."

His gaze darts to the chair then back to me, but he doesn't meet my gaze. He nods and backs out of the room with a quiet, "Good night."

"I'm happy to hear you're writing music." Doc Ulrich seems genuinely excited about my news and seems as stoked as I am that we're down to two-a-week visits. "Writing music is no different than journaling—"

"I beg to differ, doc."

He motions to my guitar with a flick of his pen. "Would you like to share what you've written?

"No can do. You'll have to wait for the single to release like everyone else."

"Fair enough." He cracks a smile and jots something on his legal pad. "Any breakthroughs at AA yesterday?"

My expression sours. "I missed my meeting yesterday because I wasn't feeling good."

He fakes concern well, but I can tell he's mostly skeptical. "Are you sick?"

I scratch my jaw as irritation crawls up my neck. "Yeah, just a... some stomach stuff."

"I see." He writes something. What could possibly be noteworthy about me being sick—well, fake-sick? "Do you need to see a doctor?"

"Nah, man. I'm good."

"You'll be attending your meeting today though, correct?"

"Yeah, and I'm going to start working out today. I'm excited about that."

He goes on and on, trying to dig out any dirt from my childhood, but I just nod or shake my head. If he's that curious about my upbringing, why doesn't he ask Ben? I'm sure he'd be an open fucking book for the doctor.

Our time finally ends and he excuses himself. I throw on a pair of athletic pants and a black T-shirt, slip on my Under Armor running shoes, and head out to hunt down my ride.

She's in the kitchen at the sink, rinsing dishes.

"Where are the keys?"

She jumps and drops a mug into the sink, where it shatters into a million pieces. "*Shit!*"

"Um, pardon me, Ms. Prim and Proper, but did you just drop an s-bomb?"

"You scared me." She glares at me, and this close, her eyes look more caramel-colored. Huh, I always thought they were just brown. "You shouldn't sneak up on people."

I rest back against the counter beside her. "Nanny, I'm six-foot-one. It's impossible for me to 'sneak up' on anyone. Maybe you should be more aware of your surroundings."

"Whatever." She picks up the ceramic pieces and tosses them in the garbage.

As often as she's here—and whenever I see her, she's always playing with the kid or cleaning—what would Benjamin do if she quit? He'd be fucked.

"Elliot, let's get a move on!" she calls down the hallway.

The little girl comes barreling into the kitchen, a big gap-toothed grin pulled tightly between her cheeks.

I'm at the door, slipping on my ball cap, while the nanny gathers the kid's crap so we can go. I snag the key fob from the kitchen table. "I'm driving."

She's in a squat, tying the kid's shoes, and peers up at me. "You can't drive. Dave said—"

"Dave doesn't want me to drive because he doesn't want me to get into trouble. I'm not going to get into trouble, so I'm driving."

"I don't think—"

I snap my fingers. "Up. Let's go."

She glares at me in that way that makes me horny, then she frowns because now I can't stop smiling. "Fine. The church is only a few miles from here. Surely you can handle that." She struts past me with a smirk.

Keep it up, nanny, and I'll have you naked and spread open underneath me by the end of the week.

She does the shit with the car seat while I get behind the wheel, adjust the seat to accommodate my much longer legs, and fix the mirrors.

She climbs into the front seat and eyes me as she clicks her own seat belt. "Aren't people like you taken everywhere in limos? When was the last time you drove?"

I reverse out of the driveway and throw the transmission in drive, peeling out just for fun.

She stiffens and braces herself in her seat. "Slow down!"

The kid laughs and squeals for me to go faster.

I press harder on the gas.

"Jesse, please!" she screams as her knuckles turn white on the oh-shit bar. "Oh my gosh!"

Not bad. I wouldn't have expected such dick-hardening passion from a woman who wears medicated Blistex as lip gloss. I'd love to hear those same words come out of her mouth in a more intimate setting.

At the end of the street, I slow and my jaw hurts from smiling. "For your information, I have a valid driver's license that has never been revoked for a DUI or DWI or for whatever else your tiny little mind has made up about me." I can feel the heat of her anger. "Jesus, nanny party pooper, take a joke."

"Can we do it again?" the kid asks and kicks the back of my seat, which is really fucking annoying.

"No," the nanny answers and turns her face away to look out the window.

I hear her sniffle. Shit, is she crying?

Women and their overactive emotions.

Another sniffle and she wipes her face.

I roll my eyes and groan. "Are you crying?"

"Just forget it," she says, but I hear the tears in her voice.

Shit. "Calm down, I was just joking around."

"You don't understand," Another sniffle. "I was in the car with my parents when my dad was *joking around* and driving too fast." She wipes her nose, still facing out the side window, most likely to hide her embarrassing tears. "He lost control of the car and... and... they were both killed."

Oh fuck... I'm an asshole.

I open my mouth to say something, but apologies never come easy. "Bethany, I..."

"I was in the ICU for three weeks." She points at a white scar the size of a paperclip on her leg. "This is a constant reminder of that day."

I pull the car over, put it in park, and stare blindly out the windshield. "I'm... look, I had no idea about your parents. I'm... really sorry."

She sniffles again and her shoulders shake.

I am such a dick. "Bethany." I reach out to touch her shoulder, but she whirls around so fast I pull my hand back.

She's smiling. Her face is dry. "Ha!" Her eyes dance with humor. "You sucker!"

"What the fuck...?"

The nanny bursts out laughing, her head falling back with the force of it, her full mouth of straight teeth on display and the sound of a hysterical donkey coming from her lips. "I can't believe you fell for that!"

"Hold on, your parents aren't dead?"

"No way! They live in Phoenix!" Now she's wiping real tears—tears of laughter. "You are so gullible!"

"What about the scar on your leg?"

"I slipped while hiking three years ago and fell on a rock."

"I can't believe you lied about your parents dying," I mumble.

"I can't believe you'd endanger the life of your four-year-old niece by driving like a maniac in a residential area." She smacks her hands together with a satisfied grin. "Now we're even."

"Even?" The corner of my mouth ticks up. "Sweetheart, we've barely just begun."

That seems to shut her up and erase the stupid smile from her face.

Game on, nanny.

BETHANY

As I sit in the car, waiting for Jesse's meeting to let out while I inspect a photo of Wyatt and Suzette on IG, I can't stop hearing that one little word.

Sweetheart.

I've been called that pet name before—usually by the elderly and once by a line cook who ended up getting fired for grabbing the hostess's boob—but this time feels different. Why would he call me that?

Wyatt never called me that. He called me honey, a few times babe, but never sweetheart. I can't decide if the term is sexy or parental.

Who am I kidding? Coming from Jesse Lee and accompanied by that smirk, it was definitely a sexy sweetheart. Why does thinking about it make my insides feel like jelly?

There's movement in the parking lot and I jump, fearing it's

Jesse and he can somehow tap into my thoughts. My eyes widen when I realize it's Wyatt. What is he doing here on a Thursday?

I scramble out of the car. "Wyatt?"

He stops and squints in my direction. "Beth?"

I walk toward him as he does the same until we meet on the Saltillo-tiled path that leads to the church doors.

"Hey." I hold back the instinct to hug him or shake his hand or greet him in some way by folding my arms and locking them around my stomach. "I'm surprised to see you here on a Thursday." *Not that I stalk you and know your schedule or anything.*

"Oh, uh... yeah, I'm kind of surprised to see you too." He shoves his hands into the pockets of his Dockers. "Beth, listen, I've been meaning to ask..."

My stomach flip-flops, and I try hard not to smile at the idea that he's been thinking about me. Maybe he's figured out that we're meant to be and he's ready to get back together. "Yeah?"

His eyebrows pinch together. "How've you been doing? You know, since... you know."

"Oh, um..." Not at all what I was expecting, but maybe it's his lead-in to more important conversation, like how he broke up with Suzette to be with me. "I've been good."

He frowns. "Good, that's good. It's just..." He shifts his weight as if he's uncomfortable. "My parents told me about what happened to your car and—"

"What? Psht... my car? Oh, yeah, that was just some freaky..." I blow air through my lips. "Crazy story, right?" Damn! My pulse is pounding and my palms are sweating. He can't know what happened. How would he? "How are you and Suzette?"

He seems a little knocked off center by the abrupt subject change. "We're good. Oh and by the way, I'm so sorry about bringing her into your restaurant. That was a dick move on my part."

"It's cool." My face grows hotter and hotter. "So you two are good?"

For the first time, he seems to genuinely smile, which hurts like hell in my heart region. Probably indigestion from the Lucky Charms I had for breakfast. "Suzette is great. She's supposed to be meeting me here." He eyes the parking lot, searching for her. "She must be running late."

The church doors swing open and Jesse walks out, pausing when he spots me and Wyatt standing close. With all the swagger and confidence of a rock god, he saunters right to us.

"Am I late?" he says and looks between Wyatt and me.

"No, I was just talking to—"

"Wait a minute," Wyatt says with surprise in his voice. "You're Jesse Lee!"

Jesse tilts his head and looks at me, his brows raised high enough to touch his low ball cap. I don't have it in me to even smile, and I can't introduce them because I'm pretty sure Jesse wants to remain anonymous. Plus Jesse already knows who Wyatt is—I can tell from the smirk on his face.

He nods at Wyatt. "I am."

"No fucking way," Wyatt says with a huge smile as he shifts on his feet as if he might piss his pants at any second. "I've been a fan for years, man. I love your music."

Jesse grins and pride shines in his eyes. "Thanks, I appreciate that."

"Whoa." Wyatt steps back, his hand in his hair. "I can't believe it. Jesse Lee. Jesse *fucking* Lee."

I hold up a finger. "Let's not forget you're on Jesus's doorstep—"

"*Jesse fucking Lee.*"

"Okay," I grumble.

"Wow, man…" Wyatt says, totally ignoring me. "What are you doing here in Arizona? Hell, what are you doing here?" He points at the ground as if he's trying to communicate the church.

"I'm taking a personal vacation."

"Cool, man." Wyatt's blue eyes are still big and round. "I have to get your autograph." He pats his pockets, then his gaze darts to the lot. "Suzette!"

A groan bubbles up my throat. This just gets better and better.

My mouth falls open when I see Wyatt's girlfriend crossing the lot in a red dress that is insanely sexy but manages to be tasteful at the same time. The cherry fabric hugs every curve of her body, from the cap-sleeves to the hemline that falls just below her knees. Her nude heels click on the pavement, flashing red soles as her long dark hair follows behind her like a Pegasus tail in the wind.

Her eyes light up when she sees Wyatt waving her over.

That, too, I feel in my guts.

"Honey, you're never gonna believe who I ran into," Wyatt says as she sidles up next to him.

Honey. Another jab to the belly. Would it be obvious if I walked away to pout in the car alone while these two fawn over the celebrity?

A female gasp later and Suzette is falling all over Jesse while Wyatt watches in fascination and awe. I take a slow step back as Jesse gets caught up in listening to the woman gush about her favorite songs, how she saw him in concert and tried to get back-stage—most likely to have sex with him because that's the kind of woman she is—*shut up, Bethany!*

Girl on girl hate is never justified.

But Suzette is the kind of woman who turns every head in a room. She's the kind of woman even faithful married men fantasize about.

"So what on earth brings you to this shithole?" Suzette says.

Shithole? The town or the church? Either way, I'm highly offended.

"Bethany."

I jump at the sound of Jesse saying my name. "What?"

He holds his arm out toward me and jerks his head for me to step closer. Numbly, I move a couple steps in only to have him throw his big arm over my shoulders and pull me into his side.

Suzette looks at me as if I grew antlers, and Wyatt's gaze settles on Jesse's hand at my bicep.

"Wait... you know her?" Suzette says.

"Yep. I came out to spend some time with Bethany. She was showing me her church." The lie slides from Jesse's lips like melted butter.

Wyatt scowls. "You never told me you were friends with Jesse Lee."

"I..."

Jesse chuckles. "You know Bethany. She's loyal as fuck. She doesn't name drop. I love that about her."

My knees wobble and Jesse holds me up as I'm forced to use him as a crutch.

Wyatt's shaking his head slowly as if seeing me for the first time.

"Yep, that's me. Loyal as eff." Why does everything I say sound so stupid!

Jesse turns his head to speak close to my ear. "We should get going," he says loud enough for everyone to hear and making it sound sexy.

His hot breath ghosts across my neck, and a shiver races down my spine. "Yeah, um... we should go."

Wyatt snaps out of a fog and checks his watch. "We should go too. We're late meeting Pastor Langley." He mimics Jesse's body language and throws his arm over Suzette. "Premarital counseling."

Those two words knock the wind from my lungs. They're engaged? A lump forms in my throat, and I sway on my feet. Jesse's arm constricts around me.

Suzette holds up her left hand and wiggles her fingers. The sun catches on a princess-cut ring the size of a laptop. "We haven't officially announced it yet."

"Congratulations." My voice must get Jesse's attention because I feel his head turn toward me even though I'm staring between Wyatt and Suzette. "Your ring is..." I swallow hard. "It's breathtaking."

"Right." Jesse turns us toward the lot. "We gotta go."

"It was great meeting you," Wyatt yells.

"You should come to the wedding!" Suzette squeals.

But Jesse ignores them and guides me to the passenger side of the car.

He puts me in and closes the door as Wyatt hollers, "I'll send you an evite!"

I stare blindly ahead as Jesse gets in, fires up the car, and pulls out of the lot. I can't feel my arms or legs as all the blood pooling in my chest drowns my heart.

"Bethany?" Jesse says.

"I'm okay."

"No, you're not."

My lips part to refuse, but the words don't come.

"Tell me how to get to your work."

I manage to mumble the directions on autopilot as my mind reassesses what happened. Wyatt said I was the kind of woman a man marries. We were together for almost a year and he never proposed. He's with her for a couple months and they're already getting married. What does that say about me?

What would I have done if Jesse hadn't been there to keep me from total humiliation?

"Hold on." I turn toward him. "Why did you do that?"

"I'm dropping you off and then going back to the church to use the gym—"

"No, I mean, now people are going to know you're here. You shouldn't have talked to them."

"And what? Just walked right past you when you had a surprise run-in with your ex-dick?"

"I mean... yeah."

He shakes his head.

I point at the restaurant up ahead. "Right there on the left."

"What time do you get off?" He pulls up to the front door.

"Um…" Every time I try to focus, all I can see is that ring and the smile on Suzette's perfect face. "I get off at ten."

"Who'll take you home?"

"I'll take the bus."

"*What?* That's fucking stupid."

Why the hostility? I'd think he's the one who just found out the love of his life is getting married to someone else.

"Says the guy who's insisting on taking the car." I shake my head, get my purse from the backseat and slam the door.

Once I'm in the restaurant, behind the safety of glass, I turn around in time to see the Lexus pull away.

"He's marrying that bitch?"

I hold the phone away from my ear as Ashleigh screeches. This is much better than the disappointment I heard in my mom's voice when I called her to relay the news. I know she didn't mean to, but her response made me feel as if I had somehow failed. So I called Ashleigh on my break to tell her what happened, knowing she'd make me feel a little better about being… well, angry. I left out the part about being with Jesse, and no one would question why I was at the church on a Thursday.

"Good for them! She'll be stuck with his needle dick and he'll be stuck with her herpes until death do they part."

Ash has no idea about Wyatt's size or Suzette's STDs, but it still makes me smile.

"I'm so sorry, Bethany. I know you hoped things would work out differently."

"Yeah, I just don't understand. He told me I was the type of woman a man marries. He said those exact words!"

"That's kind of an asshole thing to say."

I pull the phone from my ear, stare at it thinking I misheard, then press it back to my face. "Why do you think being called marrying material is an insult?"

"It's a backhanded way of saying he doesn't think you're sexy."

"That's not true." Is it?

"It is."

Is it possible I saw my relationship with Wyatt all wrong? It would make sense. Especially compared to Suzette, I am not sexy.

Ashleigh speaks to someone in the background. "I'm sorry, I have to get back to the bar. I won't be home until morning. Do you want me to wake you up so we can talk?"

"Yes please."

"I'm so sorry this happened. Hang in there and I'll wake you up with your favorite Frappuccino."

"Thanks, Ash."

We hang up, and I spend the rest of the night in a fog. My tips at the end of the night reflect my poor mood, and I blame Wyatt and Suzette for that too. I just want to go home, take a hot shower, put on my pajamas, and sleep until the pain in my chest goes away.

It's almost time to close, and since it was slow, I've already finished my side work. Good. I'll be home by eleven so I can curl up in bed and cry myself to sleep.

My gaze continues to gravitate to the booth Wyatt and Suzette occupied the night they came in. Did she have the ring on then? Surely I would've noticed.

"Bethany, I'm so sorry, but you just got a table," the hostess says and motions to the far side corner of the restaurant.

A party of four is looking over the menus. So much for getting home early. I'll have to catch the eleven o'clock bus. Great.

After my four-top eats pancakes and bacon and four pieces of pie that the cook had already put away for the night, they finally say goodbye at ten thirty. I clean up, close out, shut off the lights, and grab my purse for the walk to the bus stop.

The temperatures at night are cool and I'm grateful for the light desert breeze that accompanies me on the one-block trek.

Wyatt is getting married. The reminder pounds at my skull for the millionth time, and try I to erase the image of them together—mostly because they look so happy. I should be happy for them.

I drop heavily on the bench with the weight of my broken heart. The next bus should be here in ten minutes. Feeling fairly safe in this decently populated part of town, I watch as cars whiz by. I'm staring at my feet when I sense a vehicle slowing down in front of me.

The Lexus.

The hazard lights come on and the window rolls down.

"Jesse?"

"Hey." One of the things Jesse does that I'm getting used to is he doesn't act shy or coy. He stares boldly, almost challenging, into my eyes.

"Did you bust out?"

"I did." He grins, but it's small. "Dug a hole in the wall, covered it with Justin Timberlake's poster."

I laugh.

"No one will ever know I'm gone."

"Clever. Sounds familiar too, like maybe I saw that in a movie once or something."

"Nah…"

"Does Ben know you're gone?"

"You realize I'm a twenty-eight-year-old man, right? And no, he's asleep."

"Oh." I look down the street in the direction that the bus comes from then look back at Jesse. "What are you doing here?"

A few heavy seconds stretch between us.

"Honestly?" He frowns. "I don't know."

"Okay, well, my bus should be here any minute. You probably shouldn't be parked in the road like that." I slouch back on the bus stop bench with my purse on my lap. "I'll see you tomorrow."

"Do you want a ride?"

"You don't have to. I'm fine taking the bus."

"But I'm here so…"

I glare, hoping to be able to read his intentions. "What do you want?"

"You're fucking exhausting." He drops his head back then rolls it to look at me. "Do you want a ride or not?"

I don't have a good reason to say no—other than the fact that something about accepting the ride feels like giving in—but after the day I've had, I don't have the energy to resist. I gather my things and climb into the car. The AC blows in my face and the radio is on, but the volume is low, creating pleasant background noise.

I strap on my seatbelt and point Jesse in the direction of my apartment and try not to stare at him illuminated by the dash lights.

His great skin, gauged ears, and full-sleeve tattoos make him look every bit of the rock god the media proclaims him to be. His jeans and faded Pink Floyd T-shirt, combined with the way his hair sticks out from beneath his hat, adds a regular guy look that softens his intimidating exterior.

"Stop staring," he says as he makes a left.

"I'm not staring. I'm just trying to figure out why you're being so nice to me."

His gaze darts toward me for a second before refocusing on the road. "I'm not."

What could he possibly be doing driving around after eleven o'clock at night? I chew my lip. "Were you out looking for… you know."

His head whips around. "No, I don't know. Are you… do you think I'm out trying to score?"

My eyes practically fall from my skull. "No! I'm pretty sure you could find someone to have sex with without having to pay!"

He grimaces. "Not score pussy, genius. Drugs. You think I'm out looking for drugs?"

"No, I mean… I don't know." I catch the roll of his eyes in the headlights of oncoming traffic. He seems offended, but what else am I supposed to think? "Take a left here."

"Your intelligence is astonishing."

I cup my ear with my hand. "Wait, is that... *sarcasm* I hear?"

He shakes his head.

"I didn't mean to offend you."

He doesn't say anything, just takes my directions as the silence in the car swallows us.

I'm relieved when my complex comes into view. "I'm there, on the right."

He pulls up to the curb and puts the car in park. "How will you get to the house tomorrow?"

"The bus."

His eyebrows drop low.

"I like taking the bus. I have friends there." I grip the handle to get out. "Hey, Jesse?"

"Yeah."

"I'm sorry for what I said about why you'd be out driving around tonight. You really helped me out earlier today, and you didn't deserve that." When he looks confused, I continue. "With Wyatt and Suzette, you didn't have to tell them we're friends, but I appreciate that you did."

He nods. "I didn't say it for your benefit." He avoids my eyes by looking forward dismissively. "I said it to make Tits jealous. Did you see how hot she got when she thought I was with you?"

His words are tendrils that knot in my chest. "But she's engaged to marry someone else."

"So?"

"Do you have that little respect for the sanctity of marriage?"

"They're not married yet."

"They're in love though." I swallow back the sour bile that surges into my throat.

He tilts his head, glaring. "That chick looked at me like she wanted to lick my skin off."

"And you'd let her? Knowing she's wearing another man's ring?"

"Fuck yeah I would!"

"You're disgusting!"

"Yep."

I hop out and slam the door. I can't believe I assumed for one second that he's a decent human being. He's made it clear from day one that all he's interested in is finding the next available vagina. Of course he'd do whatever it takes to get in Suzette's pants.

Gross.

And now he has me defending my ex-boyfriend and his flippin' fiancée!

Jesse Lee is the worst!

11

JESSE

Day Thirty-Five
Less than two months to go.
Since my lapse in judgment last night, I've decided to make a few adjustments to my daily routine.

I woke up at sunrise thanks to my newfound sobriety. After my coffee and a smoke later, I'll lock myself in Ben's bedroom to write. I'll refuse to let myself leave after nine o'clock and only emerge when I'm forced to go to my meeting. I'll keep my mouth shut in the car and only speak up to let the nanny know I'm going to drop her off at work again, but this time I will not be picking her up. I've got more important things to do with my insomnia—like write songs for my next platinum album, for fuck's sake!

I never allow people to get under my skin, and it's been pretty fucking easy since adolescence. The less I care, the easier it is.

So how the fuck does this no-name girl manage to irritate the shit out of me?

I dated the actress Elise Daegar—okay, maybe dating is over-selling it, but we saw each other exclusively for at least a few weeks.

She threw a vase at me for leaving the toilet seat up, smashed in my headlights for not opening the car door for her, and insisted I send her flowers on set every day. None of that made me so mad I wanted to punch something.

I flex my hand on my guitar fret, still feeling the ache from last night's low moment.

So what? I punched the dashboard.

Back in the day, I would've drowned my irritation with a bottle of whiskey or a fresh Columbian line. That's all this is. My aggressive response last night had a lot more to do with my sobriety than the annoying woman I currently hear singing a God-awful rendition of Bon Jovi's "Living on a Prayer."

I strum my guitar and focus on the lyrics to a new song I'm working on trying to ignore the voice that sounds like cats being burned alive on the other side of the door. Why is she singing in the hallway? Is she trying to smoke me out of here?

"It's not gonna work," I growl and strum my guitar a little louder. "The thorn it sears, the smoke and mirrors..." I jot down a few chords. My hand shakes as the nanny reaches the chorus, her voice even louder.

"*Gotta hold on to what we've got.*"

I can't take another second. I jump off the bed and rip open the door.

Her back is to me as she folds towels and puts them away in the hall closet, and she has on headphones the size of coconuts. The kid is in the living room, sitting a foot from the television with the volume up. She's got the right idea.

"*It doesn't make a difference if we're naked or not! We've got each other and that's—*"

I pull off her headphones, and she jumps and whirls around.

"What did you just say?"

"What are you doing? I told you to stop sneaking up on me!" she snaps.

"Did you just say, 'It doesn't make a difference if *we're naked* or not'? Those aren't the lyrics. 'If we *make it* or not.' *Make it!*"

"That's ridiculous. He's clearly saying naked." Her brown eyes narrow. "You were spying on me?"

"You're yelling! The fucking neighbors could hear you. Are they spying too?"

"Who made you the lyrics police anyway?" Her cheeks burn red, but she covers her embarrassment by stiffening her spine. "And last I checked, it wasn't a crime to sing."

"Ha! That? What you were just doing? That wasn't singing. That was an attempt to contact alien life."

"Oh my gosh, Jesse Lee, you're so funny," she says in a mocking fangirl voice before rolling her eyes and turning her back on me.

"I need to work, but it's impossible to focus with all that racket coming out of your face."

Her shoulders bunch up around her ears. "Fine. I'll stop. You could've just asked without delivering insults."

I step away, not nearly as appeased as I thought I would be after shutting her up. I'm eager to get away from this confusing woman and back to something that makes more sense—my song—but I stop short. "What are you wearing?"

She drops her head back in exaggerated exasperation then turns around with a bored expression. "It's a dress. I would expect someone with your *experience* to know that."

"No shit it's a dress." I take another step back, not completely sure why. The dress is nothing special—simple tank top, stripes on cotton, hits above the knee. Her shoulders are tan and toned, most likely from carrying heavy trays of food. She's barefoot, and her toenails are painted a pale blue. Her feet are cute. Really fucking cute. I blink and refocus on her. "Why are you wearing it?"

She kicks out a hip. "None of your business. But!" She holds up a finger and points at me. "I'm gonna need the car."

"No."

"You can't say no. Dave said—"

"I'll talk to Dave. For now..." I look her up and down, wondering briefly what she's wearing underneath and how easy it would be to slip a hand up her thigh to find out. Not that she'd let me. If I had to guess, I'd say Wyatt's the only man she's allowed between her thighs. Judging by his Dockers and Top Siders, there's no way he rocked her world the way I would if given the chance.

"For now...?" She rolls her hand in the air.

"What?" I clear the thickness from my voice. My jeans are significantly tighter than they were before I walked into the hallway.

"You said 'I'll talk to Dave. For now... '? For now what?" Her dark eyes search mine.

"I don't know what you're talking about," I mumble and, as casually and unaffectedly as possible, walk back into the room. I don't slam the door or huff in frustration. I'm aware I have a much bigger problem on my hands—or rather, in my pants.

This makes no sense.

I date supermodels. Actresses. Gorgeous heirs with their own reality shows.

Normal girls have never caught my eye.

What the fuck is going on?

"I'm attracted to Bethany."

"Jesse? Is that you? In all the years we've been working together, this is the first time you've ever called me."

I pinch the bridge of my nose at the oncoming headache. "You're funny, dickhead."

Dave chuckles. "What's up? And how'd you get my number?"

"Can we cut the bullshit already?"

"Sorry, I couldn't help it. How're things?"

I pace the room, feeling antsy as fuck after my interaction in the hallway with the nanny. I thought a shower and my hand would take the edge off, but thirty minutes of steam and two orgasms later, I'm still fighting to keep the blood in my body equally distributed. "Everything's fine."

"How are the new songs coming along?"

"Really good, but—"

"You want to start using the car."

I stop pacing and stare at a blank wall in Ben's room. "How'd you know that?"

"I already got a call from Bethany."

I whip my head toward the door, ready to race out there and give that woman a tongue lashing. Fuck! A groan bubbles up my throat at the thought of having my tongue anywhere on or inside—*no! Stop it right now!* "She did?"

"Yeah, she said you took the car yesterday and that she needed it today for some kind of lunch date."

"A date? She said she has a date? You told her no, right? I need the car to go to the gym."

"Easy, take a deep breath. I know not getting your way all the time is going to be a difficult adjustment, but I promise you this is for the best."

"Wait, so you told her she could use the car today?" The beast inside me licks his teeth. "Whose money did you use to buy that car? I don't know what the fucking nanny told you, but I've been sober and working my ass off. I've earned the right to that car, and if you have a motherfucking problem with that, you can send in your resignation and I'll go buy myself my own goddamn car!" I'm practically panting to catch my breath.

"You done?"

No, I am not fucking done! What's happening to me? Why do I feel as though I'm about to jump out of my skin at the mention of Ben's kid's nanny?

"Bethany was cool. She said you've been working hard, that all she hears coming from your room is your guitar, and the reason she called was to make sure I was okay with you driving the car now. I told her I was fine with that until you failed a drug and alcohol screening."

"Hold up, drug and alcohol screening?"

"Every morning at nine, a nurse will show up to take a urine sample—"

"You've got to be kidding me."

"As long as you pass, you get use of the car."

I drop down on the bed and stare at the ceiling.

"And after thirty days of clean screenings, if you deliver me some songs, I'll get you a phone."

"Wow, thanks, Dad," I say dryly.

"You're welcome, son. Now go work out the driving schedule with Bethany. You're both adults. I'm sure you'll figure something out."

"Fuck."

He laughs. "Nice to have you back, Jes."

The line goes dead and I continue to stare at the popcorn ceiling.

Sixty more days and I get my life back.

Until then, I have to find something that will not only entertain but inspire me, oh, and extra challenge, I have to do that without drugs or alcohol.

I am so fucked.

The monster in my gut grumbles, "You wish."

I've always wondered why men who are losing their hair don't just shave their heads rather than comb one side over to try to cover the shining hairless scalp.

As Paul addresses the group of recovering addicts, I contemplate the many reasons why he doesn't just shave his shit. Maybe he's grateful for every last hair he has and wants to show them proudly by growing all sixteen hairs a foot long and using them as a bald shield.

God, this is where I'm at? Pondering the ins and outs of male pattern baldness?

I'd kill for an icy glass of twenty-five-year-old scotch, a cigarette, and a gorgeous woman who doesn't argue with every-fucking-thing I say to sit on my lap right now.

"And use it to replace one addiction with another. Has anyone experienced this and would like to share?" Paul's gaze comes to mine like it does after every question he asks. If he's trying to be inconspicuous about getting me to share, he's doing a shitty job.

"I've started puzzling," Oscar, the drunk who lost his wife and kids in a divorce because of his addiction to cheap vodka, says. "When I crave a drink, I head out to my dining room table and work on my puzzle."

"That's great!"

Paul's encouraging smile has other guys in the group interjecting their own stupid shit. One works on his motorcycle, the other started rolling ten years' worth of coins. Blah blah boring blah...

"This is good stuff. It's wonderful that you've all found some-thing healthy and productive to do when the cravings become unbearable." His gaze settles again on mine, and I hold his stare until he's forced to look away. "Great, let's close with the serenity prayer, and I'll see you guys here tomorrow."

They pray.

I close my eyes and imagine every woman I've ever seen naked.

Once we're dismissed, I jump up, eager to hit the gym for as long as I'm able. Back in the day before the booze—okay, before the drugs—I did my best brainstorming while working out. Wrote some of my best shit in my home gym. I feel a bit of that coming back with every workout.

I head out into the hallway and past the offices where my brother is currently working. I keep my head down to avoid being seen by one of his staff. I don't know how much Ben has shared with the church employees, and I don't really care as long as they don't bother me or rat me out to the media.

I make the last turn and head toward the glass door where I see the Lexus waiting. I grin and straighten my shoulders, strangely excited for the next verbal spar with Bethany about her fucking lunch date.

And what kind of a pussy-ass bitch asks a woman he wants to bang out to lunch?

"Hey! Jesse!"

"Fuck." I whirl around, glaring at whoever yelled my name loud enough for everyone to hear.

Suzette. She's sitting in a chair at the far end of the lobby, but she stands as I approach. She's dressed to kill in a halter top, skinny jeans, and a pair of black heels made for the club, not church. Her eyes light up in a way I've seen a million times before. "You're here."

I smirk. "What's up... uh..."

"Suzette."

"Right. Suzette." I didn't forget. The nanny's obsession with the pretty brunette and her dorky fiancé makes her a household name. But I want her to think she's forgettable. "What are you doing here?" *Let me guess...*

"I'm here for a meeting with Ben, but"—she steps closer and whispers—"I was hoping I'd run into you."

Ya don't say. I shove my hands into my pockets, feeling the stir of excitement at this kind of distraction. "Here I am. Now what?"

Her face turns red, making her seem more innocent than I'd pegged her for from the photos I've seen.

"Where's your man?" I make sure she sees me scoping out her body—her tits, hips, long legs. *You're not dressed like this for him, are you, bad girl?* "He's not coming?"

The red in her cheeks blazes a path down her throat to her breasts.

I fucking smile. See, this is fun. This is how flirting should be.

"Ms. Ortiz?"

I drop my chin at the sound of my brother's voice followed by his footsteps.

"You're here? I've been calling your cell."

I look at Ben, who studies me and Suzette as if he's expecting to find cum stains on her clothes.

"Pastor Langley, I'm sorry." She points at me. "Did you know you have a huge celebrity in your church?"

This should be fun. I watch my brother stumble over himself in an attempt to explain my presence in his tiny, humble house of worship.

"Uh..."

I lift my brows, waiting.

Ben scratches the back of his neck. "I did, actually, yes."

"Isn't it great?" Suzette looks at me. "Will you be here for service on Sunday?"

"No, I'm afraid Jesse doesn't attend," my brother says.

I scowl. He never calls me Jesse. And since when does he think he has permission to speak for me? "Actually, yes. I'll be here Sunday."

"Great!" Suzette squeezes my arm. Her long nails bite softly into my skin, a feeling I used to love from women but now have the urge to shake off. Weird. "I'll save you a seat."

Satisfaction rolls through me at the horrified expression on my brother's face. "Great. I'll see you there." I lift my chin at my brother. "Later."

I head out to the Lexus, feeling good about how that went. Not only do I have a fun new plaything in Suzette, but I've managed to send my older brother into a tailspin without even trying. This thing with Suzette could be fun, my own personal puzzle—just a hobby to keep me occupied until I get to go home.

"You're in a good mood," Bethany says with suspicion in her voice as I force her from the driver's seat and into the passenger's. "Did your meeting go well?"

"It did. I learned that to keep from wanting to drink or snort a pound of coke, I just need a hobby."

"Oh, wow." She mouths *a pound,* her eyes wide. "Do you have any hobbies?"

"Nope, not really, but I think I found something fun to do."

"Oh, is it building model ships?"

"What? No."

"Oh." She seems disappointed.

"What makes you think I'd do that?"

She shrugs. "Nothing, it was just a guess." She won't look at me.

"I don't believe you."

"It's stupid. Just forget about it."

"Wait… something stupid? From you? *No.*"

"Shhh… don't move." Her eyes dart around the space in front of her, then she smacks her hands together hard. "Got it!"

"What was it? A mosquito?"

"Nope, but just as pesky. It was your sarcasm."

"That wasn't funny."

"Then why are you smiling?" she says with humor in her voice. I know she's smiling too, but I'll be damned if I'm going to look over and see it.

"Why model ships?" I ask.

"Do you ever let anything go?" She turns her head, but I can see the flush hit her neck and that intrigues me a whole fucking lot.

"No. Just answer the question."

She sighs, shakes her head, then shrugs. "I figured you'd be good with your hands," she says in a rush of words all strung together.

I smile and stare ahead. "You think I'd use my talented hands to build toys?" *I'd love to use my hands to loosen you up, nanny. Untie her* high-strung energy and get her to melt underneath me, around me —fuck, I need to get laid.

"Are you sure you're okay taking me across town?"

"I need the car, so yeah. Are you sure you're getting a ride home?"

Of course she is. This idiot is not only taking her on a lunch date, but he's not even picking her up. He'll take her home, hoping for a hand job or an afternoon delight or whatever other shit lame guys like. I almost feel sorry for her. But she's not a kid; she knows what she's doing.

I spend the next thirty minutes negotiating the freeways while my eardrums bleed out and die a slow death. There should be a state law prohibiting this woman from singing. Ever. She's clearly hard of hearing or she'd know she's tone-deaf as fuck, not to mention she destroys the lyrics to most every song she sings.

"Exit here." She points as she bobs her head to a Selena Gomez song.

Every time I check my side mirrors, I sneak a glance at her bare thighs as her dress slides up a little higher with her dancing. Her skin is flawless and tan. Not in an over-sunned way like she's got a membership at the tanning salon, but a natural glow probably from hours spent outside.

"*I'm farting carrots.*" Her lips barely move as she sings, if what she's doing could be identified as singing. "*I'm farting carrots…*"

"Let me ask you something."

"Oh, here we ago."

"Do you actually believe the insanely gorgeous Selena Gomez would write and release a song in which she sings the lyrics, 'I'm farting carrots'?"

She shrugs. "I don't know. Maybe."

We must be getting close because she reaches into her worn (obviously fake) leather purse and grabs her Blistex. The balm looks good on her. Her lips are naturally much darker than her skin. Be a shame to cover up their dusty rose color—*what the fuck am I thinking?*

"You recorded and released a song where you were... ya know, taking matters into your own hand?" She swipes the goop on her lips. "Farting carrots could be a thing."

"It's not a thing, it's stupid, and she's singing 'fourteen carats,' not farting carrots, genius."

"Turn here."

I turn at the light. "And thank you for listening to the song where I took matters into my own hand." I smirk at her. "'Expulsion' was a worldwide hit. It climbed to the top ten twenty-four hours after it was released."

"Who's gross now?"

"Thinking of Selena Gomez farting carrots"—I shiver—"is way more disgusting than a man taking his dick in his hand."

She shifts uncomfortably, and I know she's thinking about walking in on me that first week. I love that she saw me doing that, and I really love that thinking of it makes her fidgety. Now I'm getting hard. Great.

"Let me ask you something, Mr. Expert of the Female Anatomy."

"Sure, what do you want to know? Want me to show you how to find your G-spot—"

"I'm sure you've appreciated your fair share of the female booty." She lifts her brows.

Including yours. "More than I can count."

"You realize, when you're appreciating the backside of a woman, that she poops out of that thing—"

"Fucking gross." I cringe. "Stop."

"And farts."

"No. Nope. I refuse to think about that."

"So would it be so strange for Selena Gomez to sing a song about farting carrots?" She chews her lip. "Hmm... or maybe she's farting carats, like she's so rich she farts diamonds."

"If you say fart one more time, I'm going to vomit."

She throws her head back laughing.

Now every time I check out a woman's ass, I'm going to think of... yuck. This girl ruins everything!

"Up here on the left." She points at a driveway with a sign out front that says "The Orchard Assisted Living."

I pull into the old folks' home. "Are you sure this is the place?"

She gathers her purse. "Yeah, just drop me at the front."

"Who are you meeting for lunch?"

"I volunteer here on my every other Fridays off. I help serve lunch and then lead a cut-throat game of Bingo." She pops open the door and gets one foot out before she looks over her shoulder.

Nanny volunteers with old people, how much gooder can a good person be?

"Hey, do you want to come?"

"No, I can't. I need to go work out and get to work on my songs."

Her eyes narrow. "You sure? No one in there will recognize you. They don't pay attention to anything that happened after 1990."

"I don't know, I—"

"Come on." She places her hand on my forearm, and heat slides like warm honey up my arm. Her dark eyes sparkle and she smiles warmly. "It'll be good for your soul."

"Oh, then definitely no. I need my dark soul for the sake of my music."

"Suit yourself." She jumps out of the car. "Thanks for the ride."

Even after the door closes, I watch her walk up the sidewalk. When she moves, she bounces a little as if she's lighter than air and it's only her shoes that keep her from floating away. I wonder what it would be like to be so at peace that it shows up in my steps. If I walked close enough to her I bet she'd bear the weight of my burdens without even knowing she was doing it.

12

BETHANY

"Good morning, Mr. and Mrs. Thompson, welcome to church." I hand out today's bulletin as I look just over the elderly couple's heads.

I thought I saw Wyatt's blond hair in the distance. As often as I've searched for him, I can recognize him from across the parking lot. He's not alone.

With their hands clasped, Wyatt and Suzette make their way to me. I shift on my tan ballet flats and smooth my faux-denim dress. I wore my hair down today and told myself it wasn't because Wyatt likes my hair down. I know he's happily in love, the ring on Suzette's finger a reminder that I've lost him forever, but that doesn't mean I can't look my best around him. Right?

His smile is aimed at me as they approach, and I rip my gaze away to focus on her so she won't think I'm any kind of threat. *As if a sexy and sophisticated woman like Suzette would ever be threatened by me.*

"Good morning, Suzette." I shove a bulletin toward her a little too forcefully and curse my nerves. "Welcome to church."

She looks down at me, her three-inch heels making her seem

much taller, and smirks. "Morning." She pushes by me ahead of Wyatt.

"Hey, Wyatt." Why do I sound as though I'm whispering? I clear my throat and thrust a program toward him. "Welcome to chur—"

"Ick!" Ashleigh knocks into him from behind. "What is that smell?"

He glares at her. "Long time no see, Ash."

She flashes him a cherry-red smile that's dripping in artificial sweetener. "Not long enough."

He takes his bulletin. "Thanks, Beth." Ignoring Ashleigh, he follows Suzette into the chapel.

"Why on God's green earth would you give that asshole a second of your time?" She's dressed more modestly today—a tight black dress and a pair of combat boots—her blond hair pinned in a picture perfect messy bun.

"I'm the greeter. I was greeting him, that's all."

A couple stragglers make it to the door just before the music starts. Ashleigh hooks her arm in mine, and we shuffle inside.

"We're sitting up close today. I get a better view of Pastor Langley's bulge—"

"Ash!" I whisper-hiss.

Her overly black-lined eyes widen. Ashleigh is the only woman I know who can make last night's club makeup look as though it was done on purpose. "What?"

We find a half empty pew up front, and as I sit, I feel a tug on my hair from behind. I turn, expecting to find a young child.

I was half right.

My mouth falls open when I come face-to-face with a smirking Jesse Lee. I take a quick peek at who is sitting next to him and my jaw drops further.

Wyatt and Suzette?

"Hi," I mouth. "What are you doing here?"

He's wearing his signature uniform—jeans, this time black, and a maroon T-shirt that fits him so well, it must be tailor-made. Is that even a thing? I notice this tee is long-sleeved, hiding his tattoos except for the ones on his hands. He's wearing his baseball cap pulled low, I assume to stay inconspicuous.

"Come sit with me." He motions to the empty spot next to him. "I saved you a seat."

My eyes dart to Wyatt to find him looking right at me. He looks away.

Ash must see me turned around, so she does the same. She pauses for two seconds then slowly faces forward. Her hand clenches mine. "Bethany."

Oh no… "Yeah?" I say as innocently as I can.

"Do you know who's sitting right behind you?" There's a high-pitched squeak to her voice that I worry will only get worse.

"Um—"

"Don't make me"—Jesse's hot breath is at my ear—"come get you."

I jolt upright to standing, and with Ashleigh's hand on mine in an unrelenting grip, she comes with me. We scoot around and excuse ourselves as we pass people already seated until we get to the empty spot next to Jesse. Thankfully it's wide enough to fit mine and Ashleigh's butts because her hand only grips mine tighter.

I'm hyperaware of Jesse as he leans in to whisper, "Thank you."

I close my eyes and nod, wishing I could disappear for a million different reasons. I'm two butt-lengths away from Wyatt. Suzette seems wholly unhappy at my presence. And Ashleigh is really hurting my hand.

"Oh my God, oh my God, oh my God…" she mumbles over and over. Hopefully the people around her will think she's praying rather than blaspheming. *"Jesse fucking Lee."*

Nope, there goes that hope. "Ash," I mumble, "please."

She leans into me. "Do you know him? He seems to know you! How do you know him? How did you not tell me you know—"

"Shh!" the lady behind us hisses.

"I'll tell you later," I mouth.

She slowly sits back, her spine stiff, her eyes wide, and she periodically peeks at Jesse.

"Let me guess?" he says into my ear, making my right arm explode in goose bumps. "The roommate?"

I nod, trying to be respectful to those singing around us by not talking. I wish everyone else would do the same.

Jesse leans away from me as Suzette whispers something in his ear, followed by an obnoxious giggle. Wow, she's not even trying to hide her ridiculous flirting from her fiancé. Maybe he's cool with it. He never was the possessive type.

Jesse shifts his hips, pressing his thigh to mine. The rough denim against my bare skin makes me warm. I use my bulletin to fan my face.

"Hot?" he says in my ear with humor in his voice.

"Nope," I lie, and fan faster.

The music comes to an end, and Pastor Langley takes the platform. Ashleigh's grip on my arm finally lets up a little and her posture relaxes a tad. She makes none of her usual inappropriate commentary, seeming temporarily stunned silent.

Ben opens with prayer, and while my head is bowed, I peek at Jesse. He doesn't even pretend to pray but stares straight ahead at his brother. I close my eyes, but not before catching a slight jump in Jesse's jaw, or did I imagine that?

I try to focus on the sermon but find it difficult with Jesse's leg pressed against mine. I adjust my position and cross my legs. Jesse puts his hand on my thigh in a casual way as if he's done it a million times before. I swallow a gasp and stare at his big, tattooed hand splayed on my bare skin just above my knee. What is he doing?

Ashleigh flips my hand over and scribbles something in pen on my skin before tucking my hand to my hip. I peek at her note.

You have some explaining to do!

I calmly ball my hand and refocus on Pastor Ben, but my thoughts short-circuit when Jesse's thumb makes slow swipes along my thigh. I suck my lips between my teeth. He needs to stop. He grips me ever so slightly. Oh wow… so many callouses. His thumb picks up a slow rhythm that, after a few minutes, I realize has a pattern, as if he's strumming me like a guitar. It seems less flirtatious and more like a nervous habit.

I sneak a glance at him. His jaw ticks beneath a day's worth of beard growth, and his shoulders seem tense. He's much more uneasy being here than his confident demeanor would indicate. I don't know the details of his history with Ben, but I know it's rocky. To top it off, Jesse has to worry about being recognized.

I wonder why he's here. Is this part of the conditions of his recovery? Did Ben insist he come?

Suzette glares at his hand on my thigh, and I feel a small burst of satisfaction. She whispers something to Jesse, but he keeps his eyes forward and shrugs, his hand inching a centimeter up my thigh. My muscles tense until they ache, and when I can't take his touch for another second, I gently push his hand away.

Big mistake.

He flips his over, interlocks our fingers, and pulls our joined hands into his lap.

Now my knuckles are resting on his penis!

A low rumble of laughter comes from his throat, and my cheeks warm with frustration. I continue to stew in my own juices—wait, that didn't come out right. Whatever. And Suzette doesn't stop annoying me with her whispered secrets to Jesse. Wyatt seems equally annoyed, his upper lip stiff and his eyes set forward.

Ashleigh remains surprisingly quiet until finally, and thankfully, the service comes to an end.

After the closing prayer where, again, Jesse clearly doesn't pray, the room erupts in an "Amen" and I jump to my feet only to get pulled right back down.

"What are you doing?" I ask Jesse, who hasn't made a single attempt to get up. "I'm a greeter."

"You already greeted."

Wyatt drags a pouting Suzette from the pew to the platform to talk to Pastor Langley.

I wiggle my fingers to try to free my hand from Jesse's. "I have to... ungreet. Postgreet? Whatever, I—"

"Please." His hazel eyes are flecked with gold—why did I never notice that before? "Don't leave me."

The vulnerable edge to his voice catches me off guard, so I stay put and sit back into the pew. He finally releases my hand only to throw an arm around to rest on the back of the pew behind me.

People file out of the chapel as Ashleigh leans forward, her eyes set on Jesse, who has no issues about delivering the same in-your-face stare. "What are you doing in Surprise? How do you know my best friend? And why are you acting like you two have history I don't know shit about?"

"Ash!" I shake my head.

Jesse sits up a bit, and his arm brushes against my back. I straighten my spine to put a little distance between us. He smirks, noticing and clearly finding it funny for some stupid reason.

He eyes Ashleigh. "Visiting. She works for the guy I'm staying with. And because we do."

"Works for the guy..." Her gaze wanders away. "At the diner?" When neither of us answer, she slides her gaze to Pastor Langley and her eyes brighten. "Jesse Lee is friends with Pastor Langley?"

"I wouldn't say we're friends."

Her eyes narrow as she goes back and forth between Ben and Jesse. "Wait a second, are you guys related?"

Jesse cringes.

"Holy fuck..." She mumbles.

I drop my chin and groan. "Put her in church and it's like the switch on her garbage mouth gets flipped."

"They're just words," Jesse and Ash say at the exact same time.

"Great. I should've known you two would hit it off, you're the same freakin' person." I stand and scoot past Ash to get out of the pew, grateful Jesse let me go so I won't get stuck when the bolt of lightning comes for them.

"Hey, Beth, wait up." Wyatt comes jogging up the side of the church. Suzette is still with Ben. Wyatt stops in front of me and smiles. "Let's get together sometime soon." His gaze darts to his fiancée then back to me.

The question is so shocking, I almost stumble backward. "Me?"

He nods. "Yeah, I wanted to talk to you about something." He eyeballs Jesse, and I follow his gaze to find the multi-billionaire rock star staring right at us.

Ashleigh is at his side and glaring daggers at Wyatt.

"I... guess so?"

"Cool. I'll text you."

"'Kay."

He walks past me toward the lobby, probably getting the car for Suzette. I've never understood why some perfectly healthy, capable women insist on being picked up and dropped off rather than walking with the person they love.

If I'm ever lucky enough to fall in love again, I'll brave a hot walk through a parking lot just to be together.

JESSE

Suzette finishes up talking to my brother and locks eyes on me before walking my way.

Too bad I lost my buffer.

I've never had as much fun in church as I did today. Touching Bethany was a benefit I didn't expect to enjoy as much as I did. Her skin really is as soft as it looks. She tried to act as if my touch made her uncomfortable in a bad way when I knew she enjoyed it as much as I did. The gentle shivers, the soft intake of her breath, the way the muscles in her thigh relaxed under my touch... yeah, she loved it.

The woman who didn't enjoy my touching Bethany lowers herself gracefully next to me in the pew. "What're your plans for the rest of your stay?"

A burst of hysterical laughter comes from my left, and the BFF Ashleigh angles her body toward Suzette and me. "Could you be any more obvious?"

Suzette sneers. "Do I know you?"

"Nope, but I'm sure every man in a twenty-five mile radius knows you, and I mean that in the biblical sense." Ashleigh tops off her insult with praying hands.

I laugh and swivel my head as they volley insults.

"Says the girl who always shows up to church wearing last night's tramp wear."

Ashleigh looks at me and winks. It's not overly sexual but friendly. "Can't argue that."

"Is everything okay here?" Ben steps close, noticing the women's hostile body language with little ol' me in the middle.

"Pastor Langley!" Ashleigh jumps up so fast, it catches me off guard. "Great sermon today. I like your pants."

"Now who's obvious?" Suzette mutters.

She's right. It would seem the BFF has the hots for my brother. Interesting. Ashleigh's the complete opposite of his type—meaning she looks as though she'd be fun as shit and the farthest thing from uptight and boring.

"Thank you," he says. "You're Bethany's friend. Ashlynn, right?"

She shoves out her hand. "Ashleigh."

He shakes her hand, and she dissolves a little. Wow, she really likes Ben. Why? I take in his dorky slacks, polo shirt, and loafers. He's a decent-looking guy in desperate need of a new wardrobe.

"Suzette?" Wyatt comes trotting down the aisle like a good little boy. "I've been outside waiting." His gaze darts to mine, and I smile. He frowns. "Come on, we have to meet my parents for lunch."

She allows him to take her hand, but as soon as his back is turned, she smiles and mouths, "Bye."

Ashleigh makes a gagging sound.

"You ready?" Ben asks me.

"Yep." I stand and lift my arms above my head to stretch. I

expect Ashleigh to take a good look, but she doesn't. She only has eyes for Ben.

"How are you guys related?" she asks.

The good pastor seems shocked she's figured it out.

She squints, studying him then me. "You look a lot alike."

Ben hesitates. "Jesse is my younger brother."

"Ah." She nods. "Makes sense."

That's it?

"Well, I better go find my roomie." She turns toward me. "Nice to meet you."

"You too."

"See you next week, Pastor Langley."

"You can call him Ben," I say.

Her eyes brighten a little. "Are you sure?" she asks him.

My brother actually smiles. It looks unintentional, but damn, yep, he's grinning. "That *is* my name."

"Cool." Ashleigh bounces on her toes. "See ya around, Ben."

I watch her walk away then turn and catch my brother doing the same.

He's squinting at her boots. "Odd girl."

"That there is a woman, Pastor Langley." I clap him on the shoulder. "I know you've forgotten they exist, but they do."

He frowns at the reminder of the female species, or more likely the reminder of the female he lost.

I head out the back door to the church staff parking lot to wait by the Lexus and sneak a quick smoke. I'd planned to drive myself to church, but my brother suggested we all go together, and since I refuse to be seen by anyone in his POS minivan, I drove.

I light my smoke and get in a few good drags before I have to put it out because of the kid. If Bethany were here, she'd launch into a lecture about the dangers of smoking and list all the smoking-related diseases, along with the percentage chance of contracting them. That woman really knows how to rain on a good time.

And yet here I am thinking of her, remembering the softness of her skin on my palm as I wrote music against her thigh. I came up with a killer riff too.

I put out my smoke as Ben emerges with his kid at his side. She runs up to me and thrusts some kind of color-vomit monstrosity on string into my face. "I made this for you!"

"Oh. What is it?"

She thrusts it up again. "It's a necklace! I made it in Sunday school out of noodles!"

"Awesome! Why are you yelling!"

Her dark brows bunch together. "I dunno." She thrusts the thing at me again. "Here."

I take up from her hand with two fingers, feeling the stick of wet paint. And it's pink. Fabulous. "Thank you?"

"Put it on!" She points at my throat. "It's a necklace—"

"You mentioned that, yeah…" I do not want to slip this wet-paint noodle nightmare over my head, but for some stupid reason, I can't tell her no. I take off my hat, slip it on, and return my hat to my head. "There. Happy?"

"Yes!" She races to Ben, who's at the car with the back door open for her. "He loves it, Daddy!"

I look at my chest. There's pink and purple paint on my Zenga tee.

Ben clears his throat, grinning like a fucking asshole. "Yeah, he does."

"Funny." I jump into the driver's side.

"Sorry about your shirt," Ben says under his breath. "I'll buy you a new one."

"Great. Neiman Marcus, and it cost me 395 bucks."

His jaw goes slack. "You're kidding."

"Nope."

"Huh…" He puts on his seat belt. "Would a three-pack of Hanes from Walmart do?"

I cough on my laughter and head out of the parking lot to take us home. "Yeah. That'll work."

13

JESSE

The knock on my door comes minutes after nine o'clock on Thursday morning.

I ignore it and scribble new lyrics into my notebook.

You're syrupy sweet behind a frown.

Closed off and unexpected.

You keep shutting me down.

I just want to turn you on—

Another knock on the door. "Jesse!" Bethany yells.

I scratch out the last few words and yell, "What!"

"Can I come in?"

"Yeah, come in."

The door clicks open.

"I'm naked."

The door slams closed. "Put on some clothes! My gosh!"

"I'm kidding." I laugh. "Come on in."

The door opens slowly and she peeks her head in with her eyes slammed shut. "I swear to Bob, if I open my eyes and you're naked, I'm going to be so pissed at you."

"Who's Bob?"

Her eyes are still closed. She's wearing her hair back in a pony-tail, and for the first time, I notice she has the lightest dusting of freckles on her cheeks. "Bob is no one. I mean, I'm sure Bob is someone, but I don't feel guilty swearing to Bob, ya know?"

"Not really—"

"I'm going to open my eyes now." She peeks through one squinted eye and sees me sitting on the floor, fully clothed in jeans and a Metallica shirt. "Hi."

I tilt my head, studying her because something weird is happening to her face. Her eyes glaze over a little. It's subtle, but I catch it. I know I'm clothed, but she's responding to me as if I'm not. "You okay?"

She blinks, shakes her head, and focuses on the pillows on the bed behind me. "I'm fine, of course. I'm good."

My lips curve a little. "What can I do for you?"

"Oh, right." She steps deeper inside the room and searches for somewhere to sit. "Where did the chair go?"

"Closet."

She wrinkles her nose, and fuck me, it's cute as shit. "You put the chair in the closet? Why?"

I set down my notebook and pen, cross my legs at the ankle and my arms at my chest. "Because my dad used to try to belt-whip the evil out of me on that chair, so forgive me, but I don't like lookin' at the fuckin' thing."

Her face pales and I'm feeling a little dizzy myself. Did I just slit myself open and bleed in front of the nanny?

"Your back…" she whispers.

I clear my throat to push back the fury coiling there. "I was in the middle of working, so unless you came in here for a reason—"

"I'm so sorry," she whispers and her eyes get shiny. "I didn't know."

"Bethany." I'll put an end to this shit right now. No Jesse pity parties allowed.

"Yeah."

"*What do you want?*"

She swallows hard and fidgets on her feet. I want to shake her and tell her to spit it out. "I wanted to talk about what happened at church on Sunday."

I sigh.

"I'm sure you're used to touching women the way you, um... the way you did me, and I'm also sure they have no problem with it."

I shrug.

"But I don't have a lot of experience with that kind of touch from someone who's not my boyfriend."

I stand, and her head tilts back when I cross to tower over her. "Are you saying you don't want me to touch you anymore?"

Her eyes are wide and so beautifully innocent as she stares at me. She shakes her head, but says, "Yes."

"Hmm." I wish she wasn't wearing her stupid uniform shirt. I really enjoyed seeing her in dresses the last couple days. I run my knuckles down her arm. She doesn't back away. Her breath hitches. "You may not like me touching you, but your body sure as fuck doesn't mind."

"It's not that." She swallows hard. "I like it when you touch me. It just confuses me, that's all. I thought you hated me."

"Hate's a strong word."

"Tolerated me at best."

She's right. Mostly. "I enjoy touching you."

"Why?" she says on an exhale and quickly fills her lungs with air and holds it.

I've never been around a woman as expressive as Bethany. At least not that I remember. I don't have to guess what she's feeling. Every breath she takes conveys an emotion. I wonder if I swallow her gasps, would I feel it too?

I slide my hand around the back of her neck, and she doesn't resist when I pull her toward me. "Because you're soft."

Her lips part and her warm breath ghosts across my lips. I lick my lower lip, hoping for even the smallest taste of what she's feeling. I barely brush my lips against hers.

Her weight leans slightly toward me. "What are you doing?"

"Showing you what you're gonna miss if you ask me to stop touching you." I part my lips enough to take her lower lip between mine.

She tastes like minty lip balm. Her mouth is even softer than I imagined.

She grips my biceps, bunching my T-shirt in her fists a split second before she shoves me back. "*Stop.*"

I hold my hands up in surrender and smile, feeling a little off balance for some reason. Might have something to do with the loss of blood to my head as it all races to the happy hard-on party in my dick.

Her eyes become slits of icy fire. "I come in here to tell you how your touch is confusing and you *kiss me?*"

Rejection? This is new. I don't like it.

"That was hardly a kiss." I avoid the temptation to sit on the bed at the weakness I feel in my knees.

She recoils at my counter-rejection. Good. "You're cruel."

"Don't act like a victim. You said just seconds ago you like it when I touch you."

"I do. Which is why I need you to stop."

"That doesn't make any sense—"

The obnoxious chime of the doorbell rings through the house, and Bethany jumps at the excuse to storm out of the room. I follow her, not ready to end this conversation.

When she opens the door, Pete walks in. He smiles at her in the same way he's been doing all week and she fucking smiles back.

"What's up, Beth-nanny." He holds out his arm, and they hug.

Oh, so it's okay for this asshole to touch her, just not me?

"I figured it out," she says happily, clearly not at all affected by what happened just seconds ago like I am. "Matthew Perry."

The man-nurse smirks.

"I'm right, aren't I?"

He shrugs but doesn't say anything. What kind of bullshit game are these two playing?

"I knew it!" Bethany fist-pumps like a dork.

"Knew what?"

They whip their eyes toward the hallway where I'm standing, watching their nerd-flirting.

"What's up, Jesse?"

I ignore the nurse and wait for Bethany to answer me.

"It's a game we play where I guess the celebrities Pete's been a nurse for," she says with none of the enthusiasm she showed the dick in blue scrubs.

"And on that note." Pete pats his duffle bag. "Let's get this urine test done so you can keep your driving privileges. You ready to pee in a cup?"

"Guess confidentiality means jack shit to you, eh, nurse?" I shift my hips, feeling the strain of my hard-on tucked behind the denim of my jeans. "And no, I'm not ready." Unless the nurse can catch piss, I'm going to have to jack off before I can take the test.

I've never gone this long without sex. That's all this is. There's nothing special about Bethany.

I stomp off to my room, telling myself that, but I fantasize about my hand on her thigh while I empty my balls into the toilet.

BETHANY

I'd hoped by the end of the week I'd be feeling better about how my talk with Jesse went down. I'd stayed up most every night this week talking to Ashleigh about how to explain to Jesse that he couldn't go around touching me like that. She tried unsuccessfully to hide her smile while I blabbed and blabbed about how I'd politely tell him to stop even though I didn't necessarily hate the feel of his hand on me.

His touch confuses me, is what I settled on.

I'd rehearsed the lecture a million times in my head on the bus ride to Pastor Ben's that morning. When I walked in and saw Jesse on the floor, looking like the offspring of a tortured artist and a fallen angel, I froze. I'd asked about the chair absently, and his answer was the final blow that zapped all my resolve. *Beat the evil out of him*, those where the words he'd used, but he'd said them like an afterthought, as though they'd slipped from his lips without his permission.

When I was reeling from his confession, he saw my weakness and went in for the kill.

He kissed me!

That was hardly a kiss.

His words ring through my head, embarrassment washing over me as freshly as if he'd just said them. I knew his goal was to remind me how naive I am compared to him, how innocent and prude.

"I'm not prude," I mumble and shove sugar packets into the caddy, thankful the restaurant is empty except for a few cooks in the back.

We closed ten minutes ago, but I'm in no hurry to go home. Ashleigh will grill me about how my talk with Jesse went, and I'll have to face the fact that I tried to ward off Jesse Lee and, like the entire female population, failed miserably.

The headlights of a car shine in through the front windows. During the week, we tend to get a few late-night customers who forget we're only open until ten on weekdays. They usually see the closed sign, notice the lights are off, and move on.

When the headlights turn off and I hear the slam of a car door, I peer outside to see temptation himself headed right toward me. Jesse's wearing his disguise—a baseball hat and a long-sleeved shirt. I unlock the door and open it to keep him from having to loiter too long in the open.

"What are you doing here?"

He stops just outside the door. "Can I come in?"

I didn't realize I was blocking the way. I step back. "Sure."

He stops in front of the hostess stand and looks around the semi-darkened space. "So this is where you work."

I follow his gaze, trying to see the place through his eyes. Cheap diner decorated with grandma-style curtains and photos of baked goods framed on every wall. As if he didn't already think I'm a loser, my place of employment would only confirm that I am. "Jesse, you shouldn't be here. Someone could recognize you."

"I don't care. I can't stay locked up forever."

I'm still not entirely sure why he's here. "If you're hungry, I can't help you. The kitchen is closed. I might be able to get you a piece of pie—"

"I'm not hungry."

"*Okay.*"

"Can we sit?" He motions to a booth.

"I guess so."

I direct him to the nearby booth, and I make sure we sit on opposite sides from each other. I require the distance between us because even now, there's a gravitational pull that has me leaning into the table toward him.

He takes off his hat and runs a hand through his hair. The reddish-brown mess is longer than it was when he got here, but it still looks completely Hollywood. Think Robert Pattinson post Twilight but better. "Listen, I'm sorry about what happened today. I shouldn't have touched you."

But... but... but... shut up, Bethany! This is what you wanted! "Oh, okay."

His eyes latch onto mine as if he's trying to see inside my head.

Bad idea! I can't let him see what's in there. "Do you want some coffee?"

He grins. "Yeah, that'd be cool."

I hop up and duck behind the counter to brew a pot of decaf. Motown filters in from the kitchen where the cooks, Rick and Leon, are wrapping things up. Thankfully they leave out the back door every night, so Jesse should be safe from being noticed without his hat.

I pour fresh brew into two cups and add a little cream and sugar to mine but leave Jesse's black the way he likes it.

His gaze follows me when I return with two cups. "Sexy."

"Huh?" I set down his cup and hope he doesn't notice the way my hand shakes all because of that stupid non-kiss. I can't be myself around him!

He flicks a gaze toward my apron.

"Oh. This ol' thing?" I quickly untie it and toss it into the booth.

"So this is your gig, huh? Professional waitress?"

I can't tell if he's being blatantly insulting or if he's trying to start conversation. Rather than launch into him about how much of an asshole he is, I give him the benefit of the doubt. "No, actually. I have one more year of school before I get my degree in child development."

His eyes narrow. "School? I call bullshit."

"I had to take a little hiatus." I sip my coffee and avoid his eyes. "School is pricey." A half-truth, but he doesn't need to know it all.

"So, what, you want to be a teacher?"

My stomach swirls with guilt and a lot of regret. "Is that so hard to believe?"

He shakes his head. "Nah, I can could see you being a teacher."

"What about you? Did you always know you wanted to be a rock star?"

He chuckles and braces his forearms on the table, turning his coffee mug but not drinking from it. "Yep. From day one."

"You must miss it."

He frowns. "I do. I miss getting drunk."

Is that why he's here? Is he about to fall off the wagon? *Calm down. Don't react.* I have no experience with this. What do I say?

"You drink?" he says.

Not anymore. I shake my head. "No."

He shrugs one shoulder, still focused on his mug. "I probably shouldn't have come here. I couldn't sleep, and being stuck in Ben's room, I felt like I was going stir crazy. I couldn't think of anywhere else to go." He peeks up at me shyly, which is an entirely new look from him and equally endearing as his confidence. "You ever look back on your life to one specific thing that set shit in motion and wonder if you'd done things differently, how you'd end up?"

I open my mouth to respond but close it instead.

"No. I don't suppose you do."

A twinge of irritation tightens my lips. "You think you know me so well."

"You say that like you're a mystery." He follows up quickly with, "No offense." He smiles. "You're a really good person, that's all. It's not meant to be an insult."

Rather than confirm or deny his assumption, I look away before he can see the guilt and shame flaring in my eyes. "You might want to talk to Dr. Ulrich about this stuff."

He shakes his head. "Nah. He doesn't get me. He might get paid to get me, but he doesn't, not really. He pretends. I can see it in his eyes. I'm an entitled Hollywood brat to him." He goes back to studying and turning his coffee. "Everyone looks at me like that. Except you."

"Oh no, you're wrong. I absolutely think you're an entitled Hollywood brat."

He chuckles and nods. "Even still, you don't tiptoe around me or kiss my ass like they do. When you look at me, it's like... I don't know... it's like you see me as a person."

I blink. "You are a person."

He slumps back in the booth but keeps one arm outstretched. His fingers drum on the table. He sucks in a big breath and blows it out. "Ben used to get me. We were best friends growing up."

That piece of news surprises me.

"We used to play music in my parents' church. It wasn't a laid-back church like Ben's. It was whacked, but my parents were sold on it. Ben was an amazing musician, much better than I was."

"I didn't know he could play."

"He gave it up." He drums his fingers again. "When I was thirteen, I discovered rock-n-roll. Slayer. My parents said it was from the devil. I hid CDs under my bed, and when they found them, my dad beat me pretty bad."

"That's awful."

"They were church-approved beatings, spare-the-rod type shit. But I couldn't walk away from the music. I kept getting caught, and the beatings got worse. At one point, my parents dragged me in for a cleansing ceremony that involved snakes."

I gasp then cover my mouth. "Sorry."

"No, don't apologize. It was fucked beyond belief, trust me. The shit went on and on, and the worst part is my brother never tried to stop it. He totally bought into all their bullshit brainwashing. Dedicated his life to serving the same God they followed."

I understand now why Jesse wouldn't pray in church. He's wrong, but I'm not going to tell him that. Not now.

"That chair, the one I put in the closet..."

My stomach turns at the memory of what happened on that chair, those silvery marks on his back.

"All the beatings... how can Ben have that thing in his room..." He shakes his head. "How can he even stand to look at it?"

"I don't know. I know I'll never be able to look at it again after knowing what it was used for."

The corner of his mouth twitches. "See? You get it." He frowns. "Why doesn't my own fucking brother?" He sighs. "I was seventeen the last time my dad beat me. I was bigger than him and decided I couldn't take it anymore. I fought back. My parents disowned me that night, told me I was the son of Satan and that I was dead to them. We haven't spoken since." His eyes are warm and open, fixed on mine. "They moved to some psycho religious colony or some shit. I don't think they even talk to Ben anymore."

"Probably not a bad thing."

"No," he chuckles. "I felt so free that night I left. I hitchhiked to

Hollywood, lived on the street. I was playing my guitar for money when Dave discovered me. We changed my name, and I reinvented myself as Jesse Lee. He's the only person I've ever told my story to —until you."

"I won't tell anyone."

"I know you wont." He nods and stares blindly at the table in front of him. "What's weird is now that I'm in Ben's house, watching him with his kid... I made him out to be monster, but he seems just as fucked up as I am."

I smile at his choice of words. "Why are you telling me all this?"

"I don't know. Being sober, all this shit keeps bubbling to the surface and spilling over and I don't know where to put it." Both hands go into his hair. "All I want to do, rather than think of this shit, is drink until I go numb and remember how much I hate my brother."

I want to tell him that I've been there. The confusion, shame, regret, I've felt it all. "That makes sense to me."

His chin jerks back in surprise. "It does?"

I nod.

"So what do I do? I can't drink, can't snort a line. There aren't enough women in the world to fuck this out of my system."

"Sexy." I throw his own word back at him.

He chuckles.

"Sounds like you only have one option left. Time to open up that closet and face it all head-on."

"What does that look like? Practically speaking."

I chew my lip. Do I tell him? Can I possibly share with him my deepest, darkest secret? His eyes sparkle with hope and anticipation as he waits, looking desperate for anything I have to offer. Who am I to refuse him?

"I have an idea. You game?"

He grins. "Yeah."

"Let's go."

14

JESSE

"Are you going to be able to do this?" Bethany asks and goes back to chewing on her thumbnail while staring at the disgusting antique in front of us.

"Is there a way we can do this without me having to touch it?" I fold my arms and slam my hands into my armpits, hoping to erase my memories of how the cold, unforgiving wood felt on my palms as I held on for dear life.

She spits a piece of fingernail at it. "I don't think so." Then she switches to her other thumb.

I pause to consider why nail chewing, something I usually find unattractive, is kind of cute on her. Or maybe it's the fact that she seems just as invested in this quest to destroy that's turning me on.

Bethany explained her plan on the way to Ben's house. Her face scrunched up as though she'd eaten a sour grape every time she spoke of the chair, and she became adorably flushed with excitement while laying out her plan.

We pulled the plastic baby pool into the backyard and filled it with six inches of water. Now for the hard part.

"Okay, I'll get it." I rub my hands together. "Open the door."

"You sure?" She lifts her brows then blows a long strand of hair that fell from her now-sloppy ponytail.

"Yeah."

"Try to be quiet. We don't want to wake Ben or Elliot."

I stare at the chair of nightmares. "Quiet. Got it."

She whirls around, and I hear the sliding glass door that leads from Ben's bedroom to the backyard open.

"It's just a chair," I whisper.

In one quick swoop, I grip the hand-carved wood that was passed down from generation to generation of whacked-out, brainwashed Langleys, and I speed toward the backyard. The fucker is heavy—probably because it's soaked with the tears and pride of a young Jesiah Langley.

"Good! You got it! You're almost there," Bethany cheers me on quietly as I awkwardly carry the POS to the farthest end of the yard and set it in the baby pool. "Yes! You did it!"

She holds up her hand and I smack her a high-five that feels really fucking satisfying. "Now what?"

Her grin is half evil and one-hundred percent beautiful as she takes my hand and presses a cold metal container into it. "Time to send those memories straight to hell where they belong."

My mouth stretches in a sinister smile that matches hers, and I flip open the top of the lighter fluid. "This is going to feel so fucking good."

"Yeah, it is."

I saturate the wooden chair, getting a contact high from the pungent fumes—or maybe it's the anticipated release that's giving me the floating feeling.

"How old is this thing?"

"At least a hundred years." I walk around the pool, paying extra attention to the back, where I was always instructed to hold on.

"Perfect. It'll go up like a roman candle."

The giddiness in her voice grabs my attention. "Are you a pyro?"

Her smile falls.

"I'm kidding, genius. Good girls like you don't play with fire." The double meaning behind my words is one-thousand percent intentional. A sweet girl like her would never want to get messed up with a train wreck like me.

I empty the rest of the can and toss it aside. I hold out my hand, and Bethany slaps a box of strike anywhere matches into my palm.

"Now, think back to the most painful of the punishments," she says. "Take all that anger, all that hurt, ball it up and shove it away and into that chair."

"Is this part of your child-development training?"

She rocks into my side playfully and redirects my attention to the chair. "Once you're ready, light it up."

Without hesitation, I pull out three sticks and flick them against the backs of my front teeth. They pop and ignite in a quick, hot sizzle.

"Whoa." Her eyes are bright and dart between the flames and my mouth. "That was awesome."

I smirk then toss the matches onto the chair.

In a flash of fire, the object from my past goes up in flames. The heat sears my eyes, and I hook my arm around Bethany and pull her away from the fire. The flames shoot at least seven feet high, and I'm grateful for Ben's block wall so no one will see it.

I watch in awe as the worst of Jesiah Langley's past burns. The rejection of my parents, the abandonment of my older brother, the disapproval, it'll all turn to tiny embers and be carried away in the breeze.

I can feel it.

The weight, even if only momentarily, lifts.

A surge of adrenaline courses through me. I turn to Bethany, who's watching the flames with the same intensity I'm feeling. As though she understands my pain. I've lived surrounded by people—employees, fans, sold-out arenas. But this is the first time I've not felt completely alone.

164 | JB SALSBURY

I grab her hand and pull her to me. She rips her gaze from the fire and looks at me with excitement in her eyes. The light dances along her face, and suddenly she's the most gorgeous woman I've ever known.

"I know you don't want me to touch you." I slide my hands around her waist and pull her hips flush with mine. "But for now, for tonight, can I—"

"Just kiss me." Her hands lock around my neck and she pulls my lips to hers.

There is no prelude. No gentle coaxing like I would've expected a woman like Bethany would require.

Our tongues crash together in a frenzied kiss. The meeting of our mouths isn't pretty, there is no rhythm, but it's a hot fucking mess of dick-hardening proportions.

Her fingers bite into my neck and send a delicious sting down my spine, taking all the blood in my brain with it. I fist my hand in her hair, tilt her head, and deepen the kiss. She opens up beautifully, not giving up control but pushing back with a scrape of her teeth.

I rip my mouth away and stare at her, trying to catch my breath and slow my racing pulse. "Where the fuck did you come from?"

She doesn't give me a chance to refill my lungs before she's on me again. Her mouth forms perfectly to mine as we kiss as though we've been starved of each other for way too long. The heat of the flames at my back is no match for the fire that burns between us.

I've kissed a lot of women. More than I could ever begin to number. But none have had this kind of instant effect on me. None before this one have made me lose my mind and forget my own fucking name.

She tastes even sweeter than I thought she would, and I need more.

I slide my hand up her ribcage and palm her tit over her shirt. The warm weight fits perfectly in my hand. There's no padding in her bra and the tip pebbles under my touch. I brush my thumb roughly against her and swallow her answering moan. My dick is painfully hard and I need to lay her down so I can explore her properly. I don't want to miss a single fucking inch of her skin.

I walk her backward, and she seems to understand my intention when she takes big steps back. I'm imagining all the different things I want to do, all the ways I want to touch her and make her feel good. We're not moving fast enough.

I take a bigger step at the same time she does. We're knocked off balance. She goes down, and the only way I can help her is to go down with her and try to cushion the fall.

We hit the grass hard, me on top of her, with my hands under her back and head. "Shit, are you okay?"

Her entire body shakes with wheezing laughter. "Yes."

I roll off of her once I realize she's trying to catch her breath. "Did you get the wind knocked out of you?"

She pats her chest a few times, her laughter dying a bit. "A little."

I cover her hand on her chest with my own. "Take a few deep breaths."

She nods and sucks in air a few times then looks at me, smiling. "Bet you've never had a first kiss like that before, huh?"

I can still feel her on my lips and my heart is pounding like a motherfucker. "I can't say I have." No kiss has ever come close to that.

She covers her face with her hands. "That's so embarrassing."

If she only knew how much she turned me on. I'm lying on the dirt with grass stains on my clothes after a disaster end to a hot-as-fuck kiss and I still can't get my pulse under control.

I peel her hands away from her face. "Bethany, what we just did?"

"Yeah?"

"Things between us—"

"What in God's name is going on out here?"

"Great," I mumble then peer up to see Ben standing in the glow of the fire. He looks furious.

BETHANY

I push away from Jesse and scramble to my feet, brushing grass from my clothes. "Pastor Langley, I'm sorry. It's not what you think."

His gaze jumps between me and Jesse, who is slowly getting to his feet. "It's not what I think? I don't know what to think. What happened out here?" He shoves a hand toward the fire. "What is on fire in Elliot's pool?"

Jesse scopes out the fire and smiles proudly. "Oh, that? Yeah, well, that's dad's chair."

Ben interlaces his fingers on the top of his head as he studies what's left of the chair.

"I'm sorry, Ben," I say lamely. He doesn't know it yet, but this is all my fault. The burning thing was my idea.

Jesse steps to my side, so close his arm brushes mine. My entire body sizzles with awareness, and I inwardly scold myself for feeling anything other than remorse during a time like this. "Bethany has no reason to be sorry, this is on me."

"Jesse," I hiss.

He looks at me, his gaze sliding down my neck to my chest. He grins then looks back into my eyes. Seems I'm not the only one who's having a hard time being remorseful.

"Don't lie," I whisper.

"I'm not," he whispers back. "I want you."

"What?"

He shrugs, but he's still grinning. "Nothing."

"What's going on between you two?" Ben says in a way that makes me think he already knows the answer, but he's also assuming a lot more.

"We're just friends!" I blurt.

Jesse leans into me. "Now who's lying?"

"Friends," Ben says unbelievingly.

Jesse shakes his head. "We're more than friends, but if it makes you feel better, you walked in on our first kiss." He scratches the back of his neck. "I mean, if you don't count the time she watched me jerk off."

I choke.

Ben's eyes pop open wide.

Jesse acts completely unaffected, squints one eye, and says, "We're not counting that, right?"

I gape like a fish.

He winks. "Yeah, I didn't think so either."

Ben drops to the top step of the porch and cups his head. "I knew I should've just stayed asleep."

"Speaking of sleep..." Jesse says. "It's late. I need to take Bethany home."

Ben's eyes snap to Jesse's. "You can't leave. There's a fire in my backyard."

"It's in a pool. It'll be fine." Jesse grabs my hand and drags me toward the house.

I dig my heels into the grass. "No, he's right. We should wait until it burns out. Or we should put it out before we go."

Jesse stares at the fire, and his shoulders slump in defeat. "Fine, but you know what that means, right?"

Ben and I share a confused look.

Jesse hooks his arm over my shoulders and pulls me close. "Looks like you're staying the night."

15

JESSE

The fire finally dies out after three o'clock in the morning.

On a blanket in the grass, I sit beside my brother and stare at the black water and charred pieces of the punishment chair. Bethany curled up and fell asleep shortly after she lay down, leaving Ben and me to our uncomfortable silence. I told him he didn't have to stay out here, but he insisted. Whether he did it to watch the chair burn or to make sure I didn't molest Bethany in her sleep, I'm not sure.

So here we are, with nothing but crickets to entertain us.

"It's burned out now. You can go to bed," I say, still fixated on the space where the flames once roared.

"What are you doing, Jes?" There's accusation in his voice.

Twenty-four hours ago, I would've given some smartass answer that would've made him shake his head. Then I would've said something hurtful to get him to walk away and leave me the fuck alone. But tonight feels different. Maybe burning the chair really did break the chains that shackled me to the past. Maybe I'm just too tired to put forth the effort.

"I fuckin' hated that chair. When I saw it again, it reminded me of how much my family hated me for my music. I pretended you guys were jealous because I was successful. Deep down, I knew your disapproval was bigger than that. I didn't realize how badly it hurt. When I'm drunk and high, I don't feel a thing." That felt weird. I can't say I like the way it feels, cutting myself open and exposing myself to the one man who has the ability to make me feel so fucking small.

"I appreciate you sharing that, Jes, but I already knew that. Not a day has gone by when I didn't feel horrible for not being a better brother to you. I saw the beatings. I wasn't strong enough to stick up for you because I was afraid they'd turn them on me." He picks at the grass. "Ya know…" He clears his throat. "The reason I became a pastor was because since the day you left, I've been trying to earn forgiveness for what I did to you."

I tilt my head and study him.

"I know it's long overdue." He sets sincere eyes on mine. "I am so sorry."

His apology catches me off guard, and I struggle for what to say. "Why keep the chair?" Might seem like a pointless question, but I have to know.

"I don't know. I guess keeping it was a reminder of how badly I needed God. After Maggie died, I was so mad at Him." He gazes at the sky than back at his hands. "Still am. Seeing that chair every day when I wake up is a reminder that I have sins I don't feel forgiven for yet."

"I didn't know."

He shrugs and picks at the grass. "No one does."

"Don't stay doing something you don't love just because of me, Benji."

He looks at me, and even in the dark, I can see the hope in his eyes at my calling him by his nickname.

I lean back on my hands. "The shit our parents practiced when we were kids? It's not the same as what you've got going on at your church."

"I didn't think you were listening when I preached," he says, watching me from the corner of his eye.

"Yeah, well, I did. You're different. They were brainwashed. You were just a kid."

"I was old enough to know better."

"Either way." I look at him. "I forgive you."

He flashes a half smile. "Yeah?"

I nod once and grin. "Hell yeah."

His gaze darts to my hand, and his brows furrow. "You confident about what you're doing here?"

Huh? At first I don't understand the question—until I follow his gaze. My hand is resting close to Bethany's head, and I'm absently rubbing a thick strand of her soft hair. I stare at the brown locks wrapped around my finger. I must've reached out to her while we were talking and not even realized it.

"She's not like you, Jes."

"I know."

"What's going to happen when it's time for you to leave?"

I watch the gentle rise and fall of her chest, her delicate profile illuminated in the moonlight. "I don't know."

I have no clue what I'm doing.

BETHANY

One of the most frustrating feelings in the world is waking up and realizing I still have my bra on. How much better would I have slept if I'd taken it off before I went to sleep?

With my eyes still closed, I reach back to rip at the eyehook closure and rid myself of the midnight torturer, then my hand brushes against something warm. My lids pop open, and I flip to my back only to see the sky.

"Oh good, you're awake." Jesse's deep voice is followed by the strum of a guitar. "I want you to hear this."

I push up to sitting and blink at Pastor Langley's backyard, and last night's events come rushing back to me. The chair, the fire, the kiss! I slept outside. I must look like crap. As slyly as possible, I pull the elastic band from my hair and smooth back my hair, raking through new tangles and bunching it all into a messy top knot. "Where's the pool?"

"Ben and I cleaned it up."

I turn around and find him leaning against the deck with his guitar in his lap. He's wearing the same clothes he was last night, which makes me feel better about still being in my uniform. But whereas I must look like a woman who's been living on the streets for days, he looks as if he just walked out of a *Rolling Stone* magazine.

"Typical," I mumble.

His eyes dart to mine, and his expression softens. "Did you say something?"

"Oh, what? No."

His eyes narrow. "Did you sleep okay?"

"I guess. Did you?"

He strums his guitar. "I haven't been to sleep yet. I wrote a song."

"Really? Last night?"

"Yeah."

"Huh, I assumed it takes longer than that."

"You assumed wrong." He does something with his fingers on the strings that seems really advanced or, I don't know, just sounds awesome. "Wanna hear it?"

I sit cross-legged on the blanket. "Of course."

He goes into some complicated-looking guitar playing that involves plucking strings. I begin to wonder if the song has lyrics or if he's just playing the music. But he answers my question as he opens his mouth and sings.

This is what I imagine heaven sounds like. Ethereal with dark notes that make the tiny hairs on my arms stand up. His eyes are closed, and he's not belting out the words like I expect he does when he plays those huge arenas. Instead he sings quietly, as if he's putting a baby to sleep.

The song starts out soft and almost sorrowful as he sings about pain and regret. In parts of the song, he talks about wishing he'd fought harder, wishing he'd stood stronger, and as the music builds, the passion of his lyrics, combined with his deep, raspy voice, makes tears spring to my eyes. The song climaxes when he sings of burning old picture books and ashes of a past life. His voice cracks with such emotion that I grip my chest to keep my heart from breaking along with his. His fingers beat up the strings until I expect to see blood.

There's no question why Jesse Lee is a world famous singer/songwriter. His passion and talent is transcendent.

I suck in a shaky breath as the song slows, but the heaviness of emotion in his voice doesn't let up. He sings about ashes of days gone, he sings of a future without torture. After his final chord gets swept away on the wind, his eyes open. He doesn't seem as broken as I'd expect a person to be after ripping out his soul and performing it in song.

"What's it called?" I ask through the thickness in my throat.

"'From the Ashes.' Do you like it?"

I blow out a breath and try to compose a response that doesn't involve crying and gushing. "Justin Timberlake needs to give back your MTV music award."

He barks out a laugh that showcases all his teeth and makes his shoulders jump.

"You give me his number and I'll get it back for you."

He sobers. "I bet you would."

"I would. That was…" I put my hand over my heart. "I *felt* that. I still feel it."

"Thank you."

"Don't thank me!" I pat my chest again. "This is all you. You're really incredible. I don't think the stuff I've heard on the radio does justice to—"

"Bethany, stop. What you helped me do last night? With the chair? You can't possibly understand what that set in motion." He puts down his guitar, leaning it against the deck, and crawls closer to sit on his knees in front of me. "I burned away a lot of bad shit last night. Ben and I talked. I wrote one of the best songs I've ever written, all because of you."

I lick my lips and avert my eyes, feeling insanely bashful all of the sudden. "I can't take credit—"

He cups my face. "You can." He presses a simple, closed mouth kiss on my lips. "Thank you."

"You're welcome," I whisper.

His expression changes from kind to contemplative, which has me shifting my weight.

"What time is it? I should probably get home and shower. I have to be back here at nine."

He releases my face and sits back, seeming a little dazed and not in a good way. "Ben took the day off. He said he wanted to spend some time with Elliot."

"The day off..." I shake my head. "He's never taken a day off, at least not since I've known him."

Jesse frowns.

I hop up to my feet. "Why don't I take the car home and get cleaned up? I'll be back in time to take you to group, then you can drop me off at work."

"Sure, yeah." He stands but doesn't look at me. "The keys are by the front door."

We need to talk about the other thing that happened last night. The kiss that was quickly turning into more before we butt-planted in the grass. Going off the look on his face, I don't think now is a good time.

"Right, so... I'll see you later." I stand awkwardly, wondering if I should hug him, shake his hand, fist bump? I decide to cut my losses and get the hell out of there as fast as I can.

JESSE

After a two-hour nap, a hot shower, and a mug of coffee, I'm able to get a handle on my thoughts. Bethany's reaction to "From the Ashes" was not at all what I expected. The tears in her eyes, the way she clutched her chest—she was visibly moved by my music.

The cheering I'm used to. The screaming fans... I'm accustomed to that kind of response. But her reaction was different.

Approval shone in her eyes. Acceptance. That someone as good and wholesome as her would respond to my music as if it were the worship music she hears at church... well, it did something to me. Beyond making me feel good and beyond my pride, she made me feel... worthy.

I'm grateful when the doorbell rings, signaling Pete's here for my daily drug test.

With Bethany gone and Ben and Elliot at the zoo, I answer the door myself.

Pete seems disappointed I'm not Bethany. *Horny dickhead.* "Hey, man."

I open the door for him to come inside.

"This was on your doorstep." He hands me a package that must've come when I was in the shower.

The return address is Dave's office. I rip it open and pull out an iPhone box with a sticky note on top.

Charged and programed with the only numbers you'll need.
   Don't fuck this up.
   - Dave

I pop open the top and pull out the device. It lights up with a generic screensaver, and I hit the contacts icon. Dave, Ben, Pete, Dr. Ulrich, and Pizza Hut? Asshole.

Being upset that Bethany's number isn't in the phone makes no fucking sense, so I shove it in my pocket and look at Pete. Nothing takes my mind off a woman like taking a piss in front of a man wearing rubber gloves. "Let's go."

Drug and booze tests come back clean, and before I have a chance to dick around with my new phone, there's another knock on the door.

Dr. Ulrich.

I let him inside and ask him to sit on the couch.

He studies the space. "You wouldn't prefer to do this in your room where you'll have privacy?"

I drop onto the opposite couch where Ben's been sleeping. It's lumpy and uncomfortable, which just goes to show that my brother must really care about me to save me from what must be the shittiest of night's sleep. "No chair in my room. I lit it on fire last night."

His gray eyebrows rise to his hairline. "You lit a chair on fire?"

"I did. Don't take this the wrong way, doc, I know I haven't made things easy on you, but burning that chair was the best form of therapy I've ever received."

He cracks open his leather folder and jots something down. "Would you mind elaborating?"

I want to tell him that yes, I do mind. Instead, I tell him everything. I explain in detail the beatings on that chair, the ceremony with the snakes, all of it. Even the kiss.

He listens attentively and writes things here and there. "Do you have feelings beyond sexual ones for this woman?"

"That's the thing, doc. I want to fuck her. I really want to fuck her. In every possible position and for days until she can't walk, that's how badly I want her. I can deal with that. It's familiar territory for me. I want to fuck a lot of women. But then, I also want to burn shit down with her, ya know?"

His expression turns cold as if he's shutting down because he knows I'm feeding him bullshit even though I'm not.

"I look at Ben and his dead wife, Maggie, and I can't for the life of me see what brought those two together. He may have loved her because, let's face it, we get sex when we're in love, but she's gone now and he's not moving on. You'd think he'd want to be in love again and go fuck someone else."

"So you're telling me you equate sex with love."

"Sure."

"That means you've been in love many times."

"Thousands."

"You might want to consider redefining your definition of love. It's not—"

The rumble of a car in the driveway has me on my feet. "She's here."

He checks his watch. "We ran over today," he says as if he's shocked. "I'll see you next week, but please, call me if you need to talk before then."

"Yeah, sure," I say absently as I swing open the door as Bethany gets to it.

She's wearing a clean uniform shirt and black shorts, her hair down and damp as though she just got out of the shower. She spots the doctor. "If I'm interrupting, I'll come back later."

I snag her hand and pull her inside. "Nope, you're right on time."

We say goodbye to Doctor Ulrich, and I pull her down the hallway to my—Ben's—room.

"What's wrong?"

I close the door behind her and press her against it. Our lips come together, and if I thought she might resist me, I was wrong. She presses off the door, pushing into me. I grind my hips into hers, giving her a hint of what I want so badly, I'd give up everything I own to get it.

"Wait," she says against my lips but continues to kiss me.

I smile as she sucks my tongue as though she can't get enough.

"No." She presses her back into the door, but I follow her and pin her to it.

"What? Say it quickly so I can get back to sucking those lips."

"Why..." She shakes her head as if she's trying to clear the fog of lust from her mind. "When I left, you seemed upset, like maybe you regret kissing me last night, and if you do, we really need to stop."

"I don't regret it. I only regret not doing it more."

Our mouths come back together, and I pull at her shirt and slide my hand underneath it. She arches her back, offering her tits to me. I can't stand the barrier between us, so I slip the shirt over her head and toss it aside.

I take a moment to watch my hands play with her perky breasts. "I love this bra."

"Really?" She looks down as if to see what I'm seeing.

No lace, no padding, just a thin covering of tan fabric, so thin I can see the tight, protruding tips. I dip down and suck one over the fabric. Her head drops back and a long sigh falls from her parted lips. I slip my thigh between her legs, putting pressure against her so she knows she can use it if she wants to get herself off. I lick and suck at her nipple until her bra is soaked through. She rocks against my thigh, and as much as I wish it was my dick she was using to fuck herself, I know I'd come in my pants, and we don't have enough time for the cleanup.

I move to her other breast and give it the same treatment, licking, sucking, and biting with the perfect pressure. She seems to love the shit I do to her body as she rocks harder against me. My jeans feel as if they're going to burst into flames from the friction.

I lean back to watch. Her nipples are hard and piercing against the wet see-through fabric of her bra, her hips rolling and her lips parted. "You're burning up, aren't you, Bethany?"

"I am," she says breathily in a way I feel in my balls.

"You wanna come?"

She bites her bottom lip and nods.

"Yeah, you do." I pop her tits from their cups and pinch her nipples. I dive into her neck, where the scent of her hair and skin combine, and fuck, she smells so good. The need to be covered in her overwhelms me. I want to wear her scent like clothes and be soaked in her gasping breath. "I have to feel you. Tell me I can touch you."

"Touch me."

I slip my hand into her shorts, past her panties, and into her wet pussy. "Oh fuuuck." She's so slick. "I want to fuck you." I thrust one finger inside. She's so tight I don't want to risk two. "I'm gonna open you up for me."

Her muscles coil.

"I want to use my tongue, my fingers—shit, you're so tight."

"Jesse, please."

I lick up her neck to her mouth and whisper, "I love you."

Her breath hitches, and she falls apart in my arms, my thigh between her thighs keeping her from falling. I cup her between her legs to feel how hard I made her throb for me.

"Jesse?"

"Yeah."

"You said... you love me."

I kiss her softly. "I do."

She smiles against my lips. "Really?"

"Yeah, of course." What a stupid question.

"I, uh..."

I grin, thinking of how good she must feel having come so hard it shook the fucking walls. "You love me too."

16

BETHANY

The Friday night rush hits earlier than usual because of a football game at the nearby high school. All my tables are full of teenagers who want separate checks and don't tip, but even still, I can't wipe the grin from my face.

Jesse Lee is in love with me.

"Bethany!" Leon's voice calls me from my thoughts. "Your order's up."

I blink at the six plates of food that I swear weren't there a minute ago, but judging by Leon's scowl, I've been daydreaming for longer than I thought.

"Sorry, Leon." I pile the plates on a tray and hoist them up for delivery.

My chest feels too full in the best possible way. I've been trying to sneak away to call Ashleigh and tell her before her shift at the bar, but it's already after nine o'clock, so it'll have to wait. I know I'll be getting no sleep tonight, waiting up for her so I can share my exciting news.

No, I can't wait. I'll text Ashleigh and tell her to call me on her break.

I refill sodas, drop a couple checks, and bring extra syrup to buy myself a five-minute break. "Natasha, can you keep an eye on my tables? I need to run to the bathroom."

"Sure thing," the other waitress says.

I forgive myself for the tiny white lie. I am going to the bathroom, only I'm going to use it as a phone booth. I grab my phone from my purse and lock myself inside the employee restroom.

New text message.

My heart does a strange somersault, thinking it could be from Jesse. Now that he has a new phone, we exchanged numbers when he dropped me off at work this afternoon. He suggested it, not me, but I was so happy he did. I was almost late for work because I kissed him goodbye in the car until he insisted we stop because apparently I give a "mean case of blue balls."

My lower belly warms at the memory. I open the new text message and frown.

Hey Beth, when can we get together? There's something I need to talk to you about.

"Wyatt?" I remember he mentioned something about getting together after church on Sunday. I was so eager to get out of there, I hardly thought about it then and forgot as soon as I walked away.

Huh… what does it mean that I forgot? This is Wyatt, for crying out loud.

Am I in love with Jesse?

He seems to think so, but I hardly know him. I haven't thought of Wyatt much in the last week, or even in the weeks before. Jesse has been consuming my thoughts for longer than I'd like to admit.

A knock on the door makes me jump.

"You almost done?" Natasha says. "You just got a new table."

Dang it. I pocket my phone and decide talking to Ashleigh will have to wait.

Natasha is waiting at the door with an apologetic expression. "I gave the table to you because I have to get home to my kids."

"It's fine. I could use the money."

"Table thirty-two."

I head back into the restaurant, and my gaze settles on my new table. My face splits into a grin when I spot the familiar baseball hat. Jesse.

Giggling from a nearby table catches my attention. A group of cheerleaders from the high school is staring at him, and their reaction is drawing the attention of others.

I scurry to him, realizing as I get closer that he's wearing a short-sleeve T-shirt. Those multi-colored arms draw attention from all directions. "Hi."

He grins wide. "Hi."

"You have to leave."

He frowns. "Why?"

I get as close as I can and speak under my breath. "Because there are fifty high school kids in this place right now and they all know who you are."

He smirks and stretches one arm along the back of the booth. "You worried about my safety?"

"Absolutely. You could get mobbed, they could follow you home, or—"

"Excuse me," a high-pitched voice comes from behind me. I step around to Jesse's side as the teenager in the cheerleading uniform excitedly approaches. "You're Jesse Lee."

He grins, and she visibly melts. I don't blame her. He's irresistibly charming.

"I don't mean to bother you, but could I get a picture?" She holds up her phone.

"Yeah, I can do that." He motions for her to come closer, and she practically throws herself into the booth with him.

"I can take it," I offer.

She ignores me and leans against him for a quick selfie. "I love your music."

"Thank you," he says so genuinely, as if her compliment really meant something more than "I think you're hot."

I roll my eyes, and Jesse chuckles and thanks her politely. They talk a little more about his music, and when Jesse is about to excuse her, the rest of the girls from her table inch forward.

"Can I get a selfie with you?"

"Of course." He opens his arm for them to crawl into the booth next to him and get a picture.

The area around his table gets crowded, so I back away only to get flagged down by another table. Their plates are empty.

I gather them onto my arms. "Is there anything else I can get you, or are you ready for your check?"

The teen boy leans in. "Hey, is that Jesse Lee?"

I sigh. "Yep."

"Awesome. Do you have a pen I could borrow? My girlfriend loves him. I want to get her an autograph."

"Sure." I pull the pen from my apron and leave Jesse to his room of admirers.

I drop off checks as we get closer to closing and watch Jesse sign anything from paper napkins to body parts. Word must've gotten out that Jesse is here, because five minutes before closing, the parking lot fills.

I never lock the door a minute before closing, but tonight I lock it a couple minutes early so that we don't end up here all night.

Jesse's out of the booth and talking and laughing with his fans. He's in his element, his smile genuine and his posture relaxed. I catch a little of the conversation he's having with a girl about a surprise concert he held in LA, and a guy is telling Jesse he can play his entire *Black and Blue* album on the guitar. It all seems fairly harmless. I don't know why, but I expected bras to fly and fangirls to break down crying.

"Who is that?" Leon asks.

"Jesse Lee."

"No shit?"

Something about the way he says it, as though he's shocked Jesse would be here, catches my attention. "Yeah, why?"

He wipes his hands on a towel and shrugs. "There are rumors going around that his band split up because he fucked his drummers girlfriend."

An uneasy twinge twists in my chest. "Don't believe everything you read. Ninety percent of what you read online is a lie."

That's not a real statistic, but it works to shut Leon up. I tell myself it's probably close to accurate. Jesse wouldn't sabotage his band or his friend and bandmate's relationship just for sex, would he?

He would have happily slept with Suzette. I tell myself the situations are far from the same.

"I'm outta here," Leon says. "See you next week."

"What? You're not going to get an autograph?"

"Nah, I'm more of a Justin Timberlake guy."

I wish so badly Jesse could've heard that. I'll tell him later. God knows after this, he's going to need a dose of humility.

"Just five more minutes?" the beautiful teen with the Marilyn-Monroe pout asks again.

"I'm so sorry, but I have to close this place up." I let Jesse's fans stay thirty minutes extra while I did all my side work, but now I'm exhausted and ready to go home.

"Come on"—another teen squints at my nametag—"Bethany. Just a little longer?"

I hate saying no, but this will go on all night if I let it. "I'm sorry."

"Bitch," one of the girls says beneath her breath.

"That's enough," Jesse barks at the girl who said it. "She said you need to go. You need to get the fuck out."

The girl shrivels under his glare, and they all scurry toward the door.

I unlock it and prop it open for them to shuffle outside. A couple of them thank me as they pass, but the one just keeps her eyes down. I close the door and lock it, noticing there's still a decent group of people outside, most likely waiting for Jesse to leave.

"Sorry about that," Jesse says, his voice close. "Teenage girls are vicious."

"Yeah they are." I turn around and he's right behind me, his hands shoved into his pockets and a half smile on his perfect face. "We might be stuck here all night."

"Fine with me." He doesn't take his eyes off mine.

"You seemed really happy talking to your fans. It was nice to see that side of you."

"Being surrounded by people who love my music is a great feeling. Feels even better sober."

"How so?"

He shrugs one shoulder and lets his gaze drift to the crowd in the parking lot before coming back to me. "When I was fucked up, I was always thinking about my next drink, my next high. Shit like what happened tonight got in the way."

"You know you won't be able to hide anymore, right? Word's out you're in Surprise. The place will be flooded with media by sunrise."

He closes the space between us with slow, measured steps and a predatory glint in his eye. "Don't care. I'm sick of hiding."

I suck in a shaky breath and press my back to the locked glass doors. "I hope you weren't hungry. The kitchen is closed."

He smirks. "Oh, I'm hungry." He slips his hands around my waist and dips his face to my neck. "But I didn't come here to eat diner food. I came for you." He licks a path up my throat to my ear. "You taste so fucking good."

"I..." My mind scrambles, and I struggle for coherent thought. "Thank you?"

His chuckle is dark and delicious. He nips at my ear.

A roar of applause comes from the parking lot. He pulls back and looks out over my head. "I think they want a show." He looks at me, his gaze smoldering. "What do you say we give them one?"

I open my mouth to answer—or rather, to ask if this is really what he wants and how will Dave feel—but it's too late. His tongue slides against mine, rendering me completely incapable of speech. I push my hands up his ripped abdomen to his chest, where I grip his shirt in two tight fists. He groans and tilts his head, delving deeper, sucking my lips until I'm sure they're bruised.

The crowd erupts in a symphony of hoots and hollers that have us both laughing.

"I think we should move this to somewhere more private," he says. "Why don't you let me take you home?"

JESSE

After twenty minutes of hanging out in the kitchen, where Bethany refused to make out with me—something about it being unsanitary —I decided I couldn't wait for the parking lot to clear and made a call to the local police. They had the area cleared out in five minutes and we were able to get to the car.

The drive to Bethany's apartment seems to take for-fucking-ever, but I'm sure that has everything to do with the fact that I've been dreaming about crawling into bed with her since I made her come this morning. I've been half stiff all day, and despite my efforts to relieve myself, my body told me to fuck off, that only the real thing would do.

We park in an assigned spot, and I don't wait to be invited up. Bethany doesn't seem surprised when I hop out, lock the car, and grab her hand. We get to her door on the top floor of the two-story complex, and she lets us inside. The place is simple—newer than similar apartments in Los Angeles, but generic. Her space is clean—couch, television, coffee table, and an indoor plant.

"Is your roommate asleep?" I ask as we pass a closed door.

"No, she works at a nightclub." She opens a door into her dark bedroom. "She usually doesn't get home until just before the sun comes up."

"My kind of girl."

The light clicks on and Bethany's frowning.

"Shit, that's not what I meant." I reach for her, and she comes willingly. "I mean she's a lot like me. Or the old me. You know what? Let's strike what I said from the record. I wasn't thinking."

She pats my chest. "It's all right, I know what you mean." She drops her purse and points toward the bathroom. "I need to grab a quick shower."

"Want company?"

She chews her lip.

Fuck. I'm going to need to be more aware of the things I say around her. She's not some Hollywood starlit or stuck-up socialite. I need to handle her with more care.

"How 'bout this, you take a shower and I'll wait here." I drop onto her bed with my phone in hand.

"Okay. Yeah. I'll just be a minute." She grabs a few things, closes the bathroom door, and I don't miss the click of the lock.

She doesn't fully trust me. I'm sure after what happened tonight, she's not secure about where she stands with me. I'll have to remedy that.

To take my mind off the fact that she is buck-ass naked and dripping wet on the other side of a couple flimsy pieces of drywall, I shoot a quick text to Dave. He'll be pissed when he wakes up to all the photos taken tonight at the diner. I do my best to cushion the blow.

I hit Send then spend some time studying Bethany's room. Her bed smells like her—clean and sweet. Her dresser and side tables are white but mismatched styles, and I imagine she got them from consignment stores. A cross hangs on the wall by the door, and her Bible on the bedside table looks well-loved. Her bookshelf has everything from CS Lewis to Stephen King, and she has a signed photo from Korn framed on her wall. At first I'd say the space is pure and light, but looking a little deeper, I discover the dark rebellion hanging out in plain sight. An accurate representation of the woman who lives here.

The lock clicks, and Bethany emerges wearing a pair of soft shorts and a tank top. Her hair is wet, and drops of water make her mint-green top nearly transparent in places.

"Get over here." I hear the husky lust in my voice, afraid it might scare her, but when her eyes light up and she crawls onto the bed, I see I've underestimated her.

I grab her hips and move her to straddle my lap. Her dark eyes are big and bright, her lips the same shade as her nipples, and her skin glows. I wonder why she never considered modeling, because she's better-looking than a lot of the models I've fucked.

"Jesse? Can I ask you something?"

I run my hands up her soft thighs and under her shorts, where I grasp her hips. "Anything."

"Earlier today, when you told me you love me..."

The heat of her thighs seeps through my jeans and I'm practically salivating to feel how hot she is under her panties. "Yeah, what about it?"

"Did you, I don't know..." She digs her teeth into her plump lower lip.

"Mean it?" Is she crazy? She's straddling my rock-hard dick and asking if I love her? "Yes, of course I meant it." I flex my hips. "Feel what you do to me?"

Her face flushes a gorgeous pink, and she smiles. "Okay, I get *that*, but—"

"Do you know how long I've been waiting to fu—" *Careful, Jesse...* I clear my throat. "I've fantasized about what it would be like for us to be together? How cool it would be to have someone like you in my life for more than just a few fun fucks?"

"Really?"

"Yes. So give me your mouth before I roll you over and take it myself."

She leans down, and the movement sends bolts of pleasure up my shaft to my spine. The long strands of her damp hair tickle my neck as she holds her mouth just inches from mine. "If you want this mouth, you're going to have to take it."

Fuck, I love this side of her. I squeeze her hips and rub her against me. "You sure you can handle me taking what I want?"

"I'm sure. I mean, you're no John Mayer, but—" She squeals when I flip her to her back and pin her ass to the bed with my hips.

I take advantage of her parted lips and do exactly what I told her I would. I take her mouth in a brutal kiss that has us both breathless and shaking. I roll to my back and pull her on top of me, breaking the kiss long enough to tug off her top and hurl it across the room. She rips at my shirt, and I curl up to help her strip it off me.

I reach for her boobs, but she drops to press her chest against mine. The heat from her perky tits on my pecs brings a moan up my throat, and she smiles as it rumbles against her mouth.

She pushes up, straddling my hips, her bare chest on full display. I cup her breasts and give them a gentle squeeze before licking my lips. "If I didn't know better, I'd wonder if you'd ever been with a naked woman before."

"It's been a while, I'll admit." I thumb her nipples, and she sucks in a quick breath that sounds exactly like the one she graced me with the day she caught me jacking off. "Admit you loved watching me with my dick in my hand."

Her eyes are glazed over with lust as she peers down at me, her hands splayed on my ribcage and her nails biting into my skin. "I liked it."

"You loved it." I pinch her nipples, making her moan.

Her hips gently roll, working up a sexy friction on my hard-on.

"You want that, Bethany?"

Her eyebrows pinch together as if she's fighting some internal battle.

"It's not a trick question. Simple yes or no."

Her dark brown eyes lock on mine. "I do, but..."

Lust dissolves to reveal doubt. That won't do.

With a heel on the bed, I roll and push her to her back, wedging myself between her legs to give her the pressure I know she craves. "I love you."

She blinks at me, and some of the tension melts from her body. "You say that, but—"

"I do." I thrust my hips forward, dry-fucking her slowly, giving her a taste of what is hers to take. "I love you."

"Are you sure?"

I bury my face into her neck and chuckle. "How can you ask me that when I'm right here, half-naked, and so eager to get inside you?" I kiss her until the doubt is erased from her mind. "I love you."

She flashes a shaky smile. "Okay."

I frown. "That'll do for now." I push back on my knees and hook my fingers under the elastic waistband of her shorts, pull them down her legs, and toss them away. I lift a brow. "No panties."

Her cheeks flush, and I run my knuckles between her breasts, down the center of her torso, over her belly button, to the junction of her thighs. She jumps at the contact and melts into the bed as I slip one finger inside.

The monster inside me arches his back and rears back on two legs, pushing me to fuck her fast and dirty, but I smother the urge and shove my scaly alter ego to the farthest part of my mind. He doesn't belong here, not with her.

BETHANY

I admit that I've not been witness to many sexy things in my lifetime. Most of my sexual experiences could be described as sweet and romantic, never sexy.

As Jesse sits back on his knees, wearing nothing but his jeans and the swollen rocket that punches at his zipper, I can say without question this is the sexiest experience of my life. The muscles in his powerful arm roll beneath colorful tattoos as he works his fingers between my legs. His hair is a tousled mess, one strand falling over his forehead into his eyes, but he looks positively mesmerized as he watches his hands work. His lips are parted slightly, as if he can't get enough oxygen through his nose alone, and the tight muscles in his torso seem to swell beneath his skin.

"You're beautiful," I say between heavy breaths.

His eyes snap to mine, and they're molten pools of hazel fire. "Funny." Even his voice seems to shake with barely restrained anticipation. "I was about to say the same thing to you." His gaze slides down my naked torso to between my legs. "So fucking hot."

Insecurity makes me wonder how many woman he's said that to before, how many times he's been in this exact position with someone else, how many faceless someone elses.

He must sense me locking up because he smooths my thigh with his palm, rubbing until I relax and allow my legs to fall open again. "Yes, just like that."

I fist the sheets, my back arching off the bed, and he watches it all as if trying to memorize my every response. His dark brows drop low, and he bites his lip. As if he could get any sexier…

I reach for the top button of his jeans. "My turn."

He doesn't resist. Instead, he pops the button for me and holds himself up over me so I can slide my hand down the front of his jeans.

He's long, thick, and hard as steel. I grip him in a tight fist.

A hiss slides from between his teeth. "Don't stop."

I have no intention of stopping.

He angles his lips over mine. We find a steady rhythm, kissing, touching, even biting at each other until we're both a mess of over-sensitized nerve endings. Breaking the kiss, he pushes off me and stands at the foot of the bed. He pulls a foil packet from his pocket then drops his jeans and boxers to the floor. My eyes widen to behold the sight before me.

This gorgeous man, tall, tattooed, and naked, at the foot of my bed.

I blink when another wave of reality washes over me.

Not just any man.

Jesse Lee.

How is this my life?

Before I question it further, he's over me again, and the heavy weight of his erection sheathed in latex presses firmly between my legs.

"Do you have any idea how much I love you?" His voice shakes as he stares into my eyes, giving me no choice but to believe him.

Not trusting my voice, I nod.

He grins, pecks me softly on my lips, then pushes slowly inside. I suck in a breath at the feeling of him stretching me. Inch by inch, he enters me then waits for me to adjust before sinking in deeper.

His knuckles brush along my cheek. "You okay?"

"Yes."

"More?"

I nod vigorously, and he chuckles softly while pushing in until I feel his hips touch mine.

"Fuck," he says into my neck. "We fit so good together."

I run my hands through his hair, fisting it and tilting my head to give him more of my neck.

"You want that?" He licks at my pulse point.

I do. I so do. I hate myself for wanting it, but... "Yes."

Against my neck, he makes a soft humming nose that is pure male satisfaction, then he opens his mouth and latches on. My back bows off the bed at his powerful suction, and the movement has him groaning into my throat. His hips thrust forward, pinning me down, forcing me to stay put as he sucks harder.

My breath hitches at the warm burn of his mouth combined with the force of his hips. I feel like a butterfly pinned to a board, beautifully displayed beneath him.

He breaks the seal of his lips and pulls back to admire his work. "Fuck yeah, that's hot."

If I weren't so lost to the feeling of being completely consumed by him, I might be embarrassed, but the thought of being branded, marked, owned by him is more satisfying that I ever imagined it would be.

I pull his face over mine, kissing him and locking my heels over the backs of his thighs. He seems to like that as it spurs him into action. He alternates between long, slow, deliberate and short, punchy thrusts. He rolls his hips to hit all the right spots, most I never knew I had.

I'm gasping, writhing, ripping at his arms when he pushes up over me and looks down between us.

"Watch with me," he grunts.

I do, and the vision of him lifting his hips then sinking inside me is all the motivation I need. I suck in a breath, throw my head back onto the pillow, and my orgasm whips through me like a violent tornado of ecstasy. I'm thrown into what seems like an alternate universe. My eyes slam shut as if to protect me from further stimulation as I soar then float slowly back to earth.

His pace quickens. His hand drops to grasp my backside, tilting my hips so he can gain even deeper access. He shoves his face into my throat, his teeth pull at the sensitive skin where he left his mark, then he groans, slows, and collapses on me.

We fight to catch our breath, to get oxygen back to our brains, yet hold tightly to each other to keep grounded.

"Jesse," I whisper.

He adjusts a little to take his weight off my lungs but stays put with his bare chest pressed to mine. "Yeah?" He peppers my jaw, my cheek, then my eyebrows with tender kisses.

"I think I love you too."

He pulls back and smiles. It's lazy, satisfied—for the first time since I've known him, he looks genuinely happy. "Of course you do."

I can't help it, I burst out laughing. "You're not a good person."

He shrugs. "I know. But when I'm with you"—his expression sobers—"I'm hopeful that one day I could be."

17

BETHANY

"I love your hands," Jesse says while studying our intertwined fingers.

I don't know when we woke up, only that an awareness of his body roused me from sleep. His naked chest is pressed to my back, his arm thrown over me, and our hands clasped as he flips them back and forth.

"They're so real, ya know?" The warmth of his breath against my bare shoulder sends goose bumps down my arm.

"You're not used to seeing a real woman's hands?"

"No, genius." He playfully bites me. "No nail polish, no three-inch-long fake nails, no rings or tattoos... they're just you."

"Yes, they are." I try to look at my hand, at our hands together, and see what he's seeing. "And yours are covered in ink and calloused."

"I've beat them up pretty bad."

I bring his knuckles to my lips and kiss every one. "They have character. Plus, they feel amazing against my skin."

He groans and buries his nose in my neck. "I marked you up

pretty good here." He brushes his lips against the hickey on my neck, and my face burns with embarrassment.

"That was a big mistake. I don't know what I was thinking." I was out of my mind last night, obviously. I remember how badly I wanted him to leave something on my skin, proof that I wasn't dreaming. I wasn't thinking of the light-of-day consequences of my actions.

"It doesn't look like a mistake." His voice rumbles against my throat. "It's sexy." He licks my skin. I tilt my head, opening up for his attentions, and he flexes his hips against my backside. "I'm ready to go again whenever you are."

I ache between my legs but not enough to turn down—

"Bethany!" My door flies open and Ashleigh comes stomping in. "Have you seen the news?" Her gaze darts to Jesse. "Hey, Jesse."

"Hey." He doesn't seem embarrassed to have my roommate standing feet away from our naked and very turned on bodies.

"Well?" she asks me. "Have you?"

I sink a little lower in the sheets, pulling them up to my neck. "Ash, do you think you could come back later? Like, maybe after Jesse and I get dressed?"

She blinks and shakes her head as if I've spoken in a foreign language. "Why would I do that? Neither of you have anything I haven't seen before. Dude! You two are all over the news! Local news, TMZ, ET, Extra, you name it!"

"Shit," Jesse groans and rolls away from my back. He sits up, completely bare, with nothing but the top sheet tossed over his hips. He grabs his phone from the side table. "I need to call Dave."

"Right, I'll, uh…" I fumble with the mess of sheet and comforter, trying to find the pajamas he tore off me last night. "I'll step out so you can talk in privacy."

Jesse seems entertained by my naked PJ hunt, his lips tipped up on one side. "Take your time."

I glare at him, but he's too sexy for me to even pretend to be annoyed.

"Here." Ashleigh tosses me my shorts and tank from across the room. "Nice trajectory, Jesse."

He chuckles while my cheeks burn red hot. I shimmy on my shorts under the comforter and have to drop the sheet to slip on my tank. The moment I do, I'm thrown back and Jesse's weight covers me.

He nuzzles my neck, moving downward and under the covers. "Just one taste."

I giggle and shove out from under him, flashing Ashleigh my boobs, not that she cares. She really has seen them before.

"You have no manners!" I manage to slip on my tank and get to my feet.

"Wow." Ashleigh looks at me as if I've grown a second head. "Your hair."

I pat my hair and realize I must've grown a second head because the stuff is sticking out a good six inches. I attempt to smooth it back into a ponytail. "I went to bed with wet hair, that's all."

Her eyes widen. "Nice love bite."

I slap my palm over the hickey.

Her gaze darts to Jesse. "That's impressive."

He has his phone pressed to his ear, and he smirks. "Thanks. Dave," Jesse says into his phone. "What's going on?"

Ashleigh and I tiptoe out of the room, closing the door before heading to the kitchen. There's already a fresh pot of coffee, and Ash is wearing flannel pants with her leather corset, which means she hasn't even gone to sleep yet.

"I was scrolling on my phone this morning and saw Jesse's name was trending." She grabs her phone and hits a button then hands it to me. "Apparently so are you."

The Coast-to-Coast Casanova Jesse Lee is spotted with his latest conquest.

Jesse Lee gives up Hollywood A-listers for a waitress.

Woman scorned by Jesse Lee speaks out about his latest girl.

Jesse Lee and his #slumfuck

Every headline has a photo of Jesse and me kissing in the diner.

"Slumfuck? Can't say I'm happy about that. I was hoping for one of those celebrity couple names, ya know? Like Jesany or Bethesse." I hand the phone back to Ash. "Which one sounds better?"

She blinks, stunned. "So you're okay with all this?"

"I don't care what they think. It doesn't matter."

"Don't care, huh? What about your parents? How do you think they'll feel about waking up to this on their newsfeed?"

I swallow the bitter taste in my mouth. "My parents still watch their news on TV, and my dad thinks social media is from the devil, so I'm sure I'm okay." I sip my coffee and try telling my racing heart that even if my parents do find out, they won't believe something just because they read it; they'll believe me. "And anyway, they're going to find out eventually."

Her blue eyes sparkle with confusion. "Why? Pretty soon he'll go back to Los Angeles and continue living his life, but you'll forever be known as Jesse Lee's slumfuck."

"That's not what's going to happen." I peek down the hallway, making sure he's still safely behind the soundproofing of my bedroom door. "He loves me."

She blinks. "I'm sorry. What?"

"Jesse told me yesterday that he loves me. And, Ash, I love him too."

Her brows drop, and she frowns.

"This isn't some random fling. We're..." What are we? "Look, I don't know what we are, but I know we're more than sex."

"Bethany," she whispers sadly.

"It's fine, I promise. I know what I'm doing."

"Look, I don't deny he feels something for you, but he doesn't belong to himself."

"Of course he does—"

"He can't walk away from his career. It's literally who he is."

"I would never expect him to do that. Whatever happens, we'll figure it out."

She slides onto a barstool, her shoulders slumping. "He's not going to be able to give you what you want."

"How do you know what I want?"

My bedroom door opens and Jesse emerges, fully clothed. He heads my way with the confidence and swagger of a multi-platinum recording artist—probably because he is one. I smile at my own joke as he comes around the breakfast bar. He presses up behind me, circles my waist with his arms, and kisses my neck.

I sneak a peek at Ashleigh, who's watching as if what she's seeing is causing her physical pain.

"Coffee?" I hold up my cup, and Jesse takes it from me, kissing me softly before taking a sip. "What did Dave say?"

He shrugs. "He's got it contained."

I look smugly at Ashleigh and resist the urge to stick out my tongue.

Jesse drains the rest of the coffee and kisses my jaw. "I have to go. Can I see you tonight?"

"Of course."

He looks at Ashleigh. "What crawled up your ass?"

"Oh, the list…" She sighs dramatically. "You don't have time for me to detail the many things that have been in my ass."

Jesse chuckles. "Lovely."

He pulls out his phone and types a quick text. I want to snoop, but I don't think we're at that part in our relationship yet.

But we've said we love each other.

Okay, so maybe we're going at this a bit backward, but that doesn't make it wrong.

"I gotta run." He gives me a real kiss. His tongue tastes like toothpaste and coffee, and the thought that he used my toothbrush makes me insanely hot. I pull him closer, and he breaks the kiss with a knowing smile. "I love you."

"I love you too."

He walks away and out the door, and I watch his butt the entire way.

"See!" I say to my constipated-looking roommate. "He loves me."

"Yep." She stands, still not looking the least bit happy. "I heard it."

"Everything is going to be okay."

"I hope for your sake you're right."

JESSE

Day Sixty-One.

Less than a month to go.

I've ripped my hands through my hair so many times over the last twenty-four hours, my head is numb.

After the press found out about my being in Surprise, and all the photos of me kissing Bethany surfaced, Dave said I need to "strike while the iron is hot." In Hollywood, any kind of publicity is good publicity. That doesn't mean I like what they say about me—I sure as fuck don't like what they said about Bethany—but a resurgence of my name means the public isn't over me yet. If Dave can get my new songs to the record label, it might make them consider signing me back on.

I left Bethany's yesterday on a mission to record on my phone the songs I've been working on and send them to Dave by eight o'clock, in time for a dinner meeting with a rep from Arenfield Records. I've recorded five songs, including "From the Ashes." It took me all day to get them just right. They'll sound much better with some backup vocals, a full band, and after mix and mastering, but I'm proud as shit of the stuff I sent him.

As much as I wanted to go hang out with Bethany last night, I was up against the wire, and by the time I got the songs sent off, I had a new song idea I wanted to work on while it was fresh. I completely forgot to call her until after ten o'clock, and by then I was no good to anyone and needed sleep.

Bethany was cool about it. I assured her I'd pick her up and take her to church in the morning. I'd much rather keep working, but I don't want to let her down again.

It's now nine o'clock in the morning on Sunday and I'm on hold, waiting for Dave to tell me if my career is in the shitter or if my songs bought me another chance.

"Jes, you there?"

I make sure the volume on my phone is all the way up and push a hand through my hair. "Yeah, I'm here."

"You sitting down?"

I'm on the floor in Ben's room, my back to the bed, my heart in my throat. "Would you spit it out already?"

"I listened to your songs with Mark."

"Mark Arenfield?"

"No, Marky Mark and the Funky Bunch. Yes, Mark Arenfield. I didn't want to tell you that's who my meeting was with. I thought you'd get all up in your head about it."

He's probably right. "And? What did he think?"

"Jes…"

"Fuckin' hell, spit it out already!"

"He loved 'em, man!"

"What?" I whisper.

"You're back!"

I let the phone slip from my hand and drop to the floor as I shove my fists in my eyes. "I did it. I fucking did it."

I can't believe he loved them.

Ten years in this business and I've never come this close to losing everything I've worked for. I make a vow right here and now to never let things get that bad again.

His voice sounds like a hyper chipmunk coming from the phone between my feet, and I scramble to get it back to my ear. "Sorry, what was that?"

"I said, I didn't think you were going to be able to pull it off. Not to be a dick, but it's been a long time since you've delivered this kind of quality. Mark lost his shit when I played him 'From the Ashes.' He wants you home to record ASAP."

"But I have another twenty-nine days."

"It'll take some time for us to prep the band. I'm going to fly you out for a day to meet with them, we'll discuss that later, but Mark doesn't want to sit on these. He said 'From the Ashes' is the best song you've ever written. Do you have any more besides the five you sent me?"

"I have one more I'm still tweaking and two more that I've written lyrics for but not the music. It'd be cool to work on those with the band."

"That's perfect. We'll get a new album recorded and get you back on top."

"Fuck yeah, when do we start?"

"We'll aim for two weeks, give or take, depending on the band."

"Let me call Nathan. I'll play him the songs. I think I can get him back—"

"Sorry, Jes, but Nathan made it clear he's done. I have someone who might be willing to take Nate's place. Between us? He's got the potential to be better than Nate."

"No fucking way."

"Wait til you hear him, man. You're gonna shit."

"Who is he?"

"He's out of Las Vegas. Name is Ryder Kyle. His current band just bit the dust because his lead singer went solo."

I grunt. "Never heard of him."

"Well, you will, and when you do, I won't say I told you so." There's the voice of Dave's assistant in the background. "All right, I gotta run. I'll be in touch."

Perfect. I'm finally getting out of here.

Why the hell am I not more excited?

I knock on Bethany's door harder than I need, feeling as though I'm about to explode. I haven't been able to think straight since I got off the phone with Dave. I showered, got dressed, and broke multiple speed limits on my way to Bethany's apartment. Now that I'm here, she's not opening the door fast enough.

I knock again. "Bethany, hurry up!"

"I'm coming!"

I'm bouncing on my toes when she finally opens the door.

"My gosh, is everything okay?" She's gripping a towel at her chest, her hair dripping wet, water sliding down her skin.

I step inside and right into her personal space, wrapping my arm around her waist. I press my mouth to hers, and she moans and parts her lips. I slide my tongue against hers then pull away to nip at her mouth. "Where's Ashleigh?"

"I don't know, why?"

I grip her ass and lift her up. Her legs wrap around my waist and her free hand around my neck. Still kissing, I walk her into her bedroom without bashing her against any sharp corners or walls. I shut her door and lay her back on her bed. Her towel falls open at her waist, revealing what I already assumed—she's completely bare underneath. With a knee on the bed, I open the top of her towel to reveal her perky breasts tipped with dusty-pink nipples. I run my hand from her collarbone down between her tits and make slow circles around each one with my fingertip.

"You take my breath away." I brush my thumb across her puckered nipple, and her back arches off the bed.

"You're early," she says in a breathy whisper.

I continue to tease her with barely-there touches and rough swipes against her sensitive skin. I trail my fingers over her ribcage to her belly button and finally sink them between her legs. "I have good news, but when you opened the door dressed like something I could eat, I decided my news could wait."

"What news?" She tilts her hips, taking my fingers deeper until her breath hitches.

"I said it could wait." I drop to my knees by the bed, hook her by the hips, and bring her pussy to my face.

I suck, lick, and bite at her needy flesh. She tastes so pure, clean, a delicacy a man like me doesn't deserve. But I'm an asshole and I take it anyway. I've never been the type to spend hours on foreplay, but with Bethany, I could spend days. I want to set up a tent and camp between her legs.

I lick her deep and groan. "You taste so fucking good."

Her hands grip my hair and hold me to her as she rocks against my mouth. My dick punches painfully against my zipper. I never would've guessed a woman like Bethany had this kind of drive and confidence to take over her own pleasure the way she does. A saint in the streets and a sex goddess in the sheets.

Her nails rake against my scalp, and it's all the warning I need. I push two fingers inside her and suck when her orgasm hits. Her thighs slam around my head, taking me deeper for the seconds it takes before her body turns to Jell-O. Her thighs fall limply apart, and I pull back just enough to look at her while keeping my fingers slowly moving inside.

"If this nanny thing doesn't work out for you, you might want to consider porn."

Her head pops off the bed, and despite the haze of post-orgasmic bliss, her eyes are wide. "Shut up."

"I'm not kidding, babe. You're fucking sexy when you come." I pull my fingers from her tight core and stick them in my mouth. So good.

She blushes, and damn, that just makes me harder.

I stand and open the button on my jeans. "Now bring me your mouth, I got something I want to put in it."

She's propped up on her elbows and glares at me. "Is that supposed to be sexy?"

I pull out my hard-on, gripping it tightly and slowly stroking. Staring at her naked body, her skin flushed, and her thighs wide will send me over the edge too soon. I bite my lower lip and hold back my release, but the way she's watching my hand move is too much, so I stop. "You forget how well I know your body. You like it when I talk dirty."

"Do not," she says as she pushes herself up, scoots to the end of the bed, and slaps my hand away from my dick. Those big dark eyes turn wicked as she peeks up at me with her lips inches from the head. "Maybe I do a little."

Her perfect pink tongue licks at the tip.

"Fuck."

Her grin widens and she does it again.

"Stop being a tease."

She giggles, and even though her mouth isn't on me, I swear I feel the vibration in my balls.

About to explode, I slide my hands into her wet hair and grip tightly. "Open your mouth."

"Say please."

Begging? Yeah, I can beg. For her, I'll fucking beg. "Please, baby. I want in your mouth."

She parts her lips and I press forward, sinking my dick between her hot, wet lips in one long, slow push.

"Oh yeah, just like that."

She presses the flat of her tongue against the sensitive underside as I glide in and out at a maddening pace, drawing out every sensation as she sucks me. "You're so good at this."

I don't want to know how she got so good at sucking dick. I'm just grateful she's sucking mine. My spine tingles at the base of my back as my release coils between my legs. I pick up my pace, and fuck me, she sucks me harder.

I moan and push deeper, feeling her throat open with every thrust. "Take it."

She must answer me with some kind of spoken word because her throat vibrates around me.

"It's coming."

I loosen my grip in her hair, giving her the opportunity to stop, but she wraps a tight little fist around my shaft and holds me in place.

"You sure?" I ask between panting and trying to focus and stay upright.

She nods.

This woman is perfect.

On that thought, my knees lock and the orgasm hits me like a tidal wave. My muscles shake, and I groan as each surge threatens to knock me on my ass. Stars flash behind my eyes, and I'm grateful for Bethany's grip on me as it's the only thing keeping me grounded.

Cold air hits my dick and I blink down to see her crab-walking backward and off the bed. She races to the bathroom and spits in the sink.

Unable to stay vertical, I drop back to the bed and try to remember my own name. The nanny just blew my mind.

I hear her brush her teeth, spit again, then the faucet turns off. The soft padding of her feet on the floor, then the bed dips before she crawls up next to me. I wrap a still-limp arm around her and smile when I feel she's still naked.

"You all right?" I ask.

She shifts a little and throws her arm over my stomach. "Yeah. Sorry about that."

I peek down at her, and she's ducking her head into my ribs. "What the fuck are you sorry for?"

"I'm sure you're used to girls swallowing. It's just... I have a gag reflex thing and I didn't want to throw up on you."

I run a hand through her hair. "First off, every blow job I've had in the past just became irrelevant. Second, I don't give a shit if you spit. Third, how in the hell did you learn to suck dick like that?"

She laughs. "You really want to know?"

"Not really, but kinda, yeah."

"YouTube tutorials."

"No shit?"

She shrugs. "Yeah. Is that weird?"

"No. Not at all. It was fucking amazing. But I have to wonder…"

She puts her chin on my ribs and looks at me. "What?"

I run my thumb across her swollen lips, loving that I made them that way. "Why did that fuckhead Wyatt break up with you?"

Her face pales, and she doesn't meet my eyes.

"Hey."

She shakes her head and slides from the bed. I guess I officially ruined the moment by asking about that prick, so I shove my own back into my pants while she grabs clothes. I want to tell her she doesn't have to tell me, that it's none of my business, but I want to know. What kind of man gives up a woman who's not only cute and funny but can suck dick like it's an Olympic sport?

She sits next to me on the bed and stares at her feet. "Look, there's something you should know."

My phone vibrates in my pocket. "Hold that thought." I pull out the device. "It's Ben."

BETHANY

I wonder if Ben calling right as I'm about to tell Jesse the most humiliating story of my life is divine intervention.

I've contemplated whether or not I should give Jesse all the details about my break up with Wyatt or if I should leave the past where it belongs. I've argued both sides and been stuck at an impasse each time. The only argument that I keep coming back to is I love Jesse and he loves me and shouldn't two people who love each other share all their dirty secrets?

I don't know the answer to that.

"Damn, all right," Jesse says. "Yeah, I think staying away is smart." His eyes come to mine, and a tiny smile tilts his lips. "I'll let her know. Later." He hits the end button on the phone.

"What did he say?"

"His church is covered in paparazzi. They're asking about me and about you, so Ben thinks it's best if we stay away."

A heavy sinking feeling settles in my stomach. "You mean I'm not allowed to go to church?"

He falls back on my pillows, his colorful arms folded behind his head. "Trust me when I say these assholes are never satisfied. They'll hound you until you cry."

"Ha! Cry? I'm so sure."

"I'm not kidding. They made Ronda Rousey cry outside of The Ivy. Saw it with my own eyes."

My smile dissolves. "Wow. That's surprising and really sad."

He nods. "Anyway, I think Ben just wants to protect you, and I back him up. No church until this shit settles."

"How long do you think that will take?" I love my church. A day off is one thing, but no church indefinitely? I can't handle that.

His eyes brighten, bringing out the gold in them. "I guess here is where I share my good news. Dave played my songs for Mark Arenfield."

"Who's that?"

"Forget it." He waves me off. "The good news is he loved them and I'm going back to LA to record."

His excitement is contagious, so I smile despite the horrid shattering in my chest.

"That's amazing!" I launch myself at him, wrapping my arms around his neck and burying my face in his throat. "I'm so happy for you."

He squeezes my waist and kisses my head. "I have you to thank for it." I pull back, and he must see the confusion in my eyes. "They loved 'From the Ashes,' the song you inspired."

The chair bonfire. That damn sinking feeling is back. I slide away from him, feeling exposed and bashful. "That was all you. I just planted the idea in your head."

He stares at me for a few seconds too long, making me crazy uncomfortable. "Why don't you come back to LA with me?"

"What? When?"

"This week."

"Oh, no, I can't—"

"Why not? Dave said it'll only be for a day."

"I have work, and I..." Can't think of another reason not to.

"One day." He tilts his head and unleashes the full force of his charm in a crooked smile. "Just say yes."

"I guess one day wouldn't hurt—whoa!"

He knocks me on my back and wedges himself between my legs. His mouth fixes over mine, and he kisses me until I'm out of breath. "You make me feel so good." He kisses me again, dipping his tongue into my mouth, then making me chase him down when he pulls back too soon. "I love you, Bethany."

"I love you. Now don't stop kissing me."

He grins and picks up where he left off. Before I know it, our shirts are off and our hands are grabbing hungrily at each other.

Ashleigh opens my bedroom door. "You guys about ready to go?"

"Don't you have a lock?" Jesse says, grinning at me.

"I do. I should probably start using it."

"No use." Ash jiggles the handle. "This is a standard push lock. I could have it open in seconds without either of you knowing."

Jesse stays on top of me but turns to my roommate. "No church today. Ben called. It's a media circus."

She perks up. "Oh, really? It's a good thing I'm wearing my best dress then."

Her best dress is black with a white collar and cuffs. I call it her Wednesday Addams dress, but it's a good five inches shorter than it should be.

She pushes back a panel of long platinum hair and kicks up one baby doll platform heel. "I'll go make sure the paps stay away from your brother."

"You do that," Jesse says as Ash leaves, closing the door. He gazes down at me. "She knows she's being really obvious about wanting to fuck my brother, right?"

I run my hands through his messy hair. "She doesn't care."

His gaze tracks from my eyes to my lips. "Guess this means we'll have the place to ourselves."

"Guess so."

"Fuck yeah."

18

JESSE

I got the call on Tuesday morning that I'd be flying back to LA on Wednesday. Bethany was able to get someone to cover her shifts at Pies and Pancakes, and Ben agreed to let her go for a couple days. The day trip turned into an overnight because Mark's schedule didn't sync up with the band's. Not that I'm complaining. One night in my own bed is just what I need, and having Bethany there will be a major bonus.

We pull into the private terminal at Phoenix Sky Harbor airport, where Arenfield Records's Gulfstream is gassed up and waiting.

Bethany clutches her backpack to her chest and peers out the window. "We're flying in that?"

I put the car in park and stare at her. "Yes. Is there something wrong?"

"It's so small."

An employee at the luxury terminal opens my door.

"It only needs to be big enough for the two of us." I hop out and grab my guitar from the back before I hand the guy my keys.

Bethany slides out of her seat, her eyes fixed on the plane.

"Are you a nervous flier?"

"No, but this is a new experience for me."

I snag her hand and lead her to the stairs, where I allow her to go ahead of me. "You're going to love this, I promise. And if you don't, well, it's a one-hour flight."

The wind blows her dress, giving me a quick tease of her thighs and the under swells of her ass. This woman in a dress does wicked things to my body. Once I get to the top of the stairs, I reach under the fabric and pinch her butt. She squeals and stumbles, but I catch her before she slams into the steward dressed in a white polo and tan pants.

"Welcome aboard, Mr. Lee and Miss Park. My name is Irving and I'll be assisting you on your flight." I hand the man my guitar case, and he holds out an arm to take Bethany's bag. "Would you like to stow your belongings, Miss Park?"

She slips it off her shoulder and hands it to him.

He motions to the main cabin. "Make yourselves comfortable. Is there something I can get you to drink before takeoff?"

I nod for Bethany to answer, but she's looking awestruck at the lavish interior of the plane. I hook her around the waist and get her moving. "Waters, thanks."

"Sparkling or flat?"

Bethany is still in mute-mode and I don't know which she would prefer. "Both."

I motion for her to sit on a one of the oversized leather seats next to the window, and I take the one directly across from her.

"This is the fanciest room I've ever been in." Her head swivels around as she studies the space.

White leather seats, black walls and carpet—everything screams opulence and rock-and-roll, down to the tiny chandelier lighting.

I pull out my phone and see a text from Dave that says a car will pick us up at LAX and bring us directly to Arenfield. Excited butterflies dance in my gut.

"Your drinks." Irving sets down two bottles of Fiji water and two bottles of Perrier, along with chilled glasses and lime wedges. "The pilot is ready to depart. Is there anything else I can get you before I take my seat?"

Bethany stares between the waters and Irving. "I don't think so—"

"What do you have to eat?" I'm too hyped up to be hungry, but I want Bethany to know what her options are.

"We have a fresh fruit plate, meat and cheese board, black pearl caviar, and an assortment of tropical sorbets. We also have a variety of snack foods."

"Holy crap," she mumbles.

"You want anything?"

She palms her stomach. "I'm not hungry, but thank you."

"I think we're okay for now."

"Very well." He gives a small bow. "Enjoy your flight."

She watches him walk away then snaps her gaze to me. "So this is your life?"

I shrug. "Pretty much."

She shakes her head and looks out the window. "No wonder you seem so uncomfortable at your brother's."

I snag a water and sip right from the bottle. "That has nothing to do with the lack of luxury, genius."

"I'm sure you're right, but it probably doesn't help."

The engines fire up, and the plane lurches forward. Bethany is glued to the window as the outside world passes by, and I'm glued to watching her profile as she does.

I'm so fucking happy she's here with me. If I was alone, I wonder if I'd be tempted to drink. Chances are Dave had all the booze removed from the plane though. A quiet peace settles in my chest where the monster used to be, and I don't feel even a hint of the anxious pressure I'd usually feel going into a meeting of this size. One that will determine my future.

Bethany doesn't turn back to face me until we're airborne. "That was *awesome*."

"Happy you like it."

"What are we flying over?" She peers out the window. "Farmland! Cool."

She's so easily amused.

"*I can show you the world...*" I sing the lines to one of Elliot's movies, and Bethany laughs. "*Shining, shimmering, blended—*"

"Blended! Now who's the song butcher?"

I'm smiling too. "Is it not blended?"

"Aladdin would be highly pissed at your version of his foreplay song."

"Foreplay song? I like that." I scratch my jaw. "I might have to write one of those."

She lifts a brow and smirks. "What exactly would it sound like?"

"Come sit on my lap and I'll sing it to you."

She shifts in her seat, and I fucking love the way her anticipation is so obvious. "According to FDA flight protocol, I should stay in my seat."

"Do you mean FAA, sweetheart?"

She scrunches up her nose. "What did I say?"

"Get your sexy ass over here, Bethany."

Her gaze darts down the aisle. "What about Irving?"

"This plane is owned by a recording label. You think the guy doesn't know what happens inside it?"

She looks at her seat and cringes away from the pristine white leather. "Ew. But I'm not having sex with you on a plane."

"Who said anything about sex? I just want to touch you."

She chews on her lip for a second then hops up and slides onto my lap. I run my hands up her bare thighs to her panties. I can't see the color, but they're lace and tiny. My dick swells.

"Are these new?" I skate my hands around to the front and cup her between the legs.

She falls back against me, her head on my shoulder, and her hands grasp the armrests. "Yes."

I run my fingers along the strip of lace, using just enough pressure to make her hot and greedy. If I play my cards right, I might be able to induct Bethany into level one of the mile-high club—orgasm at thirty thousand feet.

BETHANY

We just landed and I can't look Jesse in the eye, which makes things really awkward seeing as our seats face each other. Thankfully I had the window to look out during the plane's descent, but now that we've come to a complete stop, I have to face him.

When I do, my cheeks burn red hot.

"You know you're beautiful when you blush, right?" His grin is all cocky man-pride. "You have nothing to be embarrassed about."

"Shhh!" I hold up my hand. "I can't talk about it."

He stands and I follow. He motions for me to walk ahead of him, and when I pass him, he pulls my back to his front. His mouth comes down at my ear. "He didn't hear us. I promise."

I peer down the aisle to see Irving waiting at his post, facing away from the main cabin. "He did. I know he did. Maybe not for the first one, but he'd have to be deaf not to hear the second."

I feel Jesse smile against my ear. "I was shooting to give you one. That second one caught me by surprise, but you won't hear me complaining." He nuzzles my cheek and nips my earlobe. "Now I feel like I need to break a record. Tonight I'll go for three."

I turn in his arms. "Are you trying to kill me?"

"Jesse!" Dave's voice breaks us up as he comes down the aisle. "You two coming?"

"We already did." Jesse grabs my hand and squeezes it. "One of us more than the other."

Mortification crawls through my veins and makes me light-headed.

If Dave understood what Jesse meant, he has the decency to pretend he doesn't. "Bethany, it's good to see you again."

Dave's mouth is a little tighter than it was the first time we met, and insecurity creeps in. He probably doesn't want me here, thinks I'll mess with Jesse's focus. He doesn't know me well, but eventually he'll see I'm no danger to his client's career.

"Good to see you too."

His gaze snaps back to Jesse and remains there as we get off the plane and climb into a black SUV. Jesse sits in the back with me, and he and Dave talk about things like contractual stipulations and percentages, which I don't understand. I watch the city of Los Angeles fly by. Quite a bit more concrete than I imagined and a lot more palm trees than I expected.

Eventually we pull beneath a towering building in downtown LA. Dave swipes a card, and we're let through the gate. A few turns later, we park and crawl out. I grab my backpack, unsure if we'll be taking this vehicle again and not wanting to part from my meager belongings. Dave and Jesse are deep in conversation and I feel very much like the third wheel by the time we get on the elevator. Similar to the plane, the space is black and white luxury, complete with an elevator chandelier. We climb to the fortieth floor, which I believe is the top of the building, and I follow Jesse and Dave into a swanky modern-looking lobby.

Sleek black furniture sits on shining white marble floors, and above the dark reception desk is a wall fixture that reads Arenfield Records. Everyone from the receptionist to the people walking by look like celebrities, with their sculpted bodies and shining, styled hair. Not a single woman is in less than three-inch heels.

I flex my toes in my ballet flats, unable to remember a time when I felt as out of place as I do now. I gather my perfectly boring hair over my shoulder and run my fingers through the ends.

"Jesse, great to see you back." The receptionist, a beautiful redhead with bright red lipstick, smiles at him.

His eyes slide toward me and I see a flicker of worry in his gaze. Ah, so he's had sex with this girl and he's concerned I'll find out. "Thanks."

She frowns and addresses Dave. "You can go on back. Mr. Aren-field will be with you shortly."

I contemplate apologizing to the girl for Jesse's rude dismissal, but I don't want him to think I'm getting in his business. I scurry to keep up with Dave and Jesse as they navigate hallways lined with glass-walled offices. Everyone we pass does a double-take when they see Jesse, and I like that they don't seem to notice me at all. When someone like me stands close to a light as bright as Jesse Lee, they disappear in his glow.

We duck inside what looks like a conference room—the table seats at least twelve. Coffee, ice water, and assorted snack foods line the wall. I head to the floor-to-ceiling window overlooking the city. A thick layer of smog blurs the view in the distance, and I'm again underwhelmed by the Los Angeles reality.

"Jesse, welcome home."

I turn as a man with salt-and-pepper hair and a really nice suit greets Jesse with a firm handshake.

"Thank you, Mark," Jesse says with confidence and charm. "It's great to be back."

I turn back toward the window and scold myself for the twinge of hurt I feel at hearing him say he's happy to be back. Of course he's happy to be back. It would be weird if he wasn't. I tell myself that until the pain subsides.

"Bethany."

I turn at the sound of my name. Dave is walking toward me.

"Let me show you to the swag room. You can look around and feel free to take some souvenirs." He jerks his head toward the door.

I look over his shoulder at Jesse, who's in deep discussion with the man in the million-dollar suit I'm assuming is Mark Arenfield, CEO. Jesse doesn't look at me, so I nod and grip my backpack strap tighter. "Sure. Okay."

I follow Dave out of the room, sneaking one more peek at Jesse, who doesn't seem to notice I'm leaving. He probably knows I'm in good hands with Dave and he's focused on making plans for his career.

I'm led to a room the size of the kitchen at Pies and Pancakes, except rather than industrial range ovens, the walls are lined with shelves and cupboards.

"You'll find all the latest Arenfield artists' swag in here—T-shirts, hats, sweatshirts, posters. Help yourself. I'll be back to get you when we're done."

"Thank you so—"

He's already left the room.

I drop my backpack on a nearby office chair and begin my perusal. They have just about everything you'd find at a concert and more—T-shirts, stickers, posters, all sorts of things that light up.

I search for Jesse's stuff and come to a stack of Jesse Lee CDs dating all the way back to his first one, released almost ten years ago. I didn't know they still made CDs. I study a Jesse Lee baseball hat and decide it's way too cheesy to wear a hat with your boyfriend's name on it, even for me. I pick up a tiny pair of G-string panties with Jesse's name on the crotch.

"Do women really buy these?" I decide I don't want to know the answer and drop them back into the pile.

I move on to a poster of Jesse singing into a microphone, his shirt off and the light perfectly catching all the colors of his tattoos. I sift through and find one where he's wearing a regular T-shirt and jeans, his hair looking as perfect as always, as he leans back against a brick wall. He seems more boyish in this one.

Eventually I lose interest in the walls of free band merch, so I drop into the chair and spin a couple times. My stomach rumbles, and I fish my phone out of my backpack. At just after eleven o'clock, we should be grabbing lunch soon.

I text Ashleigh and tell her where I am. She responds by asking me how many celebrities I've seen and makes me promise to get photos. I tell her I'm in a room of band swag and she puts in an order for a Death Spiral tank top. I hunt them down and shove one in my bag, making sure to look around for cameras. Even though Dave said I could help myself, it still feels like stealing.

A few more spins in the chair until I'm dizzy and I give in to my hunger and eat the granola bar I stashed for emergencies. I'm mid-bite when a guy walks into the room. I don't recognize him, but I can tell by his look that he's famous. Maybe it's his edgy blond hair, or the fact that he's wearing an old Def Leppard concert shirt, faded jeans, and dirty Converse in an office where all the other men I've seen are in suits.

He smiles at me. "Hey, I wasn't expecting anyone else to be in here."

I wave, still chewing my granola bar. Without water, it's difficult to swallow, but I manage to force it down. "I'm just waiting for someone."

"Cool." He studies the MacMillionaire section of the wall.

"If there's anything specific you're looking for, I could help you find it."

He turns his head and smiles, squinting. "Really? How long have you been in here?"

I sigh. "It's been eighty-four years..." I say in my best elderly Rose voice, then I feel like an idiot. "That's from *Titanic*."

He laughs, and the sound is easy, unforced. "I know. That was a good one."

I'm grateful he goes back to studying the wall while I give my face a chance to regain its natural color.

"This is crazy, right?" He's still not facing me, and I realize how different he is from Jesse, who would love to stare at me while I squirm in embarrassment. "I can't believe I'm standing in Arenfield Records, surrounded by a bunch of shit I used to save up my allowance to buy."

Maybe that's why I don't recognize him, he's only newly famous?

I look around the room, trying to see it through the eyes of a diehard fan.

"What's your name?"

I snap my gaze to him and find him watching me. "I'm Bethany."

He seems as if he's waiting for me to finish my introduction.

"Oh, I'm no one. I mean, I'm not famous or a musician or whatever. I'm here with..." A friend? My boyfriend? "Jesse?"

His expression lightens. "Sweet." He steps forward, holding out a hand. "Nice to meet you, Bethany. I'm Ryder, Jesse's new drummer."

His palms are calloused, not his fingers like Jesse's, which makes sense if he's holding drumsticks instead of a guitar.

"Nice to meet you. Why aren't you in on the meeting?"

He leans back against the swag countertop, folding his arms. "Guess they have some stuff to work out with Jesse first. So are you Jesse's assistant or...?"

Oh no, the blush is back. "I, uh..." I suck in a quick breath and straighten my shoulders. "No. Jesse and I are dating." *We're in love.* I can't say that, it would sound ridiculous. But why?

"Dating?"

I run the word through my head a couple times, wondering why Ryder needs the clarification. Am I so hungry I've forgotten how to properly communicate? Nope, dating is what we're doing. "Yes."

"Awesome."

"Yep, it is." Ugh, I sound so stupid. I pick at the hem of my dress in the few seconds of awkward silence that fall between us.

"I take it you're not from around here?"

"Why would you say that?" There's a hint of venom in my voice that I wish I could control but can't.

He doesn't seem too annoyed by it. "Because you're nice."

"Oh, well... no, I'm not, and thank you." I slump a little under the weight of my guilt over snapping at the guy for no reason. "What about you?"

"No, I'm from Vegas. I'll have to relocate here eventually. The commute is fucking lame."

"How far is—"

"Ryder?" Dave pops his head into the room. "You're up." He doesn't even acknowledge me.

But Ryder does. "It was great meeting you, Bethany. I'm sure I'll see you around."

He follows Dave out of the room.

"Nice guy." I pull out my phone, do a quick search for Ryder the drummer from Las Vegas, and add Jesse's name in the search. "Whoa."

He might be newly famous in the music industry, but he comes from a famous family.

"Ryder Kyle, son of Universal Fighting League owner Cameron Kyle and the world famous supermodel Delilah." That would explain his perfect bone structure. Ryder Kyle hit the DNA jackpot.

JESSE

"Jes, this is the guy I was telling you about," Dave says with all the excitement of a kid with a new toy as he motions to the new guy as though he's channeling a *The Price is Right* model. "Ryder Kyle."

I shake the guy's hand, but I'm all out of pleasantries. I've spent the last however-long signing a hundred different contracts that will micro-manage the next five years of my life. From here on out, I can't even burp without it threatening my contract.

Dave made it crystal-fucking-clear that these are the only conditions under which the record label will take me back. No more mansion recording studio with free rein. Now I'm going to the on-site studio and have to clock in on time. If I'm even a minute late, I'm in breach of contract. My anger stirs up the monster in my gut, and he arches his back and preps for a fight. I'm the talent making these assholes all the money, yet they treat me like a snot-nosed kid!

You need them in order to get your music heard.

At that, the monster curls back up and disappears.

Logic is a motherfucker.

We all circle 'round the table while Mark and Dave go through

Ryder's significantly shorter contracts. His don't include curfews and consequences or the "sign over your life" clause.

I try to imagine how different things will be, having to check in frequently and get permission before leaving the city. I'm surprised they don't want to stick a tracker around my neck.

"Dave played me some of your new stuff," Ryder says, calling my attention to him. "I look forward to showing you what I've written."

I eye Dave skeptically. "Are you sure about this? I think I could get Nate back if you'd let me talk to him."

My manager looks at me as if I'm a puppy who shit on the carpet again.

"All right." I throw up my hands. "I'm just sayin' Nate was the best."

"Then you shouldn't have fucked his wife," Mark Arenfield growls from the end of the conference table.

I cringe. "Girlfriend."

"Fiancée," Dave clarifies.

Ryder stares between us, waiting for the fight to escalate, but we all take a collective breath instead.

"Right, we'll have a full band meeting at Arenfield Studios tomorrow morning at eight o'clock." Dave motions to the new guy. "Ryder and the rest of the band will play what they've written for you, and we'll get a firm recording date in the books."

"Great," Mark says, standing and looking me square in the eyes. "Last chance. You fuck this up, we're done."

"Understood."

After Mark leaves, Dave pulls out his phone. "I'll text Chris and Ethan to confirm tomorrow." He heads to one side of the room.

Ryder comes to sit next to me, and he leans in. "Between us? She seems worth it."

I glare at him. "What?"

He shrugs. "It's hard to find anyone *real* anymore, ya know? I'm not saying what you did was right, but I can't argue the outcome didn't pay off."

I blink, trying to figure out what the hell he means. "What the fuck are you talkin' about?"

His eyebrows pinch together.

"Great," Dave says. "It's a done deal."

"Good." I stand quickly. "I'm going home."

"Hold on," Dave says and addresses Ryder. "Could you give us a few minutes?"

He shrugs. "Sure thing."

Dave waits for Ryder to leave and close the door.

Fuck me, what now? I run a frustrated hand through my hair, willing my temper to cool.

Rather than take the seat across from me, he takes the one right next to me. "We need to talk about Bethany."

For a moment, my stomach turns over on itself. I'd almost forgotten she's here. I check the time. Fuck, she's been waiting for nearly two hours.

"After the photos of you two kissing surfaced, I didn't think much of it. I assumed, like in the past, you were just blowing off steam with whoever was available."

I frown, not liking the way Bethany being categorized as a random piece of ass makes me feel. Being with her has nothing to do with her being the closest woman available, even though I guess she was.

"When you told me you were bringing her here, I ran a background check."

"Jesus, Dave."

"You pay me to look out for your best interests."

"You've met the woman. She's a fucking saint."

He sucks air through his teeth. "She's pretty clean, I'll give you that. No arrest history for drugs or alcohol, the two things I was most concerned about."

"She's clean, much cleaner than me, much cleaner than any other woman I've been with. There's no way—"

"She's not clean."

I ball my fists under the table. He has no idea who he's talking about. Bethany is as good as a person can possibly get.

"Bethany has a charge for—"

"Hold on." I close my eyes and breathe deeply, giving the monster oxygen to fuel his temper. "This sit-down is because you scraped up some bullshit charge from Bethany's past?"

"Here me out—"

"No." I stand. "Unless she slit someone's throat, I don't give a fuck. Honestly, even if she did kill someone, she would've had a good reason. I'm going home."

He frowns. "Are you sure that's a good idea?"

"What are you afraid I'm going to do? Drown myself with vodka in my bathtub?"

"That would be difficult since I had the place cleaned."

Something tells me he's not talking about Merry Maids. "See? I'll be fine. Where is she?"

"Swag room." He punches something into his phone then looks at me. "Johnny will be your bodyguard while you're in town. He's waiting for you on level 2B."

I walk past him, eager to get the hell out of here.

"Jesse!" I turn around, and Dave says, "You don't want to hear it from me, fine. But as your manager, I highly advise you to ask Bethany about her past. You do not want to get blindsided with this by the press."

"Let the press throw a bitch fit over an unpaid parking ticket or a littering charge. I *know* Bethany. You need to back off."

I don't wait for his response. I storm down the hallway and past Ryder, who steps back when he sees me coming. Shit, am I that obvious? I slow down and shake out the tension in my muscles.

When I get to the swag room, I stop short in the doorway.

Bethany is on a rolling office chair, her bare feet on one wall and her dress falling to her upper thighs. "In three, two, one... blast off!" She pushes off the wall and rolls to the other side of the room, where she braces her feet again.

"Ground control to Major Tom, we are go for lift-off!" At the word off, she pushes again, this time harder, which makes her spin. Her smiling eyes come to mine, and she slams her feet to the floor to stop her spinning. "How long have you been there?"

"Only long enough to witness the last two launches." I step inside the room, feeling a thousand times lighter from just seeing her face. I nod to the chair. "Don't let me stop you."

She bunches up her perfect toes, the light purple nail polish standing out boldly against the white marble floor. "I think I'm good. Are you finished?"

"I am, but I hate to interrupt the important work of NASA."

She shrugs and scoots her chair to the corner where her shoes lie next to her bag. "I think we got what we needed." She slips on her shoes and scoops up her bag. "Don't look at me like that. It's science."

I'm trying hard to keep a straight face, but I'm losing. "Yeah, I get it."

She crosses the room toward me, her simple white sundress bringing out the warm color of her skin. She stops and smiles at me. "So? Where to next?"

"Home."

Her smile falls. "Your home?"

I pull her close, pressing her hips to mine. "Yes. Did you think we'd be sleeping in the streets tonight?"

"I thought maybe a hotel?"

"That would be weird when I have a perfectly acceptable house not far from here."

"Okay, um... any chance we can grab some food first? I'm starving."

I can't believe I didn't think she might be hungry. This is why I don't do relationships—one of the many reasons I don't do relationships. I can barely be responsible for myself, much less someone else.

BETHANY

Jesse calls Dave as we move through the halls toward the elevator. I try to school my response to hearing Jesse request a private chef come to his home for dinner tonight and breakfast tomorrow.

People stare at our clasped hands, and a thrill shoots through me at his public show of affection. When we get on the elevator, a man and two women follow us on. I tuck back behind Jesse, feeling their eyes flick toward me—or hopefully they're looking at Jesse.

The elevator pings, and when we step out into the parking garage, we're greeted by a huge man in black slacks and a black polo shirt, standing in front of a brand-new black Cadillac Escalade. His chest is wide, his arms stretch the fabric of the shirt, and I bet he only fits through doorways if he walks sideways.

"Mr. Lee." He shakes Jesse's hand. "I'm Johnny."

"This is Bethany," Jesse says. "She's never been to LA. I was thinking about a tour."

"Absolutely." Johnny pops the back door. The interior is charcoal leather, and the windows are tinted so dark that when we're inside, it feels like being in a cave.

"Where are we going?" I ask.

Johnny drives us up and out of the underground parking, and when we emerge into the bright Southern California sunlight, I'm grateful for the tinted windows.

Jesse tells the guy, "We need to get some food, then we'll go sightseeing."

"Really?"

He throws an arm over my shoulder and pulls me closer. "Yes, genius. What are you hungry for?"

I shiver at the rumble of his question against my temple. Only Jesse could make a simple lunch request sound sexual. As much as I'd love to tackle him, I am hungry, so I answer honestly. "I'd kill for an In-and-Out burger."

"Fast food?" He cringes. "With all the choices, you pick fast food." He grins and shakes his head. "All right. Johnny, can you buzz us through In-and-Out?"

"Sure thing."

"Good. And on the way, we'll drive down Sunset Boulevard."

I squeal like a little girl and press my nose to the glass while Jesse shows me his town.

19

BETHANY

Jesse played the perfect guide and indulged my tourist heart by showing me all the sites of LA, from Hollywood Boulevard to Rodeo Drive and Warner Brothers and Paramount Studios. We weren't able to get out for fear of him being recognized, but it didn't really matter. I enjoyed it just as well from the safety of the backseat behind tinted glass. We sat in traffic for an hour to get from Santa Monica to the Griffith Observatory in time to watch the sunset behind the Hollywood sign.

Sitting on the hood of the car as the final ray of light dips behind a thick layer of smog, I lean into Jesse's side. "This has been the perfect day."

His arm comes around me. "I'm glad you had fun."

I tilt up my head. "What was your favorite part?"

I expect him to say something about the meeting with his record label, maybe the new direction of his career. Strangely, he hasn't talked about that much since we left the Arenfield offices.

"Watching you power that animal-style burger was pretty impressive."

I smack his chest. "I told you I was hungry! And a gentleman never reminds a lady of her vulnerable moments."

He chuckles and hops off the hood before wiping the backside of his jeans with his hands, which is kind of funny considering there isn't a speck of dust on the car. "I'm not kidding. I've eaten a lot of meals with a lot of women." He holds out his hand to help me slide down. "I love eating with a woman who enjoys her food."

I take his hand and scoot off the hood. "That's a really weird compliment, but I'll take it."

"Let me explain it this way," he says as he circles to the back door and opens it for me. "Eating with a woman who's terrified she'll gain a pound is like fucking a woman who fakes her orgasms. Eating with you, well..." He bites his lip and grins. "It's the real thing. It gets me off watching you get off."

I hop in the car, feeling flushed. "How completely predictable of you to turn food talk into sex talk. And I highly doubt you've been with a woman who's had to fake it."

He slides in next to me. "You'd be surprised."

My eyes pop wide. "Wait, you're serious?"

"My place," he says to Johnny then angles his body toward me. "Don't look at me like that. It's not me. Some women try to boost my ego—"

"Ha! Like you need it."

"Agreed. You'd be surprised how many women act like they're hoping for an Oscar after their sex performance."

"Huh." I watch the distant lights of downtown Los Angeles fade as we make our way deeper into the Hills. "That really surprises me."

"You know what surprises me?"

I turn toward him.

"The fact that you seem completely comfortable talking about other women I've fucked."

I scrunch up my nose. "I wouldn't say I'm comfortable, but I do like hearing new things about you. It's unfortunate, but understandable, that a lot of your life happens to revolve around the woman you've... been with."

"What about you?"

"I've never been with a man who has faked an orgasm."

He laughs. "No, I don't suppose you have."

"Yours have all been real."

"Yep."

"Wyatt's too, and the guy I lost my virginity to—"

"Okay, gross. You're a better person than I am. I don't want to hear about all the dicks that have been inside your body."

Now it's my turn to laugh. "Too late!"

He blinks. "What?"

"I said it's too late. You already have."

"You're telling me you've only been with three guys?"

I shrug as embarrassment floods my veins. "Yeah. I mean, I don't sleep with people unless I'm in love with them."

His expression is blank for a few pregnant seconds before he nods.

"Whoa!" I press my nose to the window and stare at the house we've stopped in front of. "Is this yours?"

He pops the door open, and I follow him out with my backpack slung over my shoulder. The house is set back into the face of a mountain. It's lit up inside, and every wall is made of glass held together by columns of stone or wood. The exterior is simple—trim green grass, concrete rectangles set in the grass to make a walkway, and succulents everywhere. It has a mid-century modern design, but the lights and windows give it a warmer feel.

"Come on." He grabs my hand and leads me up the driveway to the garage.

He punches in a number on the keypad, and it opens to reveal a four-car garage. An old hotrod of some kind in a shining blue, a big black pickup truck, a tiny red car that I'm pretty sure is a Ferrari, and a sleek black motorcycle fill the tidy space. He pushes open the door to the house, and my nose fills with the sweet and spicy scent of Asian food.

"Mr. Lee," a small Asian man in a chef's jacket greets us in the kitchen. "Welcome home."

"Good to be home." Jesse drags me through the kitchen, only giving me a second to take in the masculine wood cupboards and stainless steel countertops.

"This place is amazing," I say as he leads me up a floating staircase to the second story. "How long have you lived here?"

"Few years." He opens a door to a room that matches the downstairs—dark gray flagstone tile, floor-to-ceiling windows that look out over a manicured lawn and—

"Look at that pool." The shimmering blue water is still and level with the horizon, like something one would find at a five-star resort hotel.

"Did you bring your suit?" Jesse says from the doorway of what I assume is his bathroom.

"No, I wasn't expecting all this."

He frowns. "Damn, I was kind of hoping to become intimately familiar with that unicorn." He winks.

"It's a Pegasus, and I only wear that suit when I swim with Elliot. I do have adult swimsuits." I turn back to the view, hopeful that he's visualizing a string bikini, not my tankini made for a much more mature adult.

I imagine the pool parties he must throw. Picture the hoards of tiny models in their barely-there suits, parading around in hopes of getting his attention. How many women have been in my very same position in this room, wondering the same thing?

But he loves me.

That thought pushes out my insecurities.

His arms come around me from behind, and his lips find my ear. "You don't really need a suit to swim in my pool." He nips at my lobe. "We can go skinny-dipping after the chef leaves."

A delicious shiver skates up my spine. "I've never swum naked before."

He nuzzles my neck, and I relax against him. "Perfect. Then I'll be your first."

I only wish I could say the same to him.

JESSE

After giving Bethany a quick tour of my house, we sit down for peppered beef and noodles, shrimp dumplings, and chocolate coconut mochi. My mouth waters for something stronger to drink than green tea and sparkling water. With four refrigerators that have always been stocked with booze, I'm having a harder time adjusting to being in my house than I thought I would.

Dave cleaned out the booze, and it's no surprise he fired Anton and hooked me up with a chef who doesn't cook using LA's finest chronic. Thank fuck for Bethany. If she weren't here, I'd have left an hour ago to pick up a bottle.

Am I that weak? With all that's at stake, would I give it up so quickly?

"I'm so full." Bethany leans back with her hands on her stomach. "That was honestly the best meal I've eaten in my entire life. I don't know how you managed to stay so fit living this lifestyle."

I push a few noodles around my plate then drop my fork. "Cocaine and a liquid diet."

She flinches a little at my tone.

I clear my throat and try to rein in these new and unfamiliar urges. This shit was a lot easier to control when I was living with Ben. Maybe those daily meetings weren't a total waste of time. "You ready for that swim?"

Her eyes widen. "Now?"

Bethany's wet and naked body in my arms is just what I need to get over the cravings.

I shrug. "I'm down if you are."

Her eyes light up, and her gaze darts to the windows overlooking the pool. "Are you sure no one will see us?"

I push my plate away and brace my forearms on the table. "Would you really care if someone did?"

"Of course I would."

"Really? Think about it. Think how sexy it would be, me pinning you to the wall of the pool, your arms locked behind my neck and your legs wrapped around my hips while I rock in and—"

"Okay!" She holds up a hand and I don't miss the way her fingers quake. "I get it."

Fuck, she's so much fun to get riled up. "So?"

Her gaze slides to the pool again, then she nods. "Let's do it."

"That's my girl."

I push up from the table and take our dishes into the kitchen. The chef left the kitchen spotless, so I rinse the dishes and put them in the dishwasher.

Bethany brings in our glasses and napkins. "How do we do this? Just strip down and go?"

I wipe my hands on a towel. "There's a robe hanging in my closet. Why don't you go get that on and meet me in the pool?"

She turns and darts up the stairs. "I can't believe I'm doing this."

As soon as she's out of the room, I pull off my shirt and toss it on the counter, along with my belt. I'm already barefoot. When I pop the button on my jeans, a flash of headlights shines in from my driveway.

Who the hell would show up here at nearly nine o'clock at night? No one even knows I'm in town except Dave and my band. I check my phone but have no new texts or missed calls. The headlights go dim, and the dark shadowy figure of a woman crosses the driveway to my front door.

Whoever it is knew my gate code. The list of people who know that is limited.

I swing open the front door as Kayla's high-heeled foot hits the doormat.

"What the fuck are you doing here?" I growl.

Her glossy pink lips part, but she doesn't answer until she steps closer. I want to back up, but doing so would put me deeper in the house and I'm afraid she'll take that as permission to come in.

"You shouldn't be here."

She blinks those long black eyelashes over icy-blue eyes. "I know, I'm sorry. I heard you were in town and I had to see you."

"Why? We've got nothing to say to each other."

Her gaze rakes over my naked torso to settle on the open top button of my jeans.

"Kayla."

Her eyes snap to mine. "I don't understand. We had plans to be together then you just cast me aside like I meant nothing to you."

"Fuck," I groan and study my feet. She's right. "I was high, drunk. I honestly don't remember much of the time we spent together."

She steps closer. "That can't be true. We talked about a future, kids—"

Kids? Damn, I must've been really fucked up.

"You told me you love me."

"I know, and at the time, I thought I did, but things change. I sobered up. I moved on."

She blinks rapidly, and tears gather on her eyelashes. "Things change?"

"What happened between us shouldn't have happened. You were Nate's, and I took what wasn't mine. I take responsibility for that, but you have to know there can be nothing between us."

"I think I have something that might change your mind." She smiles even though tears stream steadily down her face. She grabs my hand and uses the other to reach between her healthy cleavage and pull out something that she drops into my palm before closing my hand around it. "Come on, Jes, let me remind you how good we are together."

I open my hand to see a small glass vial of pristine white powder. Both of her hands cradle mine as I stare at my old vice.

A better man would drop it as if it were on fire or toss it as far as his throwing arm would facilitate.

But I am not that man.

I fantasize about what it would be like to pour out thin lines on my glass tabletop. I imagine what it would be like to feel untouchable again, to feel strong and talented and less fucking insecure. I imagine the hours I'd spend writing and fucking and writing and fucking and forgetting what day it is. I close my hand around the vial, and for a fleeting second, I want to give in.

Warm arms wrap around my waist, but it's background noise to the eager chuffing of my inner monster who wants to devour everything in sight no matter who it hurts. Soft lips on my neck send my lids popping open.

"No." I lurch back, and Kayla stumbles forward, nearly falling in my entryway. I force my hand forward to give her the coke, but she makes no move to take it.

"Why are you playing so hard to get?" Her hands grip my jeans. "Let me make you feel good. You told me you love me. Let me love you back."

In a desperate panic to get rid of her, I hook her around the upper arm and walk her out the door. "I only told you I love you so I could fuck you. I had you and now I'm done with you." I release her with a gentle but firm push. "Don't come back or I'll call the police."

I slam the door and lean against it, only realizing then that I still have the vial of cocaine in my hand. I stare at it. It feels super-glued to my palm. I have to get rid of it. I step forward and slam to a halt when I see Bethany sitting on the stairs. Her shoulders are slouched under my black robe, and her expression is etched in pain.

"How long have you been sitting there?"

"A while."

"What did you hear?" My stomach feels as if it may jump from my throat as I wait for her answer.

"All of it."

I run a hand through my hair and shrug. "Please, that was a long time ago."

She's as still as a statue as she stares through me. "How long ago?"

Fuck! I swallow hard past my suddenly-dry throat. "The day before I ended up at Ben's."

I didn't think it was possible, but her expression falls even more. "I see."

I cross to her and kneel a few steps down from her. "Don't think about her, okay? She's in the past. You're the one I want now."

"Now." She repeats the word in such an absolute way that I don't fucking like it at all.

"Yes, but... I mean, no, I—"

"What's in your hand?"

I swallow hard and grip my fist around the drugs. "I didn't want it. She handed it to me, but I didn't ask for it."

"Then flush it." There's a dare in her tone. She doesn't think I will.

"I was going to, so, yeah... fine."

I head to the guest bathroom near the front door and hear her bare feet slap the floor behind me. I take a quick glance outside, grateful to see Kayla's car is gone, then duck into the bathroom.

I flick open the vial to dump the drugs, hesitating slightly. I glance at Bethany. She's noticed. I fucking hate how weak I feel.

I upend the container, and the coke drops like white waterfalls into the toilet. I flush it and watch the water and powder drain, feeling the weight of temptation lifted from my shoulders. I would've hated myself for giving in. I hate myself for even considering it. I put the vial and lid on the counter, but Bethany snags them both and darts out of the bathroom.

"What are you doing?"

She runs through the house, my black silk robe trailing behind her as she bursts out the back door and to the edge of my yard. With a guttural grunt, she tosses the vial into the black night and down the rocky ledge.

She turns and moves past me into the house.

"Feel better?"

Her feet freeze and her shoulders climb to her ears before she turns toward me. "Did you just ask me if I feel better?"

Oh shit. She's throwing my questions back at me like Dave does.

"No, *Jesse*. I don't *feel better*. I'm going to bed."

I walk after her up the stairs. "Great, let's go to bed. I could use some—"

"Alone." She passes my bedroom door and goes into the guest bedroom, slamming and locking the door.

I stand in front of the door for minutes, staring at the wood and willing myself to say the right thing that'll fix what broke between us, but nothing comes to mind. She can't really be pissed that I have a history with other women. Just because I told Kayla I loved her doesn't diminish my feelings for Bethany. I picture Bethany in the room, her head on the pillows while she imagines a million different ways she'd like to hurt me.

A sickness twists my stomach. I put my back to the wall and slide down to my ass. I can't have her mad at me. In the past when things didn't work out in a relationship, I'd move on, no hard feelings, but I'm not ready to let Bethany go.

And what the fuck is that all about?

Love is supposed to feel good.

Whatever it is that I feel for Bethany hurts like a motherfucker.

20

BETHANY

S taying in Jesse's guest suite has got to be right up there with staying at the Ritz.

Jesse-induced insomnia gave me a rough beginning to the night, but eventually the luxurious bedding swallowed me in a cloud of comfort. I slept until the sunlight shining through the window woke me. Not ready to face Jesse, I took a long hot shower using shower products I've never even heard of because they're probably only sold in high-end salons. I pampered my skin with delicious-smelling lotion, brushed my teeth with a brand new toothbrush and toothpaste, and blow-dried my hair with one of those fancy Dyson blow dryers. Even now, as I sit on the king-sized bed staring at the Los Angeles skyline, a part of me never wants to leave this room.

As long as I stay in here, I don't have to face the inevitable conversation with Jesse.

I run my hands down the silky black robe I slept in and tilt my head to smell the collar. Sadly, it doesn't smell like Jesse. He doesn't strike me as the robe-wearing type and I'd guess all his things have been washed since he last stayed here.

Staying alone in the guest bedroom was not at all how I saw last night going, but I don't regret how this visit has turned out. Last night was a hard lesson in reality.

I only told you I love you so I could fuck you. I had you and now I'm done with you.

How familiar those words feel even though they weren't said to me. As deeply as they cut, they may as well have been.

I suck in a deep, shaky breath.

Easier to cut ties before the binds get too tight.

I slip off the bed and pull the lapels of the robe together to make sure I'm not showing any skin. I need to get my backpack and get dressed and find out when the plane to Arizona leaves.

I unlock the door and pull it open, only to pause in the doorway when I see Jesse lying in the hallway. He looks no different than he did last night—jeans, no shirt, no shoes or socks. He's on his side, using his arm as a pillow, right outside the guest bedroom door.

I nudge him with my foot. "Jesse, wake up."

He mumbles and curls up, his eyebrows pinching together as if he's in pain—which I imagine he is after a night on the cold, stone floor. He opens his eyes, and it seems to take a minute for him to place where he is. When his gaze comes to me, he pushes up and hops to his feet. "Bethany, hey."

"You slept in the hallway?"

He looks at the spot in front of my door and rubs the muscles in the back of his neck. "I guess so. I didn't want to miss you when you came out."

That's strangely sweet. I can't think of anyone who would sleep in a hallway just so they wouldn't miss me leaving. Not even Ashleigh.

"What time is it?" he says, patting his pockets for his phone.

"Seven thirty." I point past him toward his bedroom door. "I just need to grab my stuff."

"Sure." He steps back so I can exit the room. "Yeah. I should probably get cleaned up. We're supposed to be at the studio at nine."

I slip into his room and grab my backpack. As he sits on the edge of his bed with his phone, I head back to the guest room to get changed. I tell myself he's not reading a hundred different texts from the woman who was here last night, that he's not texting her back how sorry he is and making plans to meet up with her when he comes back to town. Not that any of that should concern me now.

I shake the thoughts from my head and focus on getting ready. As much as Jesse likes me in dresses, I'm grateful I brought a pair of skinny jeans and a floral top. I don't want to draw his unwanted attention. I swipe on some mascara, clear gloss, and a quick dusting of powder—just in case I find myself in the background of a paparazzi shot, I don't want to look like a corpse.

On my way downstairs, I hear the shower running in Jesse's room and decide the safest place to wait for him is outside. The morning air is crisp and filled with the scent of wildflowers and chlorine from the pool. I drop my things at the foot of a lounger and climb onto the cushions. Every single thing in this house is pure luxury. The pool water is so clear, I wouldn't be surprised if it was imported from the Swiss Alps.

I type out a quick text to Ashleigh, letting her know I should be home this afternoon and that I have a lot to tell her. She never sees things as black and white. If anyone can shed some light on what happened last night with Jesse and the mystery woman, it'll be Ash.

I close my eyes and enjoy the stillness and quiet surrounding me. I'm just able to find my Zen when I hear the door slide open behind me. Jesse appears at the lounger next to me and hands me a cup of coffee.

"Thanks." The color is perfect. When I take a sip, I find he nailed the cream-to-sugar ratio.

"Listen, about last night." Jesse doesn't face the pool but rather uses the lounger as a bench, his body facing me. His hair is damp from the shower, and he must've been in a hurry because he has a day's worth of stubble on his jaw. "I swear, I had no idea Kayla would show up here. And you have to know I wouldn't have used the coke she brought." When I don't say anything right away, he leans around to get a good look at my face. "You believe me, right?"

I grip my mug in both hands and hope the warmth will chase off the chill this conversation brings. "I believe you didn't expect her to show up. I want to believe you wouldn't use the drugs, but that's not what bothers me. You told her you love her so you could fuck her."

My words seem to deliver a quick strike, and he frowns. "I said that to get rid of her, okay? I panicked."

"You don't see the parallel," I mumble almost to myself, shocked he doesn't see how similar the woman who showed up last night is to me.

"Parallel? No. My feelings for you are real. I was so fucked up when I was with Kayla, I hardly remember it."

"I'm having a difficult time merging the Jesse Lee I know with *the* Jesse Lee."

He chuckles, but the sound is off somehow. "I'm the same guy."

I look at him and feel my eyes fill with tears. "That's what I'm afraid of."

He looks confused. "What are you saying?"

A throat clears behind us. Johnny is there, looking ever the professional, and when Jesse glares at him, the man's gaze hits the ground. "Mr. Lee, we need to get going if I'm going to get you to the studio on time."

"Shit," Jesse growls then stands.

I follow him, not wanting to be the reason he's late, and we set our mugs in the sink on the way out the door. I climb in and scoot to the far end, where my shoulder touches the door. The entire ride to the studio, I can tell Jesse wants to say something. He looks at me, parts his lips, then shakes his head and goes back to looking out the window.

Johnny pulls up in front of a non-descript building at two

minutes before nine. Jesse offers me his hand when I get out, and I take it, not wanting to cause a scene by refusing his help publicly even though I could easily remove myself from the car unassisted.

With Johnny at our backs, the door buzzes and we push inside. Jesse is instantly swallowed up in a group of men who greet him with back-thumping hugs. Only two of the half dozen men do I recognize: Dave and Ryder. The first ignores me. The second greets me with a lift of his chin. I wave and smile back.

Rather than sit in my discomfort and wish I could be back home to sort through my feelings in private, I look around the space. I don't know anyone who's been invited to a world-famous recording studio before. The walls are lined with gold and platinum records for different Arenfield bands. This room is just a lobby with a few couches. I assume all the magic happens somewhere down the hallway.

Eventually Johnny leaves and Jesse leaves his inner circle to come to me. "You okay?"

I motion around the room. "This is all really cool."

His brows pinch together. "That's not what I asked."

"I'm fine." I lean to the side to see all the guys standing around as if their waiting for Jesse. "What time are we headed back to Arizona?"

"Dave said the jet would be ready for us at one." His eyes flicker with worry. "Is that okay?"

"Great."

His expression relaxes a little. "Cool." He takes my hand. "Come on, I want you to see how we record a song."

His palm is a little damper than usual. Maybe holding all the attention in the room has made him nervous. I resist the urge to pull my hand free as his touch scrambles my brain, and I allow him to drag me down a hallway to a room the size of a hotel room. There's no bed in this room, just comfortable-looking overstuffed couches, tables, a mini-fridge and snack area, and one wall of glass that looks into what I can only describe as a fish bowl. Inside the glass room are microphones, guitars, and a drum kit.

"Make yourself at home, all right?" Jesse says close to my ear, and I refuse to shiver. "There's food if you're hungry."

I nod. "I'm okay."

He presses a kiss to my lips then smiles. "I'm so glad you're here."

I wish I could say the same.

JESSE

I've been out of practice.

After singing for only a couple hours, my voice is raspy and my throat is aching. I take a swig of water and adjust my headphones then speak into the mic. "Let's run that one more time."

Dave's voice comes into my ears. "I like the sound on this one. I know your throat must be sore, but the sound is perfect for this song."

Behind his voice, I hear the faint sound of female laughter. I can't see Bethany from the booth, but it sounds as if one of the guys is making her happy. The angry stir of jealousy rouses the monster. She's barely spoken to me all morning, and I may have caught a slight smile that may or may not have been directed at me, but that's it.

"One more time," I say.

I channel my frustration into the lyrics as I belt "From the Ashes." We had only planned to get some music down today, but the band loved the song and wrote and recorded their parts yesterday, so I thought I'd try to get the lyrics laid down so we could release a single as soon as possible. I didn't realize how much I missed this until I got in the booth.

I growl the words, the strain in my voice giving the song an edgy feel I really like.

"That was fantastic. Really fucking good," Dave says.

I pull off my headphones and exit the booth, eager to listen to it all together. Even before it's mixed and mastered, I have a feeling it's going to sound phenomenal. My excitement dies when I see Bethany and Ryder sitting on a couch, facing each other with their palms out, playing slap hand. Ryder's on top and she's on bottom. She moves fast but misses and that sends her into a fit of laughter while Ryder watches her as if he's seeing the sunrise for the first time in a frozen wasteland.

He might be one of the best drummers I've ever worked with—not that I'd ever tell him that—but I'm not above breaking his motherfucking arms if he doesn't back off.

Dave's talking about something I don't fully hear as I cross to the happy toddlers on the couch.

"You done playin' patty cake so we can get some fucking work done?" I growl at Ryder, whose eyes tighten on me.

"I guess so, yeah, but you're recording vocals so…"

"Does it look like I'm recording now, asshole?"

"Jesse," Bethany hisses, but I keep my eyes on him. "What is your problem?" Bethany tugs my arm. "Why did you snap at him? He was just keeping me company."

"I bet he was."

Her expression turns bored. "Really?"

Ryder looks between Bethany and me, and a slow grin curls his lips. "Ah. Okay. I get it." He stands and gets right in my face. "Just so you know, I'd never make a play for another man's girl." His smile widens, and he looks me up and down before saying, "I'm not like you."

I gape, trying to decide if I should kick his ass or fire him from the band. Which one would hurt worse?

"Besides." He looks back at Bethany with pity. "Don't you think she's been passed around enough?"

Bethany jumps to her feet. "What are you talking about?"

I turn and put myself in front of her, but being stubborn, she steps aside and asks Ryder again.

He smiles at her, and I want to knuckle-thump the grin off his face. "You were engaged to Nate."

Bethany blinks in confusion. "What?"

I shove the asshole. "You have no fucking clue what you're talking about."

Dave steps between us, his arms going up hold us back from each other. "Ryder, wrong girl. You're thinking of Kayla."

Bethany gasps and whirls toward me, glaring through to my soul. "What is he talking about, Jesse?"

I can't stand to witness the disappointment I hear so clearly in her voice. I turn away to see Johnny and Dave in conversation. When did the bodyguard get here?

Dave nods a few times then crosses to Bethany and me. "Jes, Johnny's going to take Bethany to the plane, but I'd like for you to stay so we can work on a couple more songs."

I'm already shaking my head. "No, I want to go back with Bethany. I'll come back next week or—"

"Jesse," Bethany says with her hand on my forearm, "it's okay. You should stay."

"No fucking way. I'm going with you."

Her gaze darts to Dave as though she wants to say something but doesn't want an audience.

"Dave, give us a minute?" I say.

He checks his watch. "Make it fast. The plane is waiting."

We watch him walk away then turn to each other.

She runs her tongue along her lower lip. "I need some time."

"What?"

She blows out a long breath and gathers her hair over her shoulder. "I'm sorry, but after last night, I just need some time to think."

I grip her hands and pull them to my chest. "I want to be with you. I feel stronger when you're with me." I can't fucking believe I'm saying this shit out loud, but it's true.

She sighs heavily. "That's the problem. I don't think we're in this for the right reasons, and I'm in no position to be throwing around words like love, trust me."

"But I do love you."

Her gaze searches mine, and tears spring to her eyes. "Was Kayla engaged to your old drummer when you told her you loved her just so you could fuck her?"

I cringe at her throwing my own words back at me.

When I don't answer, she closes her eyes and nods. "That's what I thought."

"Bethany."

"I can't lose myself to you." She pulls her hands free from mine and mumbles, "Not again."

"But I love you."

She smiles sadly. "If you love me, then please, let me go."

"I don't want to." The monster inside me shakes its head and blows steam from its nose. "If you walk away from me, you're making the biggest mistake of your life."

Her expression crumbles, and she looks at me as if she's looking at a stranger.

Dammit to fuck, the stabbing pain in my chest becomes unbearable.

Dave steps close. "Bethany. Time's up."

She shakes her head and turns away from me.

I rush after her. "Wait, I didn't mean that. I'm sorry, give me a chance to explain—"

A strong forearm slams into my chest, and Johnny shakes his head.

I throw his shit off me. "Don't fucking touch me."

When I look up, Bethany is gone.

BETHANY

The flight back to Phoenix is a lot sadder than the flight to Los Angeles was. I stare at the seat across from me, imagining Jesse sitting there with his cocky grin as he makes dirty jokes that flame my cheeks. How many times had Kayla been in my same position?

I pick at the ham and Swiss croissant Irving delivered to me just after takeoff. I assumed, having skipped breakfast, that this empty feeling in my stomach was hunger, but after only a couple bites, I realized the food did nothing to satisfy the ache.

Out the window, the barren desert landscape gives way to buildings, freeways, and city streets.

"Miss Park, we're starting our descent into Phoenix," Irving says and motions to my food. "Would you like me to take that for you?"

"Sure, thank you." I prop my chin on my palm and watch out the window as the city gets bigger and bigger. When the wheels hit the ground, I exhale a shaky breath and gather my things.

"It was a pleasure serving you today," Irving says with a polite nod.

"Thanks for everything." I climb down the stairs onto the tarmac. No one is waiting for me. No bodyguard, chauffer, or car. "I see how it is."

I make the short walk into the private terminal. Without the great Jesse Lee on my arm, I'm back to being invisible.

"Excuse me," I say to a woman wearing a Sky Harbor Elite nametag. "Can you tell me where I can get a cab?"

"I'll call one for you, Miss Park." She picks up the phone and punches some numbers while staring at me a little too closely, as if she's trying to figure out who I am. I assume they only get celebrities, politicians, and royalty through these doors.

Don't waste the energy, lady. I'm nobody.

"Have a seat." She nods toward the couches. "I'll come get you when your car is here."

"Thanks." I pull out my phone and grab a seat. I could call Ash and have her pick me up, but it's a forty-minute drive one way and she'll ask me what happened. I'm not ready to talk about it.

Not a single text message or call from Jesse. Even though it's what I asked for, it still stings.

"Miss Park, your executive car is here."

I lift my eyes from my phone to see a gorgeous black sedan pull right up to the double doors. A man in a black suit comes around the hood and into the terminal.

I stand, wondering if maybe Dave or Jesse did arrange a ride for me after all. "This is for me?"

The airport employee seems confused. "Yes, ma'am."

I hike my backpack onto my shoulder, and the driver meets me with a professional smile and nod. I follow him out to the car, and when he opens the back door, I almost expect to see Jesse in there, hiding behind the tinted glass. I'm ashamed to admit I'm disappointed to realize the backseat is empty. I slide in and tell the driver my address.

I lean my head against the glass and doze off in the cool, quiet car. Forty minutes feels more like five and we pull up to my apartment.

"We're here." He eyes me from the rearview mirror. "That'll be one-eighty."

My eyes pop wide. "One hundred eighty dollars?"

"Yes, and gratuity is not included."

Gratuity? What do I owe him a tip for? "I'm sorry." I scoot to the edge of my seat to ensure he hears me. "I requested a cab."

"The Elite terminal only uses executive cars."

Great. I pull out all my cash, which ends up being fifty-seven dollars, so I hand him my emergencies-only credit card. I never thought being stuck in a Cadillac would constitute an emergency. He runs the card and I tip him five dollars, which makes me sick. I pop the door open, thinking I should've made him do it, but I want to get out of there and go crawl into my bed.

Our assigned parking spot is empty. Ash must already be at work. I'm grateful for that. When I get inside, I drop my bag and face-plant onto my bed. The pillows still smell like Jesse. Rather than throw them away, I dig my nose in deeper and breathe him in until I fall asleep.

I jolt awake at the sound of my phone ringing. Jesse? My bedroom is dark, and I blindly search for my phone. My neck muscles protest, sore from passing out on my stomach. I hit Accept so the call won't go to voicemail and press it to my ear. "Hello?"

"Wow, you sound happy to hear from me."

My shoulders slump and I fall back onto my mattress at the sound of Wyatt's voice. "I just woke up. The phone ringing kind of startled me awake."

"Woke up? Are you sick? I assumed you'd be at work."

"No, no, I uh... I don't work tonight."

"Great! Is it too late to grab some dinner?"

Of course it's too late—like three months too late—but I don't think that's the kind of late he's talking about. "I think so. I'm sorry."

"That's all right, how about tomorrow?"

"I work tomorrow night."

"Geez, Beth, you're not making this easy on me."

"What—"

"How about Saturday night? You said you have alternating weekend nights off, right? You work Friday, so you're off Saturday. No more excuses."

He remembers that?

"Um..." But what if Jesse is back in town by then? We aren't really together anymore. Who cares, I still have no desire to hang out with my ex. Which reminds me... "Why are you doing this? Won't it upset Suzette to know you're hanging out with me?"

He chuckles. "First off, Suzette doesn't find you a threat to our relationship."

Ouch.

"But even if she did, it doesn't matter. We're taking a step back, just for a little while, until she figures some things out."

"Oh—"

"Yeah, there were a few things that came up during our premarital counseling that we need some time to work through."

Why is he telling me this? "You should keep that kind of stuff between the two of you."

"So we're on for Saturday night. Why don't you meet me at my place?"

"I can't. It's not even that I can't, it's that I don't want to. You broke up with me, and you did the right thing."

"Slow down there, turbo. I'm just asking for a dinner, not a chance to get in your pants."

I cringe away from the phone. Has he always been this much of a dickhead?

"I just need to talk to you."

"You got me on the phone now. What do you want to talk to me about?"

"I need to talk to you in person."

"I don't think you do—"

"Not at my place then. Anywhere else. I'll meet you there."

I rub my eyes and contemplate meeting him so he'll back off once and for all. "Um, okay, I guess… I'll meet you at Starbucks. Three o'clock on Saturday." That's the least romantic date I can think of.

"I guess if that's the best you can do…"

Why does every word out of his mouth feel like an insult? "It is."

"It's a date."

"It's really not."

"I'll see you there."

I drop the phone onto my stomach, and my eyelids get heavy again. I roll to my side and tuck my hands under my head with my phone cradled between them. At least when I sleep, I don't miss him so much.

21

BETHANY

The first twenty-four hours after a breakup is the worst.

The next morning, I wake feeling a little better than I did the night before. I shower and get ready to go to Ben's with only the mildest nausea turning my gut.

My stomach rumbles, forcing me to the kitchen, where I find Ashleigh at the breakfast bar, bent over her computer while her fingers tap away at the keys. "What are you doing up so early?"

She peeks up. Her face is makeup free, which means she did get home and sleep for at least a few hours last night. She closes her laptop. "Trolling people on Twitter while I wait for you to tell me how LA was."

I have my back to her as I pull an English muffin from the bag and shrug. "Good. The city isn't quite as glamorous as I thought it would be. Hollywood Boulevard was dirty and kind of terrifying."

After pressing toast on the oven, I turn and face her skeptical stare.

"That's not what I meant and you know it." She holds out her palms and flicks her fingers as if to say "give it to me." "What happened with Jesse and why do you have Bassett Hound face?"

"I don't have Bassett Hound face."

"You do."

"That's just what my face looks like!"

"No, it doesn't."

"We broke up." I flop my arms heavily to my sides. "There. Happy?"

She glares. "What did that motherfucker do? I swear to God, I'll kill him."

I sigh. "He didn't do anything. I broke up with him."

A slow smile curls her mouth. "Hold on, you broke up with Jesse Lee?"

"Yes."

A horrid snorting sound comes from her nose seconds before she bursts out laughing. "That's amazing. You broke up with him!"

"It's not amazing, it's sad. But yes, I did."

She finally calms. "Man, that had to chap his ass. I wonder how many times he's been broken up with? I'd guess none, until you."

The toaster dings and I put my breakfast on a plate before slathering it with peanut butter. Ashleigh's probably right, but I don't think most girls were with Jesse for the right reasons. I stare blankly ahead. Was I?

"Tell me everything. I want details."

In the ten minutes before I have to catch the bus, I tell Ashleigh about my stay in LA. She predictably loses her shit when I get to the part about the beautiful blonde showing up at Jesse's door, and her shit loss escalates when I tell her Jesse's gorgeous ex was his ex-drummer's now ex-fiancée.

He told her he loved her so he could fuck her.

He used her just like he probably used me.

How did I not feel the similarities to my relationship with Wyatt?

The first time a man toyed with my emotions, I made the biggest mistake of my life to help me forget, a mistake I'm still paying for.

I had to get out of this thing with Jesse before I did something I couldn't take back.

"You're saying he didn't call at all last night?" she says, visibly outraged. "Not even a text?"

I toss what's left of my breakfast and guzzle some OJ before nodding. "That's right."

She pops open her laptop. "Let's do a little investigating and see what the dickhead was up to last night, shall we?"

My gut churns at the idea of seeing Jesse live his life without me. "I'm good. I'll see you tonight."

"Wait." Ashleigh's brows pinch together. "You're passing up an opportunity to stalk your famous ex-boyfriend?"

I open the door and walk out, tossing my answer over my shoulder. "Yes. I am."

A s I make my way down Ben's street toward his house, I see the minivan in the driveway and the glaring absence of Jesse's Lexus. The twinge of pain in my chest only lasts as long as it takes to remind myself that this is what I wanted.

He didn't break up with me. I broke up with him.

I knock twice before pushing into Ben's house, and the familiar smell of coffee and sweet cereal wrap me in a blanket of comfort.

"Bethany!" Elliot races up to me and throws her arms around my thighs. "Daddy took me to the aquarium and to go see my mom!"

Ben smiles sadly at me from the kitchen table.

I rub her head and hug her back. "Sounds like fun."

She tilts her head up to look at me. "I got to pick out the flowers for Mom and I picked purple because Daddy said it was her favorite color."

Ben's never talked about Maggie much with Elliot, or with

anyone for that matter. Elliot never knew her mom, so she never asked much and I think Ben kept her from Maggie's grave to avoid the questions that would dredge up her memory and the sadness that comes with them. Why the sudden change?

"How was Los Angeles?" Ben asks.

Elliot races back to her spot in front of the television, and I join him at the table.

"It was... eye-opening."

He frowns. "I'm sorry to hear that."

I shrug. "It had to happen eventually, and for the record, your brother didn't do anything bad." At least, not deliberately. "A night in LA helped me to see myself more clearly."

That information seems to surprise him.

"I take it you haven't heard from him?" Damn the hopefulness in my voice.

He shakes his head. "Dave called and said Jesse was staying a few extra days. No clue why, but he assured me he's doing well, staying sober and all that."

"That's good." I look down the hallway. It feels weird knowing he's not behind that door, working on music. That he won't walk out any second in all his tattooed, rock-n-roll demi-god glory to tease me or piss me off. My stomach is a mess of nervous knots for no good reason at all.

Yep, that sounds like love. I groan internally at my idiocy. Can't blame a girl for getting caught up in the idea of earning the love of the great Jesse Lee.

"Bethany, I hate to see you like this."

"I didn't realize I was so transparent." I chuckle even though it's not funny.

He crosses his forearms on the table. "Don't beat yourself up. Jesse doesn't know the first thing about what it means to love someone because he was never shown it. Our parents were—"

"I know, he told me."

"So then you understand why Jesiah confuses love for a feeling."

I blink. "Love is a feeling, isn't it?"

"Probably the biggest misconception. Love is a choice. It's a commitment you make to another person that says you'll always put their happiness before your own… for richer or poorer, in sickness and in health, through all the trials that life brings." He frowns as he gazes past me at a photo of Maggie. "Until death do you part."

A wave of sadness washes over me, and I swallow back the urge to sob. "Wow, I guess I never thought of it like that." I would never commit to put Wyatt before me, and he certainly didn't consider my feelings beyond his own. That wasn't love. "Anyone can say I love you."

"Of course. They're just words."

"To be honest, Pastor Langley, I hope I never hear the word again. But man, I hope to one day feel it." My eyes dart to a photo of Maggie, one that was never there before. "I want to have what you had."

He follows my gaze to the image of his wife.

"You could have it again, you know."

He shakes his head. "I don't think so."

"Don't give up hope."

"You either." He stands and takes his empty mug to the sink. "I've got to get going."

"Have a good day."

My talk with Ben should make me feel better, but it doesn't. I thought Jesse was the one confused about what it means to truly love another person. Turns out, I'm as much of a mess as he is.

JESSE

"You look like dog shit," Ryder says from the other end of the couch inside the studio.

I eye him and take in his pale skin and the dark circles under his eyes. "You look like a strung-out Billy Idol twenty years after his prime."

After Bethany left, Ryder and I took out our anger through our music and recorded some of the best shit of my career. The music allowed us to bury the hatchet. He really is a better drummer than Nate.

I drop my head back and close my eyes. I'm so fucking exhausted. I don't know how long we've been here, but with the short naps I've grabbed on the couch, I'd say I've gathered no more than six hours' sleep in total.

Ethan and Chris left a couple hours ago, their parts finished. Ryder insisted on staying even after his parts were recorded. I respect that.

"I do my best work half dead," Ryder says, sounding halfway between sleep and awake. "We laid down some sick fucking tracks."

"The drum solo on 'Double Life' blew me away. Where the hell did you learn to play like that?"

He yawns. "Self-taught."

I blink at him through heavy eyelids. "No kidding?"

He shrugs. "What day is it?"

"No clue."

I reach for my phone then remember it died somewhere around my second nap. I could've had Dave charge it, but I thought it might be best to leave it dead—less of a distraction. And by distraction, I mean at least when it's dead, I can't obsessively check it every ten seconds to see if I got a message from Bethany.

She's back home, living her simple life, making people smile with her contagious personality and hideous singing. I hate to admit it, but I'd give anything to hear that voice now.

"Gentlemen, I think it's time we send everyone home while we mix what we have," Dave says. My manager looks exhausted, but he has dollar signs in his eyes.

Ryder pushes up off the couch. "I'll be at the hotel for another day or two, catching up on sleep before I head back to Vegas."

"Perfect." Dave checks his watch. "Why don't you both get some sleep? It's almost noon. We have enough time to make a little Friday night news while you're still in town."

"I'm going back to Phoenix." I push to stand. "I'll sleep on the plane."

"No, you're not." Dave's voice is laced with excitement. "I need you and Ryder to meet me at Spago. Eight p.m. sharp."

"Spago?" I recoil. "That place is crawling with paps."

Dave's eyes practically sparkle. "Exactly. I need to make a phone call." He disappears down the hallway.

"Fantastic, prepare to be served to the sharks." I groan and rub my eyes. My head feels like mush, and for the first time in a long time, drinking and doing drugs is the last thing I want. I want sleep. Sleep and Bethany.

"Can I ask you a personal question?"

I crack open one eye. "You can, or you can Google it. All my personal shit is online for the fucking world to see."

"How do you and Bethany do it?"

"However we want, but my favorite is when I get her on all fours and—"

"That's not what I meant."

We share a sleep-deprived-insanity laugh.

"I mean, you're you and you're here and surrounded by so many beautiful women, and she's in another state living her life, guys probably hitting on her. She's gotta get lonely when you go on tour—"

"Pretty sure you were witness to how well that's panning out for us. She fucking broke up with me."

He frowns. "Yeah, but the way she looked at you… she's into you. You'll work it out, right?"

I hold up my hand to shut him up before I charter my own damn plane and fly to Phoenix. "If you're asking so you can take a shot at her, I should let you know I will fire you from this band and cut off both your arms if you even attempt to take her from me."

"Oh shit." He rubs his spikey blond hair. "Nah, she's a sweet girl, but I'm taken."

"You've got someone back in Vegas?"

"Yeah. She's not cool like Bethany. She blows my phone up if she thinks I'm in the same room as another woman."

"You don't love her, so end it before you make LA your permanent home."

He chuckles. "What makes you think I don't love her?"

"You just said she's a pain in the ass and blows up your phone, giving you a fucking headache for shit you have no control over."

"So?"

I double-take and stare at him. "So? That sucks."

"Yes, it sucks." He blows out a defeated breath and stares blindly at the wall. "The thought that I'm hurting her fucking sucks."

"No, I mean her driving you crazy. That's a shitty thing for you."

"It's annoying, but what hurts is knowing I'm breaking her heart."

I blink and rub my eyes. Maybe I'm suffering from sleep deprivation psychosis. "Love is supposed to feel good."

"Who told you that?"

"Life taught me that."

He shakes his head. "Nah, man, love fucking kills. How could it possibly feel good when you finally get your hands around someone amazing only to have to worry every fucking day that you're gonna lose her?"

I stare at the wall of gold and platinum records as a sick feeling churns in my stomach.

"Life is much easier without love, bro." He turns to leave. "At least living without love means you don't have to walk around with a constant stomachache, fearing you'll one day lose it." He pushes open the door. "See you tonight."

Is that what this bullshit feeling is in my gut?

Johnny appears, and I numbly walk to the car, thinking about what Ryder said.

You might want to consider redefining your definition of love.

Doc Ulrich's words filter through my head. I retrace my history with woman, a train of faces and bodies that all blend together and not one of them memorable before Bethany. She's different.

I know every dip and curve of her body. The gentle sounds she makes when I touch her. Her laughter I can recall on demand as if she were sitting right next to me. I've memorized all her smiles and what they mean. I know the playful tone of her voice when she's trying to make light of something I said that really hurt her.

Oh fuck, all the times I hurt her.

I grip my stomach, trying to unwind the slow twist of pain these thoughts have induced. Grateful when Johnny pulls up to my house, I stumble out of the car and head straight for my room. I pause in the hallway and stare at the guestroom door.

Without permission, my feet carry me into the room Bethany slept in. An outsider might see nothing in the spotless space, but I see Bethany everywhere. I can smell the faint floral scent she left behind. The black robe she wore hangs on a hook in the bathroom.

I kick off my shoes, drop my jeans, pull my shirt off over my head, and stand naked in front of the robe. The monster inside me smirks and mocks my weakness, but my need for Bethany is more powerful than him.

I slip on the robe and wrap it around me. My eyes slam closed as I'm assaulted by her scent and the knowledge that I'm wearing what was once pressed to her naked body. I cross to the bed, rip back the sheets, and slide in.

Wrapped up in everything that's left of her, the pain in my gut subsides and I'm able to finally get some sleep.

22

BETHANY

"K eep it like this," Ashleigh says from the doorway of my room. "I like it this way. The bed under the window, the bookshelf, it's perfect."

I give her the side-eye because I can hear the cajoling tone in her voice, as though she's trying to talk down a rabid dog.

"What? I'm serious. I like this arrangement better than the last five or six—"

I spit a piece of fingernail. "Seven." Then I go back to chewing even though there's not much left to chew.

With nothing to do on a Saturday morning, I decided to rearrange my bedroom. The furniture has made a full circle around the space in two-foot increments, and I can't settle on which one I like best.

"You know, you could just text him back," she says softly, as if she's the voice in my head.

I close my eyes and rein in my muscles as they prepare to dive for my phone.

Last night as I got off work, I got a text from Jesse. The first words from him since we broke up. Three simple words.

I miss you.

I wanted to write him back, tell him how much I miss him too and explain that I'm a basket case and scared of the power he has over me. Then I got an alert from a celebrity-siting app Ashleigh downloaded as a joke.

Jesse Lee cozied up at Spago with ex-girlfriend actress Elise Daegar.

I sat on the curb outside work and stared at that headline, my heart in my throat, for what seemed like hours. I never worked up the courage to click on it and read the article. I didn't even have to see the picture to have the image appear with crystal clarity in my head.

Had I even been gone for twenty-four hours before he decided to move on? I deleted the app and swore to never read another word about Jesse Lee.

I wanted to text him and call him every single dirty name that came to mind, but that seemed petty. I'm the one who broke up with him, after all.

So I came home, slept, and woke up with a mission to make sure I stay too busy to text back.

"I will when I'm finished here." I push my bed over a few inches.

"It's almost two o'clock in the afternoon. You've been at this all day."

I whirl around on her. "You think I don't know that?"

She blinks, clearly surprised by my outburst.

"I'm so sorry." I take a cleansing breath. "Why is it taking so long to get to Sunday? I need to go to church."

"Are you sure you're allowed to—"

"They can't tell me what to do!" I beat my chest with my fist. "I can go if I want to."

"Okay." She holds up her hands in surrender. "But I'm going with you because if anything happens, I do not want to miss it." She walks down the hallway.

"Fine." I huff and go back to my bedroom layout, shoving my bedside table closer to the bed then standing back to do more staring.

I scratch my head and get a whiff of fried bacon. After the emotional ass-whooping I got last night, I didn't have the energy to get in the shower. Now I'm supposed to meet Wyatt in an hour and I reek like day-old breakfast.

My phone rings, and I grab it off the charger then sigh when I see it's my parents.

"Hello?" I take it with me to the bathroom and drop onto the closed toilet seat.

"Bethany, what is going on?" My dad's voice is frantic. "Your mother was at the salon and women were showing her photos of you and some famous singer? I thought you were getting back together with Wyatt?"

I groan, drop my head back, and slump. Of course my mom would tell him that. "Don't worry, it was just a fling." My heart cramps, punishing me for my lie.

"A fling? We raised you better than that."

"I know, that's why we broke up. He's moved on," I grit the words out through clenched teeth.

I tune out my dad's rambling on and on about virtue and some other crap.

"So listen"—I rub my eyes with my thumb and forefinger—"I have to go, I'm meeting Wyatt for coffee." That should shut him up.

"I know you've had a rough year," he says cautiously. "The arson on your car, the breakup."

I cringe. The arson on my car. If he had any idea that was my own doing, not some random act of violence. If I told them the truth, they'd be disappointed. They'd also sell everything they have to pay my fines. I couldn't bear either of those things.

"This is just a season," he says. "Things will get better."

"Thanks, Dad, but I really have to go."

"Tell Wyatt we say hello." I hate the joyous tone in his voice.

"Sure thing. Bye."

After locking the door and turning on the water, I stare at my reflection. "Don't do it." I shake my head at myself. "Do not look at the text again." My hand twitches on my phone. "Don't—"

I flip around the phone screen and stare at his text again.

I miss you.

Weak! You are so weak!

I try to imagine how long it took him to type the text. Did he punch it out quickly, like I've seen him do a million times? Or did he sit in bed with his phone in his hands, much like I'm doing now, and worry himself sick over what to say, wondering how I'd take it? A crazed giggle bubbles up my throat. The infamous Jesse Lee curled up with some gorgeous actress while worrying over what to say to plain ol' Bethany from Surprise? Now that is laughable.

I punch out a quick text and hit Send before I can change my mind. After placing the device screen down, I throw myself into the shower and trudge ahead.

I get to Starbucks ten minutes late, grateful that Ashleigh offered to take me or I would've been much later. When I go inside, I'm instantly seduced by the overpowering scent of coffee and the promise of good feelings it brings.

I do a quick scan and see Wyatt isn't here yet. Good. Maybe he forgot.

I order a venti iced vanilla latte frappe and pay the ridiculous price for it, then I find a table in a populated part of the coffee shop, avoiding the more intimate booths and tables for two. A four-top right next to the ten-top of what looks like some kind of moms' group. Perfect.

With my phone face up in case I get a text back—no! I'm not doing this. I shove the device in my purse that hangs off the back of my chair. "Out of sight, out of mind." Whoever made up that saying is either a fucking idiot or has never met the all-consuming Jesse Lee.

I sip the creamy iced goodness and pray Wyatt is standing me up. When I see his blond head pass through the doorway, I curse my rotten luck.

"You're here."

I spot the clock on the wall. "Yeah, I've been here for twenty minutes." He doesn't need to know it's only been ten because I was ten minutes late.

He points at my drink with his charismatic smile that I used to love but now I see right through. "I was hoping I could buy your drink."

"Then you should've been here on time." I smile sweetly and suck back a healthy gulp, giving myself brain freeze.

"I'll be right back."

He heads to the counter and places his order, but getting it doesn't take as long as I hoped. He's back with his white cup, takes a seat across from me, and studies my face, likely noticing my wet hair in a tight bun on the top of my head and the absence of makeup. I'm also wearing my GCU sweatshirt and leggings with flip-flops. What? I didn't want to give him the wrong impression. I'm only here out of the very, very little respect for the friendship we once had.

"So what's up? What did you want to talk about?"

"Oh, yeah, that." He picks at the edge of his coffee cup like a nervous little girl. "Listen, I, uh… I never really felt like we got closure after we broke up."

I narrow my eyes. "Huh, that's funny because you moved on pretty quickly. I'd say you closed out well before you even broke up with me."

He holds my gaze in awkward and prolonged eye contact. "That day I saw you outside church, when I saw you with Jesse, I realized I wasn't over you yet."

"I'm sorry... *what?*" Surely I misheard.

"I know, right? One minute I'm with Suzette and we're planning a wedding, and then boom, I see you and it's like all these feelings come rushing back and—"

"Stop."

He stares at me with anticipatory excitement.

"You saw me plenty of times when I was alone and you felt nothing."

"I know, that's the thing. I think on some level, I always knew you'd be there if I wanted you back, but seeing you with someone else—"

"Not someone else. With *Jesse*. There's a huge difference there."

He jerks his chin back in offense. "What? No there's not."

"Just say what you mean and stop wasting my time. Or better yet, I'll say it for you. You're wondering why a megastar like Jesse Lee would be interested in someone as plain and boring as me. You've imagined that a rock-god like Jesse has awakened my inner sex-kitten and that maybe you missed out on my ahhhh-maazing penis-pleasuring skills."

"That's not true. I mean, a part of me wonders how you got a guy like him, but—"

"Oh my gosh, could you be any more condescending?"

"No, no, I'm just being honest."

I roll my eyes so hard it hurts.

He reaches for my hand, but I snatch it away. "Please, listen to me. I still *love you*, Beth."

My stomach sinks to the floor and I laugh even as my eyes heat with tears. "Do you have any idea how long I prayed I'd get to hear you say that again?"

He smiles as if what I said was all the permission he needed. His gaze drops for a second to my boobs. What a fucking pig.

"I can't believe how stupid I was." I shake my head. "They're just words. It's not real."

"It was real—"

"I obsessed over you for months! I beat myself up for all the things I must've done wrong to chase you away, and I ended up punishing myself for it."

"What are you talking about?"

I run a hand through my hair, accidently pulling strands from my bun. "Do you remember the last place we had sex before you broke up with me?"

He seems to mull that over. "Um..."

He doesn't even remember!

Anger stirs in my gut. "The backseat of my car!"

"Yes, I was going to say that. How could I forget making love in the backseat of your car? Of course that's where we did it." The excitement in his face dies a little as if he's putting the pieces together.

"You told me you loved me. You told me I was the type of woman a man marries. You fucked me in my car and then broke up with me thirty minutes later in the parking lot of a Dairy Queen!"

His eyes dart to the side. "Please, keep your voice down."

"Keep my voice down?"

"Beth—"

"Did you just tell me to keep my voice down!"

His eyes widen and he drops back in his seat as if I just grew ten feet taller and three extra heads.

"I hated myself after that night, and every time I got in my car, I was reminded of my own stupidity! I just wanted the guilt to go away! I wanted it to stop, so I tossed a lit book of matches into the backseat of my car, hoping to baptize my mistake in fire."

"Jesus."

I shove a finger in his face. "Do not use his name in vain in front of me, you piece of shit." I push away from the table and grab my purse. "Leave me alone or I'll get a restraining order."

The room erupts in applause as I stomp out.

Instead of going to the nearest bus stop, I walk all nine miles home.

JESSE

By the time I pull the Lexus into my brother's driveway, the sun is setting and the string of Christmas lights illuminates his doorstep. I'm reminded of the first night I was dropped off here by Dave and how antsy I was for a drink. The hunger is still there, like a tickle in the back of my throat, but it's manageable. What isn't manageable is my need to see Bethany.

I shut off the car and read, for what feels like the millionth time, the text she sent me.

I don't care.

Just like every other time I've read those three words, my stomach turns with nausea. I hate that I chased her away and I don't know how to fix it. I considered showing up at the diner and forcing her to talk to me, but the crowds will make it impossible for me to get her alone.

I watch the blue flickering light of Ben's TV as it filters through the mini-blinds. Good, he's still awake. I hop out, grab my bag, and knock softly on the door.

He answers in his sweatpants, an Arizona Diamondbacks shirt, and a smile. "Hey, you're back."

"Yeah..." I rub the back of my neck, feeling awkward and intrusive. "I probably should've called."

"No, don't worry about it." He steps back and opens the door wider. "Come on in."

"Thanks." I linger in front of him, wondering if it would be weird if I hugged him. He seems to be toying with the same idea. Rather than fumble through an uncomfortable embrace, I head for the couch. "Are you watching the cooking channel?"

He closes the door with a chuckle. "I try to get some ideas by watching these shows, but they end up making me hungry and I have to shut them off. How was LA?"

I drop my bag at the foot of the couch and fall back onto the lumpy cushions. "Great. Recorded some of my new songs, signed a new contract with Arenfield. Life is good again."

He frowns, obviously picking up on my not-so-subtle depressed tone. He takes the couch on the opposite side, grabs the remote and hits the mute button, then turns to me. "That's good. I'm happy for you." There's a hint of worry in his voice. He's probably concerned I'll relapse. He's not the only one. "I wasn't sure you'd be back."

"Dave would've liked me to stay in LA."

He tilts his head. "Why didn't you? I would've thought you'd jump at the chance to be done with your imprisonment here." He's smiling.

I'm not. "Me too. Can I ask you something?"

"Of course."

"With you and Maggie, how did you know it was real? I mean, when you were sure that she was it for you? Like, the one."

He laughs and dips his chin for a moment before bringing his gaze back to mine. "About ten seconds after I met her."

"Really?" I frown. "It was that immediate?"

"It was for me. She was magnetic." He sinks back into his seat as the weight of her memory seems to settle on his chest. "Every time I was forced to walk away from her, I felt like I was being robbed of something amazing."

Magnetic? Huh. I suppose Bethany and I had that in the beginning, although our magnets were flipped the wrong way. Then after the night she helped me work through that shit with my brother and that godforsaken chair, it's like the magnets were made right and we stuck. "Must've been nice to be so sure so early on."

"I said I was sure. She wanted nothing to do with me for years."

"You're kidding."

"Nope." He shook his head. "I was just out of seminary and I thought I had all the answers. Believe it or not, I was a pompous, judgmental know-it-all. Maggie called me a self-righteous jerk on several occasions."

"She was probably right."

"She was absolutely right." He picks at a thinning spot on the knee of his sweatpants. "I'm so grateful she gave me a chance to grow up before she gave up on me completely."

"Why?"

He seems not only surprised but a little pissed about my question.

"I mean, she died and here you are, left alone to raise Elliot. I know you don't regret your kid, but if you take her out of the picture, you can't tell me you don't regret falling in love with Maggie."

"I don't. Never for a second have I regretted falling in love with her. I'd take all the suffering ten times over for a chance to love her again for five minutes." He stares lovingly at a photo of her across the room, starry-eyed. It makes no sense.

"But… that's stupid. You've suffered without her for almost as long as you've had her, and from the looks of things, you're going to continue to make yourself miserable for the rest of your life."

He opens his mouth to argue then closes it. Thinks for a few seconds, then nods. "Yeah, that's probably true. But love hurts. The only thing that makes the pain bearable is the memories I have of her, and I'd do nothing to change that." When I don't respond, he jerks his chin up. "Where is all this coming from?"

I groan and drop my head. "I don't know. I'm kind of a mess over a certain girl and I can't explain it."

He chuckles. "Sounds about right."

"Does it though? Because I wasn't expecting this shit to make me feel so insecure and un-fucking-comfortable. I thought when, or if, I finally met the right woman for me, it would be easy and it would feel amazing and she'd listen to me instead of being such a stubborn pain in my ass, ya know?" I fist my hands in my hair. "This woman drives me insane, and I don't know whether to run like hell and get as far away as I can or drop to her feet and beg her to continue to punish me." My eyes snap to his. "That's some sickass shit. Maybe it's a kink and I'm some kind of emotional submissive."

His face scrunches up. "No, it's not that. It sounds like you're in love, and honestly, you couldn't pick a better woman. Bethany is great girl. She's a good human being."

"But that's the thing! I didn't pick her. She crawled in like a virus and took over my central nervous system, killing me slowly by—"

He holds up his hand. "Please tell me you're not going to say that to her."

I lean forward and cup my head. "I don't know what I'm going to say to her. Every time I'm around her, stupid shit comes out of my mouth. The woman has made me crazy. "

"What do you know?"

I huff out a breath, completely exhausted. "I know that the idea of living without her makes me want to drown myself at the bottom of a whiskey bottle."

"You know, for a guy who writes songs about love, you really suck at it."

I groan. "I know. Thing is, the love I write about feels good. This shit?" I motion at my chest. "This does not."

"That's because you don't have her yet."

"What do I do?"

"That's easy. Get her back."

23

JESSE

I wake under a blur of blue fabric to the high-pitched sound of some cartoon squealing on the television. My back aches from a restless night that had nothing to do with the lumpy couch I slept on. I bat the fabric from my face only to feel something scrape against my head.

"No, you have to leave that on." Tiny, sticky hands rearrange something that pinches my head. "You're Princess Jasmine."

I stare boldly into Elliot's unwavering eyes while she's standing over me in a blond wig that goes down to her thighs. "Who are you?"

She spins, and all the wiry blond hair whips at my face. "I'm Rapunzel." Her dark curls peek out from under the wig around her hairline as she leans in to smash whatever is on my head down lower. "You have to wear this to cover your face or we can tell you're a boy."

I reach up to the plastic crown and groan. "Let me get this straight. In my sleep, you decided I'm Jasmine and dressed me up?"

She hands me a tiny plastic cup. "We're having a tea party."

I sit up and, with my feet, accidentally knock over what I assume is the rest of our tea party. At Elliot's horrified response, I try to right the fallen Barbies and tiny teapot.

"Good morning, princesses." My brother stands at the kitchen table, sucking at hiding his grin behind his coffee mug. He's dressed in a blue collared button-up, tan slacks, and brown dress shoes. "I hate to interrupt the royal tea party, but Rapunzel needs to get dressed for church."

When Elliot turns to argue, I flip my brother off over her head—with two fingers for double the fuckage.

"But Daddy, we were just getting started! I don't want to go to church, I want to stay with Jesse." Her words are edged with tears.

My brother's shoulders slump as if he's prepping for a battle he's had to fight more times than he could remember. "Elliot, take your things to your room and—"

"No! It's not fair!" She fists her hands as if she's using them to charge up for the incoming hissy fit.

"Hey, it's cool." My voice is scratchy from exhaustion and maybe an hour of sleep. "I'll help you clean up and we'll have tea later."

She starts to argue, but I already have my arms full of little plastic saucers and spoons and a couple dolls. "Fine, okay."

I follow her to her room and past a snickering Ben, who earns an evil eye from me through my blue veil.

"Where do these go?" I ask while searching for an obvious place to put fake tea party shit. My eyes snag on the wall where Justin Timberlake's poster used to be, and I grin. In its place is a poster of mine from years ago, before I started treating my body like Keith Richards. "Hey, you have one of my posters up."

She shrugs while shoving her wig into a big chest labeled Dress Up. "Bethany gave it to me."

Her name sends warmth expanding in my chest. I look at my arm as a slow slide of goose bumps trails from my bicep to my fingertips. "She's got good taste, this Bethany."

Elliot stares at me as though she hasn't the slightest clue what I mean. I clear my throat and pull off my headpiece before tossing it into the Dress Up chest.

"I wanted to keep Justin, but she said he's old news."

I grin, imagining how that conversation went and wishing I had been there to hear it. And really, what is that all about? Since when do I care about being included in a conversation between a four-year-old and a twenty-four-year-old woman?

If I didn't know for sure that my balls work properly, I'd be racing to the bathroom to make sure they do. Why am I being such a wuss?

I leave Elliot and head back out to grab some coffee.

"If you plan on coming with us, you should probably get ready."

I lean on the countertop. "You know I can't do that."

"Why? Because of the media? We'll go in my car and sneak you in the back. After you didn't show up last weekend and because you were just seen in LA, I don't think you have to worry about it."

I sip my coffee. "You think Bethany will be there?"

He nods. "I know she'll be there."

I set down my cup and grab my bag. "Give me fifteen minutes."

BETHANY

"Good morning, welcome to church." I hand a bulletin to the woman who breezes by, ignoring me completely. "Looks like you need it," I mumble then curse myself for being so salty. "Good morning, Mr. Lewis. Welcome to church."

He greets me with a smile and the familiar scent of mothballs coming from his Sunday sport coat.

I continue to greet the early arrivals to church, my stomach in knots. I don't want to end up face to face with Wyatt and Suzette. I'm not ashamed of what I said to Wyatt yesterday during coffee—I needed to get that off my chest and he needed to hear it from me—but I am humiliated that I did it so publicly. I've sworn to never go to that Starbucks again. Thankfully there's one on most every corner, so I treated my bruised ego to a Frappuccino and pumpkin loaf before church this morning.

I'm in the middle of asking Mr. and Mrs. Gaines about their weekend when I see Ashleigh racing toward the door from the parking lot. That she's able to jog in those heeled booties isn't as surprising as how her plaid mini skirt and black sweater are equal parts stripper and Sunday best.

"How does she do it?" I whisper to myself before she skids to a stop in front of me.

Her heavily lined eyes are wide. "We need to talk."

"I can't, I'm—"

She hooks me around the bicep and tugs me aside. "Listen to me." She's huffing, trying to get a full breath, which makes her running in heels a little less glamorous. "I was online this morning and I was searching hashtags."

"Okay." I continue to smile and hand out bulletins even though Ashleigh is huffing and puffing in my ear.

"I searched for—"

"Excuse me, you're Bethany Parks?" A man with longish brown hair and a goatee takes my offered bulletin.

"Yes."

I feel Ashleigh stiffen beside me.

With his free hand, he shoves a small camera in my face. "Is it true you're responsible for Jesse Lee giving up music?"

"What?"

"Are you pregnant? Are you aware of his illegitimate child count?"

"No," I say and stumble back as he presses in closer.

"Did you know he's engaged to Kayla Moore?"

I gasp and shuffle backward, hoping the distance will protect me from the foul words he's spewing.

"That's enough." Ashleigh pulls me inside the church.

Rather than drag me off to the bathroom or somewhere private where I can cry, she pulls me inside the sanctuary. I suck back my tears since the pews are filling up and the band is taking their positions. Two male ushers see the man following us and block him, turn him around, and escort him out.

"Vultures," Ash hisses as she leads me to the front row that is usually left empty for the same reason the front row in classrooms is left empty—to keep distance from the authority figure.

I'm still gripping the stack of bulletins as the weasely paparazzo's questions take up residence in my head. Engaged? Children? That can't be true. The memory of Kayla at Jesse's door flashes through my mind's eye. I close my eyes and it's as if I'm back there, watching them resolve whatever feelings were between them.

He would never fall for a woman like me. Not when he has women like her begging for his attention.

"I can't believe how merciless those little fuckers are," Ashleigh says in my ear, loud enough for the rows behind us to hear, as if she's unaware there's even a thing called whispering. "When I did my search this morning—"

I look at her, and whatever she sees in my expression silences her. "I don't care. Whatever you saw, whatever you read or heard or wanted to tell me, please don't. I just want to move on."

She frowns her perfectly-pink-painted lips. "Okay."

I turn back and do my best to focus on the music, even with my heart in my throat. During the second song, the ushers who escorted out the paparazzi head through the side door that leads behind the platform. Most likely they're going to tell Ben what happened. My cheeks get hot as I feel as if every spotlight in the room is aimed at my head.

The song ends and Pastor Ben walks out. Ashleigh and I share a look.

"What's happening?" she asks.

I slide my gaze back to the platform as Ben whispers something to the worship leader. "I have no idea."

He faces the congregation and spots me and Ash right away. He gives us a tentative smile before addressing the room. "Good morning, church. I'm so grateful you're here. I wanted to take a minute to talk about some things that have been happening here over the last few weeks. To avoid the gossip, I'd like to address the rumors that are circling."

The room erupts in murmurs, and even the members of the band seem as confused and interested as the rest of us. Well, not me. I'm pretty sure I know what he's going to talk about, and my insides are screaming for me to run away.

"First off, for those of you who're wondering about my relationship with Jesse Lee, the truth is he's my little brother."

Gasps and whispers buzz around me while my stomach sinks.

"Jesse has been staying with me for a few months, and during that time, he's made some friends here in Surprise." He doesn't look in my direction, and I appreciate that. "The media has been mercilessly hounding this church with the hope of getting the scoop on why Jes is here. They're dedicated, I'll give them that."

Laughter rings out, but I only feel sick.

"My brother is headed back to Los Angeles, but before he goes, he's got something to say." This time Ben's eyes come to mine. "I hope you'll hear him out."

"Oh God, oh God, oh God," Ash whispers.

I'm too stunned to reprimand her for blaspheming in church—because I know those weren't prayers—and instead stare dumbly ahead. Bile rushes to my throat as the sanctuary ignites with applause. *Don't throw up, do not throw up.*

From the back of the stage emerges a figure in a black T-shirt, blue jeans, and a pair of heavy-soled black boots. I fix my eyes on his feet because I can't bring myself to look into his eyes.

Engaged. Children. Affairs. Broken relationships.

"In the words of a good friend of mine," his voice rumbles through the speakers, "good morning, welcome to church."

He strums his guitar and my gut clenches at the sound, the same sound I heard all those mornings when he was writing music in

Ben's room. The same sound I heard when he played the song he'd written.

"Bethany," Ashleigh says, "you don't look so good."

Jesse strums a few more chords. "I've been working on a song I'd like to play for you all." More strumming.

My stomach twists.

"Oh shit," Ash hisses. "I think you're gonna—"

I wish I could say I could fight it. With a spine-curling retch, I double over and spill my Starbucks breakfast all over the church floor.

"Shit." Ashleigh grips my shoulders and pulls me up from the pew to guide me down the aisle toward the exit.

I keep my head down, wiping my mouth and trying not to throw up again as voices seem to scramble behind me. She kicks open the double doors and drags me sideways toward the bathroom. I hit the first stall, drop to my knees, and let loose the rest of what was in my stomach.

"I'm so sorry," Ashleigh says as she holds back my hair. "I should've gotten you out of there sooner."

"No." I shake my head and spit into the toilet. "I thought I could hold it back."

"Well, you showed him."

A small roll of laughter bubbles up from my stomach. "Yeah, I did."

Whatever lukewarm feelings Jesse had for me, I surely just killed them in a wave of pumpkin-Frappuccino vomit.

JESSE

"Just give her some space," Ben says, his eyes fixed on mine as Bethany races down the aisle and out the door.

"I can't." I pull my guitar strap off over my head and hand my instrument to him. "I have to see if she's okay."

I race down the aisle as one of Ben's staff with cleaning supplies passes me. I have a weak stomach and seeing someone throw up is so fucking gross, but I don't feel even a little nauseated as my worry for her trumps the ick factor. I push through the double doors and run out to the parking lot.

"Jesse! Jesse, over here!"

I turn to see two paparazzi rushing toward me.

"Not today, boys." I jog back inside and close and lock the glass doors. I wonder where she is—until I hear voices from the women's bathroom.

When I shove inside, Ashleigh looks at me as though she's not the least bit surprised to see me there. She's standing in the doorway of a stall, and when I lean to peek inside, she steps out and closes the door, cutting me off from Bethany.

"I just want to talk to her."

"No." She points at the door behind me.

"Bethany, please."

"Leave, Jesse!" Bethany says.

I can't take my eyes off the gray metal door of the stall or her black sandaled feet that peek out from beneath it. She looked so beautiful in her sundress, even after she threw up.

"Just go," Ashleigh says, gently shoving me away. "I know you have something to say, but now is not the time."

She's probably right. I was going for a grand gesture and all I managed to do was embarrass Bethany in front of her church.

"I'm an ass," I mumble as I step out of the bathroom and into the hallway.

She follows me but stands guard at the door. "What is your end game here?"

I run my hands through my hair and look at the ceiling, hoping it holds the answers. "I don't know what I'm doing."

"Clearly."

I drop my hands to my sides. "Tell me what to do."

"Give her some space."

"I can't do that. I'm in love with her, and I'm not talking

about the feel good kind, I'm talking about the fist in your gut"—I smack my abs for emphasis—"rip out your insides kind."

She blinks a few times then blows out a breath. "Wow."

"Yeah."

"I wasn't expecting that."

I laugh humorlessly. "No shit, me either."

She twirls a piece of her hair around her finger. "Well, I still think you need to back off until she gets back on track emotionally." She chews her lip as if mulling something over. "If this is about the video…"

"What video?"

Her eyes widen. "Forget about it."

"No, what video?"

She shakes her head, letting me know I won't get another drop of information from her.

Fine. I pull out my phone and send a quick text to Dave, asking if any new videos have surfaced that relate to Bethany or me. Ten seconds later, a video pops up.

I hit Play. The moment the audio comes through, Ashleigh curses. Bingo.

The resolution is pretty good, most likely taken on a new iPhone. When the camera zooms in, I can see it's Bethany sitting across the table from some guy at Starbucks.

Not just some guy.

Fucking Wyatt.

Bethany is leaning across the table toward him, her face twisted in anger and her hand white-knuckling her drink. *"You told me you loved me. You told me I was the type of woman a man marries. You fucked me in my car and then broke up with me thirty minutes after in the parking lot of a Dairy Queen!"*

That son of a bitch.

My blood vibrates beneath my skin.

"I just wanted the guilt to go away! I just wanted it to stop, so I tossed a

lit book of matches into the backseat of my car, hoping to baptize my mistake in fire."

"Holy shit." I watch Bethany stomp out of the restaurant to a roar of applause, and I close the video. "She's bat-shit crazy."

"That's right," Bethany says from the doorway of the bathroom, making me jump. "I am. You think I'm such a good person because I work two jobs and volunteer at the church and at a retirement home? I'm paying my way out of what should've been a felony charge for arson. That's what happens when I fall for the lies of people like you. Now you know. So now you can leave me alone."

"What? No, I'm… I don't want—"

"What about your ex, the one you were cuddled up with just the other night?" Fire lights behind her eyes, and I'm equal parts scared and turned-on by her fury.

"I was with Ryder and Mark the entire time in LA. Whatever you saw is a lie."

She steps closer, and I itch to grab her and crush her against me. "How many children have you fathered—"

"Are you kidding me with this shit? Is that what all this is about? You can't believe everything you read about me!" I fist my fingers in my hair. "You're terrified, I get that. Loving me is not a safe bet, but don't sabotage what we have because you're afraid of getting hurt."

"Just go away!" Bethany's face is flushed with anger. "I'm bat-shit crazy, you said it yourself. You don't want all this! Trust me. I'm doing you a favor."

I search for the right words and can only think of four. "But I love you."

"Anyone can say I love you." She stomps off toward the offices.

Ashleigh races after her. I shake myself to follow just as a blond guy peeks his head out of the sanctuary doors.

"Hey, Beth." Wyatt, that dickhead, goes after her.

"Yo, Wyatt!"

He stops and turns toward me, and his fake concern for Bethany morphs into anger. "She doesn't want to see you."

I step right up to him, cock my arm back, and slam my fist into his nose. "That's for what you did to Bethany."

He drops to the floor and cups his face.

I squat over him. "If I find out you've tried to speak to her, and trust me, I'll find out, there isn't a dollar amount too high I wouldn't pay to have you killed."

He garbles on his own blood and fear.

"I'll take that as a 'yes, I understand, Jesse.'"

I unlock the front doors and head outside. The paps rush to me again.

"I'll answer all your questions if you guys will take me to the airport."

"Fuck yeah!"

They show me to their car, and I climb in the back. I punch in a text to Dave.

I need a first class flight to LA ASAP.

"What's going on with you and Kayla?" one pap asks before we've even left the church parking lot.

"Nothing." I hit a quick text to Ben, telling him I'm going back to LA and I'm sorry.

"She says you two were engaged," the other pap says.

"Nope. We were never engaged."

An itinerary for a first class Delta flight from Phoenix to LA leaving in fifty-seven minutes comes up on my phone.

"What? Why not?" The first pap laughs. "She's hot."

I grip my phone and stare at the window. "Because I belong to someone else."

24

THREE MONTHS LATER...

BETHANY

"This is stupid. I look stupid."

Ashleigh's face pops over my shoulder in the mirror as she adjusts the back of my top. "No, this is necessary and you look gorgeous." She snaps a few of the straps into place. "You haven't been out in months except to go to work."

"When have I ever been the type of girl who goes out?"

"Excellent point, but it's time you get out there and see that there is life after Jesse Lee." She turns me around, stands back, and looks me up and down with an almost clinical eye. "Good." She nods. "This'll do just fine."

I turn around and study myself again. Faux-leather leggings, a red top that's nothing but criss-crossed strings in the back, and black heels that shove my five-foot-five height up a few inches. "I'm not hung up on Jesse."

I've been telling her that since the day he called me bat-shit crazy at church then ran back to LA. She didn't believe me then and she clearly doesn't believe me now. Maybe going out and meeting someone new is just what I need to get her off my back, to prove to her I'm not heartbroken over Jesse.

Because I'm not.

Not really. I suppose I would've been had I stuck around long enough to let him break me. I'm just grateful I saw who he really is before I fell any deeper.

Since he left, I've deleted all my social media and refuse to Google search him to see what he's been up to. I know if I do, I'll see images of him with his newest conquest. She'll be tall, sexy, rich, and look perfect on his arm. There's no way I can handle seeing that.

That doesn't mean I'm hung up though… does it?

Ashleigh swipes on her cherry-red lip gloss. "Come on, our Uber is here."

I sigh into the mirror. "Here goes nothing."

We arrive at the Blue Agave nightclub in Old Town Scottsdale just after eleven o'clock, and the line to get in runs the length of the street. I grab the black studded clutch Ash let me borrow and follow her out of the Uber and into a shorter line with red velvet rope that indicates VIP. An insanely large man wearing all black and sporting a manly beard gives Ashleigh a hug. She yells something into his ear over the music, and it brings his eye to me. He grins, all white teeth behind well-trimmed facial hair, before he steps aside and waves us by.

Ashleigh hooks her arm in mine and leads me through the thick throng of men and women all dressed to catch attention. "We'll go to the back bar, it's less crowded!"

I mouth okay and allow her to take me through multiple rooms, each with their own kind of music and screens showing anything from music videos to random clips of nature documentaries. The crowd thins out a bit in the back, and I'm grateful for the wiggle room as we press up to the bar. Ashleigh orders a rum and Coke, and the bartender looks at me for my order.

"I'll have the same. Minus the rum."

Our drinks are delivered, and I'm grateful Ash doesn't give me crap about not drinking. We spin around and press our backs to the bar, checking out the scenery. The dance floor in this room isn't nearly as full as the others—probably because the music is less trance and hip hop and more guitar and rhythm and blues.

"I think Big Jim the bouncer likes you," Ash says in my ear.

"The guy at the door?"

She pops her eyebrows a couple times. "Yeah. He's cute, right?"

I nod and sip my Coke. He is cute. I liked his tattoos. They reminded me of—I cut off that line of thought. I am not hung up!

"Do you want me to introduce you to him later?"

"Sure." After all, the mission for tonight is to prove I've moved on.

"That guy in the Misfits shirt is hot." She openly points at him.

The guy is hanging out with a couple other guys, but I can only see their backs. Still, I smack her hand away. "You're being so obvious."

She laughs. "It's a club. Everyone here is obvious. Want me to ask him to come have a drink with us?"

I scrunch up my nose. "If you want to. I'm not really into guys with a man bun." A memory of messy reddish-brown hair flashes through my mind. "Actually, yes. Let's meet him. He seems nice."

Ash looks at me as if I'm a second grader in a college class who just stuck her foot in her mouth. "Nice. Right."

She waves, and the guy lifts his chin in acknowledgment before he makes his way toward us, his friends watching with amusement.

"Hey," he says when he stops in front of Ash.

I wave, and Ashleigh bats her eyelashes.

"What are your names?" he asks, looking between us.

"I'm Ashleigh, and this is Bethany," Ash says.

He shakes our hands. His grip is a little flimsy. "I'm Neil. Have I seen you ladies here before? You look familiar."

Ashleigh looks like most of the beautiful bottle-blondes in this place—half-Barbie, half-porn star, one hundred percent gorgeous. I look like a small-town girl trying to fit in with big city nightlife, someone you'd easily see near any college campus.

The two of them talk about Ash's work and how maybe that's why she looks familiar, and he goes on to tell her about his job working at a record shop near the ASU campus. They talk about music, and Neil goes off on a tangent about how real music is dead and everything nowadays is overproduced.

Having drained the last of my Coke, I give the two my back and flag down the bartender for another. I may not be aiming for a booze buzz, but a caffeine-and-sugar high is better than nothing.

"I don't know if I agree," Ash says in her most flirtatious voice. "What about the new Jesse Lee album?"

My eyes snap forward and my spine stiffens. Jesse already released his new album? Warmth slowly seeps into my chest and I smile despite myself. I subconsciously block out all the noise in the room and zero in on Ashleigh and Neil's voices.

"All right, all right," Neil says, "I'll give you that one. But you have to admit his stuff in the past has been overproduced."

When I don't hear Ashleigh respond, I turn around.

She's smiling at me knowingly. "What do you think, Bethany? Do you like Jesse Lee's new album?"

What is she doing? "Um..." I shake my head. "I don't know. I haven't heard it."

Neil laughs. Hard. "Wow, you're the only living soul who hasn't. It's all over the radio."

"I don't listen to music." Not a total lie. Since Jesse left, it's been harder and harder to listen when all of it reminds me of him.

Neil scrunches up his face. "No music? I don't think we can be friends."

Ashleigh frowns at the guy. "Do you have a favorite song on that album?"

He sips his beer then shakes his head. "Nah, it's all a little too sappy for my taste."

Sappy?

"Mine is 'Anyone Can Say I Love You,'" Ash says, but her eyes are on me.

My stomach churns, tossing around a ton of Coke and coaxing old feelings back to life.

"Yeah," Neil says. "Must be everyone's favorite, it's been the number-one song in the country for two weeks."

"I'm going to go to the bathroom." I set my drink on the bar and scurry away as fast as my high heels will carry me, which isn't very fast.

Jesse put out a new album?

"Anyone Can Say I Love You?" Those were the last words I said to him. Is it possible the song is about us? No, it's a coincidence. Jesse writes music to the sound of him pleasuring himself, for crying out loud. No way his new album goes emotionally deeper than an easy orgasm.

I curse myself for being so bitter.

I am not hung up on Jesse Lee.

If I am, I'm in big trouble.

"I'm sorry!" Ashleigh yells at me from across the dance floor. After three hours of talking and dancing with Neil, we finally managed to give him the slip by disappearing into the most crowded room. My arms are lifted high and I'm in a very happy place, swaying to the beat of a Flo Rida remix.

"I've been trying to tell you all week." She gets closer to my ear. "But when I bring it up, you leave the room."

I lean close to her ear. "That's because I don't care."

She frowns. "How can you not care? You have to listen to the album! It's all about you!"

"Ha! That's funny." No, it's not, it's heartbreaking. "How could it possibly be about me? Jesse has loved every woman he's ever been with! Do you have any idea the number attached to that?" I use my hands at my temples to mime mind-blowing.

She's already shaking her head while simultaneously shaking her ass. "If you'd just listen to it, you'd understand!"

I stop moving, feeling a swell of anger behind my ribs. "Why are you doing this? You heard what he said—I'm bat-shit crazy. He left!" Dammit, my eyes burn. "I haven't heard from him in three months! I just want to move on, and you are not making that easier by refusing to give up talking about him."

I whirl around and stomp off the dance floor, knocking into people the entire way. I shove through the crowd and blink back the emotion swelling in my eyes. The bar has already done last call, so it has to be close to two o'clock in the morning.

On my tiptoes, I find the club entrance and bolt toward it. I'm knocked aside by a group of drunk girls, but I don't lose my footing as the goal comes into sight.

Big Jim.

He sees me coming and smiles. "Hey, gorgeous. Something I can do for you?"

I clear my throat and hope like hell I don't look as if I've been crying. "Yes, actually. Any chance you'd want to have breakfast with me?"

He looks around then back at me. "Now?"

I shrug. "Sure."

His smile widens, and I notice he has really dark, thick eyelashes for a man. "Okay, yeah. Let me clock out and grab my keys. I'll pick you up out front in ten minutes."

"Perfect." I hesitate for a few seconds before reaching up to his shoulders, pushing to my tiptoes, and pressing a kiss to his bearded cheek.

His laugh is low, deep, and grumbly. "Thanks for that."

"You're welcome."

"I'll see you out front." His gaze lingers a little too long on my body before it settles on my lips, then he turns and walks away.

"So that's it, huh?" Ashleigh's leaning up against the doorway. "You really are moving on?"

"Yep." I want to go on and on about how excited I am to be having breakfast with Big Jim, about how I'm going to get him to kiss me, about how I could see myself having a future with a man like him, but saying any of that is impossible. Lies, lies, all lies.

She smiles, but it's not convincing. "Good." She throws her arms around me and squeezes me tightly. "I just want you to be happy."

"I am. I'm super happy."

Now her smile is just sad. "Great. I'll see you at home."

"Don't wait up!"

She slides into an Uber and waves goodbye.

A sudden urge to slump to the ground and bawl like an infant overwhelms me, but I suck it back like an adult and wait for my date.

JESSE

"Dude, open the fucking door!"

I've been knocking on the door of Ryder's beachfront Malibu condo for what feels like two days now. I know he's here. I saw his pickup truck through the window in his garage. After a late-night rehearsal last night, I know the guy is probably passed out asleep. I pound on the door again then turn and watch a glassy set of waves roll to shore. The door clicks behind me.

I spin around as Ryder answers, wearing nothing but a pair of boxers. "What the fuck took you so long?"

He cracks one eye. The reflection of the sun from the sand is a bitch to sleep-deprived eyes. "What time is it?"

"Around six o'clock." I push past him into his house.

"Sure, dickhead, come on in." He closes the door and follows me into his kitchen.

Ryder moved to LA a month ago. I helped him go house hunting. He decided on this sickass modern condo, and he insisted on two bedrooms for when his family comes to visit him. I thought it was strange at the time—who has family come to visit? Then I imagined Ben and Elliot coming out to LA for a weekend, and yeah, I guess I get it.

"It didn't fucking work!" I pace the length of Ryder's living room.

"Let me get some caffeine before I even ask what the hell you're talking about." He grabs a mug, his eyes on the bag in my hand. "Why are you carrying a bag of Cheetos at six o'clock in the morning?"

I look at the bag and toss it onto the counter. "I don't fucking know. I can't drink, I can't do drugs, and I can't even think about fucking anyone without getting sick to my stomach. Cheetos seemed like the next best thing."

He nods. "Makes sense. Coffee?"

I drop onto his couch. "I guess."

Soon enough, he brings me a cup of coffee and sits in a leather wingback across from me.

"You want to know the kind of shit I woke up—"

He holds up his hand, silencing me as he sips from his coffee. "Wait." Another few sips. "One more." And another. He licks his lips and nods. "Okay, I'm ready."

I set down my coffee, punch my finger into my phone, and toss it to him.

He catches it and squints at the screen. "Oh *shit.*"

"Oh shit is right!" I push up from the couch, unable to contain the frustrated energy brewing just below my skin. "Can you believe that crap?"

"She looks happy."

I whirl around, my mouth gaping.

"Sorry. Too soon?"

"Yes, it's fucking too soon! I poured out my heart to her in that album. I put all my shit on the line for the world to hear to get her to hear me out and it didn't work!" I snag my phone and jab my finger at the photo of Bethany and Grizzly Adams sharing an intimate meal at fucking Denny's. "Do you see what she's wearing?"

I scroll through the images sent to me by the PI I hired to keep an eye on her after I released the album I named *Playing by Heart* because that's exactly what I'm doing. I wanted to make sure the paparazzi—oh, who the fuck am I kidding? I'm a selfish dick and I wanted to know if she'd heard it, if she loved it, if she'd moved on.

"She looks hot." He shrugs.

"That's it." I snag the bag of Cheetos. "I'm leaving."

"Easy, Jesse." Ryder points at the couch. "Put the Cheetos down and come sit."

I sit, but I don't drop the bag. "I've been losing my mind without her. Dr. Ulrich keeps saying it'll get easier, but it doesn't. I feel like I'm about to jump out of my skin. She asked for space and I gave it to her, thinking she'd eventually come back but..." Oh shit, my throat feels tight. I try to clear it, but it doesn't help. "I don't think she likes me anymore."

"You could be right—"

"Why did I come here?"

"But you're probably wrong."

My eyes snap to his. "Why do you say that?" *Tell me she still loves me, tell me there's still a chance, tell me she's coming back!*

"Women, they love grand gestures."

"I wrote her a fucking album. Songs about her or inspired by her are making top-ten lists all over the world. What more does she want?"

"That's true, but it means nothing if she hasn't heard it."

I frown.

"You need to get in her face."

"How?"

"That's for you to figure out."

"I tried that, remember? I made her throw up in front of the church and she told me to leave her alone."

298 | JB SALSBURY

"Sneak attack. Trick her into hearing you when she doesn't know it's you."

"You're talking in riddles, man."

"Hmm…" He scratches his jaw. "She did mention she likes Justin Timberlake."

I roll my eyes.

"I think it's time you patch things up with JT and ask him for a favor."

25

BETHANY

Jesse Lee is Gay.

I glare at the news article taped to my refrigerator. The photo below the headline is of Ryder walking the streets of Los Angeles with a blacked-out form of a man I'm guessing is Jesse.

"Ash!"

"Yeah?" She's in the living room, watching Netflix in her pajamas.

"I thought I told you I'm not interested in anything Jesse related."

"I blacked out his photo with Sharpie. Just read the article."

"I don't want to." I rip it from the Maytag and carry it to the trash, allowing my eyes to skim the words.

Sworn off women. Seen frequently with drummer Ryder Kyle. Has the Coast-to-Coast Casanova worked his way through one sex and is moving on to the next?

"That's ridiculous." I crumble up the paper and toss it in the trash.

Jesse is the most heterosexual man I've ever known. And I didn't pick up a gay feeling from Ryder in the time I spent with him. The media will twist anything in order to make a story.

I told you not to believe everything you read about me.

I close my eyes as Jesse's words echo through my head.

"So? You think he is?" Ashleigh asks.

I grab a water bottle from the fridge and shove it into my purse.

"No way."

She shovels popcorn into her mouth. "Weird though, right? That he's sworn off women?"

"There is no way that's true. He's just hiding it better now that he's sober."

"What time is the concert?"

I check the clock. "It starts at seven. I can't believe Ben is letting me take Elliot to her first concert. I figured he'd want to go with her."

"Nah, first concert is a mother-daughter thing. I'm sure he wouldn't have nearly as much fun swooning over JT as you and Elliot will. Which reminds me, I should put on something nicer for when I drop you off." She pops her eyebrows. "It wouldn't be right if I didn't walk you to the door."

My phone pings with a new text as Ash runs to her room to get changed.

Have fun tonight.

My chest tightens when I read the text from Big Jim. We had a great time eating Moons Over My Hammy, and since then, he's asked me out a few times. I've always politely declined. The fact is, Ash was right. I'm not over Jesse.

I miss the way he teased me—even when he called me genius because he knew it drove me nuts. I miss how he looked at me as though I was the only person in the room and how he told me he loved me no matter who heard him. Even if he didn't really mean it.

In the two weeks since Ashleigh bombarded me at the club about Jesse's new album, I've been tempted to look it up. I've gone as far as searching for the album name. *Playing by Heart.* Sounds romantic. Or maybe it's a reference to his band. I'm afraid to find out.

"Ready?" Ashleigh adjusts her pushup bra under her simple white V-neck T-shirt.

"Yeah."

The ride to Ben's is short, and I grab my purse and jump out, hearing the click of Ash's high heels behind me. I look down at my own outfit—Converse low tops, boyfriend jeans rolled at the ankle, and a pink off-the-shoulder sweater. Not at all sexy, but good enough for taking the now five-year-old to her first concert.

I knock on the door and Ben answers. "Bethany, hey—" His eyes slide to my left where Ashleigh stands. He quickly turns his head as if he's trying to avoid looking at her boobs, and honestly, looking away is the only way *not* to see them. "Hey, Ashleigh." He manages to force his gaze to her eyes.

"Hey, Pastor Langley. I was just dropping off Bethany and thought I'd say hi." She smiles and bounces a little. "I also wanted to get a picture of the girls before they take off to see JT."

"Sure, of course." He backs up and opens the door. "Come on in."

We pass him as we walk into the house.

"Nice sweatpants, pastor."

When he looks down at his pants, Ashleigh looks at me and bites her lip.

"Stop it!" I mouth.

"Uh, thank you?"

She shrugs. "You're welcome. I only ever see you in church clothes, so it's refreshing to see you have a casual side."

He shifts on his feet and rubs the back of his neck as if every word out of Ashleigh's mouth turns up the heat in the room.

"Bethany!" Elliot comes running down the hallway, her hair in a high ponytail complete with a huge black bow. "Look at the shirt the radio show sent me!" She points at her torso where there's a screen-printed photo of JT.

"That was nice of them." I hug her.

"I'm still amazed you won these tickets," Ashleigh says to Pastor Ben, who smiles awkwardly.

His eyes widen and he nods. "Mm-hm. Let's get a couple pictures so you guys don't miss the opening band." He pulls out his phone.

I squat next to Elliot, take her in my arms, and say, "Cheese!"

Ashleigh squeezes in beside him, brushes up against him, and doesn't apologize for it. She snaps a couple pictures then lowers her phone. "Okay, you two! Have fun tonight."

Ben hands Elliot her jacket. "Yeah, and call me if you need me." He hands me the keys to the minivan. "Thank you for taking her."

"Of course. I'm honored."

A flash of worry crosses his face, and I'm sure he's concerned about Elliot's safety. The radio station gave us tickets in some kind of VIP section though, so we'll be away from the crowds of fangirls and boys.

"I'll text you when we get there and before we leave."

His eyes widen. "Um. Great."

Wow, he's really a mess.

I snag Elliot's hand and walk her out, turning back to see Ash and Ben standing side by side in the doorway. Poor Ben. He's going to have one hell of a time getting rid of her.

I help Elliot into her car seat. "How excited are you?"

"I am so excited!"

"Me too."

We arrive at Talking Stick Arena right at eight o'clock. The parking takes longer than I thought, and by the time we go through security and find our seats, the opening band is mid-set.

We're in the front row, so close I can see the stud in the lead singer's nose and the snakeskin texture of his pants. Elliot's gaze is fixed on the lights, and for a moment, I feel sad that her first concert isn't her own uncle's. Not that I should feel bad. After all, Jesse is the adult and if his niece was important to him, he'd make that happen.

I try not to imagine it's Jesse on stage but find it impossible. I imagine his tall, lean body moving to the music while his raspy voice fills the eighteen-thousand-seat arena. The band on stage now, I've heard them on the radio a few times—back before I swore off music all together—and they've got nothing on Jesse.

We sway in our seats to the music, and Elliot seems completely engrossed. The seats around us fill up as the VIP section gears up for JT.

"Shouldn't be too long now!" I yell to Elliot over the music, and she nods.

Finally the band announces their last song. The crowd is much thicker now and roars when the last note rings through the cavernous space.

"Thank you!"

The lights on the stage go dark.

"What are they doing now?" Elliot asks.

"Now they have to set up the stage for Justin Timberlake."

Elliot gets antsy, so I let her run around the gated-off VIP section, climbing on the railing and scooting around it.

Ten minutes pass before the strum of an electric guitar explodes through the speakers. Elliot whips her eyes to the stage, and the arena erupts in applause.

"I'm sorry," comes a voice through the speakers, and my skin buzzes in awareness. "I couldn't think of another way to get you to hear me out."

My pulse speeds and my stomach turns. "Oh my…"

A single spotlight drops to the middle of the stage and—

"Jesse!" Elliot jumps up and down, clapping.

The walls of the arena practically crack with the force of the answering roar.

"Wow," he says and shines his million-dollar smile around the arena. "Wasn't expecting that, thank you."

The crowd discharges another deafening blast of applause.

The rumble of his chuckle pours through the speakers like warm honey. "Thank you guys so much, but uh…"

Everyone's screaming so loud, I'm tempted to cover my ears, but I don't want to miss what he has to say. Why is he here?

He laughs again. "I could really use your help. There's uh… there's something I came to say. Could I get a little more light in the VIP section?"

A blast of light shines on our section, making it look like daylight. The crowd eventually quiets enough for him to be heard.

His eyes come directly to me as if he knew right where I'd be sitting. A soft smile curves his lips. "God, I've missed looking at you."

"I'm gonna throw up," I say to myself.

"No." His eyes widen. "Please don't. Not again."

A big arm comes around me from behind, holding what looks like an airplane barf bag. I turn slowly and find Johnny smiling at me.

"Just in case," Johnny says.

I take the bag and grip it to my stomach. I turn back toward the stage. "What are you doing?"

He's close enough to read my lips, and if it's even possible, Jesse Lee gets bashful. "I wrote you a love letter in the form of an album, but it does me no good if you refuse to listen to it."

My cheeks flame and I crunch the bag in my fists. "This isn't happening."

"It's happening. It's the only way I could get you to hear me." He strums his guitar. "One song. If you walk away after hearing me out, well..." He clears his throat. "I'll have to accept your decision." Another strum, this one in a different key. "I'll hate it, but I'll accept it."

He steps back from the mic, and his fingers dance along the strings. He's shining like a dark angel, wearing all black under a single spotlight on a darkened stage. His forearms and biceps strain as he deftly works the guitar to create the most intricate and beautiful intro I've ever heard.

His lips touch the mic, and he closes his eyes.

> *You talk too much*
> *You never listen to what I say*
> *You can't sing, you're bossy*
> *I can't get enough of you anyway*

The band joins in with a raucous downbeat. My nausea fades and my heart hammers harder with every word from his lips. His voice is guttural as each note rips from his lungs with urgency and purpose.

> *You brought fire where there was sorrow*
> *You fought demons with your smile*
> *You caught my attention, gave me hope for tomorrow*
> *You taught me to fight for what's worthwhile*

> *Anyone can say I love you*
> *The word is disposable, used like a whore.*
> *I've tossed it around, wore it out*
> *But you, you deserve more*

The crowd is singing too. Lyric for lyric, they chant the words with Jesse, igniting the room. They hold up their cell phones, and I find myself in a sea of light that sways to the beat of Ryder's drums.

> *You're too good.*
> *You make everything okay*
> *I'll never be enough for you*
> *Please choose me anyway*
>
> *I miss the way you feel*
> *Your breath against my skin*
> *Wrap me up in you*
> *I want to drown in your assent*

Elliot's hand grips mine, and I squeeze hers as Jesse plays the final chords of the song.

> *Anyone can say I love you*
> *God knows I've said my share*
> *The word has been used to hurt you*
> *Guilt is my cross to bear*
> *But I'll take my lifetime to show you*
> *To call you mine is my solemn prayer.*
>
> *Say you're mine.*
> *Please, just tell me you'll be mine.*

The room explodes. The lights on the stage go dark, making it feel as if what we just saw was nothing more than an optical illusion. My pulse throbs painfully in my chest, proving it was real.

"Well?" Johnny says in my ear.

I turn to him and say the only thing that makes sense. "Take me to him."

JESSE

She said something to Johnny. I saw her. She turned around and said something, but what? I race backstage and hand the tech my guitar. He's bringing her to me, right? Or did she demand to be taken home?

I shove my hands into my hair and wait by the door. Every second feels like an hour.

"You nailed it, man," Ryder says from behind me.

"I don't know. It might have been too much. What if I scared her off?"

He nods. "It's possible."

I glare at him. "You're literally the worst friend I've ever had."

"At least I'm honest." He shoves his hands in his pockets and leans against the concrete wall. "Tell ya what, if I were gay and that song was for me, I'd choose you."

"Thanks, I think?"

"Dude, loosen up. She'll be here."

"I don't know… what if she got sick? What if I fucked everything up? What if—"

The door swings open so hard it cracks against the wall, and Bethany runs through it. Her eyes lock on mine, and I only have a second to brace myself before she jumps into my arms. Her legs wrap around my waist and I grip her ass, holding her to me while she buries her head in my neck.

"Fuck," I say against her hair. "I was so afraid I'd lost you."

Her arms grow tighter around my neck. "I'm sorry I didn't listen to your song before. I was afraid it would hurt too badly."

"I never want to hurt you. I'll do everything I can to keep from hurting you."

"Daddy!"

Bethany pulls away as Ben and Ashleigh come around the corner from the band's dressing room. "What are they doing here?"

She looks at me, and with our faces so close, her adorable look of shock is too much, so I kiss her. I want to shove my hands in her soft hair, but I can't without setting her down, and right now, it would take a team of twenty men to get me to let her go. Her tongue is sweet and silky against mine, just how I remember it. I press her back to the wall and tilt my head, deepening the kiss and grinding my hips—

"Whoa there, big guy," Ryder says through laughter. "You've got a child present."

We break apart with heated eyes, swollen lips, and panting breath. I reluctantly put her down but keep my hand on her hip and hold her close. Fuck, she feels so good at my side. I wonder how I managed to survive all this time without her.

"You guys were in on this?" she asks.

Ben scoops Elliot into his arms and eyes Ashleigh. "We were. I'm sorry, Bethany. I hated lying to you."

My woman props her hand on her sexy hip. "I can't believe it, Pastor Langley."

He groans and shakes his head. "It was for the greater good." His eyes come to mine. "And I owed my brother."

I pull Bethany tighter. "Thanks, Benji."

"All right, enough of this! Can we please go watch JT now?" Ashleigh claps in excitement and Elliot joins in.

"We're gonna pass on the concert," I say and look at Bethany. "Right, baby?"

She turns into me so her front is pressed to mine, and she peers up at me, looking conflicted as she chews her lip. "I don't know, I mean, how can I say no to a JT con—"

"Wrong answer." I scoop her into my arms and carry her toward the exit while she giggles into my throat. "Of course I had to fall in love with a Timberlake fan."

"You love it."

I lift my chin to Johnny to get the door then press my lips to hers. "I love *you*."

26

JESSE

Johnny pulls the SUV up to the private entrance at the back of the Ritz Carlton hotel in downtown Phoenix. He leads us through the service docks to the private elevator and takes us to the twenty-third floor.

Anticipation vibrates between us as we step up to the door and Johnny produces a key. I take it and he nods once before disappearing back into the elevator.

"This is so nice." Bethany's head swivels as she takes in the ornate hallway. "But ya know, I would've settled for a Motel 6."

I cringe, but I'm still smiling because why wouldn't I? I have the woman I want to spend the rest of my life with in my arms, with me for now and into the foreseeable future. "No more motels for you." I swing open the door and motion for her to walk in. "I'm going to give you all the five-star luxury I can afford."

The suite is dimly lit. A bottle of sparkling water on ice and two champagne glasses sit next to a tray of chocolate-covered strawberries. I drop the key on the dresser and my legs coil to pounce, but I can't go for sex so soon. She deserves more from me.

"Jesse, this is—"

"Wait." I close my eyes. "There's something I want to try." When I open my eyes, she's looking at me warily. "This may sound weird, but I think…" Shit, I don't know how to say it.

"Is everything okay?" She sounds worried.

"Yes." I step up to her and clear my throat. "My name is Jesiah Andrew Langley. I want you to know that." I sound so stupid! So insecure. "I want you to know me. The me who isn't Jesse Lee."

"Jesiah." The sound of my name on her lips is like a sweet seduction. I've always hated the sound of my name because it was seldom said in love, but in one moment, Bethany manages to erase all that and make it something different.

I close my eyes and step closer. "Yeah."

"I like it," she whispers, and a shiver rocks my body.

I press my forehead to hers and slip my hands around her waist. "I like you."

"Show me."

I open my eyes. "Show you?"

"Don't say it, okay? Let's only show it."

"It. You mean lo—"

She presses her fingertip to my lips. "Don't say it. Show me."

I suck her finger into my mouth, and her lips part on a gasp as she watches my lips close around the tip. I release it, and she shocks me by bringing the finger to her mouth and running the wetness along her lips.

"You are unbelievably sexy." I know she can feel how hard I am against her belly. "I want to show you how I feel about you with my body, but I don't want you to feel rushed."

"I've been waiting for what feels like forever."

I frown. "What about the guy at Denny's?" My abs flex and my spine tingles with irritation. I'm prepared for her to tell me she's going to have to break up with him soon, that she shared her body with him. I'm prepared, but that doesn't mean I'll like it.

"Were you spying on me?"

"I've been obsessed with you for as long as I've known you, so yeah, I had a guy keeping an eye out."

"That's creepy."

"I know, but that's what you do to me. You make me creepy."

She smiles and leans into my chest. "Big Jim—"

"What a stupid fucking name."

"Is just a friend."

"Bullshit."

"He is." She sighs. "And no, we never kissed or did anything more than share a late-night breakfast."

"Really?"

"I've never lied to you." Her eyebrows pinch together, and she frowns. "Oh, except for that one time I told you I wouldn't sleep with you even if we were in the midst of an apocalypse. I lied then."

"Good to know. So are you saying you're free to be with me?"

"I've belonged to you for longer than I'm proud to admit. Are you free to be with me?" The nervousness in her voice threatens to unman me.

I run my knuckles along her cheek. "I, Jesiah Andrew Langley, have belonged to you since you butchered AC/DC. From that moment on, it's only been you."

"I'm sorry, I never should've believed what I read about your ex—"

"She was at Spago at the same time we were. I didn't see her, and even if I had, I wouldn't do more than give her a polite nod. Or not even that if it makes you uncomfortable. You tell me what you need from me and it's yours."

"Right now," she whispers against my lips, "I just need you."

Our mouths come together and I feel her grin against my lips. She snakes her tongue out to brush against mine in a long, soft caress.

"We don't have to do this," I say against her lips. "We can watch TV." I grasp her hips and pull her tighter to me. "Chill and talk." I reach up her sweater and splay my fingers on her lower back. "We can take sex off the table."

She rips her lips from mine, and the abruptness has me stumbling into her. "Ohhh, sex on the table. Let's do that."

I stop her from dragging me to the six-person dining room table. "Bethany, stop." When she turns around with her eyes bright, skin flushed, and lips wet from my kiss, it takes herculean strength for me to say what needs to be said. "I want you to know how I feel about you, but I'm not sure if sex is the best way."

Truth is, I'm nervous as fuck to make love, like real love, to the woman I finally really and truly love.

She chews her lip and nods. "Okay, then how about you let me show you how I feel using my body?"

"That sounds reasonable." I grin because I can't help being downright giddy at the thought of being inside Bethany again. "Maybe you could, um…" I shrug. Feeling vulnerable sucks. "Show me how."

Her expression grows serious then heated. "Of course."

She steps in front of me, slides her palms under my shirt, up my abdomen, and slips the fabric off over my head. Her eyes devour my chest as her hands run the length of my arms to my shoulders and around to my back.

"I like your hands on me." I groan as she dips in and flicks my nipple with her tongue. "Fuck, that feels good."

I want to drop my head back and groan, but I can't peel my eyes away from her sweet mouth as she licks and sucks at my chest. My dick swells and hardens behind my fly as it presses against her, but she ignores it and continues to tease me with her teeth, tongue, and gentle suction. She drags her lips up to my collarbone and teases my neck as her warm breath ghosts against my skin. My legs wobble and my head gets light.

I sift my hands through her hair, fisting the silky locks, and holding her in place as she continues to coax me to a ridiculous state of arousal without even touching my dick. She shifts to my opposite shoulder, and I really like the way her head moves in my hands as she covers my skin in kisses.

"Don't stop," I groan.

"I'm never going to stop lo—" She kisses me again. "Making sure you know how I feel about you."

"Thank fuck."

She smiles against my throat and drops back to flattened feet before stepping back enough to lose my hands in her hair. Her grin is pure sex, but her eyes are warm with something that looks nothing like the lust I'm accustomed to seeing. A voice in my head whispers one word.

Love.

So this is love.

She grips the hem of her sweater and pulls it off over her head, tossing it aside. Her bra is pale pink, cotton, no padding.

"My favorite." Soft, round, and begging for my touch, her tight, rose-pink nipples tighten further as I stare at them. "You're perfect."

Her cheeks flush down to her chest. "I'm not."

"You are to me."

She toes off one shoe, then the other, and my heart pounds when she pops the button of her jeans, but she stops there.

"Why are you—" I moan as she touches my belt buckle, brushing the tip of my hard-on just enough to send my hips thrusting forward.

She fumbles with the belt.

"Need some help?"

Her pretty hands quiver as she finally gets to my button fly and releases me. "Nope." She shoves her hand down my jeans, outside of my boxers, and rubs the length of my dick from base to head. "I got it."

My teeth dig into my bottom lip as I try to control the way my body reacts. "Yeah, you do. For as long as you'll keep me around."

She guides me toward the table and turns me so I can sit on it. Her eyes stay on mine as she lowers herself between my knees. My vision blurs in anticipation of her swallowing me down her throat, but she instead works to untie and slip my boots from my feet.

What the fuck is she doing to me? My lungs can't seem to suck in enough oxygen and my pulse roars in my ears and I'm not even close to being inside her yet. If this is what foreplay is like when you've committed yourself unconditionally to another person, what will sex be like?

The thud of my boots being dropped aside calls my eyes back to her as she rises up to stand between my knees. "You've done nothing but touch my chest and take off my boots and I'm ready to come."

"Not yet." She reaches down the front of my boxers with two hands and my ass slips off the table.

I brace my weight with my arms, gripping the edge of the table to keep me from falling as she works me with two tight fists. I throb, swell until I'm painfully hard, and dip down to kiss her.

There is no doubt in my mind, this woman owns me.

BETHANY

The desire to let Jesse know what it feels like to be thoroughly loved in a slow, deliberate way wars with my insatiable need to jump him. I continue to touch him at a marathon pace when my body longs for a sprint.

The words he sang to me in front of a packed arena ring through my ears, and the image of him belting the words from deep in his soul only heightens my desire and devotion to him.

Love.

Oh how we have cheapened the word.

Rather than say it, I focus on the feeling that swirls and builds behind my ribs, allowing it to push me on and tend to his needs over my own.

"Lie back," I whisper and slip my hands from his boxers in order to pull off his jeans.

He watches me intently with those hazel eyes that light with excitement and attention, as if he's studying my every move and making mental notes. His boxers pool around his ankles, and he steps out of them before lying back on the table.

I blink, amazed at the phenomenal view. His tall, powerful body is laid out like a feast for my senses. The colors and images that paint his skin frame his engorged sex that stands proudly against his abdomen.

I reach for his jeans and fish into the pockets searching for—ah-ha! A black foil packet. "Am I really that predictable?"

He pushes up to his elbows, staring down the length of his beautiful body at me. "You're not predictable at all. That's just wishful thinking and preparedness. If we did make it here, I wanted to make sure I took care of you."

My heart swells and I shimmy off my jeans before I crawl up his body to straddle his hips. My bra-covered breasts are at eye level, and he doesn't pass up the opportunity to suck my nipples over the fabric. I arch my back, creating a delicious friction between my legs. His fingers dig into my hip, and I can't tell if he's trying to still me or get me to move more. I know which I prefer, so I roll my hips in a long, deliberate slide.

He sucks in a breath through his teeth then nips at my breast. "You're gonna kill me if you keep this up."

"Impossible." I grind on him again. "I think you're immortal."

He watches as I work myself against his hard-on, his lips parted to accommodate his labored breathing. When he's seen enough, he pulls the straps of my bra down my arms to free my breasts. When he alternates between long swipes of his tongue and powerful suction of his lips, my pace quickens as I bring myself to the edge of orgasm.

Finally, I scoot back and slip my panties down my legs. With the condom in hand, I lower myself to put it on him, but he grips my backside and scoots me up so that my knees rest on either side of his face.

"Jesse, I—"

His mouth latches between my legs, and I cry out as a bolt of ecstasy charges up my spine. My thighs shake with the strength it takes to hold myself up when all I want to do is drop my weight and take him deeper.

He's a mastermind of the female body, and I refuse to think about how he knows exactly what to do to keep me right on the cusp of release. He holds my hips so I can't go too far, and every time he moans against my sensitive flesh, a vibration rocks every nerve in my body.

I catch a glimpse of us in the window reflection, his cocked knee displaying the tattoos on his thigh, his hands on my butt, and me towering over his face. In the past, I've thought what we were doing was dirty, but looking at us now, all I see is two people who desperately want to love the other without having to say the word.

My orgasm reaches its peak, and as it crests, he pulls me back down his body.

"Okay, now," he says.

I rip open the condom and slide it over then down his length before positioning myself for him to sink slowly inside me. Our gazes lock as I take him inch by inch at an agonizing pace. He studies me—my eyes, my mouth, even the set of my jaw—as if he's looking for any sign of pain or regret.

He'll find none here.

When I'm finally seated, I take a deep breath and absorb the fullness of his intrusion.

"Are you okay?"

I dip down cautiously, and the new angle sends a wave of pleasure up my spine. "Of course I'm okay. I'm with you."

He cups my jaw and brings my lips to his for a soft, wet kiss. "This feels too good to be real. I'm afraid I'll blink and you'll be gone."

I shake my head. "I'm not going anywhere, I promise."

Another kiss, and against my lips, he whispers, "Marry me."

I inch back, my brain and ears unsure of what I heard. "Did you just ask me to marry you?"

Now he cups my face with both hands and brings me close. "Yes. Marry me, Bethany. It doesn't have to be tomorrow or even next year, but I want you to have me forever. I don't want anyone but you."

"That's crazy," I say through my labored breathing.

He chuckles, and the shaking of his body sends shivers through me. "I'm crazy about you."

I sit back, and he lifts his knees to support my back as I roll my hips against him. He cups my breasts, thumbs my nipples, and whispers dirty things into the space between us.

I throw my head back as my orgasm rips through me. Lights explode behind my eyes, and the feeling like I'm soaring has me falling limply onto Jesse's chest. He holds me to him then brings our lips together while he thrusts his hips and groans into my mouth. His hard-on throbs as he pumps and releases before finally slowing with an exhausted sigh.

"That was fucking beautiful," he says, his voice gravelly. "You didn't answer my question."

A lump forms in my throat at the sincerity in his voice, the warm embrace of his body combined with the vulnerability shining behind his eyes. "I'd love to be your wife, but I'm scared. I got one tiny taste of what life with Jesse Lee is like and I'm terrified."

"I can't promise it'll be easy on you. If I thought I could live even a day without you, I care about you enough to let you go, but I can't." He cups my face and brings his lips a breath away from mine. "What I can promise is that I will do anything to keep you, to make you feel safe with me, to prove to you that I'm worthy and I'll never let anyone or anything tear us apart ever again."

His words sink into the depths of my soul and wrap me in his devotion. "How do you always know what to say to relieve my fears?"

He shrugs. "No fucking clue. I've got no idea what I'm doing. I just know how I feel and I'm winging it."

I press a closed-mouth kiss to his lips. "It's working."

"So does that mean you'll marry me?"

"Eventually."

He chuckles, and the sound has me feeling lighter than I've felt in years. "Good enough."

"Should we move to the bed?"

"How about the Jacuzzi tub?"

I perk up. "There's a Jacuzzi tub?"

He wraps me in his arms and sits up while keeping us connected. With a little shimmy, he gets off the table and slides free of my body before carrying me to the bathroom. He hits the light then sets me on the countertop. Sure enough, there's a huge two-person Jacuzzi tub.

He grabs a tissue, removes the condom, and throws it in the trash, then he turns on the water. He looks over his tattooed shoulder, grinning like the cocky rock god he is. Now he's my cocky rock god. "You want bubbles or no bubbles?"

"Bubbles."

He dumps in some hotel bubble bath then turns and holds out a hand.

I take it with a smile and allow him to guide me into the tub. He lies down and sets me on top of him, my head on his chest. "I can't believe it."

"What? That you're taking a bath with a guy?" He swooshes warm water over my back.

"No. That I walked out of a Justin Timberlake concert to make a future with Jesiah Langley."

His fingers dig into my ribs. "That's it!"

"Stop!" I giggle and squirm against him.

Water sloshes over the tub. "I'll have to love you so hard you forget all about JT." His hands still on my back and he brings my lips to his. "I'm serious." I've never seen his expression so determined.

"I've made my choice. You're my priority. I'm committed to you first above all others, including myself." His wet fingers brush strands of hair from my face.

"That's the sweetest, most romantic thing anyone has ever said to me."

The corner of his mouth tilts and he blushes.

"This is a good look on you." I kiss his warming cheek and nuzzle his ear.

"It's you, sweetheart. You look good on me."

JESSE

"Stop staring at me like you're about to pounce." She points her fork at me, and I press my bare back into the padded headboard, forcing myself to stay put.

Wearing nothing but a pair of boxers, it's impossible to hide my hard-on as I watch, mesmerized, as she devours a stack of pancakes. Who the fuck knew watching the woman you love eat could be so hot?

"Finish up," I growl, my eyes hungry on her lips.

She shoves another bite of blueberry pancake into her mouth and moans. The syrup drips to her chin and she swipes at it with her finger before licking it off—

"I can't take any more." I hurl myself off the bed toward her sitting at the table. I scoop her into my arms and her fluffy robe falls open and off her shoulder, exposing one perfect nipple still red and swollen from my mouth.

"Awww…" She reaches longingly toward her breakfast with her fork-wielding hand. "But it's so good."

"I will provide a lifetime of blueberry pancakes for you. Right now, I need you more than you need those." I toss her onto the bed and climb over her. "Any chance you'd be interested in getting on the pill?"

She screws up her plump lips and squints. "What weird pillow talk."

I nip her neck. "I'm serious. And while we're at it, let's discuss living arrangements."

"Oh, Jesiah, you're making me hot with all this talk of relationship responsibility," she says in an overly affected fangirl voice.

I flex my hips, pinning her to the bed, and she gasps. I retreat and flex again until she melts, dreamy-eyed, into the bed. "Now I got your attention."

She runs her hands through my hair. "You sure you want to go down this road of conversation?" She peers down between us. "It's kind of a boner-killer."

"You're asking me what I'd rather do? Have sex or talk about our future?"

She runs her lips along my earlobe, her breath hot in my ear as she whispers, "Yep, and I'm afraid you can't have both."

I think that over for all of two seconds then roll away from her.

"What just happened?" She's on her back, her robe falling open to expose her blissfully bare body.

I pull her to my side then cover her exposed skin as well as throw the comforter over my hard-on. "You gave me a choice. I choose future talk. Even the boner-killing kind."

She pushes up to sit and folds her legs, facing me. "Not what I expected, but okay."

"Talk."

She chews her lip and her eyes move everywhere but fail to land on me. "I don't know where to start."

"How about we start with the whole 'you burning your car down in scorned-woman fury' thing, which, I must say, is fucking sexy."

Her brows pinch together. "You're so weird."

I put an arm behind my head and shrug. "So what happened?"

"It was a low point, okay? I'm not really crazy."

I frown. "That's too bad. I'm into your brand of crazy. And I remember the night we burned the chair, I saw it in your eyes. You have a wild side I would like to explore personally if you're game."

She laughs and fuck, the sound unscrews the tightness in my chest. "Apparently if you purposely light something on fire, you go to prison for arson. But, thankfully, with a personal visit from Ben and after I explained to the judge exactly what happened and because the only damage was done to my own vehicle, they took pity on me and lowered it to a misdemeanor charge with really expensive fines and a lot of community service."

"Ben knows?"

"I had to tell him. I wasn't sure he'd still want me working with Elliot if he knew what I was capable of. He's been signing off on my community hours at the church." She blows a strand of hair from her face. "I had to quit school to work, which is why I don't have my teaching certification." She puts her thumb in her mouth and chews the nail. "Now that Starbucks video is out and everyone is—"

"It's not."

Her gaze snaps to mine. "It's not?"

"Wyatt tried to sue me for breaking his nose."

She sucks in a breath between her teeth. "Oh, yeah, you hit him so hard he had two black eyes."

"He deserved worse. Anyway, my people offered him a deal— drop the charges and we'd do what we can to make the video disappear. Made it clear he'd never get laid again as long as that video was making the rounds. He saw the logic in our reasoning and agreed to take the offer."

She gapes. "Wow, what a loser."

"Enough about him. What does all this mean for us?"

She tugs the lapels of her robe closer to her neck. "I have forty-thousand dollars in fines—"

"I'll pay them. Next obstacle."

She's already shaking her head like the stubborn woman I know her to be. "No, I don't want you to do that. It's important to me that I pay them off. It's what I deserve."

"What if I offered you a job where you made over four times the amount you make now? Would that help you to pay that shit off sooner?"

She blinks. "You can't pay me to be your girlfriend."

"No shit, genius." I shake my head. "You think so little of me."

"I can't think of anything I can offer that's worth you paying for."

"Your blow jobs, but—"

She whacks my upper arm. "Jesiah!"

Hearing her say my name sends ripples of pleasure across my skin. "Just hear me out. We're planning a worldwide tour that'll kick off in about nine months. We're all getting older, our crew too, and we'd like to make it more family-friendly if we're going to be traveling for a year."

Her eyebrows pinch together.

"In order for us to bring kids along, we need a way to keep them caught up with school. If you could hammer out those last few classes, we could use someone with a teaching certificate to come with us and keep the kids up on their studies."

"Are you serious?" she whispers.

"As a heart attack, baby. You could see the world, we could be together every day, and you'd get to do what you love and make a shit-ton of money doing it."

"How much does something like that pay?"

"One hundred forty-five thousand for one tour. Plus, all expenses paid since you'll be with me, so you'll pocket every dollar."

Her eyes widen and she stares over my shoulder at nothing.

My smile falls. "Bethany." When she doesn't answer, I sit up and snap my fingers in front of her face. "Are you in shock?"

"I... I..." She shakes her head slowly. "I..."

"'I... will do it, Jesiah,'" I say, feeding her the words. "'Yes, sounds great. I'll sign the contracts as soon as you get them drawn up'?"

She snaps out of it and jumps into my arms, knocking me back to the headboard. "Yes! All that. I say yes!"

I rub her back and peel her robe from her shoulders. "Great news, sweetheart. Now... let me love you."

EPILOGUE

ONE YEAR LATER...

BETHANY

Whirlwind is the only adequate way to describe the last twelve months. I learned the morning after the JT concert that once Jesiah Langley makes his mind up about something, it's all hands on deck. A few phone calls and I was making plans to sign contracts to become the official tutor on the Jesse Lee Playing by Heart World Tour. I quit my job at Pies and Pancakes, and because Jesse wanted me to get my teaching certification as soon as possible but I couldn't enroll mid-semester, he hired a professor to catch me up. The perks of being a world-renowned superstar.

Jesiah bought a condo in Surprise and stayed there whenever he didn't need to be in Los Angeles. If I was able to go to LA with him, I would, and we managed to do regular boyfriend-and-girlfriend things—as regular as things can be when everyone recognizes him wherever we go.

He met my parents, and as predicted, my mom was captivated by the light he cast over everything. My dad wasn't as easily spellbound —until Jes spilled out his heart, and by the time we left after dinner, my dad was hugging him and giving us his blessing. I should've known Jesiah's charms would work on men as well as women.

I got my certification and found enough curriculums from an online homeschooling program to feel secure about my ability to teach while we were on the road. The night before we left for the first leg of the tour, Jesiah slipped a four-carat pave-cut diamond on my finger and asked me—in front of Ben, Elliot, Ash, and my parents at our going-away dinner—to marry him.

Since then, we've gone from tour buses to five-star penthouse hotels all over the US. The international leg of the tour isn't for another couple months. I've had to be creative in where I teach—backstage at arenas, in our bus, hotel rooms, and oftentimes outdoors at a monument or museum while surrounded by plenty of security.

I'm currently bent over the table in our tour bus, somewhere between New York and Detroit, flipping through a stack of drawings from my elementary kids. Jesiah and I are lucky enough to have our own bus. Ryder and Chris share a bus, and Ethan and his family have their own.

The door to our bedroom clicks open, and Jesiah comes out wearing nothing but a pair of boxer briefs. I sneaked out of bed an hour ago, after he woke me up using his skillful hands and mouth. I was satisfied when I left him in that halfway stage between wake and sleep, but seeing him now stirs my blood once again and my hands itch to get all over him. Since he's been sober and his life doesn't revolve around his next drink, he's been working out a lot. His shoulders are thick and rippled with muscle that bleeds down to his chest and abs. Yum. His tattooed arms flex as he runs his hands through his messed up hair and yawns.

"See something you like, Mrs. Langley?" he says with a smirk.

"I'm not Mrs. Langley yet." I still blush every time he calls me that. "And yes, actually." I make another slow pass of his body—especially his thick muscular thighs with tattoos that snake around to disappear beneath the fabric of his briefs. "I do."

He grabs his crotch and groans. "Easy, boy. Coffee first. The last round put me in a fucking coma." He pours himself a cup of coffee and drops into the seat next to me. When he leans in to kiss me, his gaze darts to the papers in front of me. "What the fuck is that?"

I follow his stare to the crayon on paper drawing of Frida Kahlo. "We're studying influential artists." I scoot the page closer to him. "That's Frida Kahlo."

He squints to study it. "Why does she have a tail?"

"That's not a tail." I study the image with him, tilting my head.

"And mouse ears."

"What?" I snag the paper, turn it one way, then the other, and... "Oh."

He sips his coffee, trying to hide his smirk. "That's Mickey Mouse, genius."

"Damn," I mumble, remembering how my second grader, Grace, kept asking questions about Disney. "That makes sense."

He chuckles, hooks me around the shoulders, and pulls me to him, kissing me sweetly on the head. "God, I fucking love you."

I run a hand up his chest and kiss his jaw. "Jar. And double the money for using blasphemy and an f-bomb in the same sentence."

He palms my hand on his chest, the rumble of his laughter vibrating our joined hands, and he thumbs my engagement ring. There really is no jar, but I do enjoy giving him a hard time. "Our realtor called."

Another thing I love is that ever since we decided to be together, everything Jesiah owns he now calls "ours".

"He got a buyer for the house."

"That's great." I pop up and stare at his perfect profile. "But are you sure you want to sell it?"

He turns on the bench seat to angle his body toward mine. One arm runs along the back of the seat and his fingers toy with the baby hairs at my neck. "Of course. I don't want to live in my house. I want to live in our house and I want you to pick it out." He kisses my nose. "All my shit from before carries too many memories of a life without you in it. That life is dead to me."

I catch my breath. One thing about Jesiah, he's never at a loss for words that make me melt. "That's really sweet."

He runs his teeth along his lower lip while staring at mine. "How much time until we hit the venue?"

"No clue, but judging by the barren roads, I'd say we've got hours."

"Come straddle me," he growls.

I throw a leg over his hips and settle on his hardness with a sigh.

He runs his hands up the sides of my Jesse Lee concert T-shirt and palms my breasts. Nuzzling my neck, he whispers, "Perfect."

"You sure you have the energy for this?" I roll my hips and watch his mouth part with heated breath. "You have four shows in a row before you get a night off."

He peers up at me. "They'll have to wheel me to the stage on a stretcher before I'd say no to getting inside my future bride."

I run my hands through his messed-up hair, and he closes his eyes as I apply gentle pressure, rubbing deep circles into his scalp.

He drops his forehead to my chest. "Feels good."

"Take me to bed and I'll make you feel even better."

He scoops me up with ease and carries me to our king-sized bed. He kicks the door shut and tosses me to the bed before crawling over me. "Let me love you."

I bite my lip and nod.

His expression turns equal parts heated and vulnerable. "Thank you for loving me. I can't wait to be your husband. I can't wait to spend every day of my life showing you how much I fucking love you."

I shimmy down my shorts and panties then kick them off. His breath hitches as I reach past the elastic of his briefs and grip his hard-on. Freeing him and feeling the heavy weight of his arousal in my hand, I'm too eager for foreplay. I widen my knees, and in one practiced slide forward, he sinks deeply and deliciously inside me.

I moan his name. "I love you."

"Say it again," he says against my lips.

"I love you, Jesiah."

His eyes slam closed and his erection throbs inside me. "Never get tired of hearing that."

He rips my shirt from me and presses his chest to mine, our racing pulses throbbing against the other, reaching for the other, communicating our commitment and devotion while he loves me fully and so completely.

JESSE

I've played thousands of shows no different than the one I'm playing tonight, yet I'm nervous as fuck. Backstage in my dressing room at Toronto's Scotiabank Arena, my knee won't stop jumping.

"Jes," Dave says from the couch behind me. I watch from the reflection in the dressing mirror as he tucks his phone in his pocket, his grin saying a million good things. "Mark loved your new songs. I knew he would. He wants to start recording as soon as the tour is over." He claps me on the shoulder, holding eye contact through the mirror.

"No can do. I'm getting married first."

Dave makes that face that says he's blowing me off. "Right, but you can do both—"

"I'm taking six months off. No recording, no talk of music. I might write some shit, but only because my woman inspires the fuck out of me."

He nods. "Sure. All right, whatever you want."

I grin at myself in the mirror. Took some time to prove myself, but I'm back to being able to call the shots in my own life and nothing is more important than that. "We'll take a couple months to plan, then the wedding, and we're going on a honeymoon for however long she wants to be gone. Once we're back, I'll need some time to settle in and then I'll get back to work."

"You're the boss," he says and his phone buzzes with an incoming text. He pulls it out and checks it. "They're almost here."

"Cool," I mumble and catch the door on the far side of the room opening. I grin as Bethany steps into the dressing room. Her eyes meet mine, and she smiles as though she hasn't seen me in months when it's only been a couple hours. I hop out of my chair and cross to her. "Hey, how was class?"

"Great." She throws her arms over my neck, and I hold her around her waist. "I love teaching those kids."

She feels so good in my arms—her slim waist, round hips and ass. Even in a sweatshirt, leggings, and her hair piled up in a mess on her head, she's the most beautiful thing I've ever seen. Her dark eyes swallow me as she gazes at me with so much love and acceptance, it hurts my chest.

After pressing a kiss to my lips, she says, "You look hot."

"Funny, I was just thinking the same thing about you."

"I'm so sure." She blushes.

"I'm serious."

"What time do you go on?"

"Why?" I nip her lips. "You got something in mind?"

The sound of her laugh sends chills of desire through my blood.

"You wish," she says, her eyes light with humor.

"I do." I press a kiss to her lips as the door opens and Ryder, Chris, and Ethan saunter inside.

"Get a room, guys," Ryder says as he passes by to the couch.

"Bethany." Chris comes up to us.

Bethany moves to releases me, but I hold her tighter, making her laugh and humor me by sinking into my chest.

"Tour's almost over and Alex is doing fourth grade math. She's going to be too smart to go back into third grade." Chris smiles at my woman. "Please tell me you'll consider homeschooling our kids once we get back to LA."

"Sounds intriguing."

I lean down to her ear. "We could turn the barn into a classroom."

After looking at what felt like thousands of homes in the Los Angeles area, we found a great house in the Pasadena mountains—a remodeled farmhouse with plenty of space for kids, pets, family, whatever Bethany wants.

She looks at me, eyes wide. "Are you serious?"

I shrug. "If it's what you want."

"Jes…" She whispers.

"Stop looking so fucking surprised." I kiss the tip of her nose and, fuck, even that does things to me. "I told you I'd do anything for you. You want to teach, I'll buy you a fucking school. Just tell me and let me make it happen."

"Bethany!"

I grin as her eyes pop wide, and this time I do let her go. She whirls toward the door as Elliot comes barreling through. The two crash into a fit of giggles and hugs.

"What are you doing here?" Bethany asks with tears in her eyes.

"Uncle Jesiah flew us out!" Elliot turns toward the door as Ben and Ashleigh walk in.

My heart pounds. I haven't seen my brother since we played Phoenix and he came to the show. He looks the same mostly— maybe a little happier, a little more relaxed. I have to wonder if Ashleigh has anything to do with it.

"Benji." I clap my brother on the back before pulling him in for a man-hug. "Thanks for coming."

He grins. "Of course. I'd never pass up a chance to see you play, Jes."

"Dude," Ashleigh says, holding Bethany's hand after a tear-filled hug, "how much sex do you think has gone down in this room?"

"Ash!" Bethany scolds and covers Elliot's ears.

Ben clears his throat and covers his smile with his palm.

"Sex ain't a bad word, genius." I pull her by the hand and kiss her perfectly sweet lips.

"You did this?" Tears spring to her eyes as she gazes at me. "For me?"

"For both of us." I turn as Ben shows Elliot around the room and watch Ashleigh laugh with Ryder and Ethan.

She bounces once, and that's all the warning I get before she wraps herself around me, her ankles locked at my ass. "I fucking love you, Jesiah Langley."

"I love you too." I kiss her softly. "More than I'll ever be able to show you in one lifetime. But I'll die trying. You have me now. You've owned me from the start. There's no playbook on how to love you, so I'll keep playing by heart."

Her lips part on a sigh. "I love that song."

"You're my muse. You inspire everything I write."

"How did I get so lucky to be the one you give your heart to?"

My face gets hot and I struggle to hold her gaze. "That's the problem. I gave it to anyone who asked, but no one ever owned it until you. Now it's yours."

"To love and to cherish."

"'Til death do us part."

OTHER BOOKS BY JB SALSBURY

The Fighting Series

Fighting for Flight

Fighting to Forgive

Fighting to Forget

Fighting the Fall

A Father's Fight

Fighting for Forever

Fighting Fate

Fighting for Honor

The Final Fight

The Mercy Series

Ghostgirl

Saint

Stand Alone Novels

Split

Wrecked

ABOUT THE AUTHOR

JB Salsbury is a New York Times and USA Today bestselling author. She lives in Phoenix, Arizona with her husband, two sassy daughters, and her boxer dogs.

Her love of good storytelling led her to earn a degree in Media Communications. With her journalistic background, writing has always been at the forefront, and her love of romance propelled her career as an author.

She spends the majority of her day behind the computer where a world of battling alphas, budding romance, and impossible obstacles claws away at her subconscious and begs to be released to the page.

For more information on her books, or just to say hello, visit JB on her website, Facebook, Twitter, or Instagram.

http://www.jbsalsbury.com/

[f] facebook.com/JBSalsburybooks
[twitter] twitter.com/jbsalsbury
[instagram] instagram.com/jbsalsbury